"OH, LUKE," SHE MOANED. "COME TO ME."

They moved together in quickening rhythm until they were writhing with longing, the fire inside consuming their entire being.

At first the distant trumpet blast registered only dimly. The second time it sounded, Andria got up from the grassy field with a start. "The alarm! We must get back at once!"

They dressed in frantic haste and started toward the village, but suddenly, out of nowhere, they were facing an army of angry bandits.

"I'll have that wench for myself," the chieftain cried. "Seize her!"

"You'll have to kill me first!" Luke spat out.

"Take him!" the chieftain ordered, "and bind him up!"

The bandits rushed him, but as Luke struggled to fight them back, he was overwhelmed by sheer numbers. Bound tightly, hand and foot, he lay there on the floor, eyes reflecting agony and horror as Andria was dragged off, kicking and screaming, crying out his name again and again.

WICKED IS MY FLESH

STEPHANIE BLAKE

PLAYBOY PRESS
PAPERBACKS

WICKED IS MY FLESH

Cover illustration by SanJulian.

Copyright © 1980 by PEI Books, Inc. All rights reserved. No part of this book may be reproduced, stored in a retrieval system or transmitted in any form by an electronic, mechanical, photocopying, recording means or otherwise without prior written permission of the author.

Published simultaneously in the United States and Canada by Playboy Press Paperbacks, New York, New York. Printed in the United States of America. Library of Congress Catalog Card Number: 79-89965. First edition.

Books are available at quantity discounts for promotional and industrial use. For further information, write our sales promotion agency: Ventura Associates, 40 East 49th Street, New York, New York 10017.

ISBN: 0-872-16610-4

First printing March 1980.

BOOK
ONE

Chapter One

Lucius Callahan stood at the port rail as the Portuguese freighter *Principe* cruised into the broad estuary of the Canton River.

"Incredible!" he murmured as his gaze traversed the sweeping harbor infested with thousands of small craft. A rag-tag conglomeration of Chinese junks, sampans, houseboats, rafts, and floating conveyances of every description swarmed around the international fleet of merchant ships at anchor or tied up at the quays.

"Indeed it is, Mr. Callahan," said the captain, who stood next to him. "Incredible. Reminds one of a gaggle of water bugs. Do you know there are human beings who go through life without ever having set foot on dry land?"

"Surely you jest, Captain Lazar?"

"Not at all, sir. Oh, they may pull into the shallows to toil in the rice paddies. But dry land—the fact is there isn't enough dry, habitable land in this poor, destitute land of the damned to accommodate the teeming masses of humanity. In most instances those brash enough to seek a living in the interior fall victim to famine or disease, or else they are shanghaied to the domain of some tyrant warlord to serve as slaves of the chieftain or fight in his army—assuming the poor devils aren't murdered in cold blood." A wry smile twisted the captain's mouth. "Yes, sir, Mr. Callahan, you couldn't have picked a more ignominious spot on earth to test your faith."

Luke Callahan flashed him a benign smile. "As our illustrious leader Joseph Smith observed in the Thirteen Articles of Faith, 'We believe all things, hope all things, we have endured many things and hope to be able to endure all things. If there is anything virtuous, lovely, or of good report or praiseworthy, we seek after these things.' "

"Pardon my French, sir," the captain said laconically, then bit his tongue to silence the rest of the sentence, "but *merde!*"

Of the scores of missionaries of all denominations he had transported to and from all parts of the world and had come to know reasonably well by the close association aboard ship, the Mormons perplexed Lazar the most.

Unlike most men of God, they abstained from fiery rhetoric about hell and damnation for those who sinned. Rather, they preached that even the meanest sinner would receive a greater gift in heaven than he could imagine.

Theirs was a sweet, optimistic, almost childlike faith. They embraced the doctrine that not only was mankind blessed with a life hereafter, but that his immortal soul had lived before he was born. They believed that each person had dwelt with the "heavenly Father" as a child in the spirit world and that in due course he would return to his Father's house once more.

"Men are that they might have joy," Callahan said more to himself than to the captain.

Lazar frowned. "Try telling that to those miserable vermin drifting about in this filthy yellow harbor. I must go forward now, Mr. Callahan. We're approaching Macao. The cesspool of the Orient."

Callahan shook his head grimly. He had done his homework assiduously. Macao was a Portuguese province, an island of iniquity. Mecca for opium peddlers, murderers, thieves, gamblers, smugglers, white slavers, and—

"Let us not forget the army of missionaries of every denomination invading the Far Eastern lands of the heathens," Luke said to himself, tongue in cheek. "The lot of us plying our own trade as enthusiastically as they apply their own."

Then again, Lucius Callahan did not serve in a society of exclusivity, as did ordained priests of the other Christian religions. In the Church of Jesus Christ of Latter-Day Saints, all males assumed the functions of priests at the age of twelve years and were encouraged to journey to all parts of the world and proselytize. In fact, since the foundation of the church by Joseph Smith and five disciples in 1830, less than twenty-five years before, thousands of converts had been won over from all over the United States and Europe by the zeal and industry of young men and women like Luke Callahan.

Three sharp blasts of the *Principe*'s whistle signaled they were about to dock at Macao. Luke went below to his cabin to fetch his portmanteau, which his father Caleb had given him before he had embarked from San Francisco. As his hand touched the carrying case, it triggered disturbing thoughts of the elder Callahan.

The quick and formidable expansion of the Mormon religion had earned the fear and mistrust of the natives of Missouri and later of Illinois, where they attempted futilely to found the Mormon equivalent of Rome— their own Holy City. After they established a headquarters in Nauvoo, Illinois, their ever increasing numbers soon earned the Mormons a balance of political power. Viewed as a threat by both the Whigs and the Democrats, they were denounced by members of both parties as "the immoral, blasphemous, nigger-loving, polygamous sons and daughters of Satan."

Joseph Smith and his brother Hyrum were subsequently jailed in Carthage, and on June 27, 1844, a mob of vigilantes invaded the jail and murdered the two men.

With Smith's demise the office of president was eliminated and the leadership of the church was placed in the hands of a council of twelve apostles, of whom Brigham Young was the senior member.

Two years later the continuing persecution of the Mormons by vigilante mobs compelled them to make a bitter, wintery exodus from their beloved Nauvoo. Young led them over one thousand miles along a torturous route to what was to be their permanent "promised land" in the valley of the Great Salt Lake.

About the same time, before departing Nauvoo, Brigham Young dispatched one of his most trusted elders, Caleb Callahan, to return to New York and lead a band of new immigrants to California, where the United States at that time, had no jurisdiction.

But by the time the company had completed the long journey by sea around Cape Horn, the United States had won the war with Mexico, and the Stars and Stripes was flying from the presidio.

Luke would never forget his father's exclamation as the *Brooklyn* sailed through the Golden Gate into the harbor of San Francisco, "All this distance and we can't get away from that damned, odious rag!"

Caleb Callahan had become disenchanted with the United States, not altogether without justification, for its failure to intervene in the systematic persecution of the Mormons by more favored American citizens. His wife and two daughters had perished in the death march from Nauvoo to Salt Lake.

From the moment he arrived in San Francisco, Luke became more and more dismayed by his father, who paid small attention to church affairs other than to collect communal funds that were supposed to be deposited in the treasury of the Latter-Day Saints at Salt Lake City. Caleb married two young women, and when he was not carousing with the two of them in the bedroom, he was gambling and drinking in the Barbary Coast's most infamous bordellos and gaming houses.

Yet, with all of his indiscretions, Caleb was a man of authority and total self-confidence who commanded respect and loyalty from the lesser men who gravitated towards him. These men, who had accrued power and riches in the gold fields during the two years following the famous gold rush in 1849, were only too eager to invest their power and riches in Callahan. He acquired vast mining holdings of his own, and the numerous newspapers of the city began to run headlines such as: 'Caleb Callahan for Mayor of San Francisco.'

Total disillusionment struck Luke when Caleb was summoned to Salt Lake City by Brigham Young to account for "the Lord's share" of all the money that the Mormons were banking in their own names in San Francisco. Not only Caleb, but increasing numbers of members of the congregation were coming to the rationalization that it was more practical to lay up treasures on earth than to wait for the distant and doubtful rewards they would receive in heaven.

Callahan's retort to Young's emissaries was, "We'll gladly pay upon a certified request from the Lord, with his signature."

When he received the report of Callahan's insolent refusal to reimburse the church, Young dispatched a private army—Destroying Angels, as they were known —to California, with orders to exterminate Callahan and, by force, to collect what was due.

Informed by spies of Young's intentions, Callahan assessed the impending showdown with cool indifference. "Destroying Angels, are they? Well, we'll see about that, my friends and I."

He proceeded to enlist an army of cutthroats from the waterfront dives of the city, men who could use a gun and a knife. Predominant among the group were a score of villainous ex-convicts who had emigrated to

California from the penal colony of New South Wales in Australia and who were popularly known as Sydney Ducks.

Callahan termed them his exterminators.

"You'll be riding with us, son?" he asked Luke on the morning they were to ride west into the desert to meet the oncoming Destroying Angels.

"I can't be a hypocrite like you, father."

Caleb's face flamed, and he lifted one huge hand as if to strike his son. "How dare you speak like that to your father!"

"I dare speak only what you, a Melchizedek priest of the church, a fountainhead of spiritual affairs, have taught me since I was old enough to read and comprehend—the Thirteenth Article of Faith:

" 'We believe in being honest, true, chaste, benevolent, virtuous, and in doing good to all men; indeed, we may say that we follow the admonition of Paul. We believe all things, we hope all things, we have endured many things—' "

"*Stop!* I will hear no more from you, Lucius!"

Luke smiled sadly. "You will hear no more from anyone, father. Including Him." He cast his eyes heavenward.

In that unguarded moment Caleb struck him, a vicious blow that almost crushed the right side of his face.

Luke remembered nothing after that until he surfaced slowly and agonizingly into consciousness, like a drowning man fighting to break through deep water to fresh air. He was in his bed in the rambling Callahan house on Clay Street.

Her face materialized out of a pink mist: Charity, his father's younger wife, a twenty-five-year-old woman with an angelic face and mousy brown hair drawn back severely in a tight bun at the back of her neck. Her chaste appearance, however, was contradicted by a voluptuous body that she tried to disguise by wearing drab, loose-fitting dresses or long skirts and neck-hugging blouses. It was contradicted as well by the passionate, animal sounds that came to Luke through the thin partition that separated her room from his, on those nights when his father honored Charity with his favor. To his credit, Caleb treated both of his brides impartially.

Now Charity was sitting on the side of Luke's bed applying a cold, wet cloth to his bruised, swollen cheek. He tried to sit up.

"No, lie still, dear." She smiled and pushed him back down gently.

Memory flooded back to him, and his voice hardened. "Where is the old—" He swallowed the curse out of deference to his stepmother.

Stepmother, indeed! Charity was scarcely three years his senior.

"—the old bastard," she finished it for him, still smiling.

Luke started, struck speechless, not believing his ears.

"It's the truth," she went on. "Caleb Callahan is a bastard, a brute, and a heretic. One day the Lord will strike him down with a lightning bolt."

Luke struggled up on one elbow. "Yet you took him as a husband?"

She shrugged. "After the death of my parents, I needed someone. Your father offered me the best chance of security."

"Then you don't love him?"

She laughed, showing small, even white teeth. "Love? What is love, dear Luke? Love of God? Love of one's parents? I have never *loved* a man in the way you suggest."

His ears were burning, and he could not meet her gaze. "But you lie with him in your bed. I hear—" He could not describe the noises he heard her making during those sessions with his father.

She laughed softly and stroked his sore cheek. "You hear the sounds of lust, Luke. Lust and love, they are quite different emotions. Have you ever known a woman in that way?"

He hesitated. Always a shy and reserved lad, cowed by his tyrannical father, Lucius Callahan had been a virgin until the Nauvoo emigrants reached San Francisco. Since their arrival, he had enjoyed sex with a variety of whores.

He nodded mutely, not caring to divulge that he had to pay for his sexual satisfaction. It would demean him in her eyes.

"You're lying," she said softly.

"I am *not!*" He was blushing furiously.

Her smile mocked him. "With imaginary girls, isn't that true, Luke? Remember, there are two sides to these walls, dear boy. And many's the night I hear *you.*"

He closed his eyes tightly, too mortified to look at her. He lay there in a trance, unable to move or protest as she drew back the covers, uncovering him. Goose bumps rose all over his naked flesh.

Naked! Until the cool air brushed his skin, he had not been aware that someone had undressed him before putting him to bed.

A tremor went through his body as her hand touched his thigh. Her fingers felt like five hot pokers branding his leg. As her hand moved upward, her fingers walking along the inside of his thigh, he made a feeble effort to push her off. Very feeble.

He shivered and moaned when she reached her objective, the hot, hard testimony of his desire and virility. Her fingers curled around him, gently caressing his manhood in a piston motion.

"This is what you do in the hot, dark night, Luke. And you pretend that you are lying with a woman, isn't that so?"

He nodded vigorously, no longer caring that she

knew his secret shame. Nothing mattered to him now other than this mounting bliss. He moved his hips to match the rhythm of her stroke.

"Do you ever think of me, Luke?"

He frowned, eyes still closed, not replying.

"Do you ever pretend you are making love to me?" There was a note of reprimand in her voice.

When he did not answer her again, she abruptly withdrew her hand from his aching erection.

"Oh, no, please!" he cried out and opened his eyes to plead with her.

"You don't think I'm desirable, is that it? All right, we'll see."

To his astonishment she began to undress. Black skirt. Gray blouse. White shirtwaist. She wore nothing now but pink satin and lace pantalets and a small frilly corselet that lifted her breasts, baring the extended nipples. Luke was shocked by her frivolous underthings. They were the kind of provocative undergarments worn by the harlots on the Barbary Coast.

She detected the bright light of lust in his eyes and smiled with satisfaction.

"You're surprised, Luke? The best is yet to come." She reached behind her back and unhooked the corselet, then cast it aside. Her large breasts dangled away from her body like ripe fruits as she stooped to step out of her pantelets.

Her smile was more lascivious now, her lips full and red and wet. She stood beside the bed, posing for him, breasts thrust out, hands on hips, one knee bent slightly in toward the other. The oil lamp on the table beside the bed bathed her body in alluring, flickering shadows.

"Do you think I am desirable now, Luke?" Her voice stroked him.

"You—you're beautiful," he whispered.

She knelt on the bed and bent over to kiss him on the lips, then lay down full length alongside him. Drawing his hand down to the moist tangle of her crotch, she directed his trembling fingers to the target. She pressed one of her breasts to his open mouth, then the other, all the while instructing him in the techniques that pleased her best.

Half crazed, he tried to roll over on top of her. "We'd better get this done quickly, Charity. I'm not certain I can wait much longer."

She pressed a hand against his chest and put him down gently once again. "You can wait, and you will."

She swung one leg across his body and straddled him. "See now, lie back and relax. You've been hurt. Let me do the work."

He sighed in ecstasy. "Work? Oh, my God! I've never felt so wonderful in my life."

"Just the same, let me do this for the two of us."

She positioned her buttocks on his thighs, grasped his turgid penis in both hands and with a deftness as accomplished as any of the women he had lain with in a house of ill repute, she impaled herself on his shaft.

The beauty of the moment was more than he could bear, and with every convulsion, tears of joy ran down his cheeks. In the dim background he heard Charity's moans of fulfillment.

"I love you—I love you—I love you—" Luke became aware that he was reciting a litany that meant no more than the rote he spoke in the tabernacle of the Latter-Day Saints.

Charity disengaged her limbs from his and kissed his swollen cheek. Her voice was throaty and mocking.

"You don't love me any more than I love you. The truth is, we both despise your father. Caleb is too strong for either of us to fight. He knows it, too. That's why he's sending you away."

"Sending me away?" Luke sat up in confusion. "What do you mean?"

She pushed him down again and kissed his eyes and

nose and lips. "By the will of Samuel Brennan, the foremost Mormon priest of California, you have been assigned to replace a missionary of the Latter-Day Saints in China."

"China?"

"Yes, China. Your steamship ticket is on the dresser. And Caleb wants you to have the new portmanteau the city council presented him last month."

Luke sat up and scratched his head. "Well, that comes as a surprise for sure." He smiled. "Still, it's welcome. Getting away from here—and him—will be just fine." He cupped one of her breasts in his hand and stroked the nipple with his thumb. "I'll miss you, though, Charity."

She laughed softly and pushed his hand away. "No you won't, Luke. There are multitudes of girls in this wide world just waiting for a man like you. Besides, even if you remained in San Francisco, we couldn't keep this deception going. Your father is much too smart not to guess his own son is cuckolding him. And then there would be hell to pay. I believe he'd kill you."

"I think so, too. Well—so long as he's gone for the night, there's no sense in wasting it. I'm ready if you are, Charity."

"I can see that as plain as the nose on your face. This time I'll teach you a new trick. I heard about it from that housemaid we had who used to be a whore in Sydney Town."

She reached behind her head and removed the pins fastening her tightly rolled bun. Her brown hair cascaded down her back almost to her waist.

Luke was astonished. "Lord! I never knew you had so much hair. And such beautiful hair. You *are* beautiful, Charity, only you go out of your way to hide it."

"Flattery will get you—" she paused and grinned— "everything. Here, lie back, that's the boy." Then she knelt over him and let her hair fan out across his loins.

Luke shivered with delight. He tried to see what she was up to, but her hair curtained his view.

Not for long was he in doubt, though. Her lips received his hard, pulsating flesh, and Luke cried out in sheer ecstasy.

Chapter Two

Another blast of the ship's whistle yanked Luke back to the present. Before he left the stateroom, he examined himself in the mirror over the small chest of drawers.

"Damn you!" he snarled. He wanted so desperately to forget his father, yet every time he saw himself in a looking glass, there he was. Caleb Callahan the way he must have looked twenty years before. The same hairline, only Caleb's was streaked with gray while Luke's was jet black. The same blue eyes, slightly slanted. The same aquiline nose, although Caleb's was blotched and streaked with veins from too much booze. So much for the Mormon Law of Health that counseled against the use of alcohol, tobacco, tea, and coffee!

Cheeks flaming, Luke stalked out of the stateroom and climbed the companionway up to the deck.

At the top of the gangplank, Captain Lazar smiled and shook hands with Luke. "Farewell and good luck to you, Mr. Callahan. I would advise you to proceed to your destination as quickly as possible and remain there until your boat trip up the river to the Mormon mission. Macao is not a place for sightseeing. The natives hate all foreigners with a vengeance."

"And who can blame them? China has been exploited unconscionably by the English, the Russians, the Germans, the French, and the United States for two decades. And since the British defeated Ching's armies in the Opium War, the situation has become intolerable. Now Britain and the major European powers trade and do about anything they want without the consent of the Chinese government. They're poisoning the Chinese people with narcotics and cheating and robbing them blind in the bargain. No wonder, captain, that Caucasians are not beloved in the Orient."

Lazar shrugged and held his tongue. He had learned from experience that it was a waste of time to argue with the missionaries who came to the Far East to spread the Christian word and bring salvation to the ignorant masses. Such nobility, such lofty ideals; a loaf of bread would save a human soul more effectively than a string of rosary beads or a crucifix!

Luke's first exposure to the teeming streets of Macao was a brutal assault on his senses. Dirt, filth, stench, raucous noises. After descending the gangplank he was immediately surrounded by a swarm of ragged beggars of all ages, their heads and bodies alive with lice and other vermin. They pawed at Luke, grabbing for his white coat and trousers, all clamoring at once. Had he been fluent in either Chinese or Portuguese, he could not have made sense of the gibberish.

Out of the chaos and confusion one voice carried to him, and his heart leaped. "Your Excellency, I speak very, *very* fine English. I will be honored if you will let this humble servant do your bidding."

The man stood apart from the throng, a full head taller than the others. He was in his early twenties, and his threadbare blue shirt and trousers and blue turban marked him as a Chinese Mohammedan. He was a mixture of several races and had strong, sharp features and a pale saffron complexion. Jammed into the sash about his waist was a dagger with a curved blade a foot long. He pushed his way through the crowd with a haughty demeanor that commanded deference from the others, and they parted respectfully to let him through.

When he stood before Luke, he bowed low and made a sweeping flourish with his hand. "I am at your service, sire. Tongdlon is my name. What is your pleasure. Food? Drink?" A glint shone in his eyes. "Perhaps a woman? There is no woman in the world who can please a man like our females here in Macao."

Luke repressed a smile. "You know perfectly well from my garb that I have not come halfway around the world to defile your women. Rather, I have come to restore them to grace."

Luke saw the hint of a smug expression cross the man's face.

Tongdlon clasped his hands together, fingers pointing upward, and bowed his head. "A thousand pardons, Your Excellency. This brash and ignorant serf should have his tongue cut out."

Luke had to smile now. "Listen, Tong-lon, or whatever your name is—"

"Tong-*dlong*, sire."

"Whatever. I want you to stop calling me sire and Your Excellency. It makes me feel like a pompous ass. My name is Luke Callahan. *Mister* Callahan to you. Is that understood?"

"Yes, *sir!* Then you do wish to honor this humble servant by engaging his services?"

Luke studied him shrewdly. "I suspect that you are about as humble as my father. Only you both have your individual ways of disguising your true natures."

Tongdlon's eyebrows lifted. "I am honored to be compared with your honorable ancestor."

Luke held up a hand. "Enough, enough. All right, I will retain your services for this one day. You see, tomorrow morning I will be going upriver to the Mormon mission."

Tongdlon's face darkened. "This is a bad season to be traveling through that country. There are many

bandits prowling in that region. The governor of Kwan-
tung only last week dispatched a detail of royal troopers
to the mission to guard it until the present emergency
is over."

"Emergency?"

"Yes, there is one very, very bad band of revolution-
aries who have sworn to destroy all foreigners in China.
They carry red banners that read, *Pao Ch'ing Mien
Yang.*"

Luke looked puzzled.

"You do not understand Chinese, sir?"

"I've been trying to educate myself during the long
sea voyage from America, but, no, that phrase eludes
me."

"It means: 'Death to the Foreigner, Long Live the
Ching Dynasty.' "

Luke frowned. "That does sound sinister, Tongdlon.
Such fanaticism. Who are these people?"

"They call themselves Boxers, and red is their badge
of honor. They would irrigate the earth of China with
the red blood of all foreigners."

"I never heard of them. Boxers, is it?"

"*I Ho Ch'üan*—Society of Harmonious Fists—and
yes, few have heard of them. But the whole world will
come to know what the Boxers stand for in time. They
are highly organized and extremely patient. They are
subversively recruiting new members from all the
provinces. It may take ten, twenty, even forty years,
but when they are ready, God help the world!"

"Aren't you being a bit melodramatic, my friend?"
Luke smiled. "You just used the word 'God'—I took
you for a Mohammedan."

"I am, sir, but God is God no matter what word
different peoples care to call him."

"An excellent point, Tongdlon. As for these Boxers,
I imagine the mission is in no danger now that government troops are protecting it."

"Do not be so confident, Mr. Callahan. There are

many law-abiding citizens, even among the police and the army who fear and respect the Boxers. You see, they claim they have divine protection, that they are sacred and immune to bullets or spears or any other weapons."

"What nonsense!"

A cryptic smile crossed Tongdlon's face. "I myself have seen some of the 'miracles' they perform for the benefit of the public. A loaded rifle is fired from a distance of ten paces directly into the chest of a volunteer. The bullet passes through his body and leaves no trace."

"Rubbish A man as intelligent as you appear to be surely doesn't believe an act like that. Why. in America and Europe there are men who make a living performing such illusions on the stage. We call them magicians."

"Ah. so Yes, you are right. Magic. Do you know how such acts are accomplished, so skillfully that they can deceive a large audience?"

"No of course not. I'm not familiar with the skills of legerdemain."

"Neither are the uneducated peasants whom the Boxers deceive. And not being as worldly-wise as their Western brethren, they accept what the Boxers tell them as truth The Chinese believe in magic and divine protection."

"And a pity it is. Well, gradually the Christian missionaries will dissipate all of these childish superstitions."

Tongdlon shook his head. "I don't know, sir. How would your people feel if an army of Chinese missionaries invaded your country and scoffed at your Bible and your belief in God, His Son, and the Holy Ghost as pagan superstitions?"

Luke did not care for the direction the conversation was taking "Look. Tongdlon, I didn't come all the way to Macao to debate theology with the likes of you."

The Oriental cocked his head to one side. "The *likes* of me, sir?"

Luke flushed. "I'm sorry, Tongdlon. I didn't mean it the way it sounded."

"Of course you didn't, *sir*."

Luke opened his mouth, then shut it. The yellow bastard is ridiculing me! he thought.

Dismissing the incident, he took a notebook from his coat pocket and thumbed through it until he found the entry he was looking for. He held it out to Tongdlon. "Do you know where the English commissioner's residence is? Here's the address?"

"To be sure. Follow me, sir. Along the way I will show you some of the tourist sights on Macao." There was again an edge of sarcasm in his voice that irritated Luke.

As soon as it had become apparent that Tongdlon had taken charge of Luke, the mob had dispersed to harass other passengers disembarking from the ship.

"Here. Let me take your luggage." Tongdlon took the heavy portmanteau from Luke, and with a light, deft motion, he deposited it atop his turbaned head and proceeded down the narrow, crowded street, balancing his burden with only the tip of a single finger.

Laughing, Luke followed after him. "That's remarkable. I don't believe I could have lugged it another hundred feet without stopping to rest."

"With all of your commercial and cultural advancements, you Westerners still have not mastered many basic problems of life."

Luke was increasingly amazed at the versatility of this young Oriental and his mastery of the English language. Although from time to time—by deliberation or by accident, Luke was not sure which—he would lapse into the form of broken English that a visiting Caucasian would expect of one of his ilk.

They had been walking for some time when Tongdlon paused before a doorway in a dingy building with mud walls and no windows.

"Here is a sight worth seeing, sir. Come along." He

took Luke inside. After being in the strong sunlight, Luke was blinded at first, even though there were candles and oil lamps in sconces along the walls. Gradually he was able to see that they were in a long, narrow room with tiers of wooden bunks against both walls. All of the bunks were occupied by people of both sexes, including children, whom, at first glance, Luke took to be asleep. They were mute and inert.

Then Tongdlon picked a candle off the wall and held it close to one of the figures, an ancient, emaciated Chinese man in rags so filthy and tattered that no self-respecting dog or cat back in America would have accepted them as a bed. He was a virtual skeleton with a thin layer of parchment stretched over his frame, a living mummy.

But it was his eyes that caused the hairs to bristle at the nape of Luke's neck. In those glazed pools were reflected such horror, pain, fear, despair, and hopelessness that Luke would see them in his nightmares for the rest of his life.

"Let's get out of here," he said hoarsely. He took a handkerchief from his breast pocket and clamped it over his nose and mouth to mask the vile stench of excrement, urine, vomit, and a sweet, cloying foreign scent he took to be opium. Tongdlon affirmed it.

"A legacy from our white brethren across the wide seas," he mused without emotion.

Luke made no reply, and they continued down the block, made a left turn, and walked for another quarter of a mile to what appeared to be a city square.

As they came closer, Luke could see that some kind of an event was in the works. Crowds milled around a raised platform in the center of the square, shouting and laughing and obviously looking forward to the forthcoming entertainment.

"What's going on?" he inquired of Tongdlon.

"The like of which you, sir, have never been privileged to witness. We'll tarry a bit." He took the portmanteau off his head and placed it on the ground.

"Some sort of show? Singing? Dancing?"

The vague smile flickered over the Oriental's face again "A show of sorts but no singing or dancing."

There was an excited stirring through the crowd as a group of people emerged from a building in the background on the far side of the square and made their way through the sea of human flesh on their way to the platform.

"What the devil?" Luke exclaimed as they clambered onto the dais There were two fierce-looking men clad in blue jackets black trousers and furred boots. They wore red sashes bound around their heads. Their belts were heavy with knives, pistols and other weaponry. Accompanying them were five young Chinese and Eurasian women in their twenties. They wore only loincloths and thin bandeaus that barely covered their breasts.

"Who are they?" Luke asked.

"Slave traders."

Luke was appalled. "You don't mean—?"

"Yes. white slavers as you call them. Am I correct?"

"This is outrageous! A disgrace!" Luke shouted. "What about the authorities? Can't they put a stop to this atrocity?"

Tongdlon was wooden faced. "I suppose they could if they cared to. You see, sir, the Occidental traders and officials who control almost all of the commerce along the Chinese coast have let it be tacitly known that such activities as we are now about to witness can be beneficial to all parties concerned. It pacifies the brutes who conduct the slave trade and makes them more tolerant of the 'foreign devils' who have established bases and legations upon Chinese soil. It solves a small percentage of China's population problems— less mouths to feed. And," he added bitterly, "not to be forgotten, think of the benefits that will accrue to these pathetic maidens standing up there when they arrive at their destination on the California Gold Coast. Good homes, three square meals a day, and more yüan a day than any of them have ever seen in their lives. All of this for bringing solace and joy to the most honorable gentlemen of San Francisco."

"They're being sold to work in the cribs in Sydney Town?" Luke was filled with such loathing he felt nauseated.

Tongdlon sighed. "Just another example of Western humanity and generosity."

Luke's mouth tightened. "See here, Tongdlon, that will be enough of your sardonic wit. Most people in the Western world deplore what's going on over here, the exploitation, the ruthless policy of national expansion and colonization by England, France, and the others. The United States, for example. Its only motive for sending our people to China and other backward countries is to help educate the people in the ways of the Western world and provide more and better methods of agriculture and raising livestock, so that underprivileged nations can better themselves and raise the poor standard of living of their populations."

"To be sure, sir. I mean, just look at you. I know your motives are honest and sincere. You have come to the Far East only to educate and inform the people."

"I think you had better take me to the English commissioner." He cast a parting glance at the platform where the female slaves were on display.

One of the bandit traders was showing off one of his wares the way a horse trader would make a selling pitch for a prize filly.

First he tore off her flimsy top. The girl, a sloe-eyed Eurasian with long black hair, covered her small breasts with her arms, but he slapped them away and, grinning lewdly, addressed the crowd.

Tongdlon translated. "He says the small-busted women are the best bargains because after they are with child their breasts enlarge to normal, pleasing size, instead of turning into udders hanging down to their waists."

Next the trader stripped off her loincloth, and the girl covered her pubic area with her hands. The man pulled them away and splayed his own hand over her.

"He says she is practically a virgin."

And to prove his point the trader inserted a thick finger between her tightly clenched thighs. He was rewarded with a hearty burst of laughter from the audience.

"My God! Can't anyone or anything stop this?" Luke turned away, his face as pale as ashes.

"Does anyone really care?"

They proceeded on, worming their way between pushcarts and peddler stands lined up end to end on both sides of the cramped street and pushing past the shoppers, who represented all the nationalities of the world. A Turk in a fez bartered for a fortune in uncut gems, and an English dandy in a pith helmet bid against a German in a spiked helmet for a hoard in silver and gold cutlery. Others vied for the best bargains in jewels, precious metals, spices, silk, and exotic artifacts.

At last they reached the commissioner's residence. It was on the outskirts of town, a small white Georgian house surrounded by a high wrought-iron fence in a setting of green grass, lilacs, roses, hawthorns, and shaded by English maple trees. It seemed strangely out of place and bizarre in the exotic world of Macao.

A British marine stood at parade rest outside a small sentry box alongside the gate. He snapped to attention at Luke's approach.

"I believe the commissioner is expecting me," he offered.

"Aye," said the marine in a thick brogue. "You'd be the priest, Father Callahan?"

Luke debated the advisability of trying to explain

that, while he was a Mormon priest, he was not an ordained Christian clergyman, but he decided it would be too complicated. Instead, he replied, "Yes, I am the priest."

"You can pass, sir."

Luke faced Tongdlon. "Well, it's time to say good-bye. I must say it has been a highly interesting experience meeting and speaking with you."

"The pleasure was all my own, *Father* Callahan." His eyes cut toward the sentry and flashed mischievously.

Luke smiled and held out his hand. Tongdlon accepted it and pressed it firmly.

"How much do I owe you, Tongdlon?"

"Not a yüan, sir. I told you it has been my pleasure, sir."

"That's decent of you, Tongdlon, and I appreciate it, but I can't accept your generosity." He took from his pocket a handful of change and paper currency. "Here, I'm not too familiar with this currency. You take what you judge is fair payment."

Tongdlon backed off, holding up both hands, palms held outward. "And I cannot accept your money." He hesitated, and his expression was thoughtful. "There is one thing I would accept."

"What is it?"

"Give me employment. Let me go along with you to the mission. I will be, how you say, your handyman. Tongdlon can do many, many things. For one thing you will need a translator if you are going to work with the people living near the mission. Moreover, I can cook, clean, sew." He grinned. "I can do most anything a good wife can do, but for one wifely service." He winked. "But I can find you a girl who will provide that satisfaction."

Luke laughed. "You are a scoundrel, Tongdlon. I really appreciate your offer, but I cannot afford such a luxury as a servant."

"Tongdlon comes very cheap. Much cheaper than a wife. One more thing—I will be your bodyguard." He slapped the long knife in his sash. "Tongdlon is a mighty warrior, and the bandits will leave you alone if I am with you when you travel about."

It was a persuasive point after all the talk he had heard about the bandits and their bloodthirsty motto, Death to the Foreigner. . . .

"Tell you what, Tongdlon, I will consider it. Sleep on it, as we say in America. Can you return here tomorrow morning before seven? Then I'll give you my decision."

"Tongdlon be here at six."

Luke shook his head. "Don't be exasperating! Stop referring to yourself as Tongdlon, as if you were some simple coolie pulling a rickshaw."

Tongdlon kept backing off, bowing obsequiously, his face twisted in suppressed mirth. "Tongdlon offers humble apologies. Yes, sire, Father Callahan. Be here sharp at six o'clock."

He turned and ran off at a leisurely trot. Luke watched him and smiled.

"Queer bloke he is, ain't he, sir?" said the marine.

"This is a queer place, Macao."

"Blimey! That it is, sir. I'll be grateful, let me tell you, when my tour of duty here is up."

"I have a hunch I may feel the same way before I'm here too long."

He proceeded through the gate and up a graveled circular drive, struggling with the ungainly portmanteau. It crossed his mind to attempt to lug it the way Tongdlon had, on top of his head, but he vetoed the idea. Someone might be watching, and he'd make a damned ass of himself.

Chapter Three

The craft that would take Luke upriver to the mission was a squat, ugly, clumsy Chinese junk propelled both by an odd membranous sail battened with bamboo and by two oarsmen sculling at the stern.

If Luke had entertained any doubts about taking Tongdlon with him, they were dispelled as soon as he set foot aboard the junk. Neither the skipper nor the two crewmen spoke any English, and all were sullen-looking fellows who regarded the missionary in his immaculate whites with obvious disdain.

At the onset of their journey, Tongdlon directed a stern tirade at the captain, punctuated with threatening gestures of his hands. In closing he slapped the knife in his belt and then drew the edge of his hand across his throat. The smaller Chinese shrank back, chattering nervously, his hands held up defensively. Then he turned to his oarsmen and commenced scolding them. In minutes the sail was unfurled, and the oarsman were sculling the craft toward the channel in mid-river.

"Whatever did you say to him?" Luke asked Tongdlon.

"I warned him that if he and his henchmen had any notion of leading us into an ambush in league with the bandits who have been preying on river commerce

31

the past weeks, I would cut out their hearts and feed them to the fishes."

Luke laughed. "I must say, my friend, you are not the soul of tact. However, I do feel more secure in your custody than if I had embarked on this trip alone."

Tongdlon grinned and bowed. "Honorable Father can rest, comfortable in the knowledge that Tongdlon will take care of him for the duration of his stay in China."

"Tongdlon takes too much for granted. I never said this position was permanent."

"Not to worry. Tongdlon will make himself, how you say, indispensable."

"How you say?" Luke mimicked him. "I told you yesterday. No more pidgin English. I wouldn't be surprised if you speak my tongue better than I do. Where did you learn English, anyway?"

"My mother was of high caste," he said with restrained pride. "Pure Ching. A distant cousin of Kwang Hsu himself. She was kidnapped at the age of twelve by a rival warlord who himself had been sired by a descendant of Marco Polo's expedition to Cambuluc. Over the span of centuries, there had been other mixed unions." He smiled ruefully. "A variety of foreign bloods flow in my veins. Almost as many strains, one might say, as the tributaries of the Yangtze."

Luke laughed. "I thought as much. And what happened to your mother after she was kidnapped?"

As indifferently as if he were describing his mother's trips to the seashore, he replied, "Oh, what generally happens in such affairs. This eminent chieftain raped her, and here you see the product of his act."

"Good Lord! The poor woman."

"Not really. Things worked out well for her in the end. He eventually traded her to a director of the East India Company, and we all ended up living in a fine mansion in Hong Kong. Colonel Bolton, a decent chap, did his best to make an Occidental out of me.

He even offered to adopt me legally. He might have succeeded, too, but for the outbreak of the Opium War." His lips curled down at the corners, and for the first time Luke read tense emotion in Tongdlon's expression. "When I saw what a cruel and merciless victor England was, how she trampled China into the dust, spat in her face as it were, demeaned and humiliated an entire people, I was convinced that my heritage lay in China and always would. No, Mr. Callahan, I take no pride in whatever trace of white blood flows in my veins."

Luke said nothing, and for a time the two men sat in thoughtful silence.

The countryside on either side of the river was drab, with craggy mountain ranges in the distance. The ascending river banks were a series of terraces, and bare-footed men, women, and children labored in the rice paddies, their trousers rolled up to their knees.

When Luke commented on it, Tongdlon told him, "Not a foot of arable land can be allowed to go to waste in China. Still the population continues to outstrip the production of food."

A thought occurred to Luke. "Last night I couldn't sleep. Too much excitement and anticipation. Anyway, I spent several hours poring over my Chinese dictionary and primer. I realize I must have translated it wrong, but your name—"

"Big Turnip. You translated it perfectly." Tongdlon was delighted. "You see, it is a nickname bestowed upon me by the other children in the village where I grew up. I was always taller and heavier than the average Chinese boy and man. That Caucasian in the distant past must have been a big man."

"Big Turnip, that is amusing."

"I like it. I never use my true name any longer. It is a decided advantage we have over you Westerners. Once you are baptized with a name, you must endure it for the rest of your life. I mean, what would your people think if you went back to America and announced, 'From now on, you will call me Big Turnip'?"

"Undoubtedly they would throw me into a loony bin."

"A madhouse. Ah, yes. Here in China everyone is tolerant of individual eccentricities. In fact even those who by your Occidental standards would be termed retarded or insane, are treated with special sympathy and even respect."

Luke nodded. "As you duly noted yesterday, Occidental culture is deficient in many areas. The white man has never been acclaimed for his humanity to his fellow men. Quite the contrary. I, and others like me, try to make amends in some small measure by doing our missionary work."

Tongdlon placed a hand on his shoulder and smiled. "I am convinced that you, Mr. Callahan, are a man of great humanity and filled with good will for your fellow man."

"Why, thank you, Tongdlon. Coming from you that is the highest flattery."

Tongdlon's liquid dark eyes were unblinking. "I am speaking with regard to you personally, Mr. Callahan. Not all of your fellow missionaries have my liking or respect."

"Even more flattering." He stood up and stretched. "These seats are intolerable. My backside feels as though it is as deeply etched as the river bank. I think I'll stretch out on the deck and grab a few winks of sleep. I'm exhausted."

"You do that." Tongdlon winked. "I'll stand watch to insure that these yellow devils don't slit your throat and toss you overboard."

"I could do without your sense of humor," Luke said wryly, then lay down on a straw mat in the shade of the sail.

Luke slept soundly for almost six hours. Tongdlon

woke him at three o'clock that afternoon. "The mission is in sight. We'll be landing in another twenty minutes."

Luke yawned and stretched. "My throat's as dry as powder. Is there any water aboard?"

"Yes, but I wouldn't advise drinking it. Cholera and typhoid are at near-epidemic proportions in this season. Better drink this." He removed a bottle of Chinese wine from his canvas rucksack and handed it to Luke.

Luke uncorked it and took a long draft. He grimaced. "God! What is it? It tastes like lye."

Tongdlon laughed and took a swig. "It's good for the digestion and kills germs, not to mention protecting one against the devil."

The mission sat on a hillside on a patch of high ground amid the terraced rice paddies. It was a long, rectangular building with red brick walls. Its flat roof and fluted parapet gave it the appearance of a fort rather than a haven for peace and prayer.

As the junk nosed into the beach below the mission, the workers in the paddies took a respite from their labor to satisfy their curiosity.

Two figures emerged from the front entrance of the mission and walked down the hill. A man and a woman both similarly attired in white silk Oriental robes.

When the junk was about a hundred feet offshore, the captain spoke to Tongdlon, who then said to Luke, "This is as far in as he can take us without grounding. We'll have to wade ashore."

He put on his rucksack and picked up Luke's portmanteau. Luke objected. "Here, I can manage it myself."

Tongdlon feigned indignation. "That is why I am here. Not to let boss-man do heavy work and tire himself. Then he will be strong and alert for his religious meditations."

"Don't be a smart-aleck, Chink, or I'll ship you straight back to Macao with these cutthroats."

Tongdlon winked and hefted the portmanteau onto his head. Steadying himself with one hand on the gunwale, he stepped over the side into waist-deep water. Luke removed his white shoes and held them high as he did the same. Together they sloshed through the muddy water to the beach.

The pair who had come down to greet them were in their early forties. The man was bald except for a wreath of brown hair, and he had a pleasant, ruddy face. His companion was plump and pasty-faced, with sad brown eyes and unkempt auburn hair streaked with gray. They beamed and hurried forward to greet the newcomers.

"Brother Luke! Welcome to the Nauvoo Mission." He extended his hand. "I am Brother Saul Carlton, and this is Sister Ruth, my wife."

Greetings were exchanged, and Luke introduced Tongdlon. Brother Saul shook hands warmly with him. "A hearty welcome to you as well, Brother Tongdlon. We can always use another strong back here."

"You are most kind, sir, but I am not one of your brothers."

"No offense, my friend. I can see by your turban that you are of the Mohammedan faith. But are we not all brothers and sisters, Mormon, Gentile, Jew, Mohammedan, whatever our creed or color?"

"Don't waste your time trying to convert him, Brother Saul," Luke said half in jest. "From my observations, he's more atheist than Mohammedan."

"Ah, then his mind and soul are fertile, virgin ground for cultivation."

"I was hoping you would bring a wife, Brother Luke," the woman offered timidly. "It's been sixteen months since I've had the company of another woman. That is a woman—" She broke off, aware of her husband's stern gaze.

"You have plentiful female companionship, my dear."

She blushed. "To be sure. The thing is, I have not been blessed with Brother Saul's adroitness in mastering foreign tongues. And as for the girls at the mission, they are very young for proper companionship."

Tongdlon's eyes danced. "You see, sire, I told you, you should have brought a woman from Macao."

Brother Saul and Sister Ruth were speechless. Luke struggled to hold back laughter. "Shall we go up to the mission? I'd like to freshen up and get out of these wet clothes."

The couple escorted them up the hillside and into the mission. The lower story was made up of a chapel, dining hall, kitchen, and a huge sitting room. The furniture was spare and austere, predominantly handmade of rough, unfinished and unpainted wood. The exceptions were a few chairs, cabinets, and a sewing machine that the Carltons had brought with them.

"Your quarters, as are everyone's at the mission, are upstairs," Brother Saul said. He led them up a flight of stone steps. A long, narrow hallway ran the length of the building. On either side of it were dormitories.

"Here's where our children sleep. At last count we had fourteen boys and ten girls, either orphaned or abandoned by their parents. "You, of course, Brother Luke, will have your own private room."

It was at the end of the hall, a fairly large bedroom with a wooden bed against one wall, a small table alongside the bed, a wardrobe on the opposite wall, a rocking chair by the single window, and a washstand in another corner.

A monk's cell, Luke thought, but said, "This is very nice. I didn't expect a mattress."

"It's stuffed with straw, I'm afraid," Sister Ruth said apologetically. "But it's free of vermin."

"What about Tongdlon?"

The Carltons looked at each other self-consciously

and then down at the floor. Brother Saul cleared his throat.

"There is a building out back where the servants at the mission live. I assumed—"

"Not an accurate assumption, Brother Saul. You see, Tongdlon is not my servant. Rather, he is my assistant, whose duties will be to make my burdens here in China somewhat lighter. The language problem for one thing. And, as you can see, Tongdlon is a most formidable-looking fellow. I don't think any of the local ruffians will attempt to harass me in his presence."

"That is an excellent point, Brother Luke," Carlton conceded. "We've been plagued with troublemakers in these last few months. In fact, there is a detachment of Chinese troops patrolling the neighborhood around the dock to ward off a band of predatory bandits who have attacked the mission on two occasions. Attack is not the precise word. They raided the barn and the chicken house, and they kidnapped two of the women workers."

"That's upsetting, to say the least. All right, then, I will appreciate it if you can arrange for another bed to be set up in my room for my friend, Tongdlon."

"To be sure," was the curt reply. "I'll see to it at once." The priest and his wife turned and left the room abruptly. As an afterthought, Carlton looked back and said, "We have choir practice at four-thirty. Perhaps you would enjoy hearing our children sing?"

"We'd be delighted," Luke told him. "Thank you again, Brother Saul, for your hospitality. You too, Sister Ruth."

"No need for thanks. This tabernacle belongs to all of our brethren."

When they were alone, Tongdlon stared thoughtfully at Luke. "You did not have to do what you did. I would have been content to stay in the servants' quarters."

Luke was amused. "Back in Macao you told me I

would need a bodyguard. How do you expect to guard me if you're out back in the servants' quarters?"

Tongdlon was pleased. "You are a good man, Mr. Callahan."

"Tell you what, Tongdlon, suppose you call me Luke?"

Tongdlon became very serious. "Oh, no! I could not do that. It would be disrespectful."

Luke was perplexed. "Disrespectful? You sly old dog. All of your little innuendoes are loaded with subtle disrespect. In fact, I believe you're pulling my leg right now."

The other man's face was wooden. "I'm sorry you think so. It's not true."

Luke shook his head. "I don't know. Talk about the 'inscrutable Chinese.' " All right, how about Brother Luke?"

"That would not be right, either. I am not of your faith."

"Go to hell!" Luke said good-humoredly. "I'm going to get out of these wet clothes and wash up for choir practice."

"If it's all right with you, I will absent myself at the singing and reconnoiter about the mission outside."

"Suit yourself."

Tongdlon studied Luke with curiosity. "For a man of God. you indulge in much blasphemy. Good Lord. Hell. Damn. How is that?"

"And that will be enough out of you, Big Turnip. Open my baggage and find me clean trousers and a jacket."

Promptly at four-thirty Luke presented himself at the chapel. a long, narrow room with wooden benches on two sides of a center aisle and a rustic altar at the front of the room. Above it was a stained-glass window depicting the crucifixion. The mission choir stood in two rows at one side of the pulpit. Luke walked down the aisle to the first row where Brother Saul and Sister Ruth were sitting.

Carlton smiled at him. "We were awaiting you, Brother Luke. Ruth, you may proceed." To Luke, he said, "Sister Ruth is the choir leader and, if I say so myself, she's done a splendid job with these children."

Luke sat down and observed the members of the choir, all looking very angelic in their billowy white robes and with hymnal books in hand.

"All right, we'll begin with 'Rock of Ages,' " Sister Ruth announced.

The choir consisted of four boys and four girls. They were predominantly Chinese, but as he studied their faces, Luke detected traces of Siamese, Portuguese, and French in two or three. There was one Eurasian girl, taller and more mature than the rest, who struck his eye forcibly. Long, straight black hair framed an oval face. Her smooth, flawless skin was the color of light tea, and she had wide-set, slightly slanted eyes that flashed like pure blue sapphires.

"What a handsome young woman," he commented to Brother Saul.

"A gem, and with a mind to match her beauty. Andria is our soloist, and her voice is like a nightingale's."

It was no exaggeration. After the choir had finished "Rock of Ages," the girl sang a solo, "O! My Father," a greatly revered Mormon hymn.

"She's magnificent," Luke said. "Her name—Andria?"

"Her given name is Sun Ying Wong, but she elected to be called Andria after a Spanish grandmother. Her father was a seaman aboard a French naval vessel. He was half French, half Spanish. Her mother was Chinese and Siamese. A most providential mixture of bloods, don't you agree?"

Luke was transfixed by her. "I'd say the blending was done by God Himself."

Brother Saul regarded him with mild disapproval. He was of the original orthodox school of Mormonism, and he had short patience with the younger "reformed" breed of priests the church was sending abroad these days.

For the remainder of the choir's practice, Luke's eyes never left the girl. At five-thirty Sister Ruth dismissed the group. As they were filing along the aisle, Brother Saul called to the girl, "Sister Andria, would you remain, please? There is someone I want you to meet. Our new priest, Brother Luke."

Andria turned and walked back toward them, all the while staring directly into Luke's eyes.

She made a little curtsy. "It is an honor to have you here with us, Brother Luke. I hope your stay here at Nauvoo will be a pleasant one."

"There is no doubt in my mind now that"—he prevented himself from saying, "I've met you," and said instead—"I've met Brother Saul and Sister Ruth and have seen all of you talented children."

"I am not a child, Brother Luke. I was fifteen last month." She spoke without any discourtesy.

Luke's eyes burned. "Forgive me, Sister Andria, it was only a slip of the tongue."

She gave him a dazzling smile.

"You have a lovely voice."

"Yes, and she is a brilliant student in the bargain," Brother Saul said. I dare say Sister Andria is as well versed on the Mormon church as you and I are, Brother Luke. Sister Andria, would you be so kind to define the sources of doctrine for Brother Luke?"

Without hesitation she launched into a recitation that astounded Luke. "The Church of Jesus Christ of Latter-Day Saints recognizes two sources of doctrine: first, the written word of God, the Bible, both the Old and the New Testaments—the Stick of Judah; as well as the *Book of Mormon*—the Stick of Joseph. The second source is direct revelation from God as exemplified by the *Doctrine of Covenants*, a collection of revelations as given through Joseph Smith; and the *Pearl of Great Price*, containing for the most part, revelations revealed by Moses and Abraham not found in the Bible.

"In addition the Mormon church believes in continuous revelation. direct communication from God, as to Moses at the Mount; by visitation of angels. as to Zacharias; and. of course. the appearance of God the Father and His Son. Jesus Christ, to the church's founder Joseph Smith."

"And what was the nature of that revelation, my dear?"

"That Joseph Smith, a mere fourteen-year-old boy, had been chosen as a prophet. Once each year after that occasion Joseph Smith was visited by a resurrected heavenly messenger, Moroni, son of the ancient prophet Mormon On the last visit Moroni revealed to Joseph the existence of a set of golden plates on which were engraved records of the settlement of America by a colony from the tower of Babel and continuing up through the fifth century of the Christian era. Moroni also delivered to Joseph Smith the key to translating the golden tablets, the Urim and Thummim of Scripture. Smith translated the records and from them issued the *Book of Mormon*."

Luke's mind was reeling as she poured forth an uninterrupted stream of Mormon dogma:

"There is but one man at a time on earth in the dispensation of the fullness of times who may receive a revelation for the guidance of the entire church. . . .

"It is the declared purpose of God to bring to pass the immortality and eternal life of man. . . .

"There is universal salvation by which all men will be resurrected through the atonement of Jesus Christ."

Brother Saul and Sister Ruth were beaming with pride, like parents at a child's dance recital.

"Our gospel, Sister Andria?"

"The gospel of Jesus Christ is the means of attaining all that God has planned and prepared for his children. And by keeping the commandments, living the law, and complying with the prescribed principles and ordinances of the Kingdom of God, the Latter-Day Saints believe that man may receive the highest blessings of heaven, which blessings include eternal progress and everlasting life with his loved ones."

Then she recited the Thirteen Articles of Faith.

"Isn't she wonderful?" Sister Ruth exulted.

"Words fail me," Luke said, looking steadily at the girl. This time her eyes refused to meet his.

"Sister Andria, why don't you show Brother Luke around our little haven? If you don't tarry, you can still see the sunset from the bluff. It's a magnificent sight. The river seems lit up by flames."

"I'd be pleased to show Brother Luke about. Excuse me while I change out of these choir vestments."

He waited for her outside on the stone steps of the mission. Shortly she appeared, clad now in what appeared to be the female uniform of the institution, a gray blouse, high necked and long sleeved, and a long, black, shapeless skirt. Her hair was tied back with a red ribbon, the one bright note of color, standing out, as it were, as a symbol of defiance against drab conformity.

The mission complex was made up of a barn, occupied by two milk cows and a plow horse, a chicken house, and the servants' quarters. There was a vegetable garden higher up the hillside. Above that, the landscape was a dazzling panorama of purple and red.

"Looks as if it were painted by an artist," Luke observed. "Bold, sweeping strokes of the brush."

"Mulberry," she told him. "The silk worms exist on the leaves."

"So I've heard."

"You speak even better English than my man Tongdlon. Surely you didn't learn it here at the mission?"

"No. My mother was educated in England. Then she returned to her native land and became a translator for the king. Her father was a royal personage and quite wealthy." There was a note of bitterness in her voice as she said, "Love was her undoing. From what I have read in novels, that is a very common thing when a woman falls in love. He was a naval lieutenant in the French fleet. He persuaded her to run off with him to Canton where he was stationed, and for a short time things went well with them. I was born there. Right after that, he was assigned to another station. He promised to send for my mother and me, but it proved to be a lie. He never saw either one of us again."

"That's tragic," Luke agreed. "What happened then?"

"She managed to support us working as a translator once again, this time with the French legation. She spoke four languages fluently."

"As her pupil, you are testimony to her fluency in English."

"Thank you."

"Where is she now?"

"She died of tuberculosis when I was nine, and I came to the mission. I've been here ever since. During the six years I've been here, everyone has been very kind to me. The Mormons are dear people, really."

He smiled. " 'Dear people,' That's a quaint way of expressing it. Are you a convert?"

"Yes, I suppose one would say so."

"I certainly would say so. You must be a staunch believer to have mastered Mormon doctrine the way you have. Amazing. I don't believe I could make such a definitive and expansive recitation such as the one you delivered before. Why, it almost sounded like you have memorized it word for word out of the *Book of Mormon* and other writings of Joseph Smith."

She laughed softly. "That is exactly what I have done. I have one of those memories that absorbs facts and words like a sponge absorbs water. A natural function, like breathing and eating."

What he had suspected earlier was reinforced. "You were just mouthing words? You are not a true believer?"

"Of course not. It pleases Brother Saul and Sister Ruth to show me off to visiting dignitaries and fellow churchmen. I wish to make them happy, so I perform, much the same as a monkey grinding an organ."

He laughed. "You're quite the little devil, Andria Sun Ying Wong."

Her deep blue eyes lit up, and her voice was gently mocking. "Do *you* believe, Brother Luke? I mean *truly* believe? All that nonsense about God and Jesus appearing to a fourteen-year-old boy! The angel Moroni and the golden tablets! Methinks that little Joseph Smith had a vivid imagination and an irrepressible lust for power!"

Luke was uncertain whether he should be shocked and indignant or dismiss her adolescent precocity with tolerant amusement. He decided on a compromise between the two.

"You should be spanked, young lady," he said with affected sternness.

"Then why don't you do it, Brother Luke?" she asked, mischief in her eyes.

His face was hot, and he stepped back a pace as she walked closer to him. No ordinary fifteen-year-old girl, this vixen, he thought. He had observed her while they were walking, unable to ignore the tantalizing suggestions of the woman's body underneath the shapeless garments—the thrust of a conical breast against the blouse, the outline of a thigh, the undulating movements of her buttocks and hips as she walked. Luke had not enjoyed a woman since the memorable night before he sailed out of the Golden Gate. And now, at this moment, his long abstinence afflicted him with a raging fever. *God forgive me!*

He desired Andria with such urgency that it was all he could do to control himself. What he wanted to do was to tear off her clothing and his own and take her right there in the high, sweet-smelling grass. He slipped a hand into his trouser pocket to subdue any manifest sign of his lust. As if she could read his intention, she dropped her eyes to the level of his belt buckle. Just a fleeting glance, yet blatant enough to mortify Luke.

Her smile was tantalizing. "Don't you feel well, Brother Luke? You suddenly look so feverish."

"Touch of the sun, I guess. All that time on the river," he mumbled. "I think I'll take a short nap before supper. I really appreciate the tour, Andria. Thank you. I'll see you later on."

He whirled and hurried back to the mission, his hand still clutched desperately in his pocket.

A trill of laughter chased after him like the musical rippling of Chinese wind chimes.

Chapter Four

Life at the Nauvoo Mission that first month was a rewarding experience for Luke Callahan. Attended by Tongdlon and by Andria, he canvassed the area around the mission seeking out unfortunates who needed God's help. Man's help as well, for disease in all varieties abounded throughout southeastern China after the monsoon season—influenza, cholera, diptheria, small-pox, and other ailments that defied diagnosis.

The medical dispensary at Nauvoo was well supplied with drugs: quinine, arsenic, belladonna, and laudanum, among other substances. And there was a medical encyclopedia that Luke pored over every night.

"On-the-job training," he told Tongdlon, as the two of them set and put splints on the broken leg of a woodsman who had fallen out of a tree. It was the first fracture he had been confronted with, and he was relieved how well the treatment had gone. "Just like the book says," he said proudly.

Then they carried the howling fellow back to his mud hut and deposited him on his sleeping mat.

"Here. This will make you feel better," Luke gave him a dose of laudanum and left a small measure with the man's wife. "When the pain becomes worse, give him another dose."

The woman grabbed Luke's hand and covered it with

kisses, all the while babbling in Chinese, too rapidly for Luke to interpret, although he was making marked progress with his language study, aided by Tongdlon and Andria.

Tongdlon translated. "She says that she and her husband and children will be in your debt for the rest of their lives. How can they repay you?"

"Tell her that there is no debt to repay. I am doing God's work. Let them give their thanks to him."

Tongdlon repeated it in Chinese. Both the man and the woman looked very serious. Luke sensed agitation in their voices as they both addressed Tongdlon at once.

"They are confused because you have a different God than they do. Your God would not acknowledge their thanks."

"That isn't so. Tell them that my God listens to the prayers of all the people on earth." He hesitated. "Tell them there is only one God for all mankind, no matter what various names he is called."

Tongdlon smiled and shook his head. "I will tell them, but—"

"Never mind, heretic. Do as you're told."

The Chinese couple nodded and exchanged words with each other.

"Wait a moment," Luke said as an afterthought. "I have an idea. If they truly want to do something for me, ask them to send their children to the mission school for just one week. If they find satisfaction in attending, then they may continue. If not, they may withdraw."

"You are learning fast, my friend," Tongdlon teased. "A wily missionary, indeed." He submitted the proposition to the Chinese.

Again the two of them engaged in energetic discussion. At last the man shrugged, and the woman turned back to Luke. She was beaming.

"They have agreed to your wish. The children will attend the school."

"Tell them I thank them and that I will be back tomorrow to have another look at that leg."

It was a typical episode in the life of a missionary. It was inherent in Chinese culture that a good deed must never go unrewarded. Kindness, generosity, and graciousness on the part of one human being demanded some reciprocity, no matter how meager.

When he wasn't attending the sick, Luke would chat with the aged and flatter them with small gifts: a tin of tea or chocolate or tobacco, sweets for the children, or a basket of fruit and vegetables for the impoverished. As his mastery of the language improved, his relationship with the people naturally became more intimate.

More and more children were recruited for the classes at the mission school, and only a low percentage dropped out after the week's trial period.

"You are by far the most successful priest we have had at the mission since I have been here," Andria told him one day while they were walking in a meadow on the far side of the hill where the mission was situated.

"I'm a pretty good medic, and you and Ruth are superior teachers."

Andria was pensive. "I only wish that I believed more in what I am teaching them."

"You don't believe in being charitable, honest, truthful, benevolent, virtuous, and in doing good to all men?"

"Of course I do."

"That's what it's all about, religion. Christianity, Judaism, Mohammedanism, Confucianism. What they all boil down to is the Golden Rule: 'Do unto others as you would have them do unto you.' Can you fault that philosophy, Sister Andria?"

She pursed her lips, and he had an overpowering desire to kiss that mouth—so sweet, so ripe, so red.

"I suppose not," she conceded. She stopped walking and looked at him oddly, her head tilted to one side. "What are you thinking, Brother Luke?"

"Nothing, nothing more than what we were talking about."

"No, that isn't it at all. I can tell." Her clear blue eyes plumbed the depths of his consciousness. She spread her feet resolutely and folded her arms underneath her breasts. "Now, you tell me the truth, Luke. You were thinking—yes, that's it! You were thinking something about *me*."

"I was not." His blush gave away the lie.

"Luke, please tell me." Her voice was soft and cajoling.

"I—I can't tell you." His gaze was fixed on the toes of her dainty slippers.

"You've got to tell me. I won't move from this spot until you tell me what you were thinking about me."

"Don't behave like a spoiled brat, or I'll—"

"Or you'll spank me." She was thoroughly enjoying his embarrassment. "You've threatened that before, yet you always back down. You're just a big bluff, Luke Callahan. I mean it. I'll stay out here all night if I have to. Maybe the wolves will eat me. Or worse, I'll be captured and raped by bandits. Ah, so! Then you'll be sorry you were so bloody stubborn!"

"All right, you snippy little wench. You want to know what I was thinking." He squared his shoulders and took a deep breath. *"This* is what I've been thinking."

He stepped up to her and took her roughly in his arms. Their eyes met briefly, and then his mouth came down hard on her mouth. And the kiss was everything he had dreamed it would be. Her lips were warm, yielding, sweet. Yielding was inaccurate, inasmuch as she responded with a fierce ardor the measure of his own.

At last their mouths parted, and she whispered against his cheek. "I have been thinking the same thing since the first time I saw you. I have been praying so long for you to do this to me. To do—more." Blue fire glinted in her eyes.

"I—I love you, Andria," he murmured, then kissed her nose, her forehead, and her ear.

"And I love you, Luke. My very own darling."

He tensed as she sank down in his arms, urging him down with her to the ground. The grass was thick and soft and smelled of earth.

They lay side by side, kissing and caressing one another. Andria sat up and began to unbutton her blouse.

"I want us to be really close. Take off your clothes."

Luke hesitated, casting an apprehensive glance back in the direction of the mission.

"No one can see us, silly. Quickly, I want you so desperately. I know you want me, too." She covered her mouth with a hand and giggled. "You imagine I don't know why you put your hand in your pocket that first day. To hide your—"

"Don't say it, please. I'm embarrassed enough as it is."

"Well, I'm not!" Skirt followed blouse and then her cotton shirtwaist and her bloomers. She sat there on her haunches, naked in the rustling grass, the breeze fanning her long, sleek black hair over her back.

"God, but you're lovely!" he said in awe.

Her cheeks reddened, and her eyes fell modestly.

"Thank you. I want to be beautiful for you."

She was everything he had envisioned her to be beneath the camouflage of her dowdy, characterless clothing. Her small breasts were perfectly shaped, the pink tips upturned pertly. Her belly was pleasingly rounded. His gaze followed the swell of her hips down the gentle tapering of her thighs, shyly avoiding the lush triangle of her pubic hair.

Trembling like a schoolboy preparing to take a difficult test, he removed his clothing. Sensing how nervous and self-conscious he was, Andria kept her own gaze demurely on the ground.

She looked up when he came to her. He knelt and put his arms gently around her shoulders. They kissed, and he pressed his feverish flesh against her. Her hands explored his body with an eagerness that inflamed him so that he almost lost control.

"I've got to hurry," he gasped.

Her hands ceased their teasing, and she lay back and spread her thighs to receive him. "Come to me, my one and only darling. I want you so badly."

She guided his erection to her, but he felt an obstruction.

"I forgot to tell you I'm a virgin," she said apologetically.

Luke was surprised and delighted. Somehow he had assumed that in this raw and primitive region of the world all females lost their virginity at puberty. He knew damned well there were no virgins in San Francisco!

"My very own Andria. Mine and mine alone." He kissed her eyelids as she surged up against him, hips twisting, trying with all her might to help him make entry.

Apprehension that the task was impossible took some of the edge off his desire. *My God! Maybe Andria is abnormal!* He had heard tales of women who were constructed so small that sexual union could never be achieved.

All at once the obstruction gave way, and he plunged deep inside her velvet sheath.

"Oh, my darling!" she gasped. "I have never been happier in my life."

"I adore you, my one and only love."

He battled desperately for control, but the excruciating passion he was experiencing could no longer be contained. No more than four or five strokes and the dam within him burst forth. He had the sensation that his whole being was vaporizing.

Andria had borne the initial pain mutely, and she was filled with joy to be one with the man she loved, but the acute desire she felt for Luke had not reached the point of climax. But she resolved to keep it secret from him. She knew instinctively that to confess he had not satisfied her needs would be an oblique reflection on his manhood, and he would be insecure in their next performance.

"I have never felt so wonderful in all of my life," she said. And that was no lie. She was filled with love and wonder.

He took one of her hands and kissed the palm. "All of your life!" He teased her. "All of fifteen years. Do you know I resent all the time that I haven't known you, my sweet."

She laughed. "I can just see the two of us as toddlers."

"We would have played 'doctor,'" he joked. "Lots of little boys and girls play that naughty game."

"Big boys and girls as well." She reached a hand between them and grasped him, rejoicing at the alacrity with which his flaccid member swelled under the gentle ministrations of her fingers. "Is this how they do it?"

"And like this." His hand coddled her mons veneris. She took his hand with her free hand and guided his middle finger to her clitoris. "This makes me feel good."

They indulged in leisurely foreplay until Andria was writhing with lust. "Now, my darling! Quickly! I am almost there!"

He mounted her and made instant penetration, smooth and painless so that Andria's desire was not blunted. They moved together in quickening rhythm until the fire in her loins consumed her entire being.

"Luke, I love you so much!" It was everything that she had read and heard it would be, the absolute expression of a man and woman's love for one another. Ravenous hunger. Unbearable bliss. The selfish hope that it would never end balanced against the tormented flesh's pleading for the ecstatic climax.

When it was over, the two of them lay in each other's arms, not speaking. The language of love required no speech, only tactile recognition. Their hands wandered idly, exploring, stroking, reassuring.

At first the distant trumpet blast registered only dimly in Luke's consciousness. The second time it sounded, he stiffened.

Andria sat up with a start. "Do you hear, Luke? The alarm!"

"Alarm?"

"From the soldiers! Alerting all that there are bandits in the vicinity. Hurry! We must get back to the mission at once!"

They dressed in frantic haste and ran, hand in hand, through the meadow and up to the summit of the hill. They paused a moment there to survey the countryside. The mission sat below them, serene as always. The workers in the rice paddies on either side went on working, indifferent to the continuing blaring of the bugle.

"No sign of bandits," Luke said. "Not yet, at any rate. Come along."

At a more relaxed pace, they descended the hill to the mission. Once inside, Luke and Andria helped Sister Ruth herd the children and the mission workers into the chapel.

"The soldiers will protect us with their guns," said Brother Saul, "but, for myself, I have more faith in the power of simple prayer. I will lead the congregation in the Articles of Faith. Let us begin."

Andria snuggled tightly against Luke on the hard wooden bench, clasping one of his hands with both of her own. The chorus of chanting voices was but a dim echo in Luke's ears. He was concentrating on sounds outside the mission. The bugle had stopped its dirge.

Now he listened for the thunder of horses' hoofs and gunshots, the outcries of bandits and soldiers doing battle.

Andria was reciting " 'We believe that through the atonement of Christ. all mankind may be saved. . . .' "

When a quarter of an hour had elapsed without further incident Luke began to relax. "The troops must have scared them off." he ventured to Andria.

"I don't know To be truthful. I do not have too much faith in the government soldiers."

Luke was startled. "Why do you say that?" He had encountered the military contingent guarding the mission on several occasions since his arrival at Nauvoo. They appeared to be well-disciplined. well-armed soldiers friendly and courteous to the missionaries.

"Because they are Chinese peasants first and soldiers second They are uneducated and just as superstitious as their fathers and grandfathers before them. They fear one very powerful sect of outlaw revolutionaries because its members claim to have divine protection."

"Yes. Tongdlon told me about them. They're supposed to be immune to bullets and knives."

"I Ho Ch'üan—The Society of Harmonious Fists."

"But that's rubbish!"

"You think so?" She was laconic. "That is what *they* say about Almighty God and Jesus. Yet millions of believers all around the world revere and fear the wrath of God."

Luke looked around the chapel. "By the way, where is Tongdlon? I haven't seen him since we got back."

"No J Luke I'm frightened. Everything is so quiet outside Still as"—she didn't want to finish it—*"death!"*

Abruptly Brother Saul ceased speaking his mouth agape his eyes glazing over. Following the direction of his gaze all heads turned to the rear of the chapel. There framed in the doorway, was as fierce-looking a Chinese as Luke had ever set eyes on.

A big man, almost as tall as Tongdlon but much broader, he was dressed in a scarlet robe hemmed with blue embroidery that reached to mid-thigh. His blue waist sash bristled with knives and pistols, and a scimitar was sheathed on his right hip. His shaved head was bound with a red cloth, and a long, drooping mustache framed a thin, cruel mouth. Grouped in back of him was a motley crew of brigands, all of whom wore the symbol of the I Ho Ch'üan, a red head sash.

Children began to cry, women screamed, and men scrambled into the aisle and fell to their knees, wringing their hands and begging for mercy.

At a signal from their chieftain, the bandits rushed into the chapel and fanned out across the back of the room, muskets and pistols held at the ready.

The chieftain then proceeded down the aisle, shoving and kicking those who blocked his way. Directly behind him, to Luke's astonishment and consternation, marched Tongdlon. His blue turban had been replaced by a red kerchief.

"I can't believe it!" Luke exclaimed. "Tongdlon, one of *them!* Impossible!" He stood up and started toward the aisle, but Andria grabbed his arm and held on tenaciously.

"Don't do anything to incite their wrath. The I Ho Ch'üan are absolutely ruthless. They would kill a white man with the same emotion they would behead a chicken."

In spite of her protestations, he called out to his friend. "Tongdlon! What's this all about? What are you doing with those murderous bastards?"

Tongdlon ignored him, but the chieftain stopped and fixed Luke with a hateful stare. He spoke harshly to Tongdlon, and Tongdlon answered him too rapidly for Luke to comprehend.

"What are they saying?" he asked Andria.

"He wanted to know what you said, and Tongdlon told him you were dismayed because he had defected

to the I Ho Ch'üan. He did not tell him that you called
him a bastard."

Still dissatisfied, the chieftain queried Tongdlon further.

"He wants to know why Tongdlon joined you in the
first place." Andria translated.

"I know, I understand that."

He was able to understand, too, Tongdlon's mea-
sured reply, that he was a fugitive from the law because he had murdered a man in Macao and that he
had sided with Luke in order to escape the island and
travel upriver so that he could make contact with the
I Ho Ch'üan and join the revolutionary movement.

As he spoke, Tongdlon cut his eyes covertly in Luke's
direction.

"He's trying to convey something to me," Luke whispered.

"He's already conveyed it, that he's a damned traitor!"

"I wonder."

Now the chieftain went to the front of the room and
stood behind the pulpit. He smashed two huge fists
down on the stand and delivered a loud, angry tirade.

Luke understood some of what he said, with Andria
filling in the gaps.

The gist of it was that his name was Yuan Kai-shih
and that he was the most powerful warlord in all of
China. It was the will of Heaven that all foreigners
should be purged from the land. He and his followers
had been chosen as the instruments to carry out the
divine decree.

At the rear of the chapel, the bandits shook their fists
in the air and chanted, "Let the will of Heaven be made
manifest! Let the minds of those who doubt be washed
clean of error!"

"Good Lord! They're fanatics!" said Luke. "Do you
suppose they're going to murder all of us?"

"I don't think so," Andria said confidently. "They

do not have enough strength or influence at this time to risk a massacre. There would be such a hue and cry from the Europeans that a massive foreign army might descend on China to hunt them down. To prevent that, the emperor would have to move against the I Ho Ch'üan first with his own troops."

"Speaking of troops, where are the government forces that are supposed to be defending the mission?"

"Fleeing with their tails between their legs," she said scornfully.

Yuan Kai-shih finished his speech by assuring Brother Saul and Sister Ruth that he held no personal malice against them and that he would grant them a six-month amnesty in order that they might clear up all of their affairs at the mission and return to their own homeland across the sea. Meanwhile, his troops would confiscate the foodstuff and livestock along with a few of the younger girls, and then withdraw peaceably.

His eyes raked the assembly in front of him and settled on Andria. Luke felt her shiver against him, and he put an arm around her.

"Easy, now, pretend you don't even notice him." His racing heart and the cold sweat beading all over his body denied his outward calm.

The bandit chieftain thrust out an arm, pointing at the Eurasian girl. He shouted at Tongdlon, "I'll have that wench for myself!"

"No! I'd rather die!" Andria buried her face in Luke's chest and clung to him.

Tongdlon intervened. "It's too dangerous, Your Excellency. The girl has royal blood in her veins. There would be repercussions. She's not worth it!"

"And I say she *is* worth it!" He directed his men, "Seize her!"

Two of the bandits, filthy and ragged but armed to the teeth, hurried down the aisle to the row where Andria and Luke were sitting together.

"You can't have her!" Luke spat out in Chinese. "You'll have to kill me first!"

Calmly one of the bandits drew a pistol from his red waist sash and leveled it at Luke. He most certainly would have pulled the trigger if it had not been for the whim of Yuan Kai-shih. "Don't kill him! I have other plans for that rash young foreigner."

As if on cue, the other bandits shouted their motto in chorus: "Pao Ch'ing Mien Yang!"

"Seize him!" ordered Yuan, "and bind him up!"

Luke rushed at them, a man crazed with outrage and terror for the safety of his beloved. The two bandits grabbed at his arms, but he possessed the strength of ten men as adrenalin surged through his body. He knocked down the first one with a roundhouse right to his temple, then, with the edge of his hand, gave the other a chop behind the ear. He went down, too, like a dead man.

Now the mob came rushing down the aisle screaming in Chinese, "Kill and burn! Kill and burn!"

Luke fought like a demon and battered down three additional bandits before he was overwhelmed by sheer numbers and bound tightly, hand and foot.

He lay there on the floor, his eyes reflecting agony and horror as he watched Andria being dragged off down the aisle, kicking and screaming.

The bandit chieftain came down from behind the pulpit and walked to where Luke was lying. A malevolent smile curved beneath his mustache. He looked at Tongdlon.

"And now we will dispose of this foreign devil!" Contemptuously he kicked Luke sharply in the ribs and stalked to the back of the room.

"I wish everyone to assemble outside to witness the execution of the devil!"

Chapter Five

Luke was carted outside to the small dirt courtyard in front of the mission. He caught a glimpse of the emperor's troops in their blue and white tunics and shako hats herded together in a corner of the yard and cowering under the brandished swords and muskets of their bandit guards. They looked anything but royal, he thought.

At Yuan's command the cords binding Luke's feet were cut so that he could stand. A red-shirted bandit, who had a scar that ran from his chin to his temple, stood directly behind him, a sword poised at the small of his back. Another bandit, clutching a fistful of small flags, stuck one into the dirt at Luke's feet. Then he backed off a yard and planted yet another. And another. Then a fourth, all in a straight line. Luke squinted, endeavoring to read the inscriptions on them as they fluttered in the wind: Pao Ch'ing Mien Yang.

"Death to the Foreigner. Long Live the Ching Dynasty," he muttered.

The bandit chieftain addressed Tongdlon. "My friend, the honor of dispatching this infidel is to be yours." He snapped his fingers, and another bandit stepped forward with a musket, a jade powder flask, a pouch containing musket balls, and a fistful of felt wads.

Yuan took the musket and presented it to Tongdlon ceremoniously. It was a cue for the I Ho Ch'üan forces to stamp their feet and chant, "Let the will of Heaven be made manifest! Let the minds of those who doubt be washed clean of error!"

"By killing the white foreigner, you will prove your loyalty to our cause and to the Ching Empire," Yuan told Tongdlon. "Proceed."

Tongdlon took the musket, braced the butt on the ground, and poured a strong charge of black powder into the muzzle. He then removed the long iron ramrod fastened on the underside of the barrel and rammed a felt wad down the barrel on top of the powder. Aware that Yuan and the others were watching him intently, he took an iron musket ball from the pouch and dropped it into the muzzle. It could clearly be heard rattling all the way down the barrel. The final step was to ram another wad down the barrel to secure the bullet.

Tongdlon took a deep breath. Taking a wad in his left hand, he wrapped his fingers around the end of the barrel so that the muzzle was hidden from view. Working quickly, he took the ramrod and thrust it into the muzzle, but in a way that pushed the wad aside, so that it was not thrust down on top of the ball. He withdrew the ramrod with a flourish and palmed the wad in his left hand. To his enormous relief, his deception had gone unnoticed.

The bandits commenced their chant again: "Let the will of Heaven be made manifest! Let the minds of those who doubt be washed clean of error!"

Tongdlon faced Yuan and snapped to attention, holding the musket at port arms.

"Your Excellency, I would tell this foreign devil what I think of him before he dies." His face was contorted by anger and hate.

The I Ho Ch'üan chieftain smiled and pulled at one end of his swirling mustache. "I would enjoy hearing you do so, but make it fast. We don't have all day to spend here!"

Tongdlon marched briskly down the line of little flags and confronted Luke. He spit in his face and, in Chinese, launched into a harangue. "Swine! Dog! Son of a whore! So low you could crawl under a viper's belly!" On and on it went. Then suddenly he looked back at Yuan. "I don't think he understands what I am saying."

"Then repeat it to him in English," the chieftain said jovially. "It would be a shame for such a glorious recitation to be wasted on his uncomprehending ears."

Tongdlon looked back to Luke and spoke so rapidly to him in English that it was almost a blur—a precaution so that no one present with a basic understanding of the language could understand what he was saying.

"Luke, pretend you're angry and listen very carefully. When I fire the gun, fall forward on your face and clutch at your heart. Shudder one time and then go limp and lay very still. Don't say a word, just do what I tell you. All right, make believe you are trying to attack me!"

Teeth bared as if in anger, Luke tried to hurl himself at Tongdlon, but he was restrained by the big bandit behind him who grabbed his bound hands.

Now Tongdlon began to jump up and down, first on one foot then on the other, all the while waving the musket around his head and under Luke's nose. The bandits were delighted with the show, especially Yuan. He was guffawing and slapping his thighs, almost on the verge of weeping with merriment.

Again the chant began. "Death to the foreigner! Let the will of Heaven be manifest! Sha! Sha! Sha!"

Tongdlon spit in Luke's face one last time and snapped at the guard in back of him. "Cut his bonds and step clear!"

Such was the gala mood prevailing, that the fellow never questioned the command. He removed a knife from his sash and cut the ropes binding Luke's wrists.

"Stand at attention!" Tongdlon said first in English and then in Chinese.

Luke obeyed promptly, to the relish of the bandits.

"The foreign devil is like a puppet," Yuan called to Tongdlon as he marched back along the file of flags to the firing position. "You have put the fear of Heaven in him!"

Tongdlon shrugged and faced his target. He dropped to one knee and braced the butt of the musket against his shoulder, sighting carefully along the barrel. His hand was steady, and his eye was keen. Yuan and his men had no doubts about the consequence. At this short range even the most inept marksman could not miss.

On the mission steps, Brother Saul and Sister Ruth looked on in stark horror. Brother Saul was white as ashes, and he kept massaging his breastbone with the palm of one hand.

"Are you all right," his wife asked anxiously.

"I'll be fine. Just a touch of indigestion."

He cast a compassionate, tortured glance at Andria at the foot of the steps, hanging limp in the grasp of the two bandits on either side of her. All of the radiance had gone out of her sapphire eyes; they were like dull blue glass marbles now. She had the pitiful, wretched aspect of an animal in a trap.

She kept mumbling to herself, much of it gibberish; she was in a state of acute shock.

"Luke, Luke, Luke. Oh, my poor darling—I can't live without you—don't want to—won't. How could you, Tongdlon—friend—no, no, no! *No!*" Tears streamed down her cheeks as Tongdlon assumed the firing stance. She shut her eyes against the horrific scene.

After an eternity the shot rang out, the echo of it sounding off the distant hills for seconds after. Fearfully Andria opened her eyes. The worst of her fears had been fulfilled. Luke lay sprawled face down, spread-eagled in the dirt. One of the little I Ho Ch'üan flags was clutched in his left hand. When the red-shirted guard stooped to retrieve it, Tongdlon rushed forward and pulled him back.

"Leave it be! It is the manifest will of Heaven. Do not touch the infidel. You will be defiled. The gods have turned their faces away from the devil. Let us do the same!"

Even as he rattled on, Tongdlon was amazed at his audacity. It was meaningless mumbo-jumbo but at perfect pitch with the superstitious, unquestioning mentality of the I Ho Ch'üan.

"Hear our new brother!" Yuan said sharply. "Keep your hands off the foreign devil! Let his own kind dispose of his remains." He came forward and threw his arms around Tongdlon. "You have proved your loyalty, your faith, your courage, my brother. Now we will ride forth to new crusades."

For a long time Andria stared numbly at the inert form of Luke. And then, mercifully, a curtain of darkness descended across her consciousness, and she knew nothing more.

She awoke with a start in pitch blackness. For a grateful moment she imagined she was in her bed at the mission and that the terrifying experience with the I Ho Ch'üan bandits had been a nightmare. But reality was restored all too grimly as she realized that she was lying on a smelly, old horse blanket on hard, cold earth.

Andria sat up gingerly and tried to determine where she was. She painfully retraced all that had transpired from the moment when the bandits had invaded the mission, up until the ghastly finale when Tongdlon had killed Luke with a musket shot.

"Oh, dear God!" She sobbed into her hands. "Oh, no, it can't be. My darling Luke, I will never see you again. You are lost to me forever." If there had been a knife or a gun or any lethal weapon handy then, Andria would have, unhesitatingly, taken her own life.

She got to her feet and walked forward, hands outstretched, feeling her way like a blind person. Her fingers brushed a rough fabric. Canvas, she thought, and then it came to her: she was in a tent. She walked sideways, searching for the entry flap. Finding it, she pulled it aside.

Outside, the night was cool, and the air was crystal clear, shimmering with the light of thousands of stars that shone more brightly than the moon. There were a half dozen campfires scattered around the area, and a circle of figures huddled around each one. She stepped out into the open.

"So you're finally awake," a gruff voice said in Chinese. Her guard moved out of the shadows and took her by the arm. "Yuan Kai-shih would see you at once."

Unprotesting Andria went along with the guard. She almost had to run to keep up with his pace, and several times she tripped over stones and exposed roots. They came to a tent, larger than the rest, and he shoved her roughly through the flap. Three large oil lamps illuminated the side of the tent.

The chieftain's quarters were luxurious compared with the Spartan accommodations of his men. There was an American army cot against one wall, covered by a thick, fleecy yak skin. There were other hides, bear and tiger, scattered over the ground and over pillows. A glowing brazier kept the temperature at a cozy level. Yuan was seated around a table with Tongdlon and one of his lieutenants. The three of them were quaffing wine from a goatskin that passed from one to the other.

The three of them turned their gaze on Andria. Yuan leered at her. "Ah, my sleeping beauty has awakened at last." His eyes moved lecherously up and down her body.

Andria became aware that her skirt and blouse were torn and disheveled. One shoulder was bared, and her skirt was torn, exposing her right leg to mid-thigh. She tried without success to arrange her attire more modestly.

Yuan dismissed the guard with a wave of the hand,

then spoke to his companions. "You are good drinking friends, but now it is time for me to indulge in an even more pleasurable diversion. If you will make yourselves scarce—" He indicated the exit.

Tongdlon and the other bandit got to their feet and prepared to depart. Hesitantly Tongdlon addressed the chieftain. "Your Excellency, if this humble servant may be so bold. I do not believe that Your Eminence fully appreciates the true value of the prize he has in this woman."

Yuan was in a good humor, anticipating a night of delights. He laughed. "Oh, but you are wrong, my friend. And I intend to extract full value of my valuable prize as soon as you two get out of here."

"Your Excellency, we speak of different values. Certainly she is desirable, a craving to the flesh. But I am referring to concrete value. In short, money to swell the coffers of our noble cause."

Yuan was losing patience now. "What are you talking about, you brash dog? This woman is worth money? Yes, I imagine she would bring more than the customary handful of yüan doled out to less endowed whores. Is that what you mean?"

"No, no, you don't understand because you don't know." He lifted his hand in supplication. "You could not know, of course, Excellency."

"Then stop babbling on like a fishmonger and tell me, and then get out of here."

Tongdlon stared at Andria in a fashion that made her sense he was trying to convey a message to her.

"Sire, do you have any idea of the price a virgin commands at the slave markets in Macao?"

Yuan stared at him incredulously. "Virgin? This mission wench a virgin? What kind of a fool do you take me for?"

"It's true." He lifted a hand. "May the gods strike me down on the spot if I am lying to you. I know because I heard the missionary woman speak of it to her husband."

Yuan scowled. "Why would she speak of such a thing in front of you?"

"Not in front of me. I was eavesdropping. As for the reason, she was concerned about the flowering relationship between the girl and the new young priest at the mission."

"Hmmm." Yuan stroked his long mustache thoughtfully as he strode around the tent, contemplating the girl from several angles. "How much would you estimate this virgin would bring on the block?"

Tongdlon mentioned an extravagant figure.

The chieftain's eyebrows went up respectfully. "That much?"

"Indeed. We would have to raid a dozen missions to reap such reward."

Yuan cocked his head to one side and rubbed his stubbed jaw with his knuckles. "I will ponder on the matter. Now leave. I want to be alone with the woman."

Tongdlon caught Andria's eyes one last time before he stepped through the tent flap. She was consumed with panic as Yuan approached her. "Don't hurt me! I beg of you to leave me alone!"

She turned to bolt out of the tent, but Yuan grabbed her by one wrist. "There is nowhere to run, my little fawn. No place to hide. If you obey and submit, then you will not be harmed."

He hooked the fingers of his other hand in the ripped neckline of her blouse and stripped it off her with one downward sweep of his arm.

She gasped and recoiled. Yuan laughed and methodically tore off her skirt and shirtwaist. Andria threw an arm across her bare breasts and began to sob softly and wrenchingly.

His eyes devoured her nearly nude body. "You are a true goddess. A woman a man would remember and speak of until old age, long after the powers of his manhood have become withered and spent. Tongdlon speaks of money! Bah! The mere possession of your body is a priceless treasure. I will wait no longer."

He grasped the waistband of her bloomers and ripped them off of her. "I have never experienced such desire!" he marveled. "I will go mad if I am denied an instant longer."

He dragged her, squirming and protesting, over to the cot and flung her down on the yak robe. He exposed himself to her without removing his trousers. Andria shut her eyes against the ugly sight of his bestial lust.

How different it had been with Luke. The vision of his nude body and his physical desire had filled her with pride and passion and tender love. Luke was beautiful. Tears squeezed through her clenched eyelids.

Luke *was*. A figment of the past.

The pig was forcing her legs apart with a thick knee. She could not resist him. Then it struck her, what Tongdlon had been trying to tell her. *Play the role of a virgin!* That wasn't difficult considering that she had been a virgin less than twenty-four hours ago.

"Don't!" she suddenly exclaimed. "I've never been with a man before! A doctor who examined me in Macao when I was twelve said I am abnormally small and may never be able to have relations with a man."

Yuan stopped just as he was positioned for the first thrust. "You speak the truth? Tongdlon was right. You are a virgin?"

She nodded her head vigorously. "You may kill me if you use force to rape me."

The bandit chieftain frowned. A voice at the back of his mind kept whispering the astronomical sum of yüan that Tongdlon had mentioned.

He made a few feeble thrusts to test her membrane. With every ounce of strength and will at her command, Andria constricted her sphincter muscle. Figuratively speaking, Yuan was confronted by a stone wall. The voice began to overshadow the urgency of his desire. His member was becoming limp.

Muttering to himself in frustration and disgust, he rolled away from her and stood up. He adjusted his clothing.

"Tongdlon is right. No woman is worth losing all of that money. You may stay where you are for this night. Tomorrow we will decide what is to be done with you. How we will dispose of you at the slave market in Macao." He turned and stalked out of the tent.

Andria wrapped herself up in the heavy robe, but her body would not stop trembling. Gradually, though, her heartbeat slowed down, and at last she lay still, exhausted and aching all over as if she had been subjected to a physical beating.

The prospect of being auctioned off at the slave market in Macao did not terrify her nearly as much as the idea of being ravaged by the bandit chieftain. There was always a chance that she could escape once she was in the city. And even if she didn't, there was an element of intrigue about the future. She had heard that the white slavers treated their girls kindly, if without respect, the same way they would feed and take care of a prized horse or cow or cat. Moreover, she would be sent to the United States, a journey she had yearned to make for several years. She had read so much about that great and marvelous land of opportunity across the wide Pacific that she was infected with a sense of nostalgia whenever she studied the map of North America on the schoolroom wall, almost as if she were an American expatriate instead of a citizen of China.

San Francisco, that is where they would be taking her—she was sure of it. Luke had lived there before coming to the mission. His family still lived there, and that introduced another appealing possibility. If she could locate Luke's father, she would tell him that she and his son had been in love, and then maybe Caleb

Callahan would save her from the seamy existence of a brothel. Her flesh cringed at the thought of being a human receptacle into which a succession of indifferent men spent their lust, night after night.

She drove such thoughts out of her mind and concentrated on Luke, as they had been so close together in the sweet green grass with the sun warming their bare bodies. She would never know that ecstasy again on this earth.

Andria wished fervently that she were a good Mormon, a true believer that all of mankind would one day reach the highest blessings of heaven, which included eternal progress and everlasting life with one's loved ones.

When at last she fell asleep, she had a smile on her lips.

Chapter Six

The next morning Andria was awakened by two of the women in the camp. "It is time for you to rise and bathe," one of them informed her.

She sat up, rubbing her eyes. "Bathe?" There in the middle of the tent was a large tin tub from which aromatic steam swirled up.

"Yes, Yuan wants you to be fresh and beautiful when they take you to Macao. You will bring a high price on the market."

The market!

It sounded as if they were speaking of a side of beef. Still, the promise of a hot bath was very appealing to her. She got out of bed and walked over to the tub. Gingerly she let herself down into the hot water. It was sheer luxury, and the perfumed bath oil was a balm to her sore, stiff limbs. The women scrubbed her back with a sponge and later dried her off with a large, clean terrycloth towel. Yuan Kai-shih had some unlikely aristocratic tastes for a professed revolutionary. Along one wall of his tent, she had observed a half dozen hampers heaped with tinned delicacies, fresh fruit and vegetables, expensive clothing, and other booty obtained in the band's raids on settlements throughout the area.

"Yuan says you may choose what clothing you wish

from his private store," a wizened woman informed her. She went over to one of the hampers and picked out a pair of black satin trousers and a mandarin jacket of Shantung silk, ornately decorated with embroidered dragons and tigers against a background of gold.

"You like these?"

Andria shrugged. "If they fit. I wish some underclothing first."

Andria rummaged through the pile until she found a pair of plain cotton pantalets and a cotton shirtwaist. She considered a petite boned corselet but rejected it on the grounds that it would be fatuous to wear such a chic garment where she was bound for.

She tried on the clothing. Although all of it was oversized, she felt comfortable enough. One of the women braided her hair in two long pigtails, after which the women served her a breakfast consisting of fried rice, bacon, and hot tea.

"I feel like a queen," she joked wryly.

"I envy you," the younger woman told Andria. "Any life would have to be better than this one. We are all whores here, anyway. But you will be paid for your services and live in a lavish bordello."

After breakfast they escorted her out of the tent where Yuan, Tongdlon, and about twenty of the bandits were waiting for her alongside a horse-drawn cart.

Yuan motioned for her to climb aboard the cart. "You will ride." He grinned evilly. "I want you to conserve your strength so that you will appear more beautiful and vital on the auction block."

She sat cross-legged in the cart, and Yuan swung aboard his mount. The driver of the cart snapped the reins down on the dray horse, and the procession started off to the southeast.

Along the way they passed the Mormon mission in the distance, and once again a lump formed in Andria's throat, and she fought back tears.

Mutely she mouthed his name. "Luke, goodbye, my

darling. I will always love you, and we *will* be reunited in some hereafter life."

At that precise moment Brother Saul was strolling along the ridge behind the mission, engrossed in his morning meditations. He spied the caravan on its way to the seacoast, but he never imagined that it was the same bandits who had pillaged Nauvoo the previous day and abducted Andria.

Reflecting on those dire events, he tried to find comfort in Luke's miraculous escape from the executioner's bullet.

As soon as the bandits were out of sight, he had rushed over to Luke's inert form and kneeled down. To his shock and astonishment, Luke had rolled over and sat up.

"No, Brother Saul, I am not Lazarus incarnate." Sister Ruth and the mission workers all crowded around him, talking excitedly.

Luke stood up and brushed himself off. "I owe my life to Tongdlon."

"But I don't understand!" Brother Saul said, awed. "I saw him load that musket with my own eyes. We all saw him."

"You only *thought* you saw him load the gun. Though actually he *did* load it, except for one detail. Instead of tamping the musket ball down with a felt wad, he palmed the wad. That way there was nothing securing the bullet so that when he put on that wild act just before he fired, shouting and gesticulating with the musket, the ball simply rolled out onto the ground, and he stepped on it and ground it into the soft dirt. It was risky, but good old Tongdlon pulled it off."

"Then he is not one of them, the I Ho Ch'üan?"

"No. He only pretended to be, in order to spy on them and find out what they're up to. I only hope and pray that he will find some way to get Andria away from those monsters." His jaw thrust out. "If there is a way, we can depend on Tongdlon to succeed."

That night Luke was awakened by the sound of someone moving about in the dark room. He sat up in bed.

"Who's there?"

"Tongdlon. Light the lamp."

"Tongdlon!" He was overcome with joy and relief. "My friend, am I ever happy to see you! At least I will be when I get this lamp lit."

He lit the lamp on the bedside table. The two men shook hands emotionally, and Tongdlon sat down on the side of the bed.

"Andria? Is she all right?"

"Up until now, she is. As for the future—" He described all that had transpired after the bandits had departed from the mission.

"Yuan's going to sell her to the white slavers?" Luke exclaimed in anger. "How could you have let it happen?"

"I had no other choice. It was either that or she would have become Yuan's concubine. I don't believe she could have endured that. This way, at least, she has a chance. I managed to buy her time. Anything could happen."

Luke leaped off the cot and grabbed for his clothes on the chair. "Come on, we've got to follow them and rescue her."

"We wouldn't stand a chance against them."

"The authorities at Macao—surely they'll intervene?"

Tongdlon laughed humorlessly. "The authorities! They are every bit the bandits that Yuan and his henchmen are, only they wear uniforms. They get paid off by all of the foreign traders for looking the other way when certain crimes are committed. And the slave traders pay the highest bribes of anyone."

"Well, we just can't sit here and do nothing. I'm going to Macao even if you won't come with me."

"Oh, I'll come with you. I have no other choice."

"What do you mean?"

"I saved your life, and by Chinese custom, I am committed to preserving the gift of life until you expire from natural causes."

Luke grinned in spite of his anguish, took Tongdlon's hand in one of his, and placed his other hand on Tongdlon's shoulder. "I have never had a better friend than you, Big Turnip, and I never will."

Luke's grin faded. "You'll have to keep out of their sight in Macao. After he discovers that you slipped away from the column, he'll guess that you're a traitor and suspect that you headed right back here. They'll be on their guard constantly until they dispose of Andria, and if they ever set eyes on you, you'll be shot on the spot. And this time the bullets will be in the guns."

Tongdlon nodded solemnly. "It was a lucky thing for both of us that one of them didn't spot that little deception."

"Little? My friend, it was the biggest thing that has ever happened to me in all of my life. It *was* life." He finished dressing.

Before they departed, they woke Brother Saul and Sister Ruth and apprised them that they were off to Macao in a desperate effort to rescue Andria. The two of them were distraught, and Sister Ruth wept at the idea of Andria being sold into white slavery.

"My darling child, she was just like my own flesh and blood. Oh, I'd rather see her dead than become defiled in such fashion."

Luke put an arm about her quaking shoulders. "You rest easy, Sister. I promise you that Andria will neither be defiled nor dead. We'll find some way to save her. Now we must be off to Macao."

*　　*　　*

The caravan of Yuan Kai-shih reached Macao at noon of the second day's march. Yuan was in a foul mood over Tongdlon's desertion. Tongdlon had told Yuan that he was going to forage the countryside for chickens or other edible commodities on the first night they had camped.

Yuan was only slightly reassured when one of his lieutenants suggested that perhaps Tongdlon had been caught pilfering by some bold landowner and had been jailed or executed.

"I don't think so," Yuan growled. "That one is too clever and quick to let some bumbling farmer catch him stealing chickens. No, that son of a whore has deserted the cause." His eyes narrowed. "But why? I mean why did he bother to join us in the first place?"

"He might be a member of the secret police of the governor of Kwangtung," another bandit declared.

"In that case he may have been setting a trap for us. There could be a legion of royal troops waiting in ambush for us at Macao." He gazed in the direction of the tent where Andria was imprisoned. "That girl, she smells like trouble. Do you gentlemen think we should dispose of her and return to our base camp?"

The votes were evenly divided, and in the end it was Yuan himself who decided to pursue the original plan.

"Tongdlon hasn't had time to alert the governor of our purpose. Besides, it takes time to mobilize troops and dispatch them to Macao." And at the back of his mind was the anticipation of the fortune the girl would bring to him at the auction. No, she had to be kept alive.

Andria's confidence and hopes were restored when they reached Macao. Amid the hustle and bustle of the teeming city, she no longer had the sense of terrible isolation she had felt in the bandits' nomad camp. Surely there was someone among all of these people who would come to her rescue. Her big hope, though, was Tongdlon. His sudden desertion the night before must mean that he was trying to find a way to help her.

Her optimism fell off sharply, however, when they arrived at that section of Macao where white slavery flourished. The vice king of Macao was a fat, swarthy Portuguese, one Paolo Mendez. His headquarters were an oasis of European luxury in a desert of squalor, deprivation, and depravity.

When Yuan and Andria were ushered into his private office by two armed guards, Mendez rose from behind his big teakwood desk and came around it to appraise the girl. His grotesque body made a travesty of the English tweed riding habit he was wearing.

His Chinese was fluent but heavily accented. "Ah! Señor Yuan, you were not exaggerating when you described your jewel as exquisite. I am tempted to buy her for myself."

Yuan shrugged. "If the price is right, you can do anything you want with her."

Mendez addressed Andria. "Little pigeon, will you kindly divest yourself of those baggy garments so I can tell what kind of a body you have?"

"I will not!" she stated firmly, and her blue eyes were as cold as ice.

"Do as he says!" Yuan snapped and moved toward her. "Or I will do it for you!"

She knew he would, too, so resignedly, she began to undress. At last she stood before him naked—not in cowering shame, but with her shoulders squared, her backbone straight, and her head held high. Her eyes regarded him with loathing and contempt.

Stroking his full beard and puffing on his long black cigar, Mendez walked around her twice, all the while nodding with approval.

She flinched as he pinched her buttocks.

"Very nice, so full and firm."

Her flesh crawled as he ran a hand over her belly, but she maintained a posture of frigid indifference.

"Flat, yet soft as velvet. A true goddess."

He cupped one breast in his hand and then the other. "Fresh fruits. From their juices are brewed the nectar of the gods.

"All right, you may put on your clothes now. Tomorrow morning we will attire you in raiment more alluring and provocative to inspire our bidders to unprecedented heights." He turned to the two guards. "Take her to the stable and lock her up for the night."

Mendez and Yuan were haggling over the minimum price that the bandit chieftain would accept for her as she followed the guards out of the office and down a long, dim hallway.

The "stable" was a large barracks with barred windows and sleeping mats along both walls. At the far end was a latrine with four seats. It was not as objectionable as Andria expected it would be because it was built out over the harbor and the human waste products that went into it daily were carried out by the tides.

She shared the space with sixteen other women of assorted sizes, shapes, and ages. Andria was the youngest at fifteen, while she judged the oldest woman to be about thirty-five. Most of them were dressed in the ragged trousers and jackets worn · by the peasants who labored in the fields and paddies.

The older woman, Lee-sou, was sympathetic, and Andria liked her immediately. "You are so young and so lovely. What a crime it is that you have come to such a tragic fate."

When Andria related her misfortunes, Lee-sou was even more appalled. "You were taken from a mission? God help you!" To Andria's amazement, she crossed herself, then explained, "I was a maid in the household of a Christian missionary many years ago, and I was baptized."

"I, too, am a baptized Christian," Andria said wearily. "But their God has proved no more benevolent than the pagan gods the peasants entreat and burn incense for."

"I hope we stay together, Andria. I will watch over you like an elderly aunt."

Andria laughed. "You are not all that old, Lee-sou. But I would like us to be together."

"Now that we will be going to America, I will drop the last part of my name. Simply Lee. Somehow it sounds more Western that way, don't you think?"

"I suppose it does."

Lee was a small, plump, attractive woman of pure Chinese descent. She had long, oily black hair, and her features were small and distinctly Oriental. Her teeth were her worst physical point, overly large, yellow, and crooked. She possessed an alert, quick mind, and she spoke English, though not as fluently as did Andria.

For a few moments Lee seemed to be deep in thought. Then she said, "I have an idea that may ensure we are sold together."

"Whatever is it?" Andria asked, her excitement rising.

"In spite of your flattery, I could be your aunt. Yes, even your mother."

"I don't understand."

"That swine Mendez would do anything to exploit our situation and wring every cent he can out of prospective buyers."

"So?"

"Suppose I were to propose to him that he should auction the two of us off as a pair, mother and daughter. Mother and *virgin* daughter, do you see my point?"

Andria grasped it at once. There was something provocative about the image of a mother and virgin daughter that was calculated to appeal to the twisted mentality of a white slaver.

"What is more," Lee went on, "selling us as an inseparable pair will bring Mendez a far greater profit than if he auctions me off as a single. An old hag like me will earn him no more than a pittance."

"It sounds promising, but how can we bring it to his attention?"

"I can't do it, but he will listen to you, Andria. You are the most expensive piece of goods he has auctioned off in years. You insist on speaking with him before the auction begins tomorrow morning."

Later, as they lay side by side on their straw sleeping mats, Andria asked her new friend, "How did you end up in Mendez's stable, Lee?"

"My father lost everything he owned playing fan-tan in one of Mendez's gambling clubs. I was the only collateral he possessed, and Mendez cancelled the debt in exchange for me." She spoke of it as indifferently as if she were telling Andria a mundane bit of gossip. "Many of the women here tell a similar story. One was even sold to Mendez by her husband. Oh, there are no shortages of slaves here in Macao. These are hard times."

Andria slept fitfully, haunted by the sighs and weeping of the other women in the barracks. From time to time one would scream out in terror in the grip of a nightmare. The one time Andria did doze off, she dreamed of Luke lying face down in the dirt, his shirt soaked with blood. She bolted upright crying, "Oh, my God!"

Something about the dream bothered her, a nagging bead of mercury rolling around in her mind, defying her efforts to grasp it. She was relieved when the oblong window above her was defined by cold gray light. Dawn at last. Soon they would be on the auction block.

A guard opened the door soon after, carrying two buckets. Another guard followed him, carrying a tray of wooden bowls and chopsticks. Breakfast consisted of thick, sticky rice and tepid tea. Andria gave her share to an emaciated young woman with a hacking cough. Then she spoke to her captors.

"I would speak with Mr. Mendez."

"Why not the emperor?" the chief guard said scornfully.

"Mendez will be displeased if you do not take this message to him. I know of a way he can double his price on this woman." She indicated Lee.

"That fat sow?" Both men laughed. But it gave them food for thought. Where money was concerned, one could not afford to lightly dismiss any proposition.

"We'll tell him what you said, but don't count on getting an answer."

Within a half hour, Mendez arrived at the cell. Ready for the day's business, he was dressed in a green frock coat, checkered trousers, and a flowery ascot. He called to Andria through the bars: "What is it you have to tell me? Be quick about it. Only ten more minutes until auction time."

She went over to him and described her plan to pose as Lee's daughter.

He stroked his beard as he considered the scheme. "Hmm, it *is* an interesting possibility. Mother and virgin daughter. Yes—I like it. All right, now get into the new clothing we have here for you."

The guard opened the door and brought in a wicker basket heaped with freshly laundered clothing. Unlike most of the slave traders, Mendez insisted that his girls appear clean and neat on the block. They commanded higher prices than the filthy, tattered women sold by other traders.

There was a special outfit for Andria, a chamois vest that laced down the front, a G-string, and a pair of gauzy, translucent pantaloons that fitted snugly at the ankles.

"I look like a concubine from a Turkish harem," Andria observed when she was dressed in it.

"I feel quite grand," Lee said, posing in her scarlet silk robe. A voluminous garment, it covered her from neck to feet and disguised her corpulence.

The door swung open, and the guards summoned them. "Time to go on the block, you whores. Be quick about it!"

Like animals going to slaughter, they were herded out into a courtyard behind Mendez's establishment, already crowded with prospective customers. The women were lined up against a brick wall to await their turn to go on the block, a raised platform in the center of the yard. Meanwhile, the buyers looked them over and made notations in notebooks and on slips of paper. Andria elicited special attention from all of them. One man clad in the uniform of a merchant marine officer —a ship's captain, Andria concluded from the gold braid on his cuffs and cap—could not take his eyes off her. A dark, saturnine-looking man with sharp features, he appeared to be Italian or French.

The auction went swiftly, and soon Andria and Lee were the sole women against the wall. It was a deliberate ploy by Mendez to whet the appetites of the buyers.

"As you can see, I have saved my prize merchandise for the end. Here we have a unique transaction. Mother and daughter, they are to be auctioned off as a single unit."

There was a murmur of surprise and approval from the spectators.

Dramatically waving his arms, he continued, "But the choicest part is yet to be heard." He paused, his avaricious eyes raking the crowd. "The girl is a *virgin!*"

This preposterous statement evoked jeers and laughter from the buyers.

"A virgin, indeed! Mendez, that is too outrageous, even for you."

"Bah! There isn't a virgin within a hundred miles of Macao! What do you take us for?"

The trader held up his hands for silence. "My friends, on the soul of my dear, departed mother, this girl is a virgin. Until a few days ago, she spent all of her life in a convent." Convent sounded more convincing than mission. "She has led the chaste, secluded life of a saint. On my word, take her to a physician if you buy her, and if he does not bear out my statement, then I will return the purchase price to you."

Attention focused on Andria now.

"Is he speaking the truth, little flower?"

"Is your hymen intact?"

"What about it, mother? Is she truly a virgin?"

Lee put her arms protectively around Andria and rebuked them angrily. "My child is as pure as the snow on the peaks of Tibet. Untouched by human intrusion."

There were still some doubters in the crowd, but a majority of the buyers were convinced that Mendez and the mother were telling the truth. There was a sudden surge of momentum to get on with the auction.

"I'll bid a thousand for the pair!" one man shouted.

Mendez laughed at him. "Take your pennies and go home, my friend. Leave the bidding to the men, sonny boy."

"Two thousand!"

In rapid succession the bids doubled and redoubled, and even Andria and Lee were impressed with their combined worth in the flesh market.

The sea captain stayed in the background, his arms folded across his chest and a superior smile on his lips. Never once did he join in the bidding.

Mendez made his final declaration. "Do I hear any further bids? No. Then I will say it for the last time. Going once—going twice—"

Abruptly the captain interrupted him. "I offer you—" And he named a sum that elicited exclamations and gasps of awe from the other buyers. Mendez's jaw went slack.

"Did I hear you correctly, sir?"

"You did. Well, get on with it. My ship sails within the hour."

"Then that is it. The two women are the property of—your name, sir?"

"Captain René Du Bois, master of His Majesty's ship, *Martinique*." He went up to the platform and handed Mendez a fat wad of currency. "Here you are. I'll take them right along with me."

"Good. I'll send two guards to see that you reach your vessel safely. It would be folly to walk the streets of Macao with such a beauty."

"That won't be necessary," the captain stated, and he opened his jacket to reveal a brace of pistols jammed in his waistband. In a motion so fast that the action was blurred, he drew the pistols, cocked them, and aimed them at Mendez's belly. "As you see, I can take care of myself and the ladies."

Mendez cringed. "To be sure, captain. Just thought I'd offer."

The captain put the pistols back in place, buttoned his jacket, and strode over to where Andria and Lee were standing.

"Let us be on our way, my good women. And if you have any notion of escaping, let me assure you that I will not hesitate to shoot you both in the back." His smile was a blade. "I think you will agree that death would be preferable to what would befall you if you fell into the hands of some of the depraved swine who frequent the streets of Macao's slave district."

"You speak excellent Chinese, captain," Andria complimented him.

"And English and French and German and Spanish," he said matter-of-factly.

"You have our word, we will not try to escape. In fact, we are looking forward to the sea voyage ahead. May I inquire as to the nature of our destination?"

"You may. The United States of America."

To his surprise and amusement, Andria clapped her hands in satisfaction. "That is what I hoped you would say. Captain, thank you for buying us."

He threw back his head and laughed. "I have a feeling that it was a wise investment."

Chapter Seven

It was long after midnight when Tongdlon wakened Luke from a deep sleep. They had made camp in a grove of trees, and after a meal of tinned meat, hardtack and tea, they had rolled up in their blankets on a mattress of mulberry leaves.

"What's wrong?" Luke sat up and stretched his arms.

"I heard suspicious noises a while ago and did a bit of reconnoitering. Yuan and his men are camped about a quarter of a mile from here."

Luke came fully awake now. "Andria?"

"I don't think she is with them any longer. It appears to me that they are heading away from Macao."

"And that means the slavers have her."

"I'm afraid so."

"Come on, let's go." Luke kicked off the blanket and leaped to his feet.

"What are you going to do? We can't take on that many men."

"I intend to take on but one man. Yuan."

They made their way to the bandits' camp and made a full circle of the clearing, keeping in the shadow of the trees. Luke singled out Yuan's tent, the largest in the compound. In front of it two I Ho Ch'üan sat on their haunches, nodding sleepily over a dying camp-fire.

Without speaking Luke motioned for Tongdlon to follow him to a spot directly behind the chieftain's tent. "Your knife," he said tersely.

Tongdlon handed it to him.

"You wait here." Knife in hand, Luke moved stealthily to the rear of the tent and placed the sharp tip of the knife against the canvas. It cut a gash four feet long through the frayed fabric, with the ease of a hot knife cutting through butter. He waited for a while to make sure that the sound of the metal against canvas had not been detected by Yuan. Satisfied that Yuan was sleeping, he eased his body through the opening into the darkened tent. He stood still until his eyes had adjusted to the darkness. There was a faint, rosy illumination from the embers in the brazier, and he could make out silhouettes of the objects in the confined space. A chair, a table, a cot. And curled up on the cot in a bedroll was a man, snoring peacefully. Quietly Luke went over to the cot and knelt down. Deliberately he placed the tip of the blade against Yuan's Adam's apple and clamped his other hand over Yuan's mouth.

Yuan wakened with a start, and his body stiffened.

"Make a move and you're a dead man," Luke said in Chinese. "I'll slit your throat from ear to ear. Now, I'm going to remove my hand so that you can speak. But remember, one false move and—" He emphasized the point by pricking the skin of Yuan's neck with the blade.

"Where is the girl? Don't waste your time lying. I know you took her to the slave mart in Macao. Whisper—or else I'll kill you right now."

The terrified bandit was trembling, and his voice quavered. "A trader named Mendez. He is the most famous in Macao. Everybody knows him, so you won't have any trouble finding him."

"I'd better find her, or I'll come after you and cut off your balls. There's nowhere on earth where you can be safe from my vengeance."

With that he delivered a powerful chop with the edge of his hand to the spot between Yuan's eyes just above the bridge of his nose. The man moaned and went limp. Luke got to his feet and went back to the opening he had cut in the canvas. He slipped through it and walked quietly back to the trees where Tongdlon was waiting for him.

"Well?" his friend inquired.

"They sold her to a trader named Mendez."

"Mendez." Tongdlon nodded dolefully. "I know the bastard only too well. He moves his merchandise extremely fast, so we'll have to hurry."

"How much further to Macao?"

"We can't make it until well after daybreak."

"Well, let's not waste time talking."

They continued on the way southeast at a clip that soon had the two of them gasping for breath. Then, when he felt that he would surely collapse, Luke got his second wind. Two hours later they paused to drink at a spring, rested ten minutes, and started out again refreshed.

It was eleven o'clock by the time they entered the white slave district of Macao.

"Mendez's place isn't far from here," said Tongdlon and led the way to the big white stucco building at the rim of the harbor. A gigantic mulatto man, armed, blocked the entrance.

"We must speak with Mendez," Tongdlon told him. "We are looking for a girl."

The guard grinned. "You're too late, brother. The girls were auctioned off hours ago. Come back on Wednesday. That's when the next batch will go on the block."

"Was there one girl who stood out from all the others in the last batch of girls?"

The guard's eyes narrowed in reflection. "You must mean the Eurasian. Mendez claimed she was a virgin. Dark hair, eyes like two blue sapphires. A real beauty."

"That's the one," Luke said excitedly. "Who bought her?"

"Some frog sea captain."

"The name of his ship?"

"He mentioned it, but I don't remember. Something about—let's see. It had the name of a place. An island in the Caribbean."

"Cuba, Haiti, Jamaica. . . ." Luke rattled off every Caribbean island he could recall before mentioning, "Martinique?"

"That's it!" the man said. "Martinique."

Luke grabbed Tongdlon's arm. "Hurry—the waterfront, the docks."

"You're too late," the guard said. "Her captain said he was sailing as soon as he took the women back to the boat. They've been at sea for at least two hours. Bound for the United States."

"Damn!" Luke pounded a fist against his leg.

He turned away and walked off slowly, followed by Tongdlon. Eventually they arrived at the docks and verified that the *Martinique* had sailed for San Francisco at 8:45 A.M.

"San Francisco," Luke mused. He walked to the end of a pier and scanned the great circle of the horizon. "She'll be put in a Sydney Town crib. Christ! What a fate for a girl! Just the thought of it makes my blood run cold. I've got to save her, Tongdlon!"

"How do you expect to do that?"

"Quit the mission. Borrow passage money from the church and get the earliest ship I can for the States."

"Can you borrow enough for two tickets?"

Luke grinned and clapped him on the back. "You don't think I'd go off and leave my good friend and lifetime protector all by his lonesome. Come on, let's go back to the mission and tell Brother Saul and Sister Ruth of our plans."

"Let's go back by boat," Tongdlon proposed. "My feet hurt from all that walking."

"So do mine. Let's see what we can arrange."

It was almost dark by the time the sampan put them ashore on the beach below the mission. When they told the Carltons that Andria had been shipped off to San Francisco, Sister Ruth was inconsolable.

"Of course you must go after her at once. Whatever the cost, the church will be only too grateful for the chance to assist our dear Sister Andria in her hour of need. That is the whole purpose of tithing. I'll fetch you the money from the safe." Brother Saul kept the mission funds in a secret cache behind the altar to insure their safety from bandit raids.

"We might as well stay here for the night," Luke said. "It's been a long and strenuous day. I'm exhausted."

Sister Ruth put her arms around him. "Yes, dear, you need the rest. And a good hot meal. I'll have the cook prepare you something right now."

After supper Luke and Tongdlon went straight to bed and slept until dawn the next morning. Brother Saul had arranged for a local fisherman to ferry them downstream to Macao. They bade the Carltons a tearful farewell on the beach and climbed aboard with their belongings.

Tongdlon had been outfitted in a white missionary's suit. "It's a uniform that carries authority," Luke advised him. "And along with your excellent English, we can pass you off as a Chinese American. When I left San Francisco, immigration was free for all. But you can never tell. Once law and order become firmly established there, the customs people will move in in force."

Tongdlon shrugged. "If necessary I can buy forged papers to establish my American citizenship."

Luke shook his head. "Is there nothing that can't be bought in Macao?"

"Nothing whatsoever."

"It might be a safeguard at that," Luke admitted. "All right, we'll buy you papers."

Upon their arrival at Macao, Tongdlon took Luke to a small printing shop in the banking district. The proprietor, a wizened Chinese man with long pigtails hanging down his back, greeted Tongdlon effusively, and they chattered away in Chinese so fast that Luke could not follow the conversation.

"I used to deliver for Chang," Tongdlon explained to Luke. "We're old friends."

Chang substantiated it by agreeing to prepare a set of identification papers for Tongdlon for a paltry sum. "They'll be ready tomorrow morning," he promised.

That task accomplished, they went to the docks to book passage for America.

"You're in luck," the clerk at the steamship office told them. "There's a Dutch merchantman sailing for San Francisco the day after tomorrow."

To conserve their funds, they found a cheap flophouse where for a few pennies one could rent a sleeping mat for a night in a common barracks that held thirty people. And the next day they marked time wandering aimlessly around the narrow, filthy streets and alleys of Macao.

"If there ever was a place that fits to a tee the expression 'den of iniquity,' this is it," Luke declared. "I can't wait to board our ship."

On the morning of their departure, they were at the foot of the gangplank at sunrise, despite the fact that the *Rotterdam* did not sail until three in the afternoon. Time seemed like an eternity to Luke, who paced the decks incessantly while consulting his pocket watch every few minutes. At last the ship's bell sounded six times, and the cry went up from the executive officer, "Cast off and raise the gangplank!"

Luke and Tongdlon stood at the stern watching the island of Macao grow smaller and smaller until it became a dot that disappeared over the horizon. Luke put an arm around Tongdlon's shoulders. "Well, Big Turnip, we're on our way."

The big Chinese man grinned and patted the new identification papers he carried in the breast pocket of his suit jacket.

"No more Tongdlon, we buried him. From now on, I'm John Yee."

"That will take some getting used to, but I'll have it down by the time we reach port. John Yee, it has a nice ring to it. And you know something, my friend, in that suit and with your new haircut, you look every bit the civilized American."

"Civilized American," Tongdlon said with faint sarcasm. "But in my heart I will always remain a noble savage."

They went below to their cabin to wash up for the evening meal.

That night Luke dreamed of his beloved Andria. They were lying in the grass, their naked bodies molded to each other, his hands caressing her velvet skin and her delicate fingers teasing and encouraging his manhood to its full potential.

A thousand miles away across the Pacific, Andria lay on her hard bunk in the cabin she shared with five other women bound for the cribs of San Francisco. Her dream was almost identical to Luke's. She moaned in bliss as his lips tantalized her rigid nipples and he entered her ever so slowly and tenderly.

Except for the overcrowded cabin, the women's living conditions aboard ship were adequate, far better than any of them, except Andria, had enjoyed in their homeland. During the day they had free run of the decks, and they were treated courteously enough. Captain Du Bois was a harsh disciplinarian, and the crew

had been warned bluntly that if any man tried to
molest the passengers he would be summarily put in
irons.

"Does that apply to the officers as well, captain?" his
first mate inquired, smiling in a way that said he was
not taking the admonition too seriously.

"Yes, it does, Dumas. And wipe that smug look off
your face."

"Yes, *sir!*"

Dumas considered himself irresistible to the ladies,
and numerous times he had left ports only minutes
ahead of an irate husband or lover. He was slim, blonde,
and debonair, with a well-trimmed mustache and brown
eyes that women frequently called soulful.

Du Bois had outfitted the women in dresses reminiscent of the shapeless garments the girls at the mission
wore, shrewdly calculated to minimize their femininity
to the horny crewmen.

Alexis Dumas, however, had what he termed "magic
vision," and in his imagination he was constantly undressing every female he met. Andria had fascinated
him from the instant she had stepped aboard. As the
days wore on and boredom intensified, his lecherous
imagination conjured up all manner of lewd fantasies
involving Andria and himself.

"I can't endure my desire for that wench another
day," he said to himself. "I must have her. I *will* have
her!"

A scheme formed in his mind. That same afternoon
he approached the captain. "Sir, I think it might be
advisable to find some small tasks to keep the women
occupied. I've heard several of them complaining about
their idleness. One has been flirting brazenly with the
crewmen."

Du Bois frowned. "That won't do at all. All right,
Dumas. What do you suggest?"

"For a start we could assign them to keeping the

officers' cabins clean and tidy. Then there is kitchen duty to which they are well suited."

"Good. I'll leave the matter in your capable hands, Dumas."

Humming gaily, the mate walked briskly to the womens' cabin and knocked on the door. Andria admitted him.

In a highly professional tone, he told them of his conversation with the captain. "Beginning this afternoon, each of you will be responsible for keeping an officer's cabin in order. Light housekeeping." He gave them their assignments. "Lee-sou, you will be responsible for the master's quarters." And so on down the line until he came to Andria. "As for you, Sun Ying, you will tend to my cabin. All right, girls, that will be all."

The women were only too pleased to engage themselves in some diverting occupation to relieve the tedium, and after the lunch period they reported for duty. Andria presented herself at Dumas's cabin.

"I am ready to begin, Mr. Dumas."

"Come in and close the door." He was lounging on his bunk reading a book, and did not immediately look up.

She stood in the middle of the room, waiting for him to say or do something. Finally she inquired, "It would be easier for me to tidy up if you would leave the cabin, please."

Dumas looked up and flashed a dazzling smile. "Oh, I have no intention of leaving, my dear." He put down the book and stood up. "Come over here, Sun Ying."

"My name is Andria."

"A rose by any other name . . . So then I must come to you."

Sensing what was on his mind, she backed away toward the door as he approached her. Like a cat he pounced on her as she turned to grasp the knob. She struggled to free herself, but Dumas was too strong for her. He wrapped one arm around her throat, bent her right arm behind her back, and dragged her over to the cot.

"You can forget about the housework, you little vixen. I have more urgent tasks that require your attention."

He forced her back on the mattress and lifted up her skirt. Futilely she kicked out at him as he forced his way between her legs and worked her pantalets down over her hips.

"If you rape me, the captain will have you strung up from the yardarm!" she shouted at him. "Remember, he paid an exorbitant price for a virgin, and if you deflower me, my value will be considerably reduced."

Damn! In his obsession to have her, that little detail had slipped his mind. He was certain he could have assuaged the captain's wrath if he had chosen one of the other women. But not this special piece of merchandise. A virgin!

"All right, you can keep your bloody cherry. There are more ways than one to skin a cat." He dragged her off the cot and made her kneel down at the side. Standing over her, he unbuttoned his trousers and dropped them to his ankles. Seating himself on the edge of the cot, a leg on either side of her, he grasped her head roughly with both hands.

"You may be a virgin, my dear, but you know what to do. Now get busy before I go mad with lust." The sight of his monstrous engorged member repelled her as nothing else ever had before in her life. Strain away as she would, his hands forced her inexorably to do his bidding.

As he watched her mouth descend on its objective, Dumas groaned with delicious expectation.

Outside on deck the crewmen went about their tasks, chipping paint, swabbing, splicing lines. It was a calm day, and the sunlight sparked like diamonds on the caps of gentle waves. Then, without warning, the serenity of the scene was disrupted by a scream, so piercing, so loud, so fraught with agony that the men were momentarily frozen like statues in a tableau. Tools clattered out of hands onto the deck.

The banshee wail persisted without stop. If anything it became more intense, a brutal torture to the eardrums. It induced more than one man to make the sign of the cross across his breast.

"*Sacre bleu!*" the bosun gasped.

His words broke the spell of immobility, and the men all scrambled to their feet and ran toward the source of the ungodly shrieking.

The second mate, Mr. Cleceau, was the first to reach Dumas's cabin, and the captain was on his heels. Just as they threw open the door, the wail abruptly ceased.

The two of them stood in the doorway, mouths agape, eyes bulging in horror and disbelief at the grisly sight that greeted them. They were struck speechless.

"What is it, captain?" a sailor behind him asked.

"Where's Dumas?" asked another.

The curious crewmen crowded around Du Bois and the second mate, trying to see over their shoulders.

"Back away!" the captain cried, and he and Cleceau gave way as Andria walked toward them. Her face was expressionless, and her eyes were unseeing. The men cleared a path for her, and she walked away like a zombie. Her mouth was smeared with blood, some of which trickled down her chin.

In his years at sea, Captain Du Bois had been witness to atrocities that had made his hair stand on end and curdled his blood. But none of what he had seen could compare with this.

"Cleceau, see that the body is prepared for burial. The sooner the better. I will be in my cabin."

On the way he stopped at the women's cabin to

check up on Andria. She was sitting cross-legged on a bunk, still in a state of stupor, while the other women cackled over her like mother hens.

"What have you done to her?" Lee demanded angrily.

"Nothing. She struck her head on the winch. Must have cut the inside of her mouth. She'll be all right."

Wearily he turned and shuffled off to his cabin where he sat down at his desk and opened the ship's log. He picked up a pen, dipped it into the inkwell, and sat there with it poised indecisively over the page.

If he accurately reported what had befallen Dumas, the authorities would take Andria away from him as soon as they reached port. It would mean all of that money he had paid for her would be wasted. As for the moral issue, he deeply regretted the first mate's horrible demise, yet he had to feel compassion for the girl. Dumas had attempted to bestialize her, and she had been driven to the point of madness. Yes, that was it, temporary madness. The chances were that once she recovered from the shock, her mind would blot out all memory of the tragic and terrifying experience.

I am judge, jury, and executioner aboard this ship. I thereby find the girl, Andria, not guilty of the murder of Alexis Dumas.

He put the pen to the log and wrote: "Today, the first mate, Alexis Dumas, was stricken with apoplexy and died shortly thereafter. He was given a Christian burial at sea. . . ."

Chapter Eight

With few exceptions there was no legitimate business on Pacific Street in San Francisco during the decade after the big California gold strike of 1849.

Also known as "Terrific Street," it was a succession of groggeries, dance halls, "dead-falls" specializing in wine and beer, and concert saloons that provided dancing and entertainment of depraved variety. All of these establishments offered girls for sale; there were no regular brothels on Pacific Street because the entire district was one big whorehouse.

Captain Du Bois had explored all of San Francisco on the three occasions he had put in there. Each time his cargo had been identical: French women hand-picked from the bagnios of Paris and Marseilles, most of them accompanied by their pimps, or "macks" as they were called in San Francisco.

One of his charges, a ravishing brunette by the name of Henrietta D'Arcy, claimed to have banked $50,000 in her first year on the Barbary Coast, and the next year she set herself up as a high-class madam in an elaborate palace of pleasure on Portsmouth Square, known as the Chez Paree; it was one of numerous elite establishments that catered to the men who had amassed fortunes.

It was to the Chez Paree that Du Bois introduced

Andria. Andria and Lee were awe-struck by its rococo elegance. Crystal chandeliers glittered from its ceilings. The walls were adorned with mirrors and lascivious oil paintings of nude women. At the end of the main gaming room on a dais, an orchestra played waltzes for the pleasure of those who cared to dance. Couples clad in evening wear swirled with abandon around the highly polished teakwood dance floor.

Henrietta's girls wore only the most fashionable gowns imported from France—silks, velvets, tulles, crepes, and tarlatans, in a rainbow of colors. They wore silk lingerie trimmed with Valenciennes lace. Their elaborate coiffures were festooned with pearls and other gems, or nets held in place by rows of gold chain.

The men in their white ties and tails were a far cry from the diggers who had eked out their fortunes toiling in the gold fields in muddy boots and filthy shirts and trousers just a few years before. What irony that the aristocracy of San Francisco for the next decade would be composed of harlots and, for the most part, rough, uncouth, uneducated laborers.

It was acknowledged in a highly popular song of the times:

> *The miners came in Forty-Nine,*
> *The whores in Fifty-One.*
> *And when they got together,*
> *They produced the native son.*

Behind the crowded gambling tables stood the croupiers, wearing the traditional black-and-white uniform of their craft. Andria gaped at the mounds of silver and gold pieces, along with gold dust and nuggets, on the tables.

Du Bois was amused and observed wryly, "It is not such an unpleasant place to work, no?"

She shook her head. "Oh, no, I would never fit in with all these grand ladies."

He laughed. "The women here and the sluts down on Pacific Street are all sisters under the skin. It is only a matter of price that differentiates between them. Come along. Henrietta is expecting us."

They were escorted up a back staircase by an attendant dressed in livery worthy of a London footman. He led them down a long hall, thickly carpeted. The walls were decorated with tapestries, again of a lascivious nature. Elegant oil lamps ensconced in wall brackets provided rosy illumination. There were at least twenty bedrooms, ten on each side of the hall, each of which had a heavy oaken door. At the end of the hall was Henrietta's chamber.

"Madam's offices," said the attendant, bowing slightly. He knocked and received a summons to enter.

"Office" was a peculiar way to describe this magnificent room, Andria thought. There were numerous, thick-piled Persian rugs, and the furniture was Empire style. A fire crackled cheerily in a massive fireplace on one wall. Henrietta D'Arcy rose from one of a pair of matching loveseats before the fireplace and came forward to greet Du Bois.

She was a handsome woman with sleek, dark hair, tightly rolled at the nape of her neck and smoldering eyes set deeply in a smooth oval face. Her skin was like pale olives. She was tall, as tall as Du Bois, and proportioned like a Valkyrie maiden. She had shown off her full bosom to good advantage in a black velvet gown that fittted her like a sheath from her bared, powdered shoulders to her ankles.

Her smile was sultry as she rushed to embrace Du Bois. "René, my darling, it has been so long."

They kissed and hugged each other affectionately.

"Seeking out new and wonderful treasures for your bevy of courtesans. I have brought you one gem the like of which you have never seen and will likely never see again."

He switched to French now and drew Andria forward by one hand. All the while Henrietta, arms folded, studied the girl intently, nodding from time to time and occasionally interjecting a word of praise. When he paused, she walked around Andria and said in English, "Her beauty is exquisite. If her form is as fair, she is a prize, indeed. It is difficult to tell with those rags she is wearing."

"I saw her without those rags, and her body is exquisite as well."

She seemed amused. *"You,* René? You saw her *au naturel,* and still you claim she is a virgin?"

"I do, indeed, and would testify to it before the bench under oath on pain of my life." His voice fell, and he glanced warily at Andria. "A virgin who will defend her virtue to the death. We will speak of that in private."

As he had suspected, when the shock of her hideous encounter with the first mate had worn off, her mind was blank as to what had occurred in Dumas's cabin.

Henrietta addressed the attendant. "Take these two to their assigned quarters and have two maids go to work on them at once." Her nose wrinkled distastefully. "I cannot tolerate lice and other vermin in my palace."

"I assure you these women are clean. What do you take me for, Henrietta? I deal in only superior merchandise."

"I must concede that, René."

When the attendant had departed with Andria and Lee, Du Bois told her of the loathsome incident that had taken place aboard the *Martinique.*

He had seldom seen Henrietta perturbed, but now she was obviously unnerved. "Mon Dieu! Poor Dumas! He was not a bad sort, though when he drank, he would sometimes become very abusive to my girls." She narrowed her lips. "I do not permit such behavior in the Chez Paree. . . . The homely one, you don't believe she is the mother? Not with a face like that!"

Du Bois grinned and shrugged. "It doesn't matter.

I saw at once the possibilities in establishing the relationship. It lends credence to the testament that she is a virgin."

Henrietta saw his reasoning. "A good point, yes, a very good point. René, what did you pay for her in Macao? I will add fifty percent to the figure as a commission."

He walked over to a table between the two couches on which rested a silver tray bearing a crystal decanter of rich ruby port wine and three sparkling crystal stem glasses.

"Do you mind?" he asked, pouring two glasses to the brim. He handed one to her.

She walked over to the loveseat and sat down again. She patted the suede cushion next to her.

"Come, René, my sweet, make yourself comfortable and confide in me your nefarious plans for the child. I want to warn you my price is adamant, regardless of how beautiful and desirable the creature is."

He dropped a hand on her thigh. "My sublime Henrietta, you don't believe I would demand usurious compensation from one who is so dear to me?" He took one of her hands and kissed the palm. "We are lovers, Henrietta. If you would let me, I would marry you and take you away from all this."

Henrietta laughed heartily at the absurdity of his proclamation, and Du Bois could not stop himself from laughing along with her.

"You would take me away from *all this*, René? And where would you take me—to your seamy little merchant ship? Hah! The only reason you would marry me is to get your greedy paws on all of this that I own. I am a rich woman, René, and you are a pauper."

"Pauper, indeed!" He liked to fence like this with Henrietta. She could be a wildcat. A hellion. Her mind was as wicked as a steel trap. And their bickering served to fan their mutual desires in preparation for the inevitable moment when she would lead him into her boudoir. René Du Bois was the only client she had serviced after her first year in San Francisco. Well, practically. She did not count the big-whig entrepreneur, Caleb Callahan. He had wanted to impress his friends—rich men as well, who dealt in sugar and pineapples from the Hawaiian Islands. Callahan had paid her $10,000 in cash for the privilege of enjoying her body.

"Well, what price did you have in mind for little Andria?"

René stroked his goatee thoughtfully. "Well, I haven't exactly made up my mind."

Henrietta's mind was racing ahead of him. If Callahan would pay her $10,000, what would he pay to possess a young virgin?

Fifteen? No, it was too paltry! Twenty—maybe even twenty-five thousand.

René put down his glass and put both hands on her shoulders. "What would you say to selling the girl outright, Henrietta?"

"Are you insane? Why, she's worth a fortune to me as a property!"

"Property has a way of declining in value," he reminded her. "Particularly if it's flesh and blood. Oh, you'll get a pretty penny auctioning off a virgin for one night. But the second time around, she is no virgin, so what's the selling point? Certainly she is still a radiant beauty, and men will pay dearly to have her, but with each succeeding interlude, the novelty wears thinner and thinner. I'd give you, I'd say, a dozen times, and then her value will balance out with the income of the other girls. After all, they are all beauties. Now think of this, my dear. What do you suppose an extremely wealthy man would pay to have this virgin beauty all to himself forever, knowing as the years pass that he was the first and the *only* man to have carnal knowledge of her?"

Henrietta's mind was leap-frogging once more. If

Caleb Callahan would bid twenty or twenty-five for deflowering a virgin, think what he would pay to have her as a household play toy. After all, he was a Mormon; he already had two wives, both sluts. He could well afford to take still a third. Rumor was that the man was worth millions.

Henrietta's eyes lit up, and she spoke resolutely. "We will ask two hundred thousand dollars for the girl!"

As accustomed as he was to the outrageous extravagances that typified the Barbary Coast, Du Bois was startled.

"Isn't that unrealistic, Henrietta? Who, even in this Sodom and Gomorrah, would give two hundred thousand for a woman, virgin or not? It's outlandish."

She slid an arm around his neck, stroked the back of his head, then kissed his chin. "Chèri, you leave everything to your little Heni." Her smile was feline. "If I do execute the transaction, you will not object to a split of the proceeds on a basis of eighty percent for me and twenty for you?"

He pretended to give it careful thought, though his mind was already made up. Forty thousand dollars was far more than he had ever dreamed to clear as a profit when he purchased Andria from the slave trader in Macao.

"You strike a hard bargain, Henrietta," he said with resignation he did not feel. "I know better than to cross swords with you. Have it as you will. Twenty percent will do nicely."

Her laughter was low and husky as she slipped the gown down over her shoulders, baring her magnificent breasts, large as melons, but still high and firm, the nipples like overripe strawberries.

"Then shall we seal our bargain between the sheets?" she asked coyly.

He placed his hands on her shoulders and bent his

head to her turgid nipples, nibbling each one in turn until they threatened to burst between his eager lips.

She was writhing and moaning uncontrollably. He lifted her hips so that he could draw the gown down over her legs and fling it off. She was naked now but for a wisp of French lace girding her loins. He disposed of that and commenced showering kisses the length of her voluptuous body.

"René!" she cried out. "I want your prettier thing!" Her hands clutched at the front of his trousers. She began to chant a bawdy French ballad:

> *A peddler proud as I've heard tell,*
> *Came into a town,*
> *With certain wares he had to sell,*
> *Which he cried up and down.*
> *And also he had many a prettier thing. . . .*

The rest of the phrase was choked off as Du Bois obliged and gave her what she was begging for.

Chapter Nine

The first week that they were in San Francisco was a sheer delight to both Andria and Lee. They shared a suite of two rooms next to the madam's quarters. Their rooms were decorated in lavish sensuality without being vulgar. All of the furniture was garlanded with satin and silk skirting, and the canopy over Andria's bed reminded her of frothy white icing on a wedding cake she had once seen in a picture book. The color scheme was virginal white and maidenly blush.

"Exactly the way I pictured what the quarters of an infamous French courtesan should be like," Andria observed. "I even feel French." She thrust her nose into the air and sashayed around the room with one hand on her hip, undulating her buttocks.

"Magnifique!" said a voice from the doorway.

Unaware that she had an audience, Andria whirled in the direction of the applause, clamping one hand over her mouth.

It was Henrietta D'Arcy with a retinue of maids in tow, their arms piled high with silk and satin undergarments, crinolines, bustles, and an assortment of gowns.

Henrietta was stunning in a bright scarlet butterfly peignoir with wide sleeves and a long, floating skirt.

Andria had never seen her in any other colors than scarlet, white, or black.

Henrietta had explained the symbolism. "White for purity, birth, and youth. Scarlet for the sensual years when the blood runs hot and red in one's veins. Black" —she threw up her hands and hung her head—"for old age when the juices dry up and the flesh withers away like a flower in the fall. Death."

"Tonight will be your debut, my dear Andria. And I caution you, none of your mimicry. 'Infamous French courtesan,' indeed!"

Andria flushed. "I—I—meant no offense."

"Of course you didn't." Henrietta came over to her, laughing, and put her arms around Andria. "It is just that a woman must not pretend to be what she is not. Now, I am a French courtesan and as infamous as they come. Before my retirement, that is. What you are, child, is a delicate, exotic flower from the East, a vestal virgin as it were. And, therefore, the role you must play is a demure one. Hands folded in front of you. Eyes downcast. Speaking only when you are spoken to."

She cast a long, appraising look at Lee. "And what are we to do with you, little *mother?*" The sarcasm was evident. "To make you a presentable parent for this glorious daughter of yours? Let me see. I suppose your plumpness and plainness are acceptable parental features. But those awful teeth! We must have Dr. Lukas do something to make them passable, at least." She turned to the maids. "All right, let us get to work on Andria."

The next two hours were very uncomfortable for Andria. She had a normal feminine interest in good grooming, but Madam D'Arcy was a martinet on the subject.

She made Andria try on a half dozen combinations of underwear alone, before she finally settled on a white camisole and French pantalets in matching silk, trimmed with lace.

"Risqué, yet innocent," Henrietta nodded approvingly.

Choosing the proper gown was even more arduous. Andria tried on twelve before the meticulous madam smiled and clapped her hands.

"Bonne bouche!"

Inspecting herself in the full-length mirror on the back of the bedroom door, Andria had to admit it was a charming gown. It was of white Lyons silk, overlaid with a shadow decoration of flowers, and was trimmed with white lace and green ribbon.

"And now for the coiffure? What do you think, Hazel?" she asked one of the maids.

"A chignon in a snood, perhaps?"

Henrietta frowned. "No, too sophisticated."

"A barrette wrapped with embroidery silk?"

"Ah, that is it. And with one end decked with a posy of flowers, violets or pansies."

They worked over her hair for at least another hour, but as Madam D'Arcy declared after it was over, "Time well spent, don't you think, mother?"

Lee's eyes were shining with admiration. "She looks perfectly adorable."

Henrietta nodded. "Adorable. Beautiful. Innocent. Yet, underneath the halo is a promise of untapped sensuality. Eh, *bien!* I do believe our 'visitors' will be extremely pleased with you, my dear."

A cold hand clutched at Andria's heart. From the day she had been on the block in Macao and had been purchased by Captain Du Bois, she had realized that this reality was inevitable. Sumptuous as it was in appearance, with its lavish appointments, beautiful women impeccably attired, and clients who had the aspect of wealth and surface gentility, the Chez Paree was, after all, a house of ill repute. No, even that euphemism was farcical. What it was was a whorehouse! She took a deep breath and forced herself to ask the crucial question.

"Am I to start work this night, Madam D'Arcy? Downstairs with the other girls? Be with a man?" She blushed and hung her head.

Henrietta chuckled and put an arm around her shoulders. "So, you are ready to turn a few tricks, no? Do you think I place such a paltry price on your virginity?"

"I do not understand."

"My dear child, you possess a commodity that no other woman in San Francisco under the age of twelve can boast of. Your cherry."

"But I thought—I mean, why else would Captain Du Bois have brought me here if not to—" Her mind balked at putting the thought into words.

"My dear child, you are an extremely fortunate girl, let me tell you. No, you do not have to prostitute your charms night after night with a variety of men. Thanks to Madam D'Arcy, you will go out of here tonight with one man. A rich man at that. Not unattractive, either. You will be established in a fine home with servants to wait on you and—"

"What are you talking about?" Andria demanded, bewildered.

Henrietta smiled and glanced at Lee. "You and your mother will become the wards of one of the three wealthiest men in San Francisco—in the entire state of California!"

Andria was, for some reason, more appalled at the implication of what Madam D'Arcy was saying than at the prospect of serving her obligation with the other harlots.

"Do you mean you are going to auction us off a second time?"

"Well, my dear, there is no more delicate way to put it. Yes, you will be auctioned off to the highest bidder. But it will not be the degrading experience you suffered in Macao at the hands of that beast Mendez. As I told you, you will become the mistress of a rich and powerful man. If you were to poll all of the women in San Francisco, or any city, I would wager that better than sixty percent of them would happily exchange places with you, my sweet. And not just single women, either."

Goose flesh rippled along Andria's arms, and she shivered and folded them across her chest. If it were not for the memory of her beloved Luke, she would have taken her own life before the horrendous moment when she had to climb into bed with some lecherous old man. Of late she sensed the presence of her beloved hovering around her night and day—his protective, loving spirit. Even now a ghostly voice echoed in her ears: *"Be brave, my darling. I am with you always, and I will let nothing befall you that is painful or harmful."*

Madam D'Arcy took her by the arm. "Come along, my dear, to our private parlor where you will meet your intended." She laughed. "One would think I am touting a courtship—your intended. Well, in a very real sense, it will be a courtship of sorts."

She beckoned to Lee. "Now as for you, little mother. I think something long and flowing would be appropriate. Black, naturally, to diminish your plumpness. All right, girls, quickly now!"

A quarter of an hour later, Henrietta escorted Andria and Lee down the hall to a parlor very similar to her private room, except that the decor and atmosphere were markedly masculine. The wall murals were not bawdy like the ones in the gambling casino, but macho —gun fighting, bucking broncos, Indians attacking wagon trains, and the like. The room smelled of rich leather, tobacco fumes, and whiskey. There was a bar with a long mirror behind it. Two men were standing at the bar, each with a foot braced on the brass foot rail. A third was acting as bartender behind the bar. As the three women entered, they turned their attention in the direction of the door.

At once Andria's attention was riveted on the big, beefy man behind the bar. Although his features were submerged in florid flesh ravaged by age, too much whiskey, and general dissipation, the resemblance was startling. The eyes, the jaw, the high cheekbones, the aquiline nose. Even before Madam D'Arcy introduced him, she *knew!*

"My child, this is Caleb Callahan."

Luke's father!

One hand clutched at her throat; she couldn't breathe. Then her entire body seemed to dissolve, and Andria fainted.

She was dimly aware of faraway voices, all talking excitedly:

"She's been under a great strain," said Madam D'Arcy.

"I dunno, 'pears to me she's sick. Don't want no ailing female on me hands."

Lee said indignantly, "She's as healthy as a horse. It's been too much for all of us these last weeks."

"Let me give her a slug of brandy. That should do the trick."

She felt a large, strong hand tilt her head up from the pillow, and then scalding liquid was coursing down her throat. Andria choked and sat upright, her head clearing rapidly. She stared numbly into the blue eyes of Caleb Callahan. When he smiled he looked even more like Luke. His voice was kind and reassuring.

"It's all right, little lady, you're going to be just fine." The smile faded into uncertainty. "Say, why are you looking at me that funny way?"

She opened her mouth to answer him, but the words stuck in her throat.

"She looks like she just saw a ghost," another man commented. His name was Spreckels, and he was a sugar dealer.

The third man, a neat, sedate-looking fellow with rimless spectacles and a high forehead, consulted his gold pocket watch. "Henrietta, can't we get this over with? I have important people from Washington waiting for me downstairs."

"To be sure, Monsieur Dole. Do you know we are serving free champagne and pineapple sticks in the faro room tonight in your honor?"

"I am flattered, madam. The girl seems to have recovered now. Gad! She is a beauty, is she not?"

"I must have her," exulted Spreckels, then, clearing his throat discreetly, added, "that is, to enter into the employment of my son in Sacramento. His wife Dolores has been ailing since her last birth, and she could use a girl with a good, strong back."

The other men laughed. "You mean that young stallion could use a girl with a strong back now that he's broken his wife's," Dole chided.

Callahan kept glancing covertly at Andria. True, she was every bit the jewel that Madam D'Arcy had claimed her to be. Yet there was something about her that put him off.

It was damnable! Ordinarily he would have entered the first bid for such a delicious wench. And a virgin, at that! It had been more than forty years since he had had a virgin.

"Stand up, Andria, and let the gentlemen have a good look at you," Henrietta said sharply.

With Lee supporting her, Andria got to her feet unsteadily.

"Turn around."

Unobtrusively, while his friends engaged in animated speculation about the girl's value, Caleb retreated to the bar and poured himself a fresh drink. He remained standing there, one elbow braced on the mahogany counter, studying the girl intently through slitted eyelids.

"I don't care much about buying the mother," Spreckels observed.

"They are inseparable," said Henrietta firmly.

"Don't bother me none," said Dole. "I'll offer twenty thousand for the pair."

Henrietta dismissed the bid with a disdainful laugh. "Caleb, did you hear the man? What does he take me for? But you, Caleb, you know the value of a beautiful woman. What will you offer?"

To the amazement of his friends and especially Henrietta, he replied flatly, "I'm not bidding. Let one of the others have her."

Hands on hips, Madam D'Arcy strode purposefully to the bar and confronted him. "I do not believe what I am hearing from you, Caleb Callahan." Lowering her voice, she continued, "You who paid ten thousand dollars for one night with an ancient hag like me. And you would pass up a virgin, ripe with her juices flowing like nectar! Mon Dieu!"

He bent closer and spoke to her confidentially. "Fact is, Henrietta, the girl spooks me for some reason. I get the feeling I know her from someplace, and I don't like the vibrations she turns out. Those eyes—God! They bore straight into your soul."

"To hell with Caleb!" Spreckels shouted. "I'll make it fifty for 'em."

"Not so fast, friend," Dole objected. "My final offer is seventy-five, and that is it." He reached for his checkbook.

"Not good enough. Make mine eighty." Spreckels was smug.

"God damn you, you stubborn bastard! All right. *One hundred thousand!* And that is final!" He started for the door. One hand on the knob, he paused, waiting for Spreckels to override him.

After a sixty-second silence, Henrietta sighed and threw up her hands. Not exactly what she had hoped for, but a very handsome sum nevertheless. She cast one more perplexed look at Caleb Callahan, who was hunched glumly over the bar, his whiskey glass cupped in both hands.

"All right then, gentlemen, I think that concludes the auction. Mr. Dole, I will accept your check now."

"Wait!" Andria thrust a hand high in the air and walked toward the bar. "Mr. Callahan, I was a friend to your son, Luke. A very good friend. We loved each other."

His face was ashen. "You're a damned liar, girl! How could you know my son?"

"He was assigned to the Mormon mission, Nauvoo, on the Canton River. I was a Sister there for six years before he came."

Caleb shook his head in utter disbelief, even though he could not deny the facts she stated.

"There's some trick here. I mean—" Then the implication of what she had said hit him forcibly. She had used the past tense.

"Where is my son now? I just received a letter from him last week."

Tears welled up in her eyes, and her voice was so thick she could barely get the words out. "Luke—Luke is—He is dead, Mr. Callahan—"

"No, you're *lying!* He said he was fine and in no danger."

She shrugged. "He was lying so as not to concern you. We lived in the midst of great danger. Surrounded by bandit armies of the revolutionary I Ho Ch'üan. One day they came to the mission and ransacked it. Luke died, trying to defend me." She burst into tears, and it was several minutes before she could continue. "The bandits abducted me and sold me into slavery at Macao"—she sighed—"and that is how I came to be here."

"That's it. . . ." He spoke to himself more than to anyone else in the room. "That's why you seemed so familiar to me. Like a face out of a snapshot. In his letter—Luke—he spoke of you. The most beautiful woman in the world—eyes like blue sapphires."

"We would have been joined in wedlock if he had

lived. I was reared as a Mormon by the missionaries, Mr. Callahan." There was an appeal in her voice that he could not reject.

Caleb Callahan looked at Henrietta D'Arcy. "Madam D'Arcy," he said without emotion, "I would like to reopen the bidding. I will offer you one hundred and fifty thousand dollars for the girl and her mother."

From the way that Dole's shoulders slumped, Henrietta knew that he would not challenge this final bid by Caleb Callahan.

Deep down she was happy things had worked out in such a way. She was fond of Andria, and her life with Caleb Callahan would be better than with one of the other two. She sensed that the girl's revelation concerning Caleb's son Luke would precipitate a different dimension into the relationship of Caleb and Andria than would have evolved if she had been just another woman on the auction block.

Henrietta smiled. Andria could well serve as a replacement for the child who had been taken away from him.

A daughter rather than a mistress!

Chapter Ten

Madam D'Arcy's intuition was correct. Caleb Callahan established her in his mansion as his ward. Her position in the household was that of a foster daughter.

Andria's fame and popularity among San Francisco's elite became widespread. Caleb Callahan was a lavish entertainer, and at least once a week the big house off Portsmouth Square was the site of sumptuous dinner parties, fancy dress balls, and masquerade balls.

Andria was awed by it all. She felt like a princess out of *The Arabian Nights*.

King Caleb, as he came to be known, swelled with pride as he observed his lovely Eurasian ward besieged at every affair by hordes of influential males, young and old, begging to sign her dance card.

The Callahan Sacramento home, where they spent the following summer, was even more luxurious. Curtains of the finest lace and drapes of crimson damask hung at the windows; carpets from Turkey and Brussels covered the floors; and the ballroom rivaled the one at the Chez Paree. In many ways the mansion reminded Andria of a pretentious palace of pleasure: crystal chandeliers, wall murals, tapestries, oils, and a great, wide, curved staircase descending from the marble foyer to the ballroom, where men and women, all clad in peacock finery, twirled around the orchestra in the center of the room like the gaudy mounts on a carousel.

On this particular night Andria was the belle of the ball and the envy of every other woman in the room. In her summer ball gown—golden butterflies on lightning blue with a wide floral border just above the floating hemline flounce; a daring horseshoe collar and a tie sash at the waist—she looked, as one swain described her, "As if you just stepped out of a dream."

Caleb came up and put a paternal arm about Andria's bare shoulders, feigning a scowl at the youthful judge, who had just complimented Andria.

"Take my advice, honey, and stay out of this rascal's dreams. Not to mention his bachelor apartment!"

The mayor joined them. He bowed to Andria. "Ma'am, judge, Caleb. Marvelous shindig, Caleb. Your parties are always the best—'specially with this little lady holding court."

"Thanks, mayor. Say, have you been speaking to Harry Love?" Harry Love was the deputy sheriff of Los Angeles.

"Yes. Did he tell you he's hot on the tail of Murieta? That bas—'scuse me, ma'am. Seems Murieta rode into Stockton last week just as the deputy was nailing up a wanted poster on him, announcing the legislature's bill offering a five-thousand-dollar reward for his capture, dead or alive. Know what he did? He got off his horse, pulled out a crayon and wrote, on the bottom of the poster: *I will add an additional thousand dollars myself!*"

"Outrageous!" exclaimed the judge.

Caleb glowered and rubbed his bearded chin. "Damn it! I've offered Harry Love the use of my exterminators over and over. Stubborn mule insists he can handle Murieta himself."

"Hardly blame him, Caleb. If the law can't do its job without the help of private citizens, then it's time we shake up the police force. Jack don't want to lose face any more than he has already."

"Then he and his boys better get cracking and catch the bastard!" Caleb offered no excuse for his lauguage to anyone, man or woman. "Stockton, you say? Maybe you ought to cancel your trip tomorrow, Andria."

He turned to the men. "She and Charity and Sada joined up with that ladies' civic group that's picnicking aboard a river schooner. They aim to scout out a site near Stockton for the new Mormon temple."

"Don't worry, Caleb," said the mayor. "That region is swarming with policemen and soldiers. Besides, long as they're on the river, nobody can get at them."

At that moment a tall, slender young man in tailored evening clothes, white waistcoat, starched shirt, and black bow tie approached the group. A visiting Mexican dignitary, he was dark and handsome and had a thin mustache. He smiled, showing even white teeth, and bowed to Andria.

"Señorita, will you do me the honor of dancing with me?"

Andria curtsied and folded her fan. "I would be pleased to have this dance with you, sir."

As the couple danced away, Caleb observed with satisfaction that he was holding Andria at a respectable arm's length.

"Nice young feller," he grunted. "For a Mex, that is."

All the men laughed.

"Joaquin Carillo," the judge commented. "Scion of a wealthy Spanish family. Hear tell he's a nephew of President Santa Anna."

Andria was thoroughly enjoying herself. Carillo was as light on his feet as a ballet dancer, and he soon had her dizzy from a series of rapid twirls.

"Please!" she gasped. "If you don't stop twirling, I shall collapse in a swoon."

He grinned. "Your wish is my command," he responded, adopting a more sedate pace. "You are very lovely, señorita."

"Thank you."

"And I think I am madly in love with you."

She laughed. "We've only just met, Señor Carillo."

"In Mexico, love at first sight is a common occurrence. Will you marry me?"

"Certainly not, and my guardian had better not hear you jest in such a brash fashion."

"Señor Callahan." His expression sobered. "Yes, he is a very formidable man."

At the conclusion of the set, the orchestra took a break, so the dancers strolled off the floor.

"Would you like some punch?" he inquired.

"Yes, thank you." She fanned her face vigorously. "And some fresh air. You've quite exhausted me."

"Then we shall have our drinks on the veranda."

He fetched two silver goblets brimming with ice-cold champagne punch. Only rich men like Caleb Callahan could afford the luxury of ice.

It was a hot night, but not sultry in the way Andria remembered summer nights being in China. Andria loved the climate of Sacramento. Even in mid-August with the sun blazing down, one could step into the shadow of a tree and feel cool instantly.

The Callahan mansion had been built on a half-acre of the most expensive property in the city and was surrounded by a ten-foot-high wrought-iron fence to insulate its occupants from the Sydney Ducks and other undesirables. In addition to the fence, two enormous bull mastiffs patrolled the grounds after dark.

Andria and Carillo stood at the veranda railing looking out over the lush, manicured lawn and garden. The bawdy, vital sounds of the city's night life carried to them, and the guard dogs gave guttural warning to pedestrians who tarried too long outside the iron gate.

"I am so tired of hearing about this Murieta person,"

she complained. "Is he really the devil everyone says he is?"

Carillo shrugged. "I suppose it depends on the viewpoint."

"Viewpoint? If it is true that the man has murdered scores of innocent people?"

"Innocent people?" His laugh was dry. "I was of the opinion that Murieta killed to avenge the death of his brother and the rape of his wife and a flogging that left him close to death."

"I didn't know that."

"The Americans are masters at sweeping dirt under the rug." He eyed her curiously. "As an Oriental, you should know that very well—the opium wars, all the other degradations they have inflicted on your race."

Andria was troubled. "Who were these people who killed his brother and raped his wife?"

"Your average, everyday gold miners. Murieta tried to stake a claim in Stanislaus County, and they would not have that. In their eyes a Mexican is only a slight step above someone Chinese." His voice was brittle. "Though they appear to accept you. Of course, *you* are the ward of the most powerful man in San Francisco."

"Well, if Murieta has killed all the people who raped his wife and murdered his brother, why does he still go on killing and pillaging?"

"Survival, I would imagine. His fate is sealed as it is. Inevitably, he will end up hanging from a rope or riddled with bullets. To the best of my knowledge, he has no wish to kill any more Americans. Only as a last resort out of self-preservation. . . . Well, as you say, there has been too much talk of Murieta tonight. Let us get on to a more pleasant subject. I understand that you plan a boat trip up the Sacramento tomorrow?"

"Yes, and I am looking forward to it."

"So am I!"

"You are going to Stockton with us on the schooner?"

"Yes. I have some family business to conduct there."

"I am pleased, Señor Carillo. Your company will be most welcome."

"Thank you, señorita, and inasmuch as we are friends, please call me Joe." He smiled. "Only my *best* friends call me Joe."

She returned the smile. "And you will call me Andria. Joe—I am glad to be your good friend."

Sunday morning dawned bright, hot, and dry, although the heat was diminished by the cool breeze blowing across the Sacramento River from the Pacific Ocean.

The ship that would take them to Stockton was a trim vessel with two masts and fore and aft sails. Her captain, Miles Stewart, was a U.S. Navy veteran of the Mexican War. He was a large, beefy man with small, deep-set eyes and red hair that sprouted profusely all over those portions of his body that were visible—head, neck, arms, the back of his hands—even his ears.

He was polite enough to his passengers, although he was decidedly cool toward Andria and Joaquin Carillo.

"Ain't I met you before?" he demanded of the Mexican.

"Possibly in Mexico City, señor. This is my first visit to California."

"You speak good English for a"—He was about to say "spick," but he caught himself. The man was a friend of Caleb Callahan, and no one insulted Callahan's friends—"for a Spaniard," he said lamely.

"Thank you, señor. I studied at the university."

Captain Stewart shrugged and put his mind to business. When the last of the cargo had been stowed away in the hatch, the order was given to cast off, and the sleek schooner slipped out of her pier and into the channel.

The voyage to Stockton was about twenty miles. On weekdays boat and ship traffic abounded on the waterway, but on the Sabbath it was mostly restricted to pleasure craft. Most of the ladies preferred to sit under the awning that been put up at the fantail to shield their delicate complexions from the sun. Not Andria. She and Carillo stood at the prow, reveling in the spray that pelted their upturned faces.

"Oh, I love this!" she exulted.

"I am pleased that you are not one of those hothouse flowers back there, afraid of sun and air and water." And with the sly innuendo she had sensed on several occasions, he added, "Then again, you and I are not of their sallow, washed-out breed, are we, Andria?"

"You claim to be a Spaniard."

He grinned. "With a bit of Indian blood mixed in, or haven't you noticed?"

She cocked her head to one side, appraising him. "More than a little, I would say."

As the morning wore on, Carillo seemed to become withdrawn and introspective. "Something is troubling you, Joe?" she inquired. "What is it?"

"Nothing, nothing at all." He smoothed out his mustache with the back of a slender, manicured finger and inclined his head at Andria. "If you will excuse me, there is something I must attend to, señorita." He turned and made his way briskly to the quarter-deck.

Captain Stewart, who was discoursing with the helmsman, frowned as Carillo climbed up the companionway.

"In case you don't know it, mister, visitors aren't allowed on the quarterdeck without the specific consent of the master."

Carillo smiled genially and walked over to him. "Do forgive me, captain. But now that I am here, it would seem foolish to deny me the opportunity of complimenting you on your fine vessel. How much longer before we reach Stockton?"

"An hour, more or less."

"I don't think so." The smile, mocking now, remained fixed on his face.

A column of hot blood shot up Stewart's thick neck, and his face turned red. His fists clenched at his sides.

"What the hell do you mean: *you* don't think so?"

Forgive me, Captain Stewart, I expressed myself poorly. I *know* positively we will not be in Stockton in one hour or even two or three or four. At least *you* and *I* will not be in Stockton at all this day."

"What the hell!" Stewart advanced threateningly on the slender Mexican. "You haul your black arse off my quarterdeck, or I'll pitch you down myself!" He raised one powerful arm as if to punch Carillo. Then abruptly he froze, and a look of total incredulity spread over his face.

Carillo had flipped back the tails of his black swallow-tailed coat and whipped two pistols out of his waistband.

"One more step and you are a dead man, captain." His voice was as slick as oil. No anger, no rancor, nor any belligerent emotion.

Stewart's arm fell to his side, and he studied the other man intently. "Say—I was right when I said I'd met you before."

"I must confess. The mining camp in Stanislaus County. That audacious little spick who thought he was good enough to work the gold fields alongside his American brothers."

"Oh, Jesus Christ!" Stewart backed away, one arm partially covering his lower face as if to ward off evil spirits. Naked terror pervaded his speech and his expression. "You—you—you're not—not *him?*"

"Joaquin Murieta at your service, Captain Stewart. And I hope to afford you the same personal, enthusiastic, and conscientious service that you treated me with back in '49. By the way, my lovely wife is looking forward to meeting you again. Very soon. Right around the next bend."

"Helmsman, start nosing her into the west bank. Around the bend there is a cove, and you will take her in there. Have no fear, the water there is deep enough so she won't run aground."

Stewart was panic-stricken. "For the love of God, man! Have pity!"

"The same pity you had for me, captain."

"I never wanted to get involved. I went along with the mob. We was all drunk."

"Funny, I don't recollect that you were drunk. You wielded the cat with exceptional strength and acumen."

Stewart fell to his knees and clasped his hands in an attitude of prayer. "I beg of you, don't kill me. I have a wife and two kids." In desperation he made a lunging tackle at Murieta's legs, but the outlaw skipped aside nimbly and kicked the captain on the side of the head with the metal toe of his heavy riding boot. Stewart was felled like an axed bull.

Murieta warned the helmsman, "One false move out of you, son, and I'll put two bullets in your gut. Behave yourself and you won't be harmed."

Pistols held high, he strode to the top of the companionway and shouted to the crew and the passengers, "Captain Stewart has suffered an accident, and I am presently in charge of this vessel, and you crewmen will obey my orders to the letter. In a short while we will be anchoring offshore. You passengers will remain in your places and be still, and when our work is completed, you can proceed on down to Stockton."

"The hell you say!" roared the first mate as he bolted for the foot of the companionway. "One damn pirate don't scare me none. C'mon, men, we can take him!"

A half dozen crewmen rallied behind him, and he was two steps up the ladder when Murieta's pistol shot echoed across the river and off the surrounding hills. The bullet caught the first mate in the right shoulder and sent him toppling back down on top of the others.

"Any other heroes among you?" Murieta asked sharply as he spun the pistols adeptly around his trigger fingers.

Their ardor for battle dampened, the sailors retreated sullenly.

As the schooner came abreast of the bend, the helmsman took her sharply into shore, his trained eye following the wide swath of deep blue water that marked the channel leading into the cove.

"Ease off now, mister," Murieta instructed him. "Bit more to the port—that's it. Steady as she goes." He walked to the head of the companionway and yelled to the crewmen below. "Drop the anchor!"

There was no need to furl the sails; in the sheltered cover, the canvas hung limp from the yards.

No sooner had the schooner entered the cove when out of the trees that lined the bank emerged a ragtag army of outlaws—Mexicans predominantly, as evidenced by their ponchos, sombreros, Spanish boots, and flowing mustaches. All of them were armed with rifles, pistols, and knives; each wore a brace of cartridge bandoleers crisscrossed across his chest. At the sight of their chieftain waving to them from the bridge, they began cheering and waving their rifles over their heads.

Murieta waved his pistols at a group of crewmen on the deck. "Lower the dinghy and dump this hulk into it," he ordered, indicating the inert form of Captain Stewart. He descended the companionway to be confronted by Andria.

"You are a contemptible pig!" she spat at him. "Pretending to be our friend and now doing a thing like this."

"My profoundest apologies, señorita, but, as I told you earlier, Murieta has no other options open to him except to survive."

"But what have you to gain by taking us as captives?"

His eyes widened. "Oh, no, you do not understand. All of you will be free to continue on your way to Stockton as soon as my men have removed the food and supplies from the hold." His lips curled disdainfully as two crewmen carried the captain down from the bridge. "And this piece of human garbage, he comes with us. You see, Señorita Andria, Stewart is the last remaining survivor of the brigands who raped my Rosita and murdered my brother Juan. Now I can rest in peace. The debt will soon be paid in full."

She shuddered. "You intend to kill him in cold blood?"

His dark eyes flashed. "Execute is the better word, my dear girl. The Bible says it all: 'An eye for an eye.' "

Meanwhile, the outlaws had launched rowboats, rafts, and canoes and were making for the schooner in great haste. The first man to clamber over the rail was an ugly little man with long, straggly hair and a cockeye. Andria recoiled as he grinned, showing stumps of blackened teeth, and extended a hand to Murieta. The hand was grotesquely mangled and had only three fingers.

"Manuel!" Murieta embraced him and nodded at Andria. "Amigo, I want you to meet the most beautiful woman in the entire world. Señorita Andria, my lieutenant, Three-Fingered Jack."

Jack removed his sombrero and made a courtly bow. "I am your humble servant, señorita."

The two men engaged in an animated exchange in Spanish as the other outlaws poured over the side. Then Three-Fingered Jack took charge of the operation.

"Open the hatches and ransack everything that is in the hold. Everything!"

"I'll see you ashore," Murieta told his henchman. "I have business to take care of." He leaned over the rail and spit into the upturned face of the unconscious captain, who was lying spread-eagled in the dinghy. He threw one leg over the rail to climb down into the small boat, then hesitated and looked back at Andria. A sly smile widened his mouth. "Do you know what I think, Andria? I think you would like this part of the country." He held out a hand to her.

Andria's blue eyes were ice cold. "I would rather be dead than go with you! I would rather be a slut in a crib on Pacific Street!"

His smile was replaced by a look of surly determination. "Seize her and put her in the boat," he ordered his men.

Three-Fingered Jack ran up to remonstrate with him, speaking in English for Andria's benefit. "Joaquin, my friend, do not do this thing. You already have a woman. A loyal woman who would give her life for you and has proved it on many an occasion."

Murieta waved a hand. "I don't want her for my woman. Rosita is the only woman for me. But think about this, Jack. She is the adopted daughter of Caleb Callahan."

Jack let out a long, shrill whistle. "Caleb Callahan! Then you are insane, my friend. If he sends his exterminators after us, then we are lost for certain. The police, bah! But the exterminators! Joe, be reasonable!"

Murieta hesitated, then said determinedly, "We are taking her captive. Think of the ransom she will fetch."

Jack rolled his eyes heavenward. "I can only think of the noose around my neck!"

But Murieta had the final word, and Andria was dragged screaming over the side into the small dinghy with Murieta and Stewart. She raked at his face with her nails, inflicting four bloody furrows from his temple to his jawbone.

"You cat!" He backhanded her across the face, sending her crashing down on top of Stewart. "Now you be still, or I'll horsewhip you when we get to shore."

Andria lay there stunned, thinking, *I came halfway across the world to get away from barbarians such as Yuan Kai-shih and the I Ho Ch'uan, and here I am in the clutches of a devil every bit as barbaric as any Chinese bandit!*

As the dinghy approached the beach, a quartet of outlaws slogged hip-deep into the water and pulled them ashore. Waiting to greet Murieta was a slender, dark woman dressed in tight black trousers and matching shirt. Her calf-high leather boots were of white buckskin ornamented with silver buckles. Under one arm she held a wide-brimmed hat with a shallow crown, black like the rest of her ensemble. Her dark hair was close cropped like a man's.

Her mouth was set in a sullen pout as she regarded Andria. Like Three-Fingered Jack she spoke in English so that Andria would not miss her meaning. "So, Joaquin, and what is this?"

"Just another piece of booty, love." He bent to kiss her lips, but she averted his mouth.

"And what do you intend to do with this 'booty'?"

He laughed lightly. "For one thing she is a valuable hostage. She belongs to Caleb Callahan."

She cursed in Spanish and slapped her forehead with the heel of one hand. "You fool! You stupid fool! Put her back on the ship at once!"

"Too late, my love." He pointed at the schooner heading out of the cove and into the middle of the river. "Don't worry. She will serve us well, Rosita."

Her lip curled contemptuously. "What will you do, throw her to the men to fight over like dogs over a bone?"

"What do you take me for?" He was growing irritated now. While she is our guest, "Señorita Andria will be treated with every courtesy and consideration. When I have made up my mind what to do with her, you will be the first to know, Rosita." He slapped her playfully on her buttocks. "I think now you should outfit the señorita in one of your riding habits. This frivolous gown she is wearing would be most inappropriate on the trail."

"My clothing for this wench! You can go to hell, Joaquin!"

Murieta gave Rosita the flat of his hand, sending her to her knees. "Do as you are told, Rosita, and be quick about it," he said quietly.

Rosita bit her bottom lip, fighting back the tears. "As you wish, Joaquin," she said with dignity and got to her feet. "Come along with me," she told Andria.

Andria followed her along a twisting path through a grove of poplars to the gang's campsite in a clearing. The horses were confined in a makeshift corral at the back of the clearing. It was evidently a site of some permanence, for, in addition to tents and lean-tos, there were several thatched huts and one square structure made of red brick. It was to this dwelling that Rosita took Andria.

"Joaquin and I live here," she said, a note of proprietorship in her voice. "I am his wife. His legal wife. We were married by a priest."

"Why do you permit him to treat you as he does? He's a brute."

The older woman shrugged. "I love him. And in his heart he loves me."

"He has a strange way of showing it. I wouldn't be married to a man who beat me."

Rosita sighed. "He was not always as he is now. Once he was a gentle, kind man who always wore a smile. A man who would stop and play with children and stray dogs. A man who loved his fellow man until—" She paused and shut her eyes. "Never mind. What has happened can never be undone. For these past four years he has been obsessed with hatred and vengeance."

"I know how horrible the Americans have been to you." She tentatively placed a hand on Rosita's arm. "You see, I, too, have been subjected to humiliation and brutality. My home was in China."

Rosita's terse defensiveness began to recede. "Yes, you are a foreigner, too, and not of white skin. How is it that Caleb Callahan took you as his mistress?"

"I am not his mistress. I am his ward. And he took me in because his son and I were in love. My Luke was murdered by a mob just as your husband's brother was."

"I am so sorry," Rosita said softly. "I am sorry, too, for behaving so badly to you—what is your name?"

"Andria."

For the first time Rosita smiled. "Andria. What a pretty name. But that is not Chinese."

"I chose to adopt the name of my Spanish grandmother," she said, a note of pride in her voice.

Rosita was pleased. "Your grandmother was Spanish! So was my grandmother." Impulsively she embraced Andria. "I am glad Joaquin brought you here. You and I will be fast friends, Andria. But for now, we must get you some suitable clothing."

She admired the smart-tailored sport suit that Andria was wearing. "How nice it must be to live in a real house and wear marvelous clothes like that."

Andria smiled. "I would like to give you what I am wearing as a gift, Rosita. Maybe one day you and Joaquin will live in a real house and—"

She stopped as pain spread over the girl's handsome face. To suggest that Rosita and Joaquin could ever live a normal life was wishful thinking of the most extravagant sort.

The interior of the brick dwelling was neat and clean, with only the sparest and most primitive furnishings: two handmade chairs, a wooden table with an oil lamp on it, a chest of drawers, and two soiled mattresses placed side by side on the floor at one side of the room.

Rosita opened a drawer and pulled out a pair of buckskin trousers and a heavy woolen shirt. "You look to be about my size. Shorter, but we can roll up the sleeves and pant legs." She also took out a pair of heavy socks and a pair of boots, not as elegant as the soft leather footwear that she herself was wearing.

Andria removed her outer clothing and looked down at her corselet and lace pantalets. She giggled.

"Will you trade me a pair of simple cotton drawers for these fripperies?"

"It's a bargain."

They both laughed.

And Andria suddenly felt a sense of exhiliration and freedom that she had never experienced in the luxurious mansion of Caleb Callahan.

Chapter Eleven

Captain Hendrik Boll was a bit of a bore on the subject of his spanking new passenger steamer, the *Rotterdam*. "The finest and most modern ship afloat," he would brag to the captive audience at the captain's table over the evening meal. "And unsinkable. Three eight-foot iron decks supported by wooden bulkheads and seven—seven, mind you—watertight compartments! And a hull constructed of solid angle iron!"

It was true the *Rotterdam* was considered without peer in international maritime circles. She was 400 feet long with a 39-foot beam; displaced almost 3,500 tons; was powered by four 125-horsepower engines fueled by coal; and had four 135-foot ship-rigged masts capable of completing any trans-oceanic crossing should the engines fail.

Captain Boll was a stocky man with a pleasantly homely face, pale blue eyes and a monk's fringe of pale yellow hair forming a semicircle about his dome from ear to ear.

This was the *Rotterdam*'s maiden voyage, and in honor of Boll's new command, the ship's Dutch owners had invited him to have his wife accompany him.

Hilda Boll was the antithesis of her husband. Ten years younger than his forty-five years, she was a petite blonde with delicate features and deep blue eyes.

135

Though slight in stature, there was a quality of powerful sensuality about her that Luke—as well as every other male aboard—was acutely aware of. Hilda flaunted it in her every movement: the uninhibited undulation of her hips when she strolled along the decks and in the very act of standing still, her hands braced on her hips and her pointed breasts thrust boldly forward.

She played the coquette with all of the male passengers, and, especially, she enjoyed flirting with Luke.

"Horseshit!" Luke demurred when Tongdlon, now firmly established as Mr. John Yee, teased him about her.

"Don't deny it, my friend. The woman has a mad passion for you. I regret to say I think the captain is deficient in the art of romance—not man enough to slake the earthy appetites of a woman such as she. I have observed the manner in which Mrs. Boll appraises you on the sly, as if she is taking your 'measure,' if you grasp my meaning."

"You keep it up, Big Turnip, and I'll measure you out on the deck. But Captain Boll's deficiencies in the boudoir don't concern me half as much as his deficiencies as a seaman."

John frowned. "Yes, I've heard several of the crewmen comment on his incompetency in handling a steamship. All of his life he's been a sailing master."

It was a failing that Boll shared with a number of ships' masters of the era, who were making the transition from sail to steam.

His archaic attitudes were clearly illustrated at dinner that night. For four days out of Macao the *Rotterdam* had made marvelous time through tranquil seas. On the fifth day high winds churned up choppy seas that impeded the ship's progress and caused it to consume enormous quantities of coal.

As the intensity of the storm increased, attendance in the dining hall fell off somewhat at lunch and sharply at the evening meal. The only ones present at Boll's table for dinner were Luke, John, the captain and his wife, Nils Brinker, the first officer, and another passenger, Hans Farben, the police chief of Amsterdam, a tall, thin, dour man with a profile like a hawk and a cleanshaven scalp.

"Chief engineer says even with the boilers going full blast we're hard put to make three knots," the first mate said apprehensively.

"Ach, you worry too much, Brinker," Boll responded.

"Sir," the first mate said evenly, "we are still four hundred miles from the Sandwich Islands, and we have less than one hundred tons of coal in the bins."

Boll waved a hand, dismissing his fears. "And we'll still have twenty left when we sight Oahu."

The island of Oahu in the Hawaiian chain was to be their refueling port before resuming the long voyage to San Francisco. Since their discovery by Captain James Cook in 1778, the Hawaiian Islands—formerly the Sandwich Islands—had become a vital link in trans-Pacific commerce between the Western world and the Far East.

"Not if this foul weather keeps up," said Brinker. "I think the remainder of the night all passengers should be remanded to their cabins."

"Considering the way the ship is pitching and rolling, I doubt many of them will object to that," the police chief offered.

Captain Boll swallowed the last of his after-dinner brandy and consulted his pocket watch. "Eight bells, Brinker. Think I'll go up to the wheelhouse. Boost the helmsman's morale."

"Yes, sir. I'll relieve you on the bridge in two hours. That's when my watch begins."

The captain excused himself, rose, and kissed his wife chastely on top of her golden ringlets.

"Don't wait up for me, my sweet."

Her eyes, bright with some private amusement, met Luke's across the table. "As you say, Hendrik. To tell the truth, I can't wait to get into bed."

John smothered a guffaw behind his napkin and with a knee nudged Luke beneath the table.

Shortly thereafter, Farben and Brinker departed, leaving Hilda Boll, Luke, and John dawdling over their coffee. To the amazement of the men, Mrs. Boll took a tin of French cigarettes out of her purse. She offered them to Luke and John.

Both declined. "We Mormons do not believe in the use of tobacco, alcoholic beverages, or artificial physical stimulants of any sort. I shouldn't even be drinking this coffee; then again, I am not particularly devout."

"What kind of stimulation do you Mormons believe in—reverend?" She used the clerical appellation in a mocking way.

Luke flushed. "I am not a cleric, Mrs. Boll. We do not have a professional clergy in the Church of Jesus Christ of Latter-Day Saints. Every competent boy at the age of twelve is ordained to an office in the church and is expected to act in whatever capacity the elders decree he can best serve his fellow man."

"And Mormon women? How do they best serve mankind?" Her tone was mischievous.

"Mormon women serve as teachers, social workers, and, yes, they assist their husbands in missionary work."

"How many wives do you have, Mr. Callahan? At least four or five from the looks of you."

John could no longer contain his laughter. Sputtering, he leaped to his feet and said, "Pardon me, but I am feeling somewhat queasy myself, and I think I'll lie down." He beat a hasty retreat.

Hilda looked after him and smiled wryly. "Mr. Yee seems to find seasickness very humorous. I could swear he is laughing."

"Yes, and at me," Luke admitted sheepishly. "Five

wives! Five wives, indeed! I couldn't even support one
wife, much less five!"

"Poor dear." She lit her cigarette from a candle on
the table.

"You know, madam, the Mormons have been unduly
maligned over the issue of plural marriages. Our belief
in polygamy stems from religious conviction, not from
salacious motives."

Her thin, plucked eyebrows lifted. "How disillusion-
ing. And all this time I've been thinking that you
Mormon fellows possessed overactive libidos, that, perhaps, it was a compensation for all of the other stimula-
tions you forgo." She sighed. "Well, it has been a very
pleasant evening chatting with you, Mr. Callahan. May
I call you Luke? After all, we're going to be shipmates
for some time to come."

"By all means, Mrs. Boll."

"Hilda." Her voice fell off an octave, and her eyes
were narrow and sultry. "Would it be an inconvenience
for you to see me to my cabin? My legs are a bit wob-
bly."

"I'd be delighted." He rose and went around the
table to hold her chair back.

She looked over her shoulder and smiled. "Thank
you, Luke. You're so gallant."

*And you are a sexy wench, my dear. What my father
commonly referred to as a cock teaser! And in that
endeavor you have sorely succeeded!*

She was wearing a dress of checkered taffeta, draped
to show off the pink petticoat underneath it. He observed that Hilda Boll required no artificial enhance-
ments such as bustle or padding to emphasize her come-
ly derriere.

Before going out on deck, Hilda wrapped a cashmere
shawl around her shoulders. It required all of Luke's
strength to open the door against the force of the wind
buffeting the ship from the northeast. Earlier in the
afternoon the crew had strung lifelines all about the

deck so that passengers and crewmen could get around without being swept overboard.

"Hang on for dear life!" he cautioned her as they stepped out into the cyclonic gale. After that, conversation was futile. Even the loudest shout could not compete with the banshee wail and roar of the wind.

At that instant a mountainous wave crashed over the *Rotterdam*, causing her to yaw precipitously to the port side. Luke and Hilda were engulfed as angry water sluiced across the deck.

Luke pushed the woman back hard against the wall and clung desperately to the lifeline with both hands, one on either side of Hilda, shielding her with his body.

They remained that way, pressed tightly together, until the cataclysmic assault by sea and wind had subsided. In the brief lull that followed, they made a mad dash for the nearby companionway that led to the captain's quarters on the quarterdeck, pulling themselves hand over hand along the safety rope. They reached the cabin just as another towering wall of water broke over the ship. It flung Luke and Hilda against the door, which crashed open, and they were catapulted into the cabin. Clinging fast to each other, they went rolling and skidding over the wet pegged planks until they slammed into the big brass four-poster bed that dominated the room.

The two of them lay there stunned, arms and legs entwined, in pitch darkness. Luke groped around blindly for some handhold. His hand came to rest on firm flesh, its warmth and vibrancy undiminished by immersion in the cold salt water. He realized with a shock that he was touching Hilda Boll's thigh.

"Good Lord!" He recoiled, but not before the tingling in his finger tips ran clear up his arm like a jolt of electricity.

He was aware of her soft, throaty laughter close by his left ear. Then she blew into his ear and whispered, "Close the door before the cabin gets swamped."

He got up on hands and knees and crawled over to the dim outline that marked the doorway, closing his eyes against the stinging spume the merciless wind flung into his face. He rose unsteadily onto his knees and leaned his weight against the resisting portal. With a mighty heave, he managed to close it and secure the latch. Groaning, he sank down again, his back against the door.

Light exploded in the darkness as Hilda lit a big brass lantern that was suspended from a swag chain in the cabin ceiling. She steadied it with both hands as she lifted it back into position. "Don't look at it for any length of time," she warned him. "It will make you seasick."

He could understand what she meant. The lamp rocked with the motion of the ship like a pendulum gone wild, swinging to and fro, north to south, south to east, and all around the points of the compass. He averted his eyes to something even more disconcerting. Hilda Boll was taking off her wet clothing.

"I'm drenched," she said casually. "You had better get out of your wet things, too."

"But—but—but—" His tongue felt like a wad of putty.

"Oh, don't worry about Hendrik. He's too concerned about his precious ship to intrude here." She laughed, a bawdy laugh. "Even if he knew what we were up to, Luke, I doubt he'd leave the bridge in this weather. Come on, be quick about it. I feel an urgent need to climb into bed with you."

Nothing remained between the lady and stark nudity except for a flimsy, peach-colored, one-piece undergarment that was wet and clinging and diaphanous. Even in the spare illumination, he could make out the bold thrust of her breasts and the lush triangle of her mons veneris. She discarded that garment and came toward him, balancing herself against the violent rolling of the *Rotterdam*.

She held out her hands to Luke. "Upsy daisy, and hold fast to me. I've got better sea legs than you."

He grasped her hands and let her help him up. Arms around each other's waist, they staggered over to the big bed and collapsed on the soft feather mattress.

"This is insane!" he mumbled as she unbuttoned his shirt.

"If you don't care to make love to me, all you have to do is to go back out into the typhoon."

"What the hell!" he said in sudden abandon. "We'll probably all be at the bottom of the Pacific in a matter of hours."

And with a zeal to match her own, he began to fling off his shirt, trousers, drawers.

"Your socks," she reminded him. "I don't want to make love to a man with his socks on. Especially wet socks."

Luke climbed in beside her and pulled the heavy comforter over them. She shivered as he took her in his arms. "God! You're as cold as ice."

"So are you." He kissed her on the lips and neck and caressed her breasts, first one, then the other. Her nipples stiffened against his palm.

"Cold, but not for long." She gasped, and her fingers encircled and stroked him. His erection swelled against her heaving belly. Quickly he entered her.

The violent motion of the ship enhanced the sensuality of their lovemaking. Their bodies kept buffeting each other in the most unexpected and exciting ways.

Hilda giggled. "We don't have to do anything but hold on." She moaned in ecstasy as the ship rolled to port and he came down so hard on her that their pelvic bones ground together.

"I feel as though I've been gored by a bull," she whispered.

"Did I hurt you? I'm sorry."

"Don't be. Do it again."

He did, and she writhed and heaved and squirmed

beneath him so vigorously that she nearly unseated him. All the while, she uttered a stream of words in Dutch.

The reality of their situation was eclipsed by passionate delirium. Ship, storm, the banshee wind, the shudders and groaning complaints of the *Rotterdam*—they were all oblivious to it all.

On the bridge, Captain Boll and the helmsman, recently joined by the first mate, peered grimly through the wheelhouse window. To compound the hazards of the storm, they were now heading into a white wall of fog.

"Christ!" exclaimed Mr. Brinker. "I've never seen anything like it. Not even in the English Channel or off Newfoundland!"

"There's no need to worry, Nils," said the captain. "Fortunately we are not in the English Channel. The chances of encountering another ship in these sea lanes is no more than one in a thousand—if that." To the helmsman, he said, "I'm going to my cabin now. Keep the same course until six bells, then call me."

The words were no sooner out of his mouth than Brinker screamed, "Lord help us! Look at that!"

Dead ahead, a white ghost came out of the fog.

"It's a ship!" yelled the helmsman.

"Hard to port!" ordered the captain, but the helmsman was paralyzed by sheer terror.

"Damn it, man!" Captain Boll pushed him aside and took the wheel himself.

He swung the wheel desperately, but it was too late. He and Brinker stared in numb fascination as the other ship bore down on the doomed *Rotterdam*.

There was a jarring impact as the other ship's bow cut through the *Rotterdam*'s hull like a cleaver slicing through meat, decapitating her bow and a good third of the ship aft of the bow.

The three men were flung to the deck. A series of explosions wracked what remained of the once-proud queen of the seas as water flooded the engine room and touched off the red-hot boilers.

When her convulsions subsided, Boll got to his feet and rushed out of the wheelhouse. He collided with the third mate.

"Sir, I've ordered the crew to close the watertight compartments."

"Good, Peter. It will give us time, at least. Prepare to lower the lifeboats."

"Sir?" the mate gaped at the forty-foot waves crashing against the wounded *Rotterdam*. "Lifeboats in *this?*"

"It's a slim hope at best, but we've got no other recourse. Give it all you've got, Peter. I've got to get my wife." He staggered down the companionway to the main deck.

The Rotterdam kept listing to the right until it seemed inevitable that she would shortly founder. The angle of her tilt made it impossible to lower the lifeboats on that side.

There were two hundred passengers aboard the *Rotterdam*, most of them British officers and their families on leave from colonial service in India and en route to England. Half of them were trapped in the lower cabins by the inrushing sea. Those in the upper-deck cabins ran out on deck half naked and dashed for the lifeboats. Panic and bedlam ensued as they battled like crazed animals for precious space in the boats, impeding the efforts of the crew to put the boats over the side. All of their genteel Victorian manners forgotten, men deserted their wives and children and began clambering into the rigging as the ship sank lower and lower into her watery grave.

Captain Boll reached his cabin just as Luke and Hilda emerged, unclothed except for their underwear.

The captain was stupefied. "What—what—is going on here? Mr. Callahan, what is the meaning of this?"

"Just a friendly little game of strip poker, cap'n,"

Luke said through gritted teeth. "Come on. We'd better get out of here."

In a state of shock and confusion, Boll stared after his wife and Luke as they dashed away, hand in hand. Shaking his head in bewilderment, he followed after them.

The scene that greeted them as they stepped down onto the careening deck was bloodcurdling. Hilda Boll crossed herself and muttered, "It is something out of a painting by Bosch!"

It was classic Bosch religious allegory, an exquisite panorama of heaven and hell as the terrified survivors, all reason and control abandoned, ran about aimlessly, seeking a salvation that did not exist. They seemed no longer human, but demons and gargoyles with faces so contorted that even their closest kin would not have recognized them.

Luke made a megaphone of his hands and shouted, "John! John Yee! Can you hear me, John?"

"I've got to find my friend John," he told the woman. "You go with your husband."

Luke scrambled about the sharply angled deck, calling for John, his desperation mounting. His heart leaped as a strong hand came down on his shoulder.

"You can't get rid of the Big Turnip so easily, my friend," a familiar voice said quietly, and Luke turned and embraced the other man.

"Thank God! John, what do you think is our best chance? The rigging?"

They looked up at the stark figures clinging to the masts, spars, and lines.

"I do not think so," John answered. "Come. We must find some axes or sledgehammers." Luke did not even question what his friend had in mind, but quickly followed him.

They went forward to the ship's carpenter's locker and acquired two axes and a thirty-pound sledgehammer. Then John led Luke to the main hatch. "We've got to break the latches on this hatch cover. Quickly!"

Fueled by adrenalin, they put forth a superhuman effort and accomplished their aim in five minutes.

"Now what?" Luke shouted above the gale.

"Lie flat and hold tight to those handholds on the cover for dear life. "When the ship goes down, we'll float free."

"Won't the suction pull us down with the ship?"

"Unquestionably. But only until the ship's displacement is compensated for by the sea. Don't panic, and take a deep breath when you feel us being sucked into the vortex."

It all happened so suddenly that Luke barely had time to fill his lungs with air before the *Rotterdam* took her final plunge and the hatch cover went spinning around the funnel sides of the giant maelstrom she created. Down and around, down and around, faster and faster. As he held on, a profound sense of calm and serenity settled over Luke. The fear was gone now, his emotion one of total fatalism and resignation.

He made his peace with God: "Our father, who art in heaven, hallowed be thy name. . . ."

As the waters closed over them, Luke concentrated on each word as if it were a priceless jewel. He thought his fingers would surely be torn off by the fierce drag of the currents within the vortex, but he hung on tenaciously. An eternity passed, and just when it seemed that his lungs would burst, the ghost of the *Rotterdam* set them free, and the buoyant hatch cover bobbed to the surface.

"Thank you, God," Luke muttered and opened his eyes.

To his astonishment the power of the storm was abating, and, in the light of the first false dawn, he made out the dim face of John grinning at him from across the hatch.

"The gods have exacted their reparation and have

seen fit to spare two unworthy mortals. See, they have called off their hounds, the wind and the sea, and have even given us a star to lend us hope."

Luke gazed heavenward, and, sure enough, through a break in the overcast sky, there gleamed a bright, friendly star.

"Now I know what they mean by a heavenly body," he said reverently.

Dawn broke over a tranquil ocean, and the sun, a blazing orange orb, rose into a sky as blue as Andria's eyes and barren of even fleecy clouds.

"How far do you think we are from land?" John asked.

"I don't know. Last night Captain Boll said we were four hundred miles from the Sandwich Islands. We seem to be drifting in an easterly direction."

"Boll," John mused. "Do you think any of the others survived?"

"It's doubtful, but then again *we* made it. So there is a chance that some of them also did."

With a twinge of real remorse, Luke thought of Hilda Boll. What a waste of a good woman, and one so young. He fervently wished that he were a better Mormon and truly believed in the immortality of man.

The hours passed slowly that first day, and in the succeeding days time seemed to stand still. The everlasting nights were the worst. John and Luke would have perished for lack of water but for the providential rain squalls that blessed them at dawn for three straight days. A yard-long trough had been gouged out of the wood at one corner of the hatch cover, and it served as a small well that held almost two quarts of rain water.

Their greatest danger, their enemy, was the tropical sun, although John and Luke were outdoorsmen and their bronzed skins provided greater tolerance to the ultraviolet rays than an average man would have possessed.

"I think my brain is frying," Luke said as daylight emerged on the morning of their fourth day afloat.

"I have an idea," said John. "We'll remove our trousers and wrap them around our heads like turbans."

It sounded like an ingenious idea, and while it gave relief to their aching heads, by late afternoon their loins and lower backs, unused to exposure to sunlight, were red and blistered.

On the following day, they decided to leave their heads exposed and put back on their trousers. By noon Luke had lapsed into a comatose state and began to hallucinate.

"Look, John! Do you see here? She's alive!"

He saw Andria, walking across the water, her arms outstretched to him. "I must go to her."

And he would have gone overboard if John had not thrown him down and straddled him. Gradually his struggles and ravings subsided, and he passed into merciful unconsciousness.

John himself dozed, for how long he did not know. He was aroused by the sound of a voice calling to him in English.

"Now I'm getting delirious," he muttered, sitting upright.

He was convinced of it when he saw the strange-looking craft that was approaching their makeshift raft. It had two separate, parallel hulls, canoes really, joined together by wooden poles strapped in place by heavy hemp line. There were four oarsmen in each half of the contraption and a single sail in the bow. The eight-man crew was as handsome a group of males as John had ever laid eyes on. Tall, erect, proud-looking fellows, their broad, deeply tanned, muscled torsos were naked but for colorful breechcloths. Their features were distinctly Polynesian for the most part, but at least half of them bore unmistakable traces of mixed ancestry— slender noses and thin lips.

"Ahoy, there!" called out a man up in the bow.

He was wearing a purple head cloth. "Where do you come from?"

John blinked and shook his head, still expecting the specter to fade away.

The man smiled at him, his teeth brilliantly white in his brown face. "Don't you speak English?" Then he said something in French.

At last John found his voice. "We were passengers aboard the Dutch merchantman *Rotterdam,* and we were wrecked in a storm by another ship. That was four or five days back, I forget which." He gave them a capsule account of all that had befallen them since leaving Macao.

"Where were you bound for?"

"Oahu in the Sandwich Islands."

All of them burst into hearty laughter, and their spokesman said: "You are right on course, my friend. Our position is no more than fifty miles from Oahu." He pointed to the west. "Come aboard and we'll take you there. Our home is the island of Maui, but what are friends for?"

John took an immediate liking to their good-humored, devil-may-care natures. As their catamaran drew alongside the hatch cover, he reached out a hand across its gunwale.

"My friend and I are pleased to meet you—how pleased you can't imagine. My name is John Yee, and he is Luke Callahan, a Mormon missionary."

"Missionary?" A chorus of groans went up from the Hawaiians. "Do you think we should leave them here?" the head man inquired tongue-in-cheek of his crew.

Grinning broadly, he said to John, "One thing we have an excess of in the Islands is missionaries. There is an old saying among our people, "When the missionaries first came to Hawaii, they had all the Bibles, and we had all the land. Now they have all the land, and we have all the Bibles.""

There was another chorus of hearty laughter in

which John joined. "That is true wherever the white man goes to spread his gospel. China has much in common with your people."

The two men shook hands, and the Hawaiian said, "I am Kiano, and my opinion of missionaries is not as bad as I suggest. Before they came there was no written language in any of the islands. They gave us an alphabet, and our ancestors were only too eager to learn to read and write." Proudly he continued, "Now we have books, newspapers, and a Bible printed in our own language. In fact, as of this time, the *Book of Mormon* is being translated into Hawaiian.

"The missionaries gave us one merciful God in place of the pagan gods whom the ancient rulers used as weapons to terrify the people into total subjugation. No, there are many things, good things, the missionaries brought to Hawaii."

He sighed. "And things not so good as well. Measles, smallpox, tuberculosis, venereal diseases. When Captain Cook's first expedition landed here, our population was over three hundred thousand. Today we number less than eighty-five thousand. . . . But we will speak of history at some other time. Let us get your friend aboard and give him fresh water to drink and a medicine made from the *kiawe* root. We never go to sea without it."

"Just what are you doing out here so far from you homeland?"

Kiano laughed. "You might say it is in the blood. For hundreds of years the Polynesian peoples have been sailing from Tahiti and neighboring islands, covering thousands of miles of uncharted ocean in open canoes to reach the Hawaiian Islands. Why, you may ask? I cannot tell you, any more than why a certain breed of white man has to climb tall mountains.

"One day last week my companions and I were sitting around drinking *'awa*—we prefer it to the white man's whiskey—and without any reason I said, 'I am very restless. Let us take a long sea voyage and cleanse our minds and bodies from the noxious vapors of the land.' And here we are."

At his command two of the supple oarsmen leaped aboard the raft and picked up the unconscious Luke as effortlessly as if he had been a child instead of a brawny man who stood six feet tall. They transferred him to the catamaran, and Kiano began to minister to him. Kiano wrapped Luke's head in a wet cloth, and the Hawaiian poured a trickle of water from a small gourd into his mouth. Next he took some powdered kiawe root from a flannel pouch and forced it between Luke's parched lips, washing it down with more water.

Almost immediately the unconscious man began to stir. Within fifteen seconds his eyelids began to flutter and open tentatively, squinting against the bright blue sky.

"Where is she?"

"It's all right, my friend," John said gently. "We are safe now."

"Andria?"

"There was no Andria. You were dreaming."

After a while Luke sat up and looked about him in bewilderment at the smiling Hawaiians. "Where did you come from?" he asked.

Kiano put a hand on his shoulder and said, "Aloha, *malihini*. Welcome to our land of paradise."

Chapter Twelve

Andria rode with the Murieta gang for the next month. In that time they committed a succession of armed robberies in small villages and mining camps along their route. From the townspeople they exacted food and supplies, and in most cases they would pay for their booty with currency and gold pilfered from banks and rich miners.

One day Murieta rode alongside Andria's white mare. "I think you no longer feel so guilty about our activities, do you?"

"I will never take pride in thievery," she replied aloofly.

"Not even if our chief purpose is to steal from the rich to feed the poor?"

"Attila the Hun excused his barbarism on the same grounds," she said scornfully, "as have all outlaws and murderers since the beginning of time. In my own country, China, it is the I Ho Ch'üan bandits who burn and kill and steal—all in the name of patriotism."

For a time he stared in silence at her perfect profile. Unexpectedly he said to her in a quiet voice, "Andria, I think I am in love with you."

She looked at him in alarm. "Don't speak to me of love. You are married to my friend Rosita."

He wore a thin smile. "Si, I am married to Rosita,

and that will always be. Do you think that because a priest says a few words over a man and a woman that forever after he will be immune to the beauty and charm of another woman so desirable as yourself?"

She turned away from him. "I do not wish to discuss it, Joe—please. Someone may hear you. It would break Rosita's heart if she knew what you have been saying."

He slumped in the saddle, and his voice was bitter. "Rosita's heart has been broken so many times in the past few years that it has become as hard as stone." He reined his horse about abruptly and rode off at a gallop to the east.

Three-Fingered Jack rode up beside her, frowning. "What is it with Joaquin? Where is he going?"

"He seems to be restless. I'm sure he'll catch up with us."

But when they reached their campsite at Lake Tulare, Murieta still had not rejoined them. He finally appeared at dusk as the bandits were sitting around their camp-fires, preparing the evening meal.

"Where have you been?" Rosita demanded.

He swung down off his black stallion and swaggered over to the fire where she, Andria, and Jack were sitting cross-legged, eating out of their mess tins. Laughing, he bent and kissed Rosita wetly on the lips.

"Making an honest day's wages for a change." He withdrew a fat pouch of gold dust from his saddlebag and tossed it down in front of her. "I've been into town at the Silver Slipper. And I won handsomely at the dice table and the faro table."

Three-Fingered Jack looked troubled. "You should not expose yourself in the gambling halls in this region. You are too well known. And alone at that." He shook his head. "You are a crazy one, Joaquin. Who were you gambling with?"

"Billy Burns, among others."

Jack was aghast. "Billy Burns? You are even madder

than I imagined. He is one bad yanqui, and he despises *Chilenos* more than any white man I have ever met."

Murieta grinned as he stooped to dip a tin into the communal stew pot. "No more than we despise him, but he respects me, and we play well together.

"Here, Rosita, pass me the goatskin." She did, and he angled it deftly across one shoulder and tipped the spout to his mouth. Red wine gurgled down his throat and spilled out of the corners of his mouth, then ran down his chin.

Sitting around the fire after the meal, Joaquin continued to drink. By the time darkness had shrouded the lake, he was in high spirits—not drunk, but at that border where reason and good judgment give way to abandon and irresponsibility.

Andria yawned and stretched. "I think I will go to my tent. It has been a long and tiring day."

Since her abduction, Andria had been provided with a pyramidal tent stolen from a U.S. Army supply depot and a folding army cot. She lit the lantern hanging from the center pole and undressed. In the morning she would bathe in the lake. Naked, she lay down on the cot and wrapped herself in a light cotton blanket. She fell asleep almost at once.

She awoke with a start, her heart hammering wildly against her breastbone. There was not a sound to be heard except for the chirping crickets and the night cry of a loon soaring over the lake. The campfires were out, or she would have seen a red glow filtering through the canvas sides of the tent. She lay there rigid, waiting.

Still no sign to trigger alarm, but she knew intuitively that someone was in the tent. Someone or something—possibly a wild animal foraging for food. She cursed herself for not washing her eating utensils before retiring; the scraps could well attract a hungry forest creature.

No such luck! A hand came down quickly over her mouth, and she knew that she was confronting a human predator.

"Do not be afraid. It is I, Joaquin."

She struggled furiously, but he pinned her down with the weight of his body.

"Stop it at once! I promise not to harm you. You know that already, Andria. I love you too much."

She went slack, and he said, "Promise you will not scream, and I will let you speak."

She nodded her head mutely. Guardedly he removed his hand from over her mouth. Andria was true to her word. What good would it accomplish in any case to make a frantic scene over his indiscretion? Andria possessed a strong degree of Oriental stoicism. Besides, the pain and humiliation it would cause for her dear friend Rosita was unthinkable.

"Stop this nonsense, Joaquin," she said in a whisper. "You are drunk."

"Drunk with desire for you, my darling." He bent to kiss her lips, but she turned her cheek to him.

"Don't you feel anything for me at all?" he implored her.

"I used to think you were a good friend and a gentleman, but you've proven me wrong this night."

The truth was that Andria felt a strong physical attraction to Murieta. The long-dormant sexual feelings that Luke Callahan had awakened in her woman's body had been reawakened by Joaquin Murieta.

He flung off the blanket and cupped his hands over her small, firm breasts. She shuddered, and her nipples hardened against his palms. He laughed softly and kissed her throat, noting with satisfaction how her pulse quickened against his lips.

"Your mind says one thing, *querida,* but your flesh and blood tell quite a different story."

He ran one hand down over her smooth, flat belly and around the curve of her hip. Down to her knee, then working it inside her clenched thighs.

"Don't, Joe, I beg of you!"

"And I beg of you: don't fight me, *querida*. Don't fight your own emotions."

Andria exerted all of her willpower to resist, but her body had turned to jelly. She was powerless to stop the caressing, exploring hand. His fingers moved up the inside of her thighs like little mice seeking out their nest.

"Oh! Oh! *Oh!*" she cried out softly.

She offered no resistance as he took her hand and guided it to his rigid member. With an upward surge of her hips, she guided it eagerly to its goal. He filled her until she thought she would surely burst.

"*Mia cara,*" he murmured in her ear, "you are the most beautiful girl in the world."

She was consumed with lust, yet, even as she achieved her climax, at the back of her mind was the realization that what she was experiencing was sheer physical pleasure and emotional release. It could not approach the warm, tender, and blissful love she had known with Luke.

He peaked with her, and they rocked back and forth on the creaking cot until their bodies were thoroughly spent. He groaned and rolled on his side, still caressing her buttocks.

"*Carita de angel,*" he said.

Suddenly Murieta sat up, his head cocked to one side.

"What's wrong?"

"Did you hear anything?"

"No."

"I did." He bounded off the cot and put on his trousers, tiptoed to the tent flap and held it ajar, no more than an inch.

"*Caramba!*"

"What is it?" Andria swung her legs to the floor and wrapped the blanket around her naked body.

"The law, unless I miss my guess. Querida, I must leave you now." He ran to the back of the tent, took out his knife, and slashed an opening in the canvas. Soundlessly he slipped through it into the night.

Shots sounded from all sides of the clearing, catching the unsuspecting bandits in a murderous enfilade. Three-Fingered Jack was cut down beside a smoldering mound of embers; he died instantly. Some of the bandits ran for their horses. Others threw themselves down in order to surrender before they were killed. Murieta made it safely to his stallion, vaulted onto its back, and the horse, trained to make quick getaways, galloped off into the trees. He would have made it easily, but for a chance shot by some California ranger.

After the brief fracas was over, they found Murieta a hundred yards from the camp, lying on his back with a fatal bullet in his spine.

Back at the clearing there was mayhem as the triumphant lawmen herded the prisoners into a circle. Andria, dressed now, stepped out of her tent to be confronted by a tall, burly man in a Stetson hat.

"Ma'am, I'm Captain Love, deputy sheriff of the Los Angeles Rangers. Would you be Miss Andria Callahan?"

"I am ward to Mr. Caleb Callahan."

"Thank God! We thought you might be dead by now. Caleb has been going out of his mind since they carried you off."

"He had no cause to worry. I was treated very courteously by all of them. Where is Joaquin?"

"Joaquin?" His eyebrows lifted at the informal use of his name. "You mean Murieta? He's hit real bad. Most likely he'll die before too long."

"I would like to see him."

"Ma'am?"

"I would like to see Joaquin Murieta," she repeated firmly.

He shrugged, mystified. "If you say so. Come along."

There were two rangers standing over the fallen outlaw, holding torches.

Andria knelt down beside him and spoke softly. "Joaquin—Joe, it is I, Andria."

His eyes opened, and he smiled up at her.

"Carita de angel—" His voice was so weak she had to bend her ear close to his mouth to hear him. "Now more than ever, your face is that of an angel. Why, I may even be in heaven already, do you think? No, I fear I am headed in just the other direction." He coughed violently. "Querida—one more thing. Always remember that—that"—the coughing wracked him again, and she barely caught his final words—"I love you."

Captain Love helped Andria to her feet. To keep from crying, she bit her lip until it bled. Rosita ran up, her face wet with tears. She clasped her hands to her face in horror and grief when she saw her dead husband.

"Joaquin! My darling! What have they done to you?" She would have thrown herself on top of his prostrate body, but two rangers restrained her.

"We're sorry, Mrs. Murieta," Captain Scott said kindly. "But we all knew it had to come to this in the end. He knew it better than any or one of us. Do you know what he said to me when we found him? He said, 'Captain, my work is done, and now your work is done. Farewell, amigo.' "

Andria put her arms around Rosita and clasped her head to her bosom. "He said one more thing—just before he died."

"What was it?" asked the disconsolate wife.

Andria took a deep breath. "He said to me, 'Tell my darling Rosita that I love her dearly and that one day we will be together again in the hereafter.' "

And now Andria cried along with Rosita, grieving for her own lost love.

"Miss Callahan, you'll be riding back to San Francisco with us," Captain Love said. "That's where the Callahans are now. Think you're up to it? We could put you on a coach at Stockton, of course. That would be easier for you."

"And slower. No thank you, captain. I prefer to ride with you." She smiled. "Since my abduction, I've been in the saddle every day. San Francisco will be nothing." She hugged Rosita fiercely. "What about my friend? What will happen to her?"

"She'll have to stand trial with the rest of the gang. Being she's a woman, I'm sure the court will show her leniency."

After a tearful farewell, Rosita was led away by a ranger to join the other prisoners. And at dawn the company headed west on its way to San Francisco.

The long trip was uneventful. By the morning of the third day, they were approaching the suburbs of the sprawling city.

"Hey, cap'n, look at this fog we're coming into," one ranger commented.

Love wrinkled up his nose. "Fog? Smells more like smoke to me."

An air of consternation spread through the ranks.

"Must be Frisco."

"And from all this smoke, it must be a dilly of a fire."

Andria's heart accelerated. Caleb Callahan and his wives were the closest thing to a family she had known since the missionaries had taken her into the temple at Nauvoo. And there was her dear friend Lee.

"Captain Love, is it all right if I ride on ahead? I'm worried about my family."

Love pushed back his Stetson. "I dunno, ma'am. If Frisco is burning, all hell will break loose. Them scum from the Barbary Coast will run rampant. It's happened before. Murder, rape, pillage—there's nothing they'll stop at."

"I'll take my chances."

"I can't stop you, but take this, at least." He offered her a pistol. "Can you use this?"

"I learned to shoot with Murieta and his men. Thanks, captain. For everything. Now goodbye." She put the spurs to her mount and galloped off in advance of the column.

The closer she came to San Francisco, the thicker the smoke became. At last she reached the hills overlooking the city, and from that vantage point she looked down upon a scene that took her breath away. It was a raging holocaust of such proportion that it defied description. Chinatown, the Barbary Coast, scarcely any part of the city was unscathed. Portsmouth Square was an inferno. Thousands were fleeing in blind panic just ahead of the flames.

Firemen and civilian volunteers battled valiantly to hold back the fire to afford the populace a chance to evacuate the city. Not that they held even a remote hope of putting it out. San Francisco, built almost entirely of wood, was a tinderbox. Flames raced out in all directions from Portsmouth Square—up Kearney Street, down Clay Street, along Depont. Consumed were the customhouse, seven of the city's best hotels, the post office, and scores of office buildings.

The firefighters concentrated their herculean efforts on demolishing the wharves before the flames could incinerate them and reach the ships at dock and jammed in the harbor. With the police occupied helping battle the fire, the Sydney Ducks pillaged private dwellings, shops, office buildings, and banks. They ransacked bars and swilled whiskey, wine, and vintage champagne.

On the outskirts of the city, Andria passed droves of people stumbling about aimlessly, their eyes glazed over from shock. A girl wearing only a satin chemise and high-heeled slippers wandered among the mob of poor wretches huddled next to the few household possessions they had managed to salvage. She was dispensing champagne from a galvanized bucket. She was one of dozens of prostitutes dispossessed from their cribs and gaming clubs, who with typical resourcefulness were busily engaged in setting up tents so that business could carry on as usual.

Riding into the city, Andria found herself in a zone where the looters were engaged in their savage desecrations. Three men blocked her way.

"Look at that little Chink cutey," one said, and they all leered at her with unmistakable intent.

One grabbed the horse's bridle, and the other two moved in to unseat Andria. Calmly she snatched the pistol from her waistband and drilled a shot into the shoulder of the **one** closest to her.

She covered his companion with the gun and snapped, "Now get out of my way, you vermin, or you'll get the same! Only this time it will be in the gut!"

They sped away, leaving their pal writhing in the ashes and dust.

Andria rode until she came to a warehouse where a crew of workmen were emptying kegs of liquid all over the roof and sides of a building.

"What are you doing?" she shouted.

"Vinegar," one told her. "We just got in eighty thousand gallons of it. Nothing better to fireproof wood."

"Has anyone seen the Callahans?"

"Caleb and his brood were heading for the docks last I saw of him. No chance to save his place."

"Thank you." She turned her horse in the direction of the docks. The animal trembled nervously as he trotted through the smoldering ruins. As they approached the conflagration that raged all along the waterfront, he spooked and reared high in the air. Caught by surprise, Andria was sent flying, and the terrified horse raced back in the direction they had come from.

She got up, brushed herself off, and continued on foot.

"You'd better get the hell out of here!" a fireman warned her. "These structures are going to give way any time now."

Towering over them on all sides were the flaming skeletons of the once-proud metropolis. The water supply was exhausted, so the firefighters were beating at the flames with blankets soaked in wine or beer.

"I'm looking for Caleb Callahan. They told me the Callahans were headed this way."

"Yup! I saw old Caleb awhile back. He was trying to break up the wharves with that bunch."

Andria raced along the street, just escaping a fiery death as a tall building collapsed in a shower of embers. She would have been cremated had she remained there an instant longer.

She made it through to the docks where the firefighters were celebrating their victory over the fire, passing around bottles of wine and whiskey. She pushed through the mob, shouting for Caleb Callahan.

"Andria!"

She whirled in the direction of the voice and saw him.

"Caleb!" She rushed into his arms, and they embraced.

He hugged her so hard, her ribs creaked. "This is the miracle I've been praying for. I've been praying morning, noon, and night since they took you away from us." He wept unashamedly. "I don't deserve his forgiveness, an old sinner like me. But *you,* you are all purity and light, and that's why he answered my prayers."

He put a protective arm around her shoulders and led her toward the demolished docks. "No time for palaver now. We've got to get out of here."

"Where are we going?"

"I've booked passage for all of us on a ship. This city is in ruins. No future for us here now. The women are aboard."

"Lee?"

"She's there, too, your mother." He grinned. "Never did buy that crock about you and her, child. No matter. She's a good soul."

"Where are we going after we're on the ship?"

"The Hawaiian Islands. Ever hear of 'em?"

"Yes, the Sandwich Islands they were called in China. What on earth will we do there?"

"I've been buying up land there for a long time. Me and the Doles and the Spreckels. They say it's the perfect climate to grow sugar cane, and the world-wide demand for sugar is insatiable."

At the water's edge a skiff manned by two oarsmen awaited them. Caleb helped her aboard, then climbed in after her.

"All right, you swabbies, shove off." He put an arm around her shoulders and said, laughing, "Hawaii, here we come!"

Chapter Thirteen

Luke would never forget his first sight of the Hawaiian Islands. A high, magnificent rocky bluff loomed out of the mist like the figurehead of a giant ship.

"Diamond Head," Kiano told him. "Forged out of stone by the ancient gods to be sentinel of the heathen temple, *Puuk a hola*. There—you can see the temple now atop that hill."

It was an awesome and ominous-looking structure, terraced on the sea side, at least two hundred and fifty feet long, he judged, and over one hundred feet in depth. Lava walls enclosed it, walls fifteen feet high and ten feet thick at the base.

"It looks more like a fort than a temple," Luke mused.

"In a sense it was a fort," Kiano said. "A fort's purpose is to keep out one's enemies. The function of those thick walls was to keep one's enemies inside. A prison, really. Ah, if those walls could only speak. What manner of unspeakable atrocities they could describe that were inflicted on hapless victims. Men and women dismembered, piece by piece. First the fingers, one by one. Then the hands. Next a forearm. And so it went, all done diabolically slowly and methodically, until all that remained was a head and a torso, still alive and screaming in indescribable agony."

Luke shivered. "I'm glad that is ancient history."

"For the most part, but there are still die-hard sects in the hill country faithful to the old rites."

"We shall steer clear of the hills," John said.

Both Luke and John commented on the fluency of the Hawaiians' English.

"One would almost believe it was your native tongue," Luke said. "The same as with my Chinese friend here. I envy you both for being bilingual."

"Our people have always had an ear for foreign tongues," Kiano said. "French as well as English."

When they spoke among themselves in their native tongue, it was a pleasure to Luke's ear. The Hawaiian language was soft and musical and flowed like oil.

"I must learn to speak it," John vowed.

Kiano grinned, showing perfect white teeth that had never had a cavity in all of his twenty-five years. He was a handsome man with Roman features and straight black hair.

"I will teach you, my friend," promised Kiano.

"I'm afraid we won't have time to spare for lingering in your paradise," Luke said regretfully. Even before they had sighted land, the exotic aromas of the tropical Eden were a euphoria to the nostrils.

"Is the climate like this all of the time?" Luke asked.

"Year round, with rare exceptions. You see, our mountain ranges act as barriers to the tropical trade winds, so we are blessed with northeast winds from over the cold ocean currents. Throughout the seven main islands, temperatures average around seventy-five degrees all year."

"Someday I would like to come back here and make a home," Luke said. "But first there is someone I must find and take her with me."

Kiano laughed. "You would travel halfway around the world for a woman? She must be quite a woman."

"An angel."

A glint shone in the Hawaiian's eyes. "Wait until you

see our *wahines*. You may change your mind. There are no women on earth more beautiful than Hawaiian women."

"I don't doubt that. You are a beautiful people, all of you. But love goes deeper than mere beauty, and I am in love with my Andria."

As the catamaran sailed into Honolulu Harbor, a similar craft, only much larger, headed out from shore to meet the returning adventurers. There was a dais of a sort mounted between the twin hulls and covered with an awning. Seated on a chair upon the platform was a large regal-looking man with white hair, swathed in colorful ceremonial robes. Two attendants standing behind him held flags that Kiano identified as *"kais* rods."

"He is King Kamehameha, my uncle," Kiano exclaimed. He leaped up and began shouting and waving his arms. "He must be visiting Oahu! What a wonderful surprise!"

As the royal barge approached the smaller craft, the oarsmen lifted their thin-bladed paddles from the water and held them straight up in the air.

Kiano crossed over to the other vessel, bowed to his eminent relative and said something in Hawaiian. It was obviously a request for permission to mount the dais.

The king smiled and made a beckoning motion with his right hand. The formality observed, Kiano leaped up onto the platform. Kamehameha rose, and the two men embraced in more familial tradition.

After their amenities, the king gestured at Luke and John, and it was evident that he was more than a little curious about them. After Kiano had described what Luke imagined was an account of how he and his crew had rescued them, His Highness beamed at them and spoke in English as fluent as his nephew's.

"Welcome to Hawaii, malihinis. In our world there are no strangers. Only newcomers."

Luke and John moved to stand up in the small

catamaran out of deference to their benefactor, but the king motioned for them to remain seated.

"No, please. You both must be very weak after your harrowing ordeal. It is my wish that you be my guests at the royal palace on Oahu. It is more modest than the permanent palace on Hawaii, but I am sure we can make you comfortable."

"That is most kind and generous of you, Your Highness, and we accept with the utmost gratitude."

Kiano leaped back into his own boat. "Then we will head shoreward with all dispatch." He waved a parting salute to his uncle, took his place with the other oarsmen, then shouted a final word to the king," I will bet you, sir, that we dock before you do!"

Kamehameha laughed and shouted back, "You have a bet!"

The small, slim catamaran beat the king's clumsy craft handily. After they were all ashore, Kamehameha rewarded Kiano with a gold coin. Then, accompanied by his retinue, he was whisked away in a carriage to the royal dwelling. He called back a reminder. "I will expect you for tea and crumpets at four o'clock."

Luke chuckled. "Tea and crumpets? That's the last thing I expected to be served way out here."

"My uncle and his brother, Prince Lot, are pro-British and devout members of the Anglican church. As youths they traveled all over Europe, and if any uncles could have their way, they would restore an absolute monarchy here in Hawaii, as well as the ancient traditional culture that was subverted by the missionary invasion."

"But it was my impression that the missionaries accomplished so much good. You said so yourself. Literacy. A democratic, liberal government."

"Again, it all depends on what side one is on. The monarchists or the *haole*—the white establishment, that is. Again, its the old joke, which I told your friend, about how the missionaries had all the Bibles when they arrived in Hawaii, and the Hawaiians had all the land—"

John Yee snorted. "And now the missionaries have all the land and the Hawaiians have all the Bibles."

"There is a more profound truth in the statement than its surface meaning. It is ironic that because we were such apt pupils and adapted to the Western-economy society far ahead of their timetable, the clergy turned its attention to other areas. Money and political power. The clergy's descendants and future descendants may well become the nucleus of economic and political power in the islands for all time to come. When my Uncle Liholiho, Kamehameha the Fourth, became king last year, it signified the inevitable showdown in the power struggle between the monarchists and the haole."

"What is to be gained by either side?" Luke demanded.

"Are you serious, Luke? The stakes are exceedingly high. There is a fortune to be made in Hawaii from sugar, coffee, beef, pineapples. The ultimate goal of the haole is to achieve a monopoly over the economy and push for annexation to the United States.

"The Kamehameha's aims are equally as selfish, but with the added incentive that the royal line is battling for survival. The big issue both are confronting, as of this time, is the drafting of a new constitution. The Americans are pressing for even more liberal amendments to the old constitution, with an eye toward establishing a mere puppet monarchy with economic policies favoring local whites and the United States. It stands to be a long and bitter battle, and there could be bloodshed."

"A grim prospect," Luke admitted. "How can you be so pragmatic about it?"

Kiano shrugged. "I suppose I am of a new breed torn between irreconcilable social and cultural crosscurrents. I can argue the case for either side. I am aware that that is not an especially redeeming trait in a man."

Not without a hint of sarcasm, Luke said, "Where I come from, they say, 'He runs with the foxes and hunts with the hounds.' "

"An apt metaphor. But come—we have discussed politics too long as it is." He flipped the gold coin the king had presented to him in the air and caught it. "Now I must introduce you to some genuine Hawaiian food." He winked. "And also to some genuine wahines as well."

Luke looked down at his tattered shirt and trousers. His shoes and socks had been torn off in the maelstrom when the *Rotterdam* went down.

"John and I are not exactly in a presentable state to meet anyone—much less take tea and crumpets with your uncle, the king."

Kiano laughed. "Look around you, my friend. You blend into the scenery as if you had lived here for years."

There was truth in the statement. Kiano, like his boating companions, wore a *malo,* a colorful, decorative loincloth.

"We *kanakas* wear as little clothing as possible, except for certain ceremonial and festive functions."

There was an infinite variety of attire to be seen on the streets of Honolulu: men wearing only a malo like Kiano and women in rustling grass or paper skirts that displayed provocative glimpses of long, shapely legs when they walked. Most of the women wore shawls or halters to cover their breasts, but some of the younger girls with firm, high bosoms flaunted them proudly bare. The older females preferred muumuus, the long, loose flowing garment patterned after the shapeless Mother Hubbard gowns the first missionaries had compelled the native women to wear. Many of the native men and white beachcombers wore dirty canvas trousers cut off at the knee, and shirts with the tails worn outside the pants. They appeared no better nor worse than Luke and John. And there were the missionaries in their pure white suits and white shoes kept immaculate through daily applications of chalk.

There was about Honolulu an aura reminiscent of the American West; it was an exciting, crude, swashbuckling, hustling city. Kiano took them on a tour of the neat geometric streets. On each side were rows of straw and adobe huts, many adorned with cream-colored pebbles and coral and shells inlaid in cement. There was an occasional white frame wood-and-brick structure.

"The rich whites live in those," Kiano informed them.

When they saw their first coconut tree, both Luke and John had to laugh. "Looks like a dust mop struck by lightning," Luke observed.

They paused by a street stand where a merchant, squatting on his haunches, was surrounded by piles of strange-looking vegetables that resembled corpulent yams. There were others boiling in an iron pot suspended over a fire. Cooking turned them an unappetizing purple.

"Corms, the roots of the taro plant," Kiano explained. "The Hawaiians' staff of life. It is boiled, pounded into mash, baked underground, mashed again, and mixed with water to make a dish we call poi."

Then Kiano purchased a large gourd of what appeared to Luke to be wallpaper paste. The three of them squatted around the gourd, and Kiano instructed them how to partake of the delicacy.

"The proper manner to eat poi." He dipped a finger into the mushy contents, deftly swirled it around, then withdrew the well-coated finger and jammed it into his mouth.

"Delicious! Please, eat."

Luke looked at John and grimaced, swallowed hard, and bravely followed Kiano's example. He thought it tasted vile, but he could not insult his host.

"Delicious," he said.

Kiano laughed. "You're a liar, but it grows on you. Before long you will appreciate poi as much as we do."

"I know I'm not going to be in Hawaii *that* long!"

From another stand Kiano bought three coconut shells filled with an exotic-smelling beverage. He passed them around.

" 'Awa, our version of your whiskey."

Luke took a swallow and almost choked. Liquid fire seared his gullet; tears flowed freely from his eyes. When he found his voice, he asked hoarsely, "My God! What is it?"

"I'm not sure myself, but one must have a government license to brew it. In fact, it's much worse than whiskey. If one imbibes too frequently, he can become a raving addict."

"I've seen it happen with whiskey."

"Yes, but 'awa is a narcotic. Its distillers claim it can cure everything from impotency to measles."

Luke grinned. "Snake oil medicine. We have it back home."

On the outskirts of town they passed a row of cottages that, from a distance, had the furry appearance of bearskin. Closer scrutiny showed huts constructed of long gray grass bound together with vines. High, steep roofs and thick walls gave them a cool and pleasant atmosphere. A group of three young women sat in the shade of a tall tree at the side of one dwelling, dangling their feet in a sylvan pool. A commonplace scene but for one thing: all three were stark naked.

All had long black hair streaming halfway down their backs, dark sultry eyes, and a sensual fullness about their mouths and noses. Classic Polynesian. They smiled and waved at Kiano, calling to him in Hawaiian.

He grinned and turned to Luke and John. "They wish us to bathe with them."

"I could sure use a bath," Luke observed wryly. "But it could prove embarrassing."

"Why do you white men entertain such guilts about

the human body, male and female? Almost everything you do has some remote sexual significance. God made male and female to complement and please one another. The different parts were intended to fit together smoothly; that is obvious even to a child. If I meet an attractive girl who arouses desire in me, I simply ask her, 'Wahine, I want to bed down with you and make love.' If she finds me desirable, she simply replies, 'I would like that, too.' And she takes me by the hand and leads me to her shack. If not, she smiles and answers, 'No thank you, Kiano. I am not in the mood.' A transaction that is not nearly as complicated and lengthy as the ritual you people call courting. We have not the time nor the patience for playing such childish games."

Luke threw back his head and laughed. "I like that, Kiano. You speak the truth. What about it, John? Shall we join the ladies?"

"By all means."

The three of them commenced taking off their shirts as they walked toward the pond. Kiano introduced them. "These are my friends Luke and John from across the sea. Here are Kokua, Leilani, and Uli."

They were all pretty girls, but Luke was captivated by Leilani. Taller and slimmer than the other two, she had the graceful neck of a swan and breasts and buttocks that looked as if they had been carved out of tan, flawless marble.

To Luke's surprise, bathing in the nude with a member of the opposite sex was not in the least erotic. As an adolescent in Illinois, he had been consumed with lust, swimming in the buff with schoolmates, knowing that a bunch of curious girls were watching them from behind nearby bushes; the boys had floated on their backs and brazenly flaunted their aroused manhood.

All three girls spoke English, though not as well as Kiano. At first they engaged in no more than innocent gambol. Then, inevitably, they paired off, John with Kokua, Kiano with Uli, and Luke with Leilani.

"Leilani—what a pretty name. What does it mean?" he asked her.

She blushed and laughed shyly. "Oh, something very silly. I won't tell you."

"Then I'll find out from Kiano." He called to his friend. "Kiano, what does Leilani mean?"

"Flower of the heavens," said the Hawaiian. "In English, you might say that she is an angel."

"That she is, for sure," Leilani was the most beautiful girl he had ever seen, with the exception of Andria.

At one point he and Leilani waded up the gently flowing stream that fed the pond. It traced a sinuous course through a tall fern forest draped with *ie* vines and fragrant *maile*.

"This *is* paradise," he mused.

She giggled. "And you and I are Adam and Eve."

And there is the forbidden fruit, he thought. Gazing at her pear-shaped breasts, he experienced a stirring in his loins. To his mortification, he was powerless to subdue the physical manifestation of his sexuality. He let go of her hand abruptly and turned away.

"We had better go back with the others. It's getting late." He walked several steps ahead of her.

"Luke, what is wrong?" she asked in concern. "Did I do or say anything to displease you?" She ran after him and placed her hand on his shoulder.

"Don't!" He pulled away roughly.

"Luke!"

"I'm sorry, Leilani," he apologized. "No, you do not displease me in any sense. Quite the contrary. In fact, you please me too much. Far too much."

"Too much?" She was bewildered at first, but soon it dawned on her. She laughed in relief. "But I want to please you, Luke." She came up behind him and wrapped her arms around his waist, pressing her body hard against his. One had glided down over his belly and grasped his rigid erection. "I am pleased that I so please you," she whispered.

"You little vixen." He whirled, took her in his arms, and kissed her passionately. Her lips, her eyes, her throat. She took one of his hands and guided it between her thighs. She was wet and slippery to the touch.

"You see, you please me very much, too. Right from the beginning, I wanted you so badly."

Leilani took his hand and led him to the bank. They lay down amid a bed of silversword and forest moss.

"You're not a virgin?" he murmured as he slipped between her beckoning thighs.

"Not since I was ten years old," she answered without any self-consciousness.

"Ten years old?" He laughed. "I didn't even know what sex was at that age."

Leilani giggled. "When did you first have a girl?"

"I was close to twenty," he admitted.

"Twenty?" She rolled her eyes in disbelief. "How did you endure the torment all those years, not making love with a woman?"

"There is an old American expression that applies to puritanical little boys like I was: 'I went steady with my hand.' "

"With your hand? I do not understand."

"Keep quiet and concentrate on what we're doing now."

Her rhythm matched his, and the pace quickened to a frenzied dance, and they peaked together. His tumescent member never faltered, and they climaxed a second time.

Afterward, they dozed on the soft forest moss, his hand on her breast, her hand on his satiated manhood. A distant voice roused them. "Luke! Leilani! Where are you?"

"Sounds like Kiano," he said. "We'd better be getting back."

They washed in the stream and headed back to the pond. Their four companions were all grinning like Cheshire cats when they arrived.

"What were you two up to?" Kiano asked, smiling knowingly. "As if I didn't know."

"Leilani was showing me the flora and fauna of Hawaii," Luke said with a straight face.

Kiano appreciatively ran his eyes up and down the girl's lissome body. "And her flora and her fauna are certainly something to see. However, it is getting late, and we don't want to keep my uncle, the king, waiting. No more time for fun and games. Put on your pants, my friend, and we will be getting on."

King Kamehameha's residence on Oahu was a white Georgian mansion with four pillars supporting the portico. The grounds were a faithful reproduction of the grounds of an English town house in Surrey—oaks, and elms, ivy, brier and privet hedges.

The rooms had beamed ceilings and pegged floors, all of the wood darkly varnished. It was furnished with a meticulous eye to traditional British appointments of the period.

"The most civilized people on earth, the British," King Kamehameha said as he, Kiano, Luke, and John reclined on chaise lounges in his garden, sipping a beverage made from pineapple juice, coconut milk, and 'awa.

The king had put aside his native garb for a costume more appropriate for an English drawing room: dark trousers, a maroon swallow-tailed coat, ascot, and patent leather shoes. He had insisted on outfitting Luke and John Yee from his considerable wardrobe, and his personal tailor had made the necessary alterations. They were both wearing tweed town suits with waistcoats, white shirts, string ties, and brown leather short boots.

"The British support our nationalist position thoroughly," the king was saying. "We must restore political and economic power to the Hawaiian royal family. American missionaries have held sway in Hawaii far too long. They have prospered, and we do not deny them the fruits of their labors. In truth, we owe much to Western technology and business acumen. Our burgeoning industries in sugar, pineapple, coffee, beef. The white man taught us how to take our place in the civilized world.

"The next problem we will have to cope with as our economy expands is a growing labor shortage. Our native population keeps declining, and what we must do is to encourage immigration, primarily from China and Japan."

"Cheap coolie labor," John said with a trace of sarcasm.

"I don't deny it, Mr. Yee. What about you, sir, can I interest you in making Hawaii your home? Our government could use a man of your intelligence and versatility. In fact, you could head up my new program for building up the labor force. You speak Chinese as well as excellent English."

"I am highly honored, Your Highness," John said humbly, "but my friend and I have urgent business on the mainland."

"Luke is chasing a girl all the way to San Francisco," Kiano teased.

The monarch chuckled. "I would look on that girl, she must be very special. Have you met no one of our native maidens who could dissuade you from your quest?"

"I am afraid not, sir. Your *wahines* are the equal of lovely women from all over the world, but there is more than beauty that makes me seek out my Andria. We love each other dearly."

There was a twinkle in Kamehameha's brown eyes. "There will not be a ship bound for San Francisco for another three weeks. Perhaps you will change your mind by then. As for you, Mr. Yee, my offer stands. You would do me a great service if you would accept a post as my advisor on labor development. I would even consider establishing a special cabinet post for you. After all, what is your concern with this girl who Mr. Callahan covets so desperately?"

"John saved my life back in China," Luke explained, not without humor. "By his custom that obligates him to look after me for the remainder of my life. A sort of big brother."

"That is a noble sentiment, Mr. Yee. There is much to be said for ancient customs. My predecessors permitted the missionaries to impose their religion and philosophy of life—what the English would refer to as stuffy or strait-laced—upon our people. Their rigid morality. And the result is that we are fast becoming as inhibited and neurotic as the white man. In my reign I intend to undo much of the harm they have caused."

His contempt and ridicule for those aspects of Western culture was obvious. "Covering up the beautiful female form in those gunnysacks called Mother Hubbards. Obscene! Outlawing the hula! Can you imagine? Have you ever seen girls dancing the *hula,* Mr. Callahan?"

"No, sir, but I look forward to being a spectator before we leave Hawaii."

"And you shall be, my friend. Tonight after the *luau.*"

Chapter Fourteen

The luau, or feast, is one of the most hallowed of all
Hawaiian traditions.

The dress for the royal luau that evening was purely
ceremonial, for it was considered an occasion of great
importance. King Kamehameha looked every bit the
proud monarch in his silk robe elaborately embroidered
with gold and silver threads, the design symbolic of the
fire goddess, Pele, and other ancient deities.

John and Luke wore the same raiment as Kiano,
princely garb, not as ornate as the king's robe, but
highly distinctive.

Included among the female guests were Leilani,
Kokua, and Uli. The women, most of them with familial
ties to the royal family, were breathtaking in their fine
silk robes in all of the hues of the rainbow. They wore
their long hair bound up in fine nets of spun silver and
gold thread, decorated with blossoms. Their delicate
slippers also were decorated with flowers. And around
their necks they wore necklaces made from the exotic,
multi-tinted blossoms of the ohi'a tree.

Leilani sidled up to Luke, her smile radiant, and put
one of the necklaces around his neck.

"A *lei* from Leilani," she whispered. Standing on tip-
toes, she kissed his cheek.

Kiano leaned over and said to him in a low voice,

"After this afternoon you are as good as engaged to that *wahine*."

Luke blushed to the roots of his hair and said nothing.

The assembly sat cross-legged on the ground on straw mats around the *imu,* the underground oven—a long pit covered over with sand and leaves—where the main course, the *kalua,* a pig wrapped in ti leaves, was baked whole.

The dining area was covered with tapa cloth and layers of fern and ti leaves. Arcing trestles over the diners' heads were strung with ginger vines, jasmine, oleander, orchids, and other fragrant flowers. A red hibiscus was placed at each setting.

As they waited for the main course to be served, they sampled from platters heaped with pineapples, bananas, guavas, pears, mangoes, coconuts, papayas, and other tropical fruits.

There was *laulau,* fish, chicken and pork wrapped and steamed in taro leaves; *limu,* an edible seaweed; salmon, shrimp, moray eel, squid; *alemihi* crabs with their shells cracked and stuffed with *haupia*—coconut pudding; yams, breadfruit—so many different kinds of food that Luke and John stopped counting and tasting to save room for the *kalua.*

Naturally, before each place there was a coconut shell filled with the national dish, poi. They discovered that taken along with the other foods, it had a piquancy all its own, and it seemed to enhance the flavor of fish, beef, and pork.

The highlight of the feast was the *kalua.* As the sand, leaves, and canvas were removed from the roasting pigs, the heady, aromatic steam assailed the nostrils of the anticipating diners. "It quite literally makes the mouth water," Luke marveled.

The roast pigs were served on wood platters surrounded by yams and wild bananas. The well-done meat was tender and moist on the inside and brown and crackling on the outside.

During the banquet, musicians strolled among the guests playing native instruments, both wind and string, as well as an unusual nose flute. There were also the cheerful, twanging melodies of the ukulele; Kiano explained that the instrument had been introduced into the islands by Portuguese sailors.

Among the king's guests were a number of American dignitaries and their wives: Hiram Bingham, the most influential missionary ever to preach Christianity in the Hawaiian Islands, and the man responsible for developing a written Hawaiian language; John Ricord, who had been appointed attorney general after the United States had insured the Hawaiians of American protection against the threats to Hawaiian independence posed by the British and French in the 1840's; and W. L. Lee, chief justice and drafter of the penal code of 1850 and the liberal constitution of 1852, who was currently working on a new civil code. One of his most constructive reforms was the Great *Mahele,* or division of lands, a blueprint for modern land titles. Ultimately the Great *Mahele* eliminated the ancient feudal tenures; and the rights and interests of government, crown, chiefs, and the common people were determined impartially by a board of which Lee was chairman.

Last but not least there was R. C. Wyllie, the Hawaiian minister of foreign affairs, to whom Luke took a great liking. Wyllie was unstinting in his praise of the Kamehameha dynasty.

"You might say the power behind the throne in this royal family has been Kekuanaoa, father of the present king and Prince Lot," Wyllie told him. "Under the rule of the Kamehamehas, Hawaii has become a civilized nation with a democratic constitution guaranteeing its people inalienable rights and with a legislature and an executive and judicial branch second to no country on earth. That may sound like hyperbole to you, son, but

I am exceedingly proud of these wonderful people and the great strides they have made in a remarkably short span of years. Personal and property rights are secured —allodial tenures. Our industries are expanding in leaps and bounds. And, what is equally as important, Hawaii has earned the respect of the other nations of the world, thereby ensuring its independence."

"My friend and I find Hawaii a beautiful and exciting land," Luke said. "If I did not have urgent business back in the United States, I would like to settle here."

"Urgent business? Would I be imprudent to ask what nature of business, sir?"

"Not at all, Mr. Wyllie. I am seeking the woman I love." And he related the tragic circumstances of how he and Andria had been separated in China.

The foreign minister looked grave and stroked his goatee. "Luke Callahan—Callahan—hmmmm . . ."

Luke's brow furrowed. "Yes. Does that name have any special significance to you?"

"Yes, indeed. You are of the Mormon faith, as I was led to believe?"

"Yes, I was performing ministerial duties at a Mormon mission in China when it was attacked by the bandits."

"Of course, it just might be a coincidence, but is your father one Caleb Callahan?"

Luke grinned. "One and the same. How do you know my father?"

"I have recently had occasion to correspond with your father. He has large landholdings in Hawaii, you know."

"I never did pay much attention to my father's business dealings. I believe he had invested in a sugar refining mill outside San Francisco."

"Precisely. And the land he bought here on Maui and the big island of Hawaii is for the purpose of cultivating sugar cane."

"I'll be damned!"

"He also has interest in raising livestock in Hawaii. Cattle, mostly. By Jove! This is a most remarkable coincidence. Just last week I received notification from the U.S. State Department that Caleb Callahan intends to emigrate from the mainland and settle here. In fact, in our personal correspondence, your father has suggested more than once that he would like to supervise his sugar plantations personally."

Luke smiled bitterly. "My father never did trust anyone else to do work for him. I don't expect our paths to cross, inasmuch as I am sailing for San Francisco in three weeks."

"In the statement of intent he filed with our department of foreign affairs, Caleb Callahan listed the names of his wives, since they will be coming with him."

"Yes, Charity and Sada. Neither is mother to me. My mother died along with my sisters in the long, deadly Mormon march from Nauvoo to Salt Lake City."

"I was about to say, Mr. Callahan, that your father has since taken a third wife."

"A third wife?" Luke laughed. "Why the old roué!"

"Yes, and I think you should know that—"

He was interrupted by the announcement that King Kamehameha had ordered the hula to commence.

The guests filed into a fragrant rose garden where bamboo chairs and lounges had been arranged in a circle. It was an uncommonly cool night, and men and women alike donned *kiheis,* a togalike robe. The king put on an elaborate and ornate robe made of feathers, the symbol of high royalty.

And in the center of the ring stood the dancers, three of the most exquisite girls Luke had ever seen. Their only raiment was a *pa'u,* a grass skirt, and the traditional lei. In the light of the torches, their bare breasts shone like polished brass.

At a rolling signal from the hula drums, they began to dance. The dancers moved in precise coordination, as if they were part and parcel of a single creature possessing the fluidity of a many-legged centipede. Their hands and arms described the narrative of the song, while their facial expressions were a moving picture of passion, fear, sadness, and joy, the highs and lows of feeling.

Kiano translated the voiceless speech of the *hula* for Luke and John.

Hands posed vertically on their outstretched arms: "Now the lovers are faced with a serious obstacle."

Fingers pointing upward, arms held high: "He is of royal blood, and she is a commoner."

Arms outstretched, hands, wrists, forearms, and upper arms all undulating sinuously in the motion of a snake: "His father, the king, sends him on a journey to another of the islands."

Arms extended, fingers spread, palms downward: "The night before he leaves her they are on a sandy beach."

Arms extended, back of the hands advanced, then alluding to the *pa'u:* "They disrobe. . . ."

And now the drums commenced to roll in sensual rhythm, and the dancers swung their hips from side to side in ever quickening frenzy, their faces contorted in passion, pelvises grinding and rolling.

"I can make that one out for myself," Luke whispered to Kiano.

The dancers mimicked the gestures of oarsmen. "He departs the next morning in his canoe. . . ."

It was a simple and not profound little tale, like such folklore from countries and cultures all around the world and with a universal theme and conclusion.

Finger tips pressed together and suddenly drawn apart with a flourish and lowered until the palms faced the sand: "And our hero is killed by the king's enemies on the other island."

Hands pressed over their left breasts; eyes closing slowly; heads drooping until their chins rested on their chests; then gracefully collapsing to the sand in perfect harmony, shuddering and lying still: "And the grieving lover left behind dies of a broken heart."

There was resounding applause for the dancers and the musicians. One by one the girls approached the king and made a Hawaiian version of a deep curtsy and backed off. The third girl, carried away by emotion, grasped Kamehameha's hand and kissed it.

As the gathering disbanded, the minister of foreign affairs took Luke aside. "Mr. Callahan, there is something you should know. I tried to tell you before, but the *hula* prevented me from finishing what I had to say."

"Yes, what is it, Mr. Wyllie?"

"This woman you are endeavoring to find, her name is Andria?"

"That is her name. Why do you ask?"

Wyllie squirmed uncomfortably and avoided Luke's gaze. "Her Chinese name was Sun Ying Wong?"

Luke was astonished. "Yes—but how could you know that?"

Wyllie let out a long, shuddering sigh. "Mr. Callahan —I don't know quite how to tell you this. You see— your father's third wife—that is—she is—your Andria."

Luke felt as if a torpedo had exploded inside his head. There was a blinding pain, and red film fell over his vision. Outraged, he groped at the minister, and his fingers locked on the old man's lapels.

"What in the hell are you trying to tell me? That my father and my Andria—? That is absurd! Positively ridiculous! How could my father have met Andria?"

"Mr. Callahan, take hold of yourself. You told me yourself that this girl was abducted and sold at the white slave market in Macao; she was bound for the cribs of San Francisco. Don't you understand? Your father purchased her at an auction from Henrietta D'Arcy, the most notorious madam on the Barbary Coast."

"My father *bought* Andria?" Luke was appalled.

"I am afraid that is the truth. Mr. Callahan, are you feeling ill?"

Luke was too weak to reply. He had the eerie sensation that all of the blood was draining out of his body. His nose, cheeks, mouth, and finger tips felt like wax. He attempted to speak, but his tongue was a useless piece of meat in his mouth, like the tongues of cattle and pigs they pickled at the marketplaces in San Francisco. Lifeless.

Darkness closed over him like a shroud, and he slumped to the ground unconscious.

Later, in a private bedroom in King Kamehameha's residence, the royal physician made the grim pronouncement:

"I regret to tell you, Your Highness, but this man has diptheria. The ordeal he has been through"—he shrugged hopelessly—"has taken its toll. He must be kept in isolation. But I must be honest—I do not hold out much hope for his recovery."

John Yee cradled his friend in his arms and buried his face in Luke's chest. His sobbing reverberated through the royal mansion.

Dr. Lester, Foreign Minister Wyllie, and King Kamehameha turned away, their heads bowed, and walked sorrowfully out into the corridor.

BOOK
TWO

Chapter One

Andria began her diary on the long, monotonous sea voyage from California to Hawaii. Gifted with near-total recall, she retraced her life from an early age to her present condition as a ward of Caleb Callahan.

Her entries were in the form of letters addressed to her beloved Luke. The hours she spent writing were the most pleasurable and satisfying time of the day for her. While she was writing, she could believe that he was alive and well and living in another world where she, one day, would be reunited with him. There was a deeply ingrained sense of Oriental mysticism in Andria's soul. She was convinced that as the words flowed onto paper, they were being projected telepathically at the same time to Luke in the hereafter.

By the time they reached their destination, the diary was up to date.

My darling Luke,
This morning we sighted Hawaii. It was so beautiful tears came to my eyes. Standing out like Atlas bearing the sky on his back was the magnificent mountain Mauna Kea. Thirty miles wide at the base, so Captain Haines informs us, and almost 14,000 feet high. The early morning sun glittering on its snow-capped summit was a spectacular vision, something out of a fairy tale. A fleecy girth of clouds encircled its massive

waist, gradually dissipating as the sun's rays warmed the air. As our ship approached the island, we saw that the mountain's base was furrowed with ravines and a labyrinth of streams. Beyond that, bright green grass and tropical shrubbery ascend midway to a belt of lush ohia forest. Mauna Kea's terminal peaks are surrounded in blue ice at their bases and topped with snow, a breathtaking contrast of perpetual summer and perpetual winter. There are no seasons to speak of in the Hawaiian Islands, the captain says. The temperature hovers at an average of seventy-five degrees year round.

At first glimpse of the broad swath of beach running as far as the eye could see, I imagined the pure white sand was snow.

Over thousands of years, these islands literally grew out of the Pacific Ocean from the ocean floor, coral, and volcanic debris. And even presently Hawaii's great volcanoes are active and might erupt at any given moment.

The natives tell a story of Keoua, a great chieftain from Hilo, our destination, who camped on the summit of the volcano Kilauea on his way to do battle with a rival tribe. That evening he and his men took recreation in throwing boulders into the fire pit. This so angered the goddess Pele that she hurled fire and stones high into the air and raked the sky with thunder and lightning. Keoua and his army fled the scene, but not before a third of his forces were annihilated by molten lava. We shall take care not to offend that sensitive lady inasmuch as one of your father's plantations lies directly in the path of the historic northeast flow of Kilauea's major eruptions.

On the Hilo—Haina—Koloa side of the island, rainfall may exceed three hundred and fifty inches a year, while on the west shore of Hawaii as little as four inches may fall. Drainage is excellent throughout the island because of the high porosity of the volcanic rock and soil, ideal for the cultivation of sugar cane.

Your father has gone ashore to inspect the house

where we will be living. Tomorrow Charity, Sada,
Lee, and I will join him.

I am nodding over the paper and am so exhausted
from all the excitement that I can no longer hold the
pen. So I will say good night to you, my darling.
Hopefully you will come to me in my dreams.

All my love and devotion,
Your Andria

The Callahan homestead sat on a hillside overlooking
a small village where the plantation workers resided. It
was a quixotic community in that it lay squarely in the
middle of a shallow taro pond. On the other three sides
of the hill there was sugar cane. The cane, somewhat
like corn in appearance, was a tall perennial grass. It
required fourteen to twenty-four months to mature, and
two or three crops, at various stages of development,
were cultivated simultaneously. Before a given field was
harvested, it was set afire to burn off the worthless
leaves. After the cane was cut, it was prepared for
shipment to the mills in California by a process called
centrifugal drying. In California it was refined and sold
to customers throughout the world. It was a very pros-
perous industry because the demand for sugar was
always far greater than the supply.

The house, built by an American missionary, was a
long, low, rambling dwelling of wood with a red brick
facade. The interior was of dark oak and plaster and
had Gothic overtones. There were long galleries, bay
windows, elaborate carvings, and dreary halls that
formed a quadrangle.

The house lay in the ominous shadow of Mauna Loa,
twin to Mauna Kea, the world's largest and most active
volcano. The elongated caldron at the summit encom-
passed almost four square miles.

Andria felt more at home in Hawaii than she had
ever felt in China. "I was born to live here," she told
Caleb and his wives.

The two Callahan women wore the same garb they had worn in the United States, fashionable dresses with heavily flounced skirts; crinolines; bonnets; and shawls.

Andria, to the contrary, fancied the casual dress of the native girls, a single garment loosely draped from shoulder to ankle, made of colorful silk or cotton. She wore her long, dark hair done up in a fine net, and necklaces and ankle bracelets of ohi'a blossoms. She smelled of jasmine, oleander, and pride-of-India.

Life on Hawaii was lazy and idyllic, but after a few months Andria experienced a sense of isolation that she had not felt in the vast landspread of China. Although it was the biggest island, it was only ninety by seventy-five by sixty miles long on its three sides. Compounding the feeling of insularity was the nature of the terrain. Except for along the coast, the interior of Hawaii was interlaced with crevasses, ravines, and steep saddles formed by overlapping lava flows, which made communication between various settlements difficult.

The two Callahan wives occupied themselves by paying obsessive attention to household chores and sewing. Andria worked off her own restless energy through riding. Her favorite mount was a chestnut stallion with a diamond-shaped patch of white on its forehead. She promptly named him Diamond Head.

Her riding habit was the costume of Hawaiian young women of high social and economic order—a long silk sash of brilliant scarlet trimmed with black embroidery. It was wrapped around her loins, passed between her thighs, then was wrapped around once more and passed over the opposite leg and between the thighs a second time in such a way that the excess cloth streamed out far behind in the breeze. A gay gypsy hat garlanded with blossoms and soft leather slippers completed her attire. Sitting militarily erect in the saddle, her breasts thrusting against the narrow bandeau that confined them, she was a striking picture as she galloped mile after mile across the snow-white beaches, with the horse's hoofs churning through the surf.

In the first year on Hawaii, Caleb Callahan was scarcely home for more than two or three days every two months. With a retinue of lieutenants, he was constantly traveling about the big island on horseback, inspecting his holdings in sugar, coffee and, more recently, beef; or traveling by ship from one island to the other, looking for new lucrative investments and conferring with other speculators like himself—men who were the founders of what would become known one day as the Big Five families in the Hawaiian Islands.

This meant the running of the plantation was left to his *lunas,* or overseers, who were accountable to Charity and Sada. His wives, however, had neither the ability nor the inclination for business or bookkeeping, so the responsibility fell squarely on Andria's shoulders.

Her grasp of figures and the mechanics of cultivating and harvesting cane were a source of marvel to Caleb. "Hard to believe that inside a head so pretty there lies the brain of an Arizona horse trader."

She would make daily rounds of all the fields, notebook under her arm, a black crayon in the pocket of her riding blouse. While doing her professional chores, she wore a more severe riding habit, breeches, long boots, and a high-necked blouse.

Caleb had made it bluntly clear to all of the *lunas* that "that gal is speaking for me, and what she tells you, you get to it as fast as if the order came out of my mouth."

She got along well with all of them but for one surly Swede who had jumped ship to take a job with Caleb, a common occurrence in the formative years of the Islands. Olaf Olson was engaged in a brazen affair with Charity Callahan; more than once Andria had seen him leaving her bedroom in the wee hours of the morning.

One day, while out riding over the plantation grounds, she came upon Olson heaping verbal and physical abuse on a frightened native cutter.

"Stop it, Mr. Olson," she said in a deceptively calm voice. "Stop it at once."

"I was just teaching the dumb *kanaka* a lesson," he growled. "Only way you can get 'em to learn anything, these coloreds, is to beat it into their thick heads."

"Isn't that what Jack Treudeau said about you last week?" she asked icily. "That you were a dumb Swede with a thick skull? It took ten men to pull you off of him."

His jowled face turned crimson, and he took a step forward and grabbed hold of Diamond's bridle. His small blue eyes were bright with hate.

"I don't take that from anyone, much less a Chink whore."

Before he could duck away, her riding crop lashed across his face, leaving a welt from jaw to forehead. He staggered back, holding his cheek. He recovered and lumbered toward her again. He would have dragged her from the saddle, but Andria whipped a pistol out of her waistband and cocked the hammer.

"That's far enough, Mr. Olson. I can shoot as well as any man, and you know it."

Caleb was always boasting about her skill with firearms, honed by her association with Joaquin Murieta.

The big towheaded man backed off, mumbling sullenly, "I didn't mean anything by what I said, miss. Just lost my temper."

Andria replaced the pistol in her belt and warned him, "If I ever catch you beating your workers again, I will dismiss you at once. Now get back to work."

As she rode off, Olson glared after her. "I'll get even with that little Chink if it's the last thing I do."

To his shock he suddenly found himself surrounded

by a number of workers, all of whom held machetes or shovels in a manner most menacing.

"You ever lay a finger on that girl and we'll tear you apart with our bare hands," their spokesman warned him. "And we'll accept the consequences."

"Aw, I wouldn't touch her with a ten-foot pole. Now get to work." They obeyed, but Olson was left with a sinking sensation in his chest. Spurred by their loyalty to Andria, the workers had successfully defied the bully. Never again would he have his former power over the men.

One morning Andria announced to Charity and Sada, "I'm going to ride up to Mauna Loa."

"Whatever for?" Sada asked.

"The *kanakas* say it's acting up again. The last eruption was only a few years back. I want to have a look for myself."

"Heaven preserve us! Whatever will we do if it does?"

Andria laughed. "We'll run the other way, just as the Hawaiians have been doing for centuries."

"Well, you're not going up there alone," said Lee. "I'll go with you."

Andria embraced her fondly. "*You* ride a horse? Lee, you know you're terrified of horses."

"I'll walk then," her friend said determinedly.

"Thirty miles? No, I think not. Look, I can take care of myself, you all know that. Besides, these are the friendliest people on earth. No harm will come to me, I assure you."

She donned heavy riding breeches, boots, and a cotton shirt. In her saddlebags were a change of warmer clothing and a woolen jacket lined with fleece.

"It frequently gets below freezing up in the mountains," she told Lee.

She packed two days' rations: tinned meat, biscuits,

fruit and vegetables that Sada had canned, and a jar of *poi*.

"I can supplement it with wild fruit and berries along the way," she said.

She tucked her pistol in her belt, put on her gypsy hat, and bid the other women goodbye. "I'm going to take my time, so you probably won't see me until day after tomorrow." Giving them a parting wave, she headed for the stables.

Diamond Head was saddled and waiting. When he saw his mistress, he snorted and pawed the ground.

"He's been fidgety and excited for the past hour," the stable boy told her. "He senses that you two are off on an adventure."

Andria let him nuzzle her neck, stroked his nose, and mounted him. "Goodbye, Paki."

The boy admired the spread of her buttocks in the tight pants as she rode off. "She has one handsome *okole*," he said to himself. "She would make one fine *hula* dancer." And he scratched his crotch.

For the first few hours, Andria held Diamond to a leisurely trot. The road ran through thick tropical forests where the air was cool and sweet with the aromas of a potpourri of exotic flowers and fruit.

At noon she stopped for lunch by a mountain stream. Diamond had a drink and nibbled on the long grass. Andria's meal consisted of crackers, cheese, and a mango for dessert. The sweet-sour, sticky juice of the yellow fruit ran down her chin. Later she washed her face and hands in the brook and had a cool drink.

She approached Diamond and patted his side. "Time we're off again, my friend." She remounted, and they continued on their way. From time to time they would break out of the forest and from a high spot have a view of towering Mauna Loa. The closer she got to it, the more beautiful and awesome it appeared. Its snow-capped spires flashed in the sun, and sinister, dark vapors belched forth from its fiery caldron at the summit. She gripped her arms and shivered, not from cold, but from foreboding.

Near four in the afternoon, she rounded a sharp bend in the road and emerged into a broad, grassy clearing. To her surprise she was confronted by a party of men making camp. Although they were clearly Hawaiians, they were dressed in Western outdoor gear, reminiscent of the attire worn by California diggers and hikers. They were even equipped with canvas campers' tents.

A tall, handsome man with piercing black eyes and an aquiline nose walked up to her. His smile was beautiful, she thought.

"This is too good to be true," he said. "I pray to the great goddess Pele and almost at once, my wish has been granted."

Andria looked at him, head cocked to one side in bewilderment. "What might your wish be that I have satisfied it for you?"

"I wished that before the sun set over Mauna Loa, I would meet the most beautiful woman in the world. And lo and behold, here you are!"

Andria put a hand to her tingling cheek and laughed self-consciously. "That was a very pretty speech. *Mahalo.* But I know very well how I must look after all day in the saddle."

"And it is about time that you were out of the saddle. You must do me the honor of being my guest for supper, and you will have one of our tents in which to spend the night."

Andria hesitated. Her experiences with Yuan Kaishih and Joaquin Murieta had left her with a distrust of strange men. "Thank you again for your hospitality, but I really must ride on a bit further. I have my sleeping bag and plenty of food. I am accustomed to the outdoors."

"Nonsense! I won't hear of you spending the night

alone in the woods. I know what you must be thinking, and I wish to assure you that my motives are honorable. Allow me to introduce myself. I am Prince David Kalakaua, and these are my traveling companions. Lopaka here, my close friend; Keawe, our cook and handyman; and Lakana, a palace courtier who keeps tabs on me for my aunt, Queen Emma."

As Lakana opened his mouth to protest, the prince laughed and clapped him on the shoulder. "I am only teasing you, you handsome dog."

Lakana was indeed handsome, Andria thought—too handsome, with his long, wavy black hair, delicate facial features and soulful eyes. Pretty was what he was. She preferred more masculine types, such as Prince Kalakaua.

"We are on a hiking holiday," he explained. "All the way from the other side of the island, Kailua-Kona."

"I am on a holiday of sorts myself," she told him. I want to climb Mauna Loa and see what is in the crater."

The four men looked at her with astonishment mixed with respect.

"That is a tall order for a young woman, no matter how beautiful she is," the prince said. "And all by yourself. I can tell you that if you were my wife, I would forbid it vehemently."

Andria's chin tilted up. "I am nobody's wife, but if I were, he would not forbid me to do anything I cared to do. Oh, he could, I suppose, but I wouldn't listen to him."

Standing with his arms folded across his chest, Prince David shook his head. "You have spirit, and I like that in a woman as well as a man. But you haven't introduced yourself yet."

"I'm sorry. Forgive my poor manners. My name is Andria—" She hesitated. For purposes of satisfying the immigration authorities, her papers had been made out in the name of Andria Callahan. Caleb Callahan had been like kin to her, and she resolved to bear his name with pride. "Andria Callahan," she said.

His curiosity was obvious. Certainly she did not look like a Callahan.

She answered his unspoken question. "I am formerly of China, but now I am the ward of Caleb Callahan."

"Caleb Callahan—ah—yes. My uncle, King Kamehameha, has spoken of Mr. Callahan."

Prince David refrained from saying that Caleb Callahan was not a popular figure with the ardently pro-British royal family.

"Then you will accept our humble hospitality for this night?" the prince entreated her. "Please say you will."

Andria smiled and dismounted. "All right. And I am indebted to you for the offer."

"Not at all, the debt is on my own side. I cannot provide us with a proper luau, but I do have a decanter of *okoleohao* and half of a *kalua pun'a,* along with wild rice and pineapple." He nodded to Keawe, a portly fellow with a moon face. "You may prepare dinner now."

"Is there any place nearby where I can freshen up?" she inquired.

"Just beyond the edge of the clearing there is, a sylvan pool." He pointed to the south side of the campsite. "Lakana will take care of your horse. A gorgeous animal."

"That he is." She opened her one saddlebag and removed a bar of soap, a small towel, and a clean shirt. "I'll be back shortly."

The pond was about fifty feet through thick brush and quite private. Andria stripped off her sweaty shirt and cotton undervest and proceeded to wash her face, arms, and underarms. She was unaware that David

Kalakaua was observing her from the concealment of a thick tree bole at the other side of the pond.

Desire licked at his loins as she raised her arms, one by one, to dry herself. Her breasts looked as firm as alligator pears, high and proud, with the nipples tilting upward. Magnificent, he thought. He was not in the least contrite that he was spying on her, invading her privacy.

Prince David was a Hawaiian traditionalist and believed in royal privilege. When she had finished her toilet, Andria washed out her vest and shirt. Standing, she hung them up to dry on a low tree branch. Then she donned a fresh vest and shirt.

Prudently the prince faded back into the brush. When Andria returned to the camp, he was seated cross-legged around a cook fire with his traveling companions.

"Do you feel refreshed?" he asked casually.

"Much so, thank you."

"Please sit down."

She sat down beside him, and he handed her half a coconut shell filled with an aromatic beverage.

"Okoleohao," he said.

She accepted the cup reluctantly. "I do not drink strong spirits."

"Just a sip or two. To toast our climb tomorrow."

Her eyes widened. *"Our* climb?"

"Of course. You didn't think I'd let you make such a hazardous journey by yourself."

"I was unaware that it was hazardous. Many people have climbed Mauna Loa."

"True, but not when it was in such a turbulent state. Our chief topographical expert in Kailua-Kona predicts that we could have a major eruption any time within the next few months."

"Then I will accept your offer to act as my guide."

He raised his cup. "To the great goddess Pele, may she smile favorably upon us tomorrow."

Andria took a small taste of the sweet liquor.

The prince smiled and said, "Now I would like to propose still another toast. "My congratulations to the man who will one day become your husband."

Prince David was confident that he was drinking to his own good fortune.

Chapter Two

They rode their horses as far as the crater of Kilauea, an independent volcano that was only a third as high as Mauna Loa.

"The fact is," David told her, "Kilauea is merely a hole in the side of the big girl, but it is the largest and most active of any volcano in the world. What's more, it is the home of the fire goddess Pele. In the old days the summit of Kilauea was hallowed ground. Visitors would never dare to cut down a tree or bush up here or eat a berry—not even move a rock or disturb the earth, for fear of offending Pele."

"I know. I've heard about Keoua and his army."

"A charming fairy tale."

"You don't believe in Pele?" she teased.

"As a matter of fact, it was an ancestor of mine, Princess Kapiolani, who put Pele to rest once and for all. Ignoring the entreaties of the people and the high priests, she picked berries from a bush and descended into the crater, which at the time was in the throes of a tremor, with molten lava churning like a stormy sea.

"Then, while the spectators watched in awe, she ate Pele's berries and rolled stones into the pit. Laughing at the spectators on the rim of the crater, she said, 'I will not die from the wrath of Pele because the

fire was kindled by my god.' Calmly she recited the
Lord's Prayer.

"She made the ascent and went home. And that was
the end of Pele. Oh, there are always superstitious
people in the world who will continue to worship fire
gods and sea gods and thunder gods, but it is a harmless
diversion."

David gave her his hand, and they made the long
climb up the walls of the fire pit. At last they stood
on the rim of the outer crater.

"It's almost three miles down to the walls of the
central crater," he told her. "The Lake of Fire."

"I can't wait."

The journey down was easy enough at first. The
landscape was surprisingly beautiful. There were
stunted ohi' as with fragile scarlet blossoms, ferns of all
varieties, and silvery grass.

David picked a handful of red berries. "The sacred
whortleberries that Kapiolani ate."

Andria gazed down at the great gray lava bed. "It
looks like a petrified ocean."

"It is, rather. The result of centuries of overflows,
one overlapping the other."

Now they plunged into the bed itself, and the journey
became more arduous. Lava had hardened in countless
bizarre shapes and formations: intertwined coils that
resembled a tangle of gargantuan snakes; angular
blocks of every geometric design; folds hanging from
high crags like rich black satin draperies; and waves
of black glass with iridescent glazing.

"It's like another world," she gasped as they climbed
a hill close to a hundred feet high and down the other
side into a sea of translucent blisters.

Andria cried out and clutched his arm as the lava
crust gave way under her feet.

David laughed. "It's all right. You'll get used to it."

Every step of the way from then on, the lava
crunched and split with even the most gingerly impact.

Andria went up to her knees at one point. "How deep are the deepest fissures?" she asked nervously.

"No more than that one you just stepped into."

The beauty of a black frozen waterfall with a dazzling rainbow running through it displaced her apprehensions. "Isn't that magnificent?" she exulted.

He stooped and picked up a handful of finely spun, varicolored glass. *"Lauoho-o-Pele*—Pele's hair. When the fire pit sends up geysers of molten rock, the wind catches the spray and turns it into this. The birds line their nests with it."

Andria sank down exhausted. "How much further? We must have walked ten miles."

"A slight exaggeration. Maybe three. There—up ahead."

Andria groaned in despair. Looming up a half mile away was what appeared to be a mountain close to six hundred feet in height.

"The ring of the central crater. Each time Kilauea has an upheaval, the walls get higher."

It was the worst part of the journey, for they had to walk over highly brittle, crusty lava.

"You will think all of this has been worth it once you gaze into the Lake of Fire," he encouraged her. "Here give me your hand." The last one hundred feet he practically dragged her along. And, at long last, they stood on the brink.

Andria was speechless. It was the most awesome sight she had ever looked upon or ever hoped to look upon again. Waves of liquid fire crashed against the walls of the crater like ocean waves breaking against cliffs, then rushed out again in great waves to the far side of the crater. In the center of this frothing hell was an enormous maelstrom.

"I can almost believe there is a Pele down there at the bottom of that whirlpool," she said reverently.

"Look just below us." Like a waterfall of fire, a torrent of molten lava came tumbling out of a cavern.

Andria stepped back from the edge. "I've seen enough of Kilauea for one day."

"Yes, it's getting late. We'll go back to the base camp. Then tomorrow we'll have a go at the big one."

That night the moon was full, and the little lagoon where Andria had washed earlier was bathed in a silvery, luminous glow. She and David sat on a bank dangling their feet in the tepid water.

She reached an arm into the air. "The moon looks so big and close I almost feel I can touch it."

"If you want the moon, then I shall give it to you," he said solemnly.

She laughed. "Do you always get whatever you want, David?"

He looked at her meaningfully. "Yes, I suppose I have always gotten what I wanted—up until now, at least."

"Until now?"

"Yes. Now that I've met you, I—"

She placed a hand gently over his mouth. "Don't, David. We've hardly known each other for more than one day."

"Long enough for me to know that you are in my blood like a fever. I love you, Andria."

"You don't love me. You want me. There is a difference."

"I love you, and I want you."

She looked away at the sky. "It's no more than the magic of this heavenly evening. The air and the water, so warm and sensual. The fragrance of maile, hibiscus, jasmine and ginger."

Beyond the trees at the camp, Keawa, Lopaka, and Lakana were harmonizing as one of them strummed a ukulele.

"What a lovely song," Andria said.

"It's an ancient Polynesian love song."

"Polynesia—so very far away. Why did your ancestors leave there to come here?"

"For many reasons. Chiefly to get away from the incessant tribal wars, I imagine."

"But long after your people settled here, they were still warring among themselves."

"That is so, until my eminent ancestor, Kamehameha the Great unified the different island kingdoms."

"Why doesn't your uncle the present king like Caleb Callahan and the other Americans?"

"Because they exploit our people and want to take our country away from us and make it part of the United States."

Andria sighed. "You speak the truth. Not just the Americans, but all white men. They think of themselves as great white fathers and think of people with colored skins as children who need looking after. I do believe they mean well but—"

"I don't think they mean well at all. They are a predatory race. Cruel, selfish, avaricious, indifferent to the human rights of those weaker than themselves. Take your mentor, Caleb Callahan. He professes to be a man of God, a priest in his Mormon religion, but his true god is wealth, power."

"I cannot deny it. Yet I must be grateful to him for all he has done for me," she told him.

David gave it some thought, then said, "He treats you well to make up for the way he treated his son. Guilt, nothing more."

"No. Caleb loved his son, and I think he loves me."

"Let's not spoil a night like this by speaking of the *haole*. . . . Listen, Andria, I have a splendid idea. Why don't you come back to Kailua-Kona with me? Have you ever been to the other side of the island?"

"No, and I would like to visit Kailua-Kona, but you see, when Caleb is away, the responsibility of the plantation falls on my shoulders. He doesn't trust his lunas."

"A short visit. Four or five days. The plantation will not fall apart in such a short time. We will travel by ship from Hilo. The royal yacht is due to pick up my party there the day after tomorrow. You and my Aunt Emma will get along famously. You will like the king, too, although he is scarcely ever home. He loves to travel—England, Europe, the world."

"Where do they live?"

"Hulihee Palace." He smiled. "Actually, it's more of an English town house than a palace. The king and queen are ardent Anglophiles and staunch Episcopalians. Just as my aunt and uncle are more the family patriarch and matriarch than king and queen." He yawned. "We had better turn in if we hope to get an early start tomorrow. It's quite a climb, you know."

He took her hand and helped her to her feet.

Outside her tent, Andria put a hand to his cheek and gave him a sisterly kiss.

"You are a dear man, Prince David," she whispered.

"Only you don't love me?"

"I didn't say that. I hardly know you. What I do know about you I like very much indeed."

He smiled and squeezed her hand. "I will settle for that—but only for the time being. Good night, sweet Andria. I do love your name as well as your body. You know, some day I will be a king. Think how nice it would sound. Queen Andria."

Laughing, she slipped through the flap into the tent.

That night she dreamed of Luke. He was with her in the Islands. Coconut trees shook their tousled crowns in the soft, warm wind above a lagoon as sapphire blue as Andria's eyes. She and Luke were swimming nude in the pool. He took her in his arms, and her breasts flattened against his muscular, hairy chest. They were locked together.

In her sleep Andria moaned in ecstasy and writhed about sensually on her sleeping mat, feeling his masculinity rising hard against her belly. The smile of pleasure gradually faded, to be replaced by a frown, as the girl in the dream turned her head and looked back over her shoulder at Andria. *At* her!

"No, no, no!" she protested. It couldn't be! The woman in the dream was a voluptuous, pretty Polynesian girl. Her beloved Luke was making love to a strange woman!

"Stop it!" she screamed and sat up.

Moments later Prince David charged into her tent. "Andria, what is it? Is anything wrong?"

She came awake slowly and brushed a lock of hair back off her forehead. "Ah—I—I'm sorry, David. I was dreaming."

"It must have been a very bad dream from the way you were carrying on."

She covered her face with both hands. "It was. A nightmare. I'm sorry."

"There's a good girl. Only a dream. Now go back to sleep. Good night."

"Good night."

She fell back on the mat and stared at the dark top of the tent. His words echoed in her brain: "Only a dream."

She slept restlessly for the remainder of the night.

Chapter Three

"Sure you three won't come with us?" David asked his companions prior to the ascent of Mauna Loa.

Keawe grinned. "Not on your life. I've made that climb as a youth more times than I can count."

David and Andria bid their farewells and set forth, knapsacks on their backs, with a blanket rolled around each one.

"It can get very cold at the summit," David told her. "And we might have to spend the night on the mountain."

"Is it a hard climb?"

"Not really. But it's a long climb. That's why they call Mauna Loa the long mountain. In spite of its height, the gradient is quite low."

They began the trek through uneven terrain laced with ravines and gushing streams and covered with grass and shrubbery. With increasing altitude the clouds girding the mountain drew closer and closer.

"It's an eerie feeling," Andria said. "As if we were climbing into the heavens. There is an ancient Chinese fable about a boy who climbed to the top of the tallest tree in the world and found himself in a new, strange land."

He laughed. "There is a similar fable in every culture. Well, in a sense you will find yourself in a new, strange world when we reach the summit."

They stopped to rest in a ravine and filled their canteens from a trickling stream. While they were sitting on a grassy bank, David cocked his head to one side and frowned. "Shh—don't speak. Listen."

Andria heard a distant roaring sound like the noise that precedes a typhoon. "What is it?"

"Quickly! Up to high ground." He grabbed her hand and dragged her up the steep bank to a rocky knoll.

To her amazement, moments later, a wall of water came rushing down the ravine, engulfing the spot where they had been seated to a depth of ten feet.

"Somewhere higher up there has been a local cloudburst," he explained. "One must be alert to the hazard."

They resumed their journey, and now they passed into the thick of the clouds, and their vision was limited to a distance of eight or nine feet.

Suddenly they broke out into bright, glorious sunshine, and now, the higher they climbed, the more the clouds receded behind them.

When they reached the timberline, Andria sank to the ground. "I can't walk another step today. Let's camp here for the night."

"All right. I'll gather wood and build a fire."

Soon David had a welcome blaze going, and Andria huddled close to it, her hands outstretched. With the setting of the sun, cold descended upon the mountain.

"This doesn't feel like Hawaii any longer."

"Wrap a blanket around your shoulders."

He took a pot and a can of tinned British bully beef from his pack. He broke up the beef in the pot and added an assortment of vegetables and spices: chili peppers, *kukui* nuts, *limu*—seaweed and kelp—all dusted with *pa'akai* salt. He stuffed the mixture into coconut shell halves and baked the shells in the embers.

"You are really very domestic for a prince," she commented.

"Wait until you taste my *sushi* and *saimin*."

The meal was delectable, and they washed it down with coffee brewed in a saucepan and seasoned with sugar and ginger.

Over David's objections, Andria insisted on washing the utensils in a nearby stream. "I want to earn my supper," she said.

His smile was whimsical. "It isn't proper for a future queen to do servants' chores."

"No more improper than for a future king to cook supper."

They exchanged affectionate banter while she washed and dried the implements, and after David had packed them away, they stoked the fire with wood and rolled up in their blankets. They lay on their backs looking up at the countless twinkling stars. A meteor flashed across the dark heavens.

"Make a wish," he told her. "The gods have given you a sign. They will grant you one wish."

Bring my darling Luke back to me.

"Well? Did you make a wish?"

Andria shut her eyes and pretended to be asleep.

Andria awakened to the warmth of the sun on her eyelids.

"No bad dreams last night?" David asked as he prepared the coffee.

"I was too tired to dream. I'm famished. What do we have for breakfast?"

"Breadfruit, bananas, pineapple, and *poi*."

They ate quickly and resumed their trek to the summit of Mauna Loa. They entered a thick forest of ohi'a trees. After they emerged from the forest, the foliage began to thin out until at last there was no vestige of vegetation at all. It was the barren, bleak landscape of Kilauea all over again.

The higher they climbed, the colder it became. And Andria became aware of an awe-inspiring feeling.

Despite their high altitude, she had the queer sensation that they were standing at the bottom of a symmetrical bowl and that the island and the sea around it were lifting up into the sky.

"I don't believe it!" she exclaimed. "I am looking *up* at what is thousands of feet below us."

David laughed. "I told you that you would be moving into a strange, topsy-turvy world. Actually, it's a common hallucination perpetrated by isolated great altitudes."

She moved into the comforting circle of his arms. "I can't help it, it frightens me, David."

"Nothing to fear, not even from Pele. Come along, not much further to go."

After a while she grew accustomed to the phenomenon and regained her true perspective. Below, the island was laid out like a child's toy. A checkerboard of grayish brown squares, forests reduced to mossy tufts, and immense sugar plantations that looked as if they could be erased with a smudge from Pele's thumb.

At last they reached the summit and peered into the elongated crater, or caldera, as David called it. It was putting on a display even more angry than that which they had witnessed on Kilauea.

"Pele's caldron," Andria mused.

David completed the thought. "A witch's brew of molten rock, sulfur, and thunder and lightning. Oh, there is no doubt about it. The old girl is getting ready to blow any time now."

Andria shivered. "Not until we get down off her, I hope."

"Nothing to fear, my dear. I am highly sensitive to Pele's vagaries. Soon, but not this soon."

That night they slept near the rim of the caldron, where it was warmer, and the molten pit cast a cherry glow against the low-hanging clouds.

The next morning Andria awakened with a start. Clouds were drifting and swirling all around them, obscuring the view of everything within a radius of twenty feet or less from where they were lying.

Below, in the pit, lower clouds drifted lazily through chasms in the crater wall and heaped up until the crater resembled an abyss filled with balls of cotton.

Andria hugged herself. "I feel like we're the last two people alive on earth."

David chuckled. "Then you would have no choice but to marry me."

As they watched, the sun rose majestically and penetrated the gray pall, its rays piercing through the cumulus curtain like shimmering, probing fingers, enriching the cloud cover with a spectrum of sublime shades that made Andria think of cathedrals with stained-glass windows and fairy-tale palaces in the sky. Tears glistened in her eyes. "It is so beautiful I could cry."

She did not resist when he took her in his arms.

"I could not stand to see you cry." He kissed her eyelids, her nose, and then her lips.

The chill and stiffness from sleeping on the hard, cold mountain were miraculously dissipated from her body. Warmth and tenderness welled up inside her, and flesh and blood overcame the protest of her intellect. Her arms crept around his neck, and her body responded hungrily to his need.

"Come." He led her to his blanket and pulled her down gently. Then he covered them with her blanket. Slowly and tantalizingly he undressed her, unfastening her shirt one button at a time and drawing her riding breeches down over her hips, thighs, and feet.

He fondled her breasts through her thin undervest. His hand slid across her soft, heaving belly and down inside the waistband of her drawers. His fingers played on her, striking resounding, melodious chords.

"Take off your clothes—quickly!" Her voice was tremulous and urgent.

David obliged and lay beside her. Her eager fingers sought out his sturdy shaft and caressed him lovingly.

"Quickly!" he gasped. "Before I—"

The rest of his sentence was drowned out by the fierce pounding of her blood in her ears. Her thighs opened to him like a hibiscus opening to the warmth of the morning sun. She showed him the way with her hand. Her moistness facilitated his smooth entry, and there was no trace of discomfort to dull her own pleasure.

There was a sense of bliss about their consummation, enhanced by the celestial aura of the dawn atop Pele's citadel, that she had not experienced since the first and only time that she and Luke had made love.

It burst forth. "I know now I can love you, David," she whispered in the sweet, contented aftermath.

"My own darling! I have never been happier in all of my life." He lavished her with kisses, moving from her face, to her neck, down her breasts, her belly, to her thighs. Her thighs seized his head like a vise, and she cried out in a resurgence of desire and ecstasy.

And she, in turn, adored him with her hands and her lips, leaving no part of him untouched by love.

When they were thoroughly satiated, they lay in each other's arms beneath the blanket. "We will have a wedding such as never before has been seen in all of the islands," he declared.

She teased him. "First you must request my hand from my guardian, Caleb Callahan. Is that not the custom?"

"I think he will be pleased at the prospect of his ward one day becoming queen."

"You have a high opinion of yourself. You said you are not pure stock of the Kamehameha line."

"There is only the king's brother, my Uncle Lot, in line ahead of me." He frowned. "No, that is not true. There is also Prince William Kanaina to be reckoned with. His family has strong ties to Kamehameha the Great. No matter. William is a frail man."

The light of ambition glowed so fiercely in his eyes that Andria was vaguely dismayed. "Does being king mean so much to you?"

"Ascending the throne when one is summoned is a royal obligation. Now put on your things, my sweet, and we will be on our way down."

Before they set forth, David hurled a large boulder into the crater and sang out, "I thank thee for the gift of Andria, Pele. Had you not worked your magic on her, she might not have fallen victim to my charm."

Andria was solemn and silent. His choice of the word did not please her: *victim*. It had an imperial ring to it. She looked up at the bright heavens and said a silent prayer. *Forgive me, my beloved. In spirit, in soul, I will always be yours and yours alone. But there are worldly needs that cannot be denied. I am lonely. I need warmth. I need companionship. I need love.*

One week later Andria was introduced at the royal palace at Kailua-Kona.

Hulihee Palace, as David Kalakaua had pointed out, did not fit the average person's image of a royal dwelling aglitter with crystal chandeliers, corridors of mirrors, polished marble, silver, and precious gems. It was, in fact, a plain, unadorned two-story Georgian town house comfortably furnished in the dark, austere Victorian tradition.

Queen Emma and David's sister, the Princess Liliuokalani, were women of the same tradition. Except for their Polynesian features and the color of their skin, they epitomized British womanhood, for they wore elaborately flounced skirts and high-necked blouses with sleeves of puffed muslin trimmed with lace.

For the occasion Andria had replaced her favorite informal Hawaiian wear with a formal gown. The skirt was supported by a hoop and molded to the upper body to give the effect of a triangular silhouette.

Queen Emma was a handsome matron, on the buxom side, but tightly corseted. Her keen black eyes appraised the young Eurasian woman. "You are very lovely, my dear." She turned to David and affectionately said, "My nephew here keeps finding pretty girls no matter where he travels. Even on top of Mauna Loa."

"My sublime Aunt Emma, I met Andria on the way to Hilo. Climbing Mauna Loa was an afterthought. A whim of hers that I indulged."

Andria gave him a sweet smile, but there was a tartness to her retort. "I did not seek his indulgence, Your Highness. Prince David insisted on accompanying me to the summit."

"Bravo!" cried his sister, clapping her hands. "David can be a pompous ass at times, but we all love him in spite of his inflated ego." She went to her brother and kissed him fondly on the cheek.

Princess Liliuokalani was a petite, slender girl with long, dark hair upswept and fastened with gold combs inlaid with ivory. Her nose was pert, and her large, limpid eyes were wide-set. She and Andria took an immediate liking to each other.

"You must call me Lili," she chided when Andria persisted in addressing her as princess.

Tea and crumpets were served by servants attired like English parlormaids.

After the conventional amenities had been exchanged and Andria had recited the ordeals she had endured before coming to Hawaii, David questioned his aunt about more personal affairs.

"Is the king still gallivanting about as usual?"

"Not at this time. After all, he has just returned from a canvass of all of the major islands, exerting his magnetism and strong personal appeal to his people to support the monarchy against the annexationists."

"I am confident of his success," said David staunchly and lapsed into his native tongue. *"Ua mau ke ea o ka aina i ka pono."*

"The life of the land is perpetuated by righteousness," Andria translated promptly.

Queen Emma regarded her with pleasant surprise. "You speak Hawaiian, my child?"

"Oh, I've managed to pick up the ability to communicate with the people."

"Don't you believe her. The girl has a mind like a sponge. And she possesses a natural aptitude for languages. English, French, Spanish—Chinese, of course—and now she's conquering our complex tongue."

Queen Emma looked thoughtful. "And you have been active in religious work?"

"Yes, while at the Mormon mission."

"Although I am an Episcopalian, I have always admired the Mormons," said the queen. "Basically, we believe in the same good things. We believe in God, the Eternal Father, and in His Son, Jesus Christ, and in the Holy Ghost. At present King Kamehameha and I are engaged in founding Queen's Hospital here in Hawaii and a Church of England. Recently the U.S. Board of Missions has decreed that the Hawaiian Islands are qualified to graduate from the field of Christian missions, and, henceforth, its work will be assigned to a Hawaiian board. Tell me, Andria, how would you like to be a special assistant to me in my work? Your latitude in speaking foreign languages will be invaluable, not to mention your very obvious intelligence and alacrity."

"Not to mention her good looks, either, Aunt Emma," David quipped.

Andria was at a loss for words. "Your Highness, I am highly flattered that you would entertain such an idea that I would be qualified for the post."

"More than qualified. Then you will consider it, at least?"

"With a sense of highest honor. I would like to consult with my guardian, Mr. Caleb Callahan, before I reach a final decision. Will that be agreeable?"

"Perfectly agreeable, my dear. Here, dear, have another cup of tea and some of these delicious cucumber sandwiches."

"Did I hear the name of Caleb Callahan mentioned?" a deep voice called from the archway. Andria turned her head and saw a tall, imposing-looking man who could only be King Kamehameha the Fourth, so noble was his mien.

He was dressed like an English dandy, fawn-colored trousers and a dark swallow-tailed coat with velvet collar and silk lapels. His white ruffled shirt was set off by a wide bow tie.

David and the women rose and paid their respects to the king, who dismissed their formality with a self-conscious wave of his hand. "Please, we are not out in public. I no longer have to be reminded of the king's responsibilities."

Kamehameha kissed his consort on the cheek and embraced Prince David. "David, my boy, it has been a long time. I have missed you. What have you been up to?"

"Traveling, mostly. England, the Continent."

The monarch let out a nostalgic sigh. "England. Ah, how I yearn to return to London again before I die. The theaters—the music halls—Picadilly Circus—Buckingham Palace. I say, did you have an audience with Queen Victoria?"

His nephew smiled. "I'm afraid not, Your Highness. You see, Keawe, Lakana, and I were traveling incognito. Just like any other gawking tourists. You know how I hate protocol."

The king frowned. "An aversion unworthy of a future king, my boy."

David laughed. "Far distant future, uncle. Until then I will continue to be the playboy of the Eastern world." His eyes shone mischievously. "Recently I have been on a hunting expedition across the island. Near Hilo."

"Hunting? And were you successful?"

"Quite."

"What kind of game?"

"Wahine—and I landed a whopper. Uncle, I take great pleasure in presenting Miss Andria Callahan."

The king was clearly impressed with the ravishing Eurasian girl. He acknowledged her curtsy by bowing low over her right hand and kissing it.

"Miss Callahan, your fame has preceded you. I have heard talk of your reputed beauty through all of the islands, and not one bit of it was exaggeration. To the contrary, your beauty exceeds mere words."

Andria blushed. "You flatter me too excessively." Her eyes lit up with mischief. "David comes by his gift of hyperbole quite naturally."

When the laughter had subsided, King Kamehameha became sober. "I hesitate to say that the reason we have not met sooner—to my sincere regret—is that the relationship between your guardian, Mr. Callahan, and the royal government has always been rather strained."

"So I understand, and that is regrettable, Your Highness."

"I must say, however, that I find Caleb Callahan's son a most engaging young man."

"His son?" Andria's hand flew to her throat to hide her quivering pulse.

"Yes, Luke Callahan. His good friend John Yee, as well. In fact, John is my special labor minister and adviser."

Andria's head began to spin, and David rushed to her side. "What's wrong, Andria? You're so pale. Do you feel faint?"

"I—I think I'd better sit down," she said weakly.

He eased her down on the divan, and the king and queen joined him beside her.

"Was it something I said, child?" the king inquired anxiously.

She gazed up at him imploringly. "Luke—Luke Callahan is alive? You have seen him?"

"Why, of course. He did have a precarious bout with diptheria when he and John first arrived on Oahu. He hovered between life and death for weeks. But I am pleased to say that he has fully recovered and is now gainfully employed raising pineapples on the island of Lanai."

The king looked perplexed. "You mean to say that in all this time he has not been in touch with his father?"

In a daze she shook her head. "No—not once. I do not understand. Perhaps he doesn't even know that we are in Hawaii."

"Oh, he knows that full well. If memory serves me, there was some sort of an estrangement between Luke and his father. John Yee was vague about the details. And rightly so. It is none of my affair."

She swallowed a hard lump in her throat. "Are you certain that Luke knows that *I* am here with the Callahans?"

"Yes, he does. In fact he was on his way to the United States in search of you when his ship was wrecked in a storm two hundred miles off Oahu."

Andria was distressed and bewildered. "Then *why?* If he knows I am here in Hawaii, why did he not come and find me?"

King Kamehameha looked uncomfortably from Prince David to Andria. He cleared his throat. "I am afraid that our foreign minister, Mr. Wyllie, was misinformed about your status in the Callahan household when first you arrived in the Islands."

"In what way?"

"You see, my dear, in our immigration records, you are listed as Caleb Callahan's wife?"

"His *wife?*" She was incredulous. "How can that be?"

"It facilitated permission for you to enter Hawaii. Cut through red tape, that sort of bureaucratic nonsense."

"His wife." She kept repeating it listlessly. "And Luke believed it—how could he? The whole thing is insane. Your Highness, I must go to him and tell him the truth." She went to David and clasped his shoulders. "David, will you help me to travel to Lanai?"

David Kalakaua was stony faced and grim, his lips tight.

"David, please."

"You love this man very much?"

"With all my heart." Sudden realization of what he must be thinking jolted her. "Oh, David, I—I—" What could she say to this man she had become mistress to and who had professed his undying love for her and his intent to make her his queen one day? She was overcome with grief for him and terrible shame for herself. He was a brave man. A noble man. A man of impeccable integrity.

David compelled himself to smile, and his voice was gentle and understanding. "Of course I will help you find Luke Callahan. My yacht is at your disposal. We can leave whenever you wish, Andria, my—" He omitted the "darling."

A maid appeared in the doorway and curtsied. "Your Highness, Mr. Yee has arrived. He says you are expecting him."

"Good. Please show him in." He explained to the others. "As you are aware, our native population continues to decline at an alarming rate, while our industry expands in leaps and bounds. Mr. Yee and the legislature are drafting a bill that would provide for the importation of a mass labor force from the Far East—China, Japan and from the Portuguese colonies. Ah, here he is now."

Andria's shock at seeing "John Yee" was only slightly less great than of learning that Luke Callahan was in Hawaii.

Her mouth flew open, and she could only gape.

John stared at her coldly. He spoke to her in Chinese, employing her native name. "Well, Sun Ying Wong, so we meet again. It has been a long time."

Andria found her voice. "Tongdlon, so you are John Yee now. Tongdlon, I just learned that Luke is alive and is right here in Hawaii. The shock of it, my mind is all sixes and sevens. I can't think straight. But how can he be alive when I saw you shoot him right before my eyes in front of the bandits at the mission?"

"A small illusion I staged to preserve his life. No matter. That is all in the past." He compressed his lips. "And we learned some time back that you were in the Islands." The ice grew thicker. "With your husband, Caleb Callahan."

She rushed over to John and seized the lapels of his dark business suit. "But that is a horrible mistake. I was just telling the king. I am not now and never have been Caleb's wife. True, he rescued me from a brothel in San Francisco when he learned that Luke and I were in love. He did it for his son, and he has treated me like a daughter all this while. *Never* as a wife!" It suddenly dawned on her. "Caleb believes that Luke is dead, just as I have believed since that hideous day at the mission. Tongdlon! Caleb loves his son. How cruel of him not to let his father and me know that he was alive."

"He thought it would be better for all concerned, for him to remain dead. He has changed his name to Luke Jennings. It was his mother's maiden name."

"Cruel! Stupid! Pointless!" She kept shaking her head in mindless rhythm. "How could he believe that I was married to his father? How could he be so blind to my character?"

"Luke is not the only one who continues to believe that you are Caleb's third wife—or mistress, call it what you will. Polygamy is not a popular institution here in Hawaii. Besides, Caleb does nothing to discourage such fancy."

She was stunned. "Do you mean to infer that Caleb lets people think that he and I—?" She could not bring herself to say it. "I cannot believe he could be so deceitful."

John shrugged. "It is all academic now in any case. You see, Andria, Luke is married to a Hawaiian girl."

"Tongdlon, oh, no!"

"My name is John Yee," he said impatiently. "Tongdlon is as dead to his past as is Luke Jennings. Let sleeping dogs lie, Andria."

"No! No! I will never give him up! You are lying to me to keep him away from me! You never did like me, John Yee!" She raised her fists as if to strike him in the face, but David caught her from behind and restrained her.

"No, don't blame this man for your plight, Andria. I must confess that, until I met you and came to know that you were a woman of integrity, I, along with countless others, was of a mind that the designations guardian and ward, describing the relationship between you and Caleb Callahan, were an obvious flimflam."

"David!" His face was becoming blurry, fading into the distance. She closed her eyes and sagged in his arms. Merciful unconsciousness settled over her like a shroud.

Chapter Four

There was a rustic atmosphere about the island of Lanai that appealed to Luke Callahan from the first day he set foot on the white strip of sand at Shipwreck Beach, a veritable graveyard of ships of all sizes, shapes, and ages that had, over the years, been driven ashore and wrecked by the savage surf curling about the small island.

Prowling among the skeletons that littered the beach for as far as the eye could see, Luke had the eerie sensation that he was treading in a vast outdoor cathedral.

"Do you sense the presence of ghosts?" he asked his companion, John MacIntire, a former Scotch merchant seaman.

"Aye, laddie," replied MacIntire, and he paused to have a swig from a flask he always carried on his hip. "Will ye have a wee nip?"

"No, thanks, Johnny. That *okoleohao* will be the death of you yet."

MacIntire was squat, paunchy, and ruddy faced, with a bulbous nose and gray side whiskers fringing an otherwise bald pate. Ignoring the admonition, he took yet another defiant swallow of the liquor and capped the flask.

"Drives away the evil spirits," he said solemnly.

"I'd question that, considering the demons you professed to see after your last drunken bout."

"Never you mind. Now let's have a look at our bountiful acreage."

"Your acreage, John, boy."

The older man put an arm about his shoulders. "No, laddie. Our land. Gor! I wouldn't be standing here alive today if you hadn't pulled me out of that brawl with limey sailors in Honolulu. Yes, sirree, you and me is equal partners. Wait until you see our spread."

MacIntire had come to the island in the late forties with a modest poke he had acquired in the first days of the California Gold Rush, before the official word spread around the world that there was a horde of treasure in the substrata along the Sacramento River.

It was pure chance that had brought MacIntire to Lanai, which was the outcast runt of the archipelago. His financial resources, as well as his political and social naivete, were inadequate to compete with rich and powerful entrepreneurs such as Caleb Callahan and the other families who dominated Hawaiian commerce and who bought up most of the rich, virgin land from which would spring vast sugar and coffee plantations and grazing land for livestock.

An unscrupulous petty bureaucrat "sold the Scotty a bill of goods," as the official later bragged to fellow politicos after selling MacIntire land on Lanai.

His initial visit to his newly acquired real estate was a bitter disappointment to MacIntire. Lanai, it seemed to him, was as primitive as the day Captain Cook had stepped ashore.

The only white man on Lanai, as far as MacIntire could discern, was a Presbyterian missionary who lived in a small adobe-and-straw bungalow alongside his drab mission house. The Reverend Sila Thatcher was conducting Sunday morning services when MacIntire stumbled upon the congregation.

Befitting the solemn, pious nature of the occasion,

the men and women were adorned in the best finery
that the preacher had been able to provide them with
from the mission's wardrobe: colorful muumuus and
calico robes, hats, gloves, and shoes. What was disconcerting was that these garments were being worn in
a highly unconventional way. A voluptuous young
woman wore a bonnet and gloves and nothing more! A
man of splendid proportions was decked out in a bowler
hat with his trousers tied by the legs around his waist,
comprising a sash of sorts that concealed nothing of
what trousers are intended to hide from public view.

Afterward, over tea and biscuits, Thatcher lamented
to MacIntire, "God only knows, I've done my best to
make them see the way. But they refuse to abide by
Christian doctrine and dogma. They are like spoiled,
mischievous children. I mean, did you see that hussy
in the front row, sitting with her limbs all askew,
directly beneath the pulpit? I tell you, Mr. MacIntire,
it was a highly distracting spectacle."

MacIntire hid his smile behind a biscuit. "I can well
imagine how you felt, sir. I experienced a similar reac-
tion myself." He shifted about to relieve a tightness in
his crotch that had persisted since witnessing the young
wahine's lascivious attitude.

When MacIntire told Thatcher that he had purchased
land on the island, with an option to augment his holdings within one year, the missionary was scornful.

"Good God, man! They must have seen you coming
over at the land office. The only thing that will grow on
this patch of jungle and rock is pineapple."

"Pineapple—yes—" There was a fruit bowl on the
table holding a pineapple of a dimension that MacIntire
had not seen matched anywhere else in the Islands. He
picked it up and hefted it in his palm.

"I must say this is an exceptionally tasty variety,"
Thatcher said. He handed MacIntire a knife.

The Scot proceeded to slice off a wedge of fruit.
His hand was filled with juice. "My word!" He took a

healthy bite of it, and his eyes lit up. "This is without doubt the finest pineapple that I've ever tasted since I came to Hawaii," MacIntire exclaimed.

"Something to do with its geographical location and the extensive interior plateau. Lanai is protected from inclement weather by the sister islands of Maui and Molokai. I'll explain further as I show you the island."

Luke and MacIntire made a complete tour of the island that day, and when it was over, Luke's doubts had been resolved. He clapped the older man on the back.

"I like it here, Scotty. It's got an aura about it that smacks of the Garden of Eden. And the pineapple! I've got a feeling, man! With a little luck you and I can make this place into the greatest pineapple plantation in the world. An empire."

The Scotsman smiled wryly. "Only thing, laddie, do you think that pineapples will ever replace apples and oranges in the Western world?"

"Once they taste *our* pineapples, the nations of North America and Europe will be vying for them just as they vie for Hawaiian sugar cane."

When he returned to Oahu, Luke consulted with his good friend Kiano. "What do you think of our venture?"

Kiano was reserved about the idea. "Assuming you can drum up a world demand for pineapples, how will you get started? Capital, for one thing."

"Scotty owns the land."

"Yes, but it must be cultivated. Workers must be hired. Labor does not come cheap any longer. We can't get enough help to maintain the sugar plantations."

"John Yee and your uncle are currently working on that problem. Cheap coolie labor imported from the Orient."

"All right, but you still must face the initial problem of cultivating pineapple on a large scale. What do you know about growing pineapple commercially?"

"Nothing at present, but I intend to rectify that lack as soon as possible. Tomorrow Leilani and I are boating over to Molokai to visit with John Butler."

"Ah, yes, Butler. He owns a small pineapple plantation up north. Not far from the leper colony." A glint came into his eye. "Did you know Butler has an eye for Leilani?"

"I understood he is married."

The handsome Hawaiian's teeth flashed, white as the sand on Waikiki Beach. "Since when does having a wife deter a man from desiring another woman?" A hint of sarcasm. "You Mormons surely understand that?"

"I'm not worried about Butler as far as Leilani is concerned."

"Pretty sure of yourself, eh?"

"Sure enough to ask her to marry me."

Kiano grabbed his friend's hand and wrung it vigorously. "That's wonderful! I'm so happy for the two of you. We must have the wedding at King Kamehameha's residence."

"I don't think so, Kiano. Both Leilani and I wish to have a small, intimate ceremony with no more than a few close friends present."

"No *luau?* No hula dancers?"

"To be sure, but nothing ostentatious."

Kiano grinned. "When will this marriage take place?"

"As soon as Scotty and I are settled on Lanai and have our plantation progressing. Also, I want to have a cottage ready for my bride."

"I understand, my friend. But you still haven't answered my question about capital. Neither you nor MacIntire has more than five pounds between the two of you. I tell you, I will lend you the money to get started.

"I wouldn't hear of it, Kiano. There's no better way to destroy friendship than to borrow from a friend."

"The king will be delighted to help you. It would be a mere pittance out of the royal coffers."

Luke frowned. "It would set a bad precedent. Everyone and his brother would expect the king to finance them in business ventures."

Kiano took a deep breath and posed a subject he knew would incense Luke. "What about your father? Caleb Callahan would be only too overjoyed to set his son up in a worthy business venture."

Luke did not hide his displeasure. "I respectfully request that you do not bring up my father again, Kiano. Oh, he would lend me money, without a doubt, to assuage his miserable conscience—if he has one at all. More than that, it would restore his sense of power over me. No, as far as Caleb Callahan is concerned, I am dead. And I prefer to keep it that way."

Kiano eyed him shrewdly. "Is it possible that I detect something far less worthy than altruism in your adamant position? Perhaps you enjoy punishing your father by letting him go on thinking that you are dead?"

Luke sighed. "A germ of truth, I concede. You seem to forget, my friend, that my father married the girl I loved more dearly than anything else in life."

"Even Leilani?"

Luke dropped his eyes in shame. His voice was low. "I—I—that isn't fair to ask me, Kiano. Andria is lost to me. The past is as dead as I am to Andria and to my father. Leilani and I have the whole future ahead of us. Let it be so."

The two friends embraced each other.

"May God be with you always, Luke Callahan."

"Luke Jennings."

The next morning Kiano bid Luke, Leilani, and MacIntire farewell on the quay at Honolulu. As Luke and the girl boarded the skiff that would make the short haul to Molokai, Kiano took Scotty aside.

"There is something I must speak to you about privately. You are going to need financing for your plantation."

The Scotsman was crestfallen. "Aye, laddie, and I've just about exhausted all me avenues. So has Luke."

"Not entirely. Only Luke has too much pride to pursue this source. Will you do what I tell you and promise never to divulge our secret to him?"

"I'd deed you my right arm if you can help us raise the capital we need to go into business."

"You'll lose that arm surely enough if you break your word to me, Scotty," Kiano said unsmilingly.

"No fear. So what is it, laddie?"

Aboard the skiff, Luke said impatiently to Leilani, "What are those two cooking up, do you suppose?" He shouted, "Scotty! Stop that palavering and come aboard. We're late as it is."

"Aye, lad, right with you." The old man pounded Kiano on the shoulder and leaped nimbly from the dock onto the deck. From his pocket he took his ever-present flask and uncorked it. "A little nip to fortify us against the chill sea air?" He offered it to Leilani and Luke.

The girl smiled and shook her head. To Scotty's surprise, Luke grinned and took the flask from him. "I think this is a special occasion, so, aye, my partner, I'll drink a toast with you."

John and Melody Butler's sprawling, erratic home reflected their background in the Australian bush. "Put together piecemeal," John observed. "We've been adding a room here and a room there for the past decade, whenever we felt the need to expand." And expand they had. The Butler family now consisted of six boys and three girls.

Butler was a tall, slim man with piercing dark eyes, black hair, and an intense, saturnine face. His wife was a short, plump, and pretty redhead.

Luke and Scotty marveled at Butler's comprehensive knowledge of pineapple. His plantation was small but efficient, and as he put it, "Our output is double that of most plantations twice the size, and the quality of my fruit is unmatched anywhere in the Islands." He took them on a tour, lecturing as he displayed prize specimens of the crop.

"Look at this fellow. Four feet high, at least. See how the long, spiny leaves grow around the short stump. That stalk rising from the center of the cluster bears the flower. This one is sixteen months old. Note the purplish blossoms. Each flower is protected by a bract, and the fruit itself represents the union of all the flowers and bracts into a fleshy mass. In four more months the fruit itself will mature."

"That's a long time," Luke observed.

"Growing pineapple is a long-term proposition. No quick returns. You have to have the cash reserve to ride it out until your first crop is ready for harvesting."

Luke and Scotty exchanged a gloomy look.

Butler took them to another section of the plantation where the fruit was ready for harvesting.

"While it is ripening, the pineapple absorbs sugar from the stump. Here—this one is perfect. The hard, horny rind and prickly leaves are protective. The pineapple is a hardy fruit indeed, and can withstand considerable rough handling and long storage."

Day after day Luke and Scotty worked in the fields with the hired hands and listened attentively to Butler's dissertations on pineapple growing and care.

After three weeks Luke told Leilani, "I eat, sleep, and think pineapple all day and all night."

She snuggled up to him in the big brass bed they shared and said shyly, "Is that all you can think of at night? Pineapple?" Her slim, soft hand settled on his chest and worked its way down slowly, kneading the rippled muscles of his belly. Then her fingers walked downward and closed over his penis, coaxing it into full, vigorous bloom.

"True, my mind is distracted from pineapple at this moment," he admitted, taking her in his arms. He kissed her mouth, her throat, her breasts. Her pink nipples hardened under the ministrations of his lips.

He got on his knees and straddled her, their positions reversed. His tongue teased her navel until she cried out in pleasure. He parted her thighs, just as he parted the purple blossoms in the fields, and his hands curled under the backs of her limbs and pressed the sides of her thighs.

"Oh, Luke, my wonderful, marvelous lover!" She moaned in ecstasy, thrashing about in uncontrollable passion, and her thighs clapped viselike on his bent head.

Leilani, in turn, adored every part of him her eager lips could reach, and shortly the two of them were convulsed in simultaneous orgasms.

Without cessation he turned and mounted her in what the *kanakas* and *wahines* referred to as the missionary position, poking fun at their white mentors.

This time they made love leisurely, savoring every nuance the way island gourmets linger over the many courses of a luau. The climax was less intense, but sweet and liquid.

They fell asleep still locked in loving embrace, with Leilani's legs wrapped loosely around Luke's waist.

On the other side of one bedroom wall, in a small, dark linen closet, John Butler's right eye was glued to a small aperture that looked into the guest room. Breathing heavily, he rose from his knees on unsteady legs and tiptoed out of the closet and down the hall to his own bedroom.

Melody was sitting up in bed, reading a newspaper by the light of an oil lamp. She looked up startled at his lurching entry into the room.

"John, have you been drinking too much again?"

It was true he had been drinking, but his present intoxication was of a different form than that induced by alcohol. His mind still reeling with lurid fantasies of what he had just witnessed, he threw off his clothing and strode to the bed. Melody's eyes bulged at the sight of his male arousal.

"Whatever brought *that* on?" she asked, her own breathing picking up tempo now. Of late Melody had been deprived of her husband's marital attentions, to her mounting restlessness and frustration. She threw back the covers, pulled up her nightgown, and opened her arms and her thighs to him.

"Come, my darling, quickly."

He took her roughly, and she liked it that way. Like a stallion mounting a mare. Her body was pleasurably gorged, and in seconds they were rocking back and forth in the most satisfying intercourse Melody had enjoyed in many a moon.

Chapter Five

On the day that Luke, Leilani, and MacIntire returned to Honolulu from Molokai, John Yee visited them in the small grass-and-adobe cottage where Leilani and her mother had resided before Luke moved in with Leilani.

Leilani's mother was a short, plump, jolly woman who wore muumuus the size of a small tent. When Luke and Leilani had told her of their marriage plans, she had kissed both of them enthusiastically and said, "Bless you, my children. I will move in with Aunt Uli. She's has been trying to persuade me to join her for years."

"I wouldn't hear of it," Luke had protested. "I can't dispossess you from your own home."

"Besides, there is plenty of room, mother," Leilani had said.

Her mother had chuckled and nudged Luke in the ribs with an elbow. "There is never too much room for young lovers. In any case Aunt Uli and I will be company for each other. Old widows."

The fact that her daughter was sleeping with a man without benefit of clergy did not faze her in the least, although she attended church services every Sunday. She herself was a common-law wife.

Nevertheless, before she departed Luke had assured her, "Don't worry, mother, I intend to make an honest woman out of Leilani as soon as we get to Lanai. There's a Reverend Silas Thatcher who lives there, and I think he will be delighted to officiate."

The woman shrugged. "She will always be an honest woman in any case. *Aloha.*"

John Yee arrived as Leilani was preparing supper. He kissed her warmly and shook hands with Luke. "And have you mastered the fine art of pineapple growing, my friend?"

"I'm almost as expert as John Butler. He's a good teacher."

Leilani sniffed. "And a dirty old man as well. Always pinching and feeling."

The men laughed. "I'm always pinching and feeling too," Luke quipped.

She slapped his face playfully. "Yes, but at least you are a dirty *young* man. Now, the two of you go out on the porch and let me finish making dinner."

Luke filled two mugs with pineapple juice, coconut milk, and a healthy swig of rum, and then he and John retired to what they laughingly referred to as the porch. In truth it was a flagstone patio with a thatched overhang to shield it from the sun and rain. They sat cross-legged on the ground as was the local custom, and John proposed a toast.

"To your future success, my friend. May you one day be the greatest pineapple tycoon in all of Hawaii."

"I'll drink to that." They touched mugs, then drank of the delicious and aromatic concoction. Abruptly Luke's jovial mien grew solemn. "There is but one drawback. Capital. Do you know how long it requires to harvest one crop of pineapple? Almost two years!"

"That is precisely why I am here, Luke." He took another swallow. "I think I can arrange financing for the venture."

"You must be joking."

"No, and it was quite by chance. Last week the

foreign minister was telling me about a rich American from New York City who is desirous of investing in undeveloped foreign real estate—China, Australia, and the Hawaiian Islands. He was principally interested in sugar and coffee, but Mr. Wyllie informed him that these commodities were pretty well taken up, owned, or on option to local investors like Caleb Callahan, the Doles, and the Parkers. So, when Wyllie suggested pineapple, he was extremely enthusiastic and gave the minister carte blanche to buy up all the arable pineapple land that is available. What it means is that you have pretty much a blank check to start cultivating your holdings on Lanai."

Luke was dumbfounded. "That's positively incredible! Just who is this remarkable benefactor, and how can he be so naive to invest in a proposition sight unseen?"

"Rich and powerful men like that—he's one of the Astors—don't worry about being cheated by pygmies such as we. In essence the Hawaiian government will be his watchdog. They'll keep a watchful eye on you, my friend, to insure that the interests of your silent partner are protected."

Luke could still scarcely believe his good fortune. "Amazing! Outlandish! Incredible!" He leaped up and rushed into the house to tell Leilani the good news.

She was as overjoyed as he was. The two of them danced about the small kitchen like children, hugging and kissing each other and shrieking with delight.

John Yee poked his head through the doorway and grinned. "Where's my supper? I'm famished. Enough of this nonsense, you two."

They feasted royally that night on roast pork, fish baked in kelp, candied yams and poi, along with a variety of exotic vegetables. And the rum and the *okoleohao* flowed in countless mugs and cups.

Luke and Leilani were quite tipsy by the time they fell into bed. Still the alcohol had not quite slaked the heat of the blood and the flesh. Before they slept they made love twice, and the last thing Luke remembered was Leilani nibbling on his ear and whispering, "Mrs. Luke Callahan. Yes, I will like that very much indeed."

On the day that Luke and Leilani arrived on Lanai, they went immediately to see Reverend Thatcher with the request: "Will you do us the honor of marrying us, sir?"

Thatcher was more than happy to oblige. And he even offered them the use of his house while he was away in Hawaii, the big island. "I must attend a convention of the Christian Missionaries League at Hilo," he told them. "I'll be leaving in three days' time, and, meanwhile, you may live and sleep in the mission house."

"God bless you, Mr. Thatcher." Leilani, eyes brimming with tears of happiness, went over to the little man, put her arms around his neck, and gave him a resounding kiss on the mouth.

Reverend Thatcher turned beet red and sputtered, "My word! You are a dear child. And you, sir, are a very lucky man." He shook Luke's hand.

John MacIntire brushed a tear from his cheek with his sleeve and took out his flask of liquor.

"Just a wee nip in celebration. Join me, reverend?"

"Don't mind if I do, sir."

And the flask was passed around.

Even with unlimited funds to back their venture, Luke and MacIntire worked side by side with the hired hands, local men, up to twelve hours a day throughout the first year.

A house for Leilani had taken first priority. All of his life Luke had been impressed with colonial American architecture, and he drew the plans in his own hand. He hired men to build it, but he worked with them on every phase of its construction. He instructed the workmen in every detail of Western carpentry: how to ham-

mer a nail; set a peg; install a miter joint, a post and
lintel; and hang a ceiling beam. It was hard, painstaking
labor, but it was a labor of love, and so a joy rather
than a hardship.

Leilani marveled as the structure assumed shape and
character, a harmonious blend of Georgian and Grecian,
simple yet regal, with pillars, porticoes, and cornices
of white stone.

In the interior Luke deviated from the classic form—
no long, dark corridors or gloomy wood paneling. The
house was light and airy, with large windows, and
sweeping, high-beamed ceilings. All of the furniture
was of native wood, mostly koa.

"I can't wait until we move in," his wife exulted.

They did so on a Christmas Eve, a balmy evening.
That was one aspect of Hawaiian existence that left
Luke nostalgic for past Christmases back home, when
he had toasted marshmallows over a roaring fire as the
north wind whistled under the eaves and the snow
drove hard against the windowpanes.

John Yee was invited to Lanai for the occasion, as
well as Leilani's girlhood friends, Kokua and Uli. Luke
was pleasantly surprised when John arrived aboard a
familiar-looking catamaran. Then he spied Kiano at
the tiller and his friend Kana, a lean, lithe man who
looked more Portuguese than Polynesian.

Luke rushed down to the beach and greeted them
effusively. He embraced all three of them. "My dear
friends, having you in my new home for the holidays
is the best Christmas gift I could have received. Come,
we must celebrate at once with a cup of hard pineapple
cider."

"Pineapple cider?" Kiano laughed. "Whatever is pineapple cider?"

"Same as the apple cider we made back home, only
with pineapples. Sadly not with my own crop, not this
Christmas, but everything is going marvelously well.
Here, let me help you with your luggage."

"None to speak of for Kana and myself," said Kiano. A *malo* or two serves us very well, but at the Christmas *luau,* we promise to dress more formally." He looked at John Yee and winked. "Hasn't our friend John become the dandy, though? That's what comes of being a civil servant."

"These are my play clothes," John said, indicating the colorful shirt he was wearing, adorned with embroidered birds, flowers, and fruits. He wore his shirt-tails outside his white linen trousers, *aloha* style, as it would come to be known.

Leilani welcomed them at the house with hugs and kisses. She was especially affectionate to Kiano.

"It was all because of you that I met my Luke," she told him.

"Some people might consider that grounds for hating me for life," he teased. And he presented her with an elaborate *lei* made of flowers, seeds, coral, shells, and nuts.

"It's absolutely gorgeous," she said enthusiastically and kissed him once again.

"Hey, enough of this spooning with my wife," Luke joked.

"Spooning?"

They all looked at him curiously.

"An old American term for playing around with one's girl."

Kiano presented Luke with a jug of *'awa.* "Only for this very special occasion. It is the finest quality to be bought in all of the islands."

They relaxed on bamboo lounges and sipped Luke's pineapple cider, cooled in an icy spring at the back of the house. The spacious flagstone terrace lay in the shade of two stately koa trees almost one hundred feet high, their shaggy crowns wagging in the ocean breeze.

"How is your labor importation program progressing?" Luke asked John.

"Far ahead of schedule. We expect a shipment to arrive from Hong Kong right after the first of the year."

"I'd like to contract for at least fifty more plantation workers," Luke said. "I want to expand our operation twofold by next summer when we'll be getting ready for the first big harvest."

"I'll draw up the contract as soon as I get back to Kailua-Kona," John promised.

Later in the afternoon while the women were preparing for the grand Christmas *luau,* Luke inquired casually—too casually—of his friend John, "How is Andria? Do you see her often?"

"Andria is fine. As radiant as always. And extremely busy. She's become Queen Emma's right arm, what with the new hospital, the church, and all of the queen's social work among the deprived populace. I am trying to persuade her to lend support in my department. Andria would be indispensable in dealing with the immigrants, especially the Chinese women. They are a shy, frightened lot."

Kiano helped himself to more pineapple cider. "I must say that in the few short years you three have been in Hawaii, you have become pillars of Hawaiian society. Indispensable civil servants."

"Not I," Luke objected. "I'm just another farmer."

"Farmer, indeed. In no time your name will rank with the foremost families in these islands."

"Jennings or Callahan?" Luke asked flatly.

Kiano and John Yee exchanged a meaningful gaze.

"Why, Jennings, of course," John answered quietly.

There was an awkward silence, broken by Luke. "You claim that Andria knows I am alive. How is it that she has never spoken to my father about it?"

John shrugged. "Why don't you ask her yourself, my friend?"

"I do not appreciate your sense of humor, John," Luke snapped. "Does she still see your cousin David, Kiano?"

"Frequently. It is no secret that he would make her his wife if she would have him."

Luke's smile was bitter. "Would he now? And what does my father think about that?"

"I think he approves. Caleb Callahan is proud of his ward and her popularity with the royal family."

"I'll bet he is, the opportunistic old bastard! He'd sell his soul to the devil for political influence of that magnitude. Andria Callahan, adviser to the king and queen."

John Yee put a hand on his friend's shoulder and said seriously, "You cannot accept that Andria has never been wife to your father. You feel more comfortable with the lie than the truth because it helps to ease your own conscience."

"Look, my friend, Dame Fortune is a sadistic mistress. She manipulates our mere mortal existences as the puppeteer pulls the strings of his marionettes. She deluded Andria into believing that you were dead and then, in turn, persuaded you that Andria was mistress to your father. False in each instance. But time aided and abetted the deceit. You fell in love with Leilani and—"

"And Andria became mistress to David Kalakaua," Luke said leadenly. "Ah, what's the use of belaboring the issue? It's water under the bridge."

To their common relief, the discussion was interrupted by the appearance of John MacIntire and Reverend Thatcher.

Scotty whipped off his wide-brimmed bush hat and fanned his ruddy face. "We've just come from the north grove. Gor! I tell you, partner, them 'apples are goin' to be monsters."

"You both look parched. Help yourself to some punch, reverend. It's laced with rum."

"I do believe I will," said the wizened, gray-haired missionary. But first he brushed off his white shoes with a handful of koa leaves.

"Know what the reverend was telling me, Luke? He says on some of the islands to the west they make cloth from the spiny leaves of pineapples."

"And tough fiber at that," acknowledged Thatcher. "It's quite valuable."

"I must make a note to look into that," Luke said. "That's one of the secrets of successful business. Find a way to turn your waste products into additional profit. John, you might mention it to the foreign minister to pass on to our benefactor. See what he thinks of branching out into fabric production."

"I certainly will. It sounds like a good idea to me. We'll get in touch with Astor as soon as possible."

Leilani appeared on the patio to announce to her husband, "Darling, I think the *kalua* is done. Would you please do the honors?"

The men stared at her in unabashed admiration. "A picture of beauty and grace," John Yee murmured.

She was, indeed, a picture in a wraparound garment of georgette crepe that just covered half of her breasts, sheathed her waist, hips, and thighs like second skin, and terminated at knee level. In its dazzling flower print were all the colors of the rainbow. Around her neck she wore the *lei* that Kiano had given to her. Her long hair trailed down her back, tied back with a pink ribbon and crowned with a halo of morning-glories, *ohi'a* blossoms, and ginger petals.

Kokua and Uli, who had followed Andria to the patio, wore ceremonial muumuus with long trains.

Luke went to his wife, kissed her chastely on the brow, and led her around to the far side of the garden where the banquet had been laid out around the oblong imu pit. When the party was all seated cross-legged at their places, Luke and Kiano dug away the sand from the pit and cut away the canvas and the ti and banana leaves.

Sighs and mutterings of appreciation went around the group as the sweet, savory aroma of roast pork assailed their nostrils. They hoisted the *kalua* onto the *papapuaa*. Then Luke commenced carving the succulent, fragile meat onto serving platters.

It was a feast to end all feasts. In addition to the pork there was *laulau*—fish, pork, and chicken mixed with taro leaves; salmon and tomato; shrimps and crabs; coconut pudding; breadfruit, bananas, pineapples, papayas, and mangoes.

"In my country they describe a luau such as this as a 'groaning board,'" Luke told his guests. "In lieu of a table, we must call it a 'groaning earth' feast."

"Your country?" Kiano quipped. "America is no longer your home. You are one of us, a Hawaiian."

"And glad to be one, old friend. "Luke lifted his glass of *kava* and drank.

In the middle of the feast, Luke stopped eating and listened, his mouth agape. "I must be dreaming," he murmured.

In the distance he heard a symphony of wind, percussion, and stringed instruments, punctuated by the unique twang of a ukulele. What was even more unique was the tune they were playing.

"'Silent Night'! I can't believe it!"

Leilani, who was smiling smugly, leaned over and kissed his cheek.

"Niveu, your chief foreman, has been practicing with a group of the men for weeks to learn a medley of American Christmas songs and carols in appreciation for your kindness and generosity. To them you are no longer a *malihini*. You are a *kamaaina*."

"An old-timer." Kiano grinned and proposed another toast. "To my blood brother, Luke Calla—" He caught himself. "Luke Jennings."

They drank as the music drew closer, and at last the musicians were serenading them from the perimeter of the flickering fires. "Jingle Bells," "We Three Kings," "Holy Night"—a wide gamut of nostalgic Christmas music that brought tears to Luke's eyes.

Reverend Thatcher leaned over to him and whispered, "This is all very grand, but I must say I do miss the roast turkey or goose, chestnut stuffing, and plum pudding."

Luke smiled and nodded. "Most of all I miss the snow."

And as if to answer his wish, a shower of white blossoms cascaded down onto the banquet area from the trees overhead. He gathered up a handful of them and buried his nose in the soft petals.

"Merry Christmas, darling," he said very quietly.

But not so quietly that Leilani did not overhear him. "Thank you, my love," she said, then kissed his lips. And a Merry Christmas to you."

Luke's eyes glazed over, and suddenly he started, as if awakening from a trance.

"What? What did you say?"

"Merry Christmas, darling, you silly goose." Her eyebrows arched. "Or perhaps you were talking to Kokua or Uli?"

He shook his head to clear it, as the other girls erupted into peals of laughter.

"I—I'm sorry," he said faltering. "It's the *'awa*. It's making me dizzy."

The truth of the matter was that he had been talking to Andria!

Chapter Six

The banquet room of Hulihee Palace was filled with illustrious celebrities of both the Hawaiian aristocracy and the white establishment. On occasions such as this, an armed truce prevailed between the monarchists and the annexationists. It was a birthday party for the Princess Liliuokalani.

Formal attire was required, and both men and women were dressed as fashionably as any peer group in a London or Paris grand ballroom.

The princess was glittering in a gown of lime organdy overlaid with a shadow decoration of native flowers and trimmed in white lace and green ribbon. Her hair was done up in a ribbon headdress of buttercups.

Andria had gone to great pains in selecting her own gown, so as not to overshadow the princess, who had become her best friend, aside from Lee who still played the role of mother, confidante, companion, and part-time lady's maid.

"Do I look inconspicuous enough?" she asked Lee before going downstairs to join the other guests.

She was wearing a simple, billowing black satin skirt and a coordinated white satin blouse with a flaring collar that framed the V-neckline. Her breasts were modestly concealed. Puffed sleeves and a ribbon over the waistband of her skirt endowed her with a girlish innocence calculated not to compete with the sensuality of the princess.

"You could never appear inconspicuous among an army of beautiful women." Lee hugged her and said, "Has the prince proposed again, dear?"

"None of your business, nosy body."

"I know he has. I heard him last night on the front veranda," Lee said matter-of-factly.

Andria pretended to be outraged. "This is too much, really! Not only are you overly curious, but now you are eavesdropping as well!"

David, handsome in his evening clothes, white ruffled shirt, and black cravat, was waiting at the foot of the stairs as she descended. He held out a hand to her.

"You look divine, my love."

"Indeed she does, and I claim the first dance, Miss Callahan." It was R. C. Wyllie, the minister of foreign affairs.

"I would be honored, Mr. Wyllie."

David was good-natured about her flirtatious snub, and, with arms folded, he watched them sweep onto the floor. The couples moved gracefully, forming ever changing patterns and colorful designs, like the dancing chips of glass in a kaleidoscope.

Andria smiled and nodded to friends as they whirled past—John Ricord, the attorney general; W. L. Lee, the chief justice, and others. Halfway around the floor, Caleb Callahan cut in.

"May I, Mr. Minister?"

The wily Scotsman cackled. "Caleb, you rascal, I was just getting on to it."

"I'll save you another dance, Mr. Wyllie," Andria vowed.

Caleb looked awkward in formal wear, as if everything were two sizes too small for him. And on the dance floor his awkwardness was compounded.

" 'Can't make a silk purse out of a sow's ear,' " my mother used to say. "And how right she was. Listen.

Waltz over to them French doors, and we'll get a bit of air. I want to speak privately with you."

Outside on the porch the air was as soft and sweet on the skin as a caress. Andria inhaled the sensual tropical fragrance of jasmine, oleander, honeysuckle, and ohi'a blossoms.

"God, but you are a beautiful creature," Caleb told her. "I can't tell you how proud I am of you. No less than if you were my own kin." He frowned. "Speaking of which—what have you heard lately about Luke?"

"Just that he and his wife are very happy and that his plantation is prospering."

"And expanding every month, so John Yee tells me. Damn it, Andria! When am I going to get to see my son? It's been over a year since we've known he's alive. I may die without seeing him. Hell, I'm no spring chicken."

Andria smiled and patted his arm. "You'll live to be a hundred, Caleb. Look. If you were to reveal yourself at this critical stage of his endeavor as his benefactor, it might wreck his whole life. Luke is a very proud man."

"Too proud to accept help from his own father?" Caleb asked sullenly. "Does he really hate me all that much?"

"He doesn't hate you, Caleb. He wants to believe that he is as good a man as you are and that he can achieve success on his own."

"He is as good a man as I am. Hell! That capital I advanced him is a pittance, and I stand to double, even triple, my investment. That's just plain good business sense. Luke is the one making a go of the plantation."

"I know, and in time he will come to realize that, and then it will no longer matter that you put up the money for him to get started."

"Well, I'm not going to wait too much longer."

"A few more months. Until he reaps the rewards of his first big harvest."

"If you say so. I respect your opinions, Andria, you

know that. So do the king and queen." A sly note that displeased her crept into his conversation. "When are you going to come to your senses and marry David Kalakaua? Now, there's a lad with a head on his shoulders. And my bet is that one day David will be king."

"You and David agree on a lot of things," she said, her tone faintly sarcastic. "He is too ambitious to suit me sometimes."

"Nothing wrong with ambition. I'm telling you that if David were king, this stalemate over the tariff the United States levies on Hawaiian sugar would be fast ended. These God-damned Kamehamehas with their stuffy pro-British attitudes and their reactionary approach to government! It's no wonder they get Uncle Sam's back up! Now Kalakaua, he's altogether different. He wants to be friends with the U.S. Do you realize what would happen to Hawaiian sugar if the import duties on Hawaii's trade with the United States were removed? Sales would soar, go out of sight!"

All at once the sky to the east lit up with an ever expanding and ever intensifying reddish-orange glow, followed shortly thereafter by a series of earth tremors that rattled the palace chandeliers and sent cups of punch and other beverages skidding off tables and crashing onto the floor.

The guests, all shouting with excitement, poured out of the house onto the porch.

"Listen, it's a naval cannonade! We're being attacked by the British or the French!"

David Kalakaua shook his head grimly. "No, those are not naval guns. I expect Pele is on the verge of fulfilling the promise she has been warning us of for the past few months."

"Mauna Loa!" a score of voices said in unison.

"And our plantations lie directly in the line of the northwest and northeast rifts," Caleb said tersely. "Now we'll see if those stone retaining walls will do the job I intended them for."

One of the top-priority projects Callahan had instituted as soon as he began cultivating sugar cane was the erection of ponderous stone walls along the flanks of his land facing the rifts on the slopes of Mauna Loa that marked the principal flows of molten lava in past eruptions.

"That's standard procedure in Italy around Vesuvius and Mount Etna," he had answered critics. "You wait and see, when and if a big blowup comes, you'll be laughing out of the other sides of your mouths."

Now he turned to King Kamehameha. "Sorry to miss this great shindig, Your Highness, but I've got to get back to my sugar fields, see what I can do to save them."

"I'm coming with you," Andria said firmly, and she was adamant against the objections of both Caleb and David.

"All right, the prince conceded finally. "But if you go, I go with you."

She smiled and squeezed his hand. "I'll feel brave with you at my side, David."

"Well, let's skedaddle," Caleb told them. "No time to lose."

At the time of the eruption of Mauna Loa, Luke Callahan was visiting Kiano's cattle ranch in northern Hawaii, just north of Mauna Kea.

"What I'd like to do is to invest in coffee land," he told his friend as they sipped rum and pineapple juice on the white beach in front of Kiano's bungalow.

"The best coffee land is over in the Kona district," Kiano advised. "Why don't you go into a partnership with me? I tell you, this is the best beef country in the world, and within ten or twenty years, I'll be able to sell out for ten times what I paid for the acreage. There's a rich American corporation that has been sounding me out about joining their combine."

"No thanks, Kiano. I'm going to stick with the pastoral life. What has John been up to of late?"

"Working night and day, I hear, on his immigration program. I believe he's planning to go to China personally, to promote the idea."

"I hope to see him before he leaves." He hesitated, and Kiano read his meaning.

"This is your first visit to the big island, isn't it? The closest you've been to Andria in the years since you were separated in China?"

Luke waved a hand in a deprecating gesture. "I never think about her anymore, Kiano. I love my wife. I'm the happiest man in the world."

Well, almost, anyway . . .

That evening in Luke's honor Kiano had a small supper party attended by a handful of his neighbors. A modest *luau* on the beach in front of his house. They had just uncovered the *imu* when the first tremors shook the earth, followed by thunder and a panorama of fire that lit up the southern sky like a bold sunset.

"So it's come," Kiano said with native stoicism. "Tomorrow morning we will ride down there and have a look, my friend."

Luke could not conceal his apprehension. "There is no danger to the residents in that area, is there?"

Kiano laughed. "In most cultures people flee from the scene of a volcanic eruption. We Hawaiians are of more sturdy stock. We seek them out. There is nothing more spectacular than to witness Mauna Loa, or Kilauea for that matter, in action. From a safe distance, that is." He smiled. "You need not fear for Andria. She will be perfectly safe."

"Tomorrow morning, you say? You aren't in any hurry to get there, are you?"

"No, the old girl's eruptions commence on the floor

of the caldera, Mokuaweoweo. It will be two or three days yet before there is any flank activity."

All that night the volcano's angry rumblings shook the island, and a curtain of fire surged and ebbed continuously in the sky.

They rose at dawn. Clad in denim trousers, *aloha* shirts, and Stetsons, they mounted two of Kiano's farm horses and set out for Mauna Loa.

It was a two-day ride, and at camp that night on a high ridge, they could see the flat dome of the "shield" volcano silhouetted starkly against the curtain of fire.

The following day they reached their goal. Hundreds of sightseers had preceded their arrival and, from safe vantage points, were avidly watching the spectacular display of pyrotechnics within the fire pit.

"See—there is the new fracture along the rift zone." Kiano pointed out to Luke a succession of fiery fountains of lava spewing hundreds of feet into the air along the new fissure. "That is what produced the curtain of fire we saw last night."

Later in the evening a team of American geologists, who had been making observations from the summit since the first earth tremors, began hurriedly to pack up their gear and instruments.

Their leader, a Professor Wagner, informed Luke and Kiano, "I think the time is fast approaching when the flanks will give way. In my considered opinion the principal flows will occur on the northwest and southwest rifts. Probably the major flow on the northwest."

"As much as I respect the professor's opinion, I think it is time for us to evacuate the mountain, even though we are on the east side," said Kiano. "When lava first breaks out of the flank, it may flow as fast as twenty-five miles an hour, spreading out as it descends, slowing down and thickening when it reaches the lower slopes. When the flow divides, it leaves high spots like small islands in the molten stream. We call them *kipukas.*"

Luke's brow was furrowed. "If the professor is correct and the outbreaks occur on the northwest rift, how will it affect the Callahan plantation?"

Kiano looked glum. "Not too favorably, I fear. Some of your father's richest sugar cane lies in the path of the northwest rift."

"But you say they will have ample warning to evacuate if the lava overruns the plantation?"

Kiano did not answer immediately, and Luke sensed his hesitation was prompted by reluctance to reply to the question.

"What is it, Kiano? Are they in danger?"

"It is just that Caleb Callahan is a man of great courage and daring. Also very stubborn. Anticipating an eruption of major proportions at some point in the future, he has erected this great stone wall."

"My God! He must be insane! How could a wall stop a river of flaming lava?"

"It has been successful in other parts of the world—depending, of course, on the magnitude of the eruption."

"What you're saying is that my father will remain on the land, like King Canute, defying the ocean's tide. Or an even more apt metaphor, 'He will go down with his ship,' as a good captain should!"

"It is possible."

"And you can be damned sure that Andria will stand by him. She has a measure of courage and single-mindedness as well."

Kiano did not reply.

"Come on, Kiano! To the horses!"

"Where are we going?"

"To my father's plantation, where else?"

Chapter Seven

Caleb Callahan stood on the top of his wall and stared defiantly up at the flaming summit of Mauna Loa. The curtain of fire climbed higher, ever higher, into the sky, black with smoke and ashes now.

All around the plantation there was a mass evacuation of workers and residents of neighboring villages, staggering toward the seacoast under absurd loads of valuables and cherished possessions.

Standing off the beaches was a small armada of boats of every size and variety—sailboats, skiffs, power boats, catamarans, and private yachts such as Caleb Callahan's. There was only a remote possibility that the lava would reach as far as the sea, but the authorities were of the opinion that it was better to be safe than sorry.

Back at the sprawling Georgian mansion that Caleb had built in almost the exact proportions of his San Francisco dwelling, Andria and David were in charge of evacuating the most valuable appointments of the house, paintings, sculptures, tapestries, and silver and gold objets d'art.

"Just in case," as Caleb determined in a taut voice.

The servants piled all of the valuables on carts and wagons and covered the lot with water-soaked canvases to protect them from ashes and embers spewing out of the crater. In the midst of all the swarming confusion, two horsemen rode into the front yard along the sweeping graveled drive that curved up from the roadway.

Andria paid them scant attention. Neighbors and strangers had been coming in and going out since daybreak to confer with Caleb and assess what the best course of action should be when the volcano's giant magma chamber disgorged its lake of fire down the side of the mountain.

When the two riders were almost on top of her, Andria looked up, and her eyes widened in disbelief. She put a hand to her throat and steadied herself against one of the white columns that supported the porch roof. Her vocal cords were paralyzed.

Luke swung down off his mount and climbed the steps. He removed his hat, and his smile was lopsided and somewhat self-conscious.

"Andria—I—" To say anything at all pertaining to their personal lives would be maudlin. So he simply offered, "We've come to help. Just tell us what to do."

Andria took a deep breath and swallowed with difficulty. "Luke—how good of you. Then again, you always were—" She paused to avoid the pitfall he was avoiding.

"Where's my father?"

"Out by the southwest boundary—at his wall." There was an element of scorn in her voice. She addressed Kiano. "It is good to see you again, Kiano. Your cousin David is here with us. Here he is now."

David Kalakaua came staggering out of the front door with an armload of leather-bound books. Kiano sprang to his side. "Here, let me help you."

David's face lit up with surprise. "Kiano! What the devil are you doing here?" He handed over a portion of his burden.

"The same as you, cousin. To do battle with Pele as our illustrious ancestor Kapiolani did."

David grinned. "I fear a handful of berries and the

Lord's Prayer will not stop the old girl this time. It's going to be a big blow, Kiano. Maybe the biggest of all time."

The grin dissipated as he took notice of Luke speaking with Andria. She turned to him.

"David, I would like you to meet Luke Callahan."

Luke's mouth opened to correct her, but he thought better of it. His secret was out in the open now, so what was the difference.

"So you are Luke Callahan," David said softly.

Luke offered his hand. "It's a pleasure. I've heard a great deal about you."

"And I about you." He declined the proffered hand. "Excuse my rudeness, but as you can see, I am loaded down."

"Not at all."

"Let us dispense with amenities, my dear friends," Kiano said. "This is not a tea party. We are all on the brink of disaster."

"Kiano, you help out here," Luke said. "I am going to see my father." He climbed onto his horse. "I'll see you all later."

"Not too much later," Andria called after him. "Persuade Caleb to come back to the house before it is too late. We must flee to the coast as soon as possible."

About a hundred yards from the wall, Luke swung down off his horse and tied the bridle to a tree. His father's brawny figure was a formidable silhouette against the darkening sky. Caleb looked as indomitable as the stone he was standing on. In the distance the immense lava dome of Mauna Loa presented a strange illusion. It appeared to be a living, breathing thing, shuddering and pulsating in preparation for the holocaust. Claps of thunder shattered the atmosphere, and bolts of lightning zigzagged across the sky above the caldera.

Luke strode purposefully toward the wall. He was

less than halfway there when Caleb turned, almost as though he sensed another presence.

An expression of astonishment froze his face. He wiped a hand across his eyes, blinked and shook his head. "I must be dreaming," he muttered.

"No dream, father. It is I, Luke. Back from the dead." His eyes narrowed craftily. "You did think I was dead, didn't you?"

Caleb was equally as crafty. "I never really believed you was dead, boy."

"But you never expected me to turn up here in Hawaii?"

Caleb started to deny it, then shrugged. "I never— oh, what the hell! Word gets around. The islands ain't all that big."

"And who spread the word? Was it John Yee or Kiano?"

"Like I said—No, you might as well know. It was King Kamehameha himself who told Andria you was alive and growing pineapple on Lanai."

"How come you didn't try to find me?"

Caleb's face was hard as stone. "How come you didn't try to find us?"

Luke's mouth curled up scornfully on one side. "I couldn't stand the thought of my Andria being your wife."

"You damned fool! I had to list her as my wife to bring her to Hawaii. I love Andria, that's true. But like a daughter, not a wife!"

Luke threw up his hands. "It doesn't matter anymore. Water under the bridge. I'm married to a wonderful woman."

"To spite Andria?"

"No, I love Leilani."

"Not in the way you love Andria and the way she loves you. You've caused her much grief, boy."

"I'm not a boy, father."

Caleb appeared to sag. "I know that. I'm sorry,

Luke. Look, what are we standing here palavering for, when the whole world may blow to kingdom come any second now."

He bent down to retrieve a barometer from the stones at his feet. His brow furrowed. "Jesus Christ! It's hit rock bottom!"

No sooner had he spoken when the ground began to tremble. The tremors were more severe than any of the others in the past three days.

"This is it!" Caleb dropped to his knees to keep from being thrown down.

Mutely the two men fixed their gaze on mighty Mauna Loa. Suddenly a giant fissure opened in the mountain's flank. It was accompanied by a tremendous explosion that sent Caleb flying off the top of the wall to the ground. Fortunately his fall was cushioned by heavy foliage. As father and son gaped in stupefied horror, great balls of fire and smoke erupted from the gaping wound, and a river of lava—the blood of the goddess, as awed, superstitious natives described it—roared down the mountainside, spreading out to a width of one mile. It traveled with the speed of a tidal wave at first but slowed as it approached the lower slopes.

Everything in its path was obliterated—sugar-cane and tobacco fields, livestock, houses. Small villages were carried off intact on the crest of the molten wave before disintegrating in the blinding heat.

Caleb and Luke got shakily to their feet.

"We'd better get out of here fast," Luke said. "It's heading straight for us."

"No," snapped his father stubbornly. "My wall will hold."

"You're crazy!" Luke shouted over the crackle and roar of the deadly stream and the screaming of hurricane winds. "Come on, be sensible."

He took his father's arm and tried to pull him back in the direction of the house, but Caleb shook him off.

"I know what I'm doing."

"You always were a pigheaded son of a bitch, and you haven't changed a whit!"

"Don't you speak like that to your father, you disrespectful whippersnapper!" Enraged, Caleb rushed at Luke and swung a roundhouse punch at his head.

Luke ducked under and drove a hard right into Caleb's gut. It was like hitting a steel wall, but the older man grunted and gave way briefly.

Then Luke caught a punch on the left shoulder that sent him sprawling, but he was up at once and circling, bobbing, weaving as Caleb kept charging at him like a bull. Like a piston, Luke's left kept flicking into Caleb's face, and before long a trickle of blood issued forth from Caleb's punished nostrils. His left eye was puffed up as well, and he was breathing laboriously.

"You bastard!" he wheezed. "One thing I'll say, you've become a man since the last time I saw you."

Luke thought he detected a note of pride in the statement, and he repressed a smile of satisfaction.

A random punch struck him on the side of the head, and his knees gave way. He backed off clumsily and sat down.

His father stood over him, fists clenched and at the ready. "Well, you had enough?"

"The hell you say!" Luke got up slowly and backed off, determined not to be enticed into a toe-to-toe slugging match that he was sure to lose. Caleb was the heavier and stronger of the two, and there was more power behind his blows. Luke resumed his sparring, torturing Caleb's face with the annoying left. When he saw a chance, he crossed over with a hard right. Twice he jolted his father, and the combination of left hook and right cross finally felled Caleb.

He was on his hands and knees, shaking his head to clear it.

"You had enough?" Luke goaded.

"I'll die first." Painfully he got to his feet and put up his fists.

Luke experienced a touch of panic. The old man meant what he said. He would die before he would give in to any man.

At that critical moment, Kiano and David came running up. "Have the two of you gone mad?" the prince demanded.

He and Kiano interceded between the two combatants, neither of whom offered any strenuous objections.

"There is only one enemy we must face this day," said Kiano. "Pele. See, lava is already halfway here."

"The wall will divert it," Caleb maintained, mopping his bloody nose with a bandanna.

"Not against that colossus," David disagreed.

Caleb wiped his face with the bandanna. "When I first came here, I did a lot of studying up on volcanoes in preparation for this day. Etna, Mount Pele.

"Here's how it works. As the lava proceeds, a pahoehoe crust hardens on the surface, and walls of scoriae, a kind of volcanic slag, build up to channel the flow. What they are, really, are giant tubes that insulate the molten lava inside so it can't harden and the flow can continue for miles with no loss of heat."

Luke was beginning to grasp his father's intent and marveled at the boldness of his concept. "Maybe the direction of the lava could be diverted by punching holes in those tubes?"

"Exactly—and that would slow up the forward lip of the river, certainly reduce its speed and height."

Prince David was awed. "Has this ever been successful?"

"Yup, a Baron Papalardo diverted lava from Catania in Sicily back in 1669. Come on. Let's go back to the house and round up a crew with hooks, crowbars, and sledgehammers."

There were ten of them who clambered up the mountain, skirting the main flow of the lava. They were bundled up in heavy clothing, hats, face cloths, and gloves, all soaked in water.

About a half mile above the forward lip of the flow, Caleb signaled that here was where they would make the bold effort. It was the widest part of the stream, and the scoriae walls of the natural channel were bulging under enormous pressure of both lava and gases.

There were already hairline cracks in the barrier, and they had to sidestep and leap away from numerous little rivulets of lava that crawled among them like fiery serpents. Red and blue flames licked at their feet and legs and ignited the brush. As they got nearer to the river of fire, the heat became scorching.

"We got to get this done fast and get out and up the hill before the dam breaks," Caleb instructed them. "All right, let's rush in and get to work with these picks and crowbars, whatever you're equipped with."

It was the kind of job that required absolute concentration on one's own part of the task. Luke swung his longshoreman's loading hook at a break in the slag wall from which issued a steady trickle of lava. In seconds he had widened the breach to a diameter of a foot, and now the lava continued to enlarge the gap with its own weight and pressure. The heat was stifling, and for one bad instant he thought he would perish on the spot. But with adrenalin pumping through his veins, he managed to stagger away and on up to higher ground. Kiano, David, Caleb, and the other men were right behind him.

From a comfortable distance they watched to see if their handiwork had accomplished its purpose. There were a dozen rents in the scoriae of the sort that Luke had effected. Building from thin trickles to fiery spouts and, at last, to a steady gush of molten lava, all merged into one stream as it flowed down the gulley to the northwest.

All at once the scoriae around the expanding openings began to tremble, and there was a loud crackling noise like a thousand window panes shattering at the same time. Caleb whipped off his hat and slapped it hard against his thigh.

"We did it, men! She's aiming to come apart. *There!*"

The rest of them sent up a cheer as a portion of the containing wall at least fifty feet long disintegrated with a deafening reverberation. A waterfall of liquid fire tumbled down the draw, sending up a shower of flaming sparks that dazzled the eye.

"Let's go up higher where we can get a look at the forward lip," Caleb yelled.

From a jutting vantage point on a bluff that commanded a fine view of the retaining wall and of the plantation behind it, they studied the main flow of the lava. Without any doubt it had diminished and slowed down. Meanwhile, the rate of the diversionary flow continued to accelerate as the chasm widened.

"What's gonna happen," Caleb predicted, "is that all that stuff down there is gonna harden, now that it's losing heat and pressure from behind."

They looked on in tense silence as the front lip moved closer and closer to the wall below. It reached the stone and commenced to climb. One foot. Two feet. Three.

"Stop, you bastard!" Caleb shouted and shook his fist as if it were a mortal enemy.

"Don't, you will offend Pele," David said dryly.

Caleb gave him a savage glare, but said nothing further.

At a height of five feet, the rise was so gradual that it was almost imperceptible. Still the gap between the pahoehoe crust and the top of the wall kept getting narrower and narrower.

Caleb swore softly to himself.

Only six inches stood between the relentless river of fire and the plantation and house behind the wall.

"I think—" Luke was afraid to say it, lest the fates punish him for his brashness.

Five minutes, ten minutes, fifteen minutes passed.

The gap had remained constant, and the shiny, glassy whorls on the surface of the pahoehoe began to darken and glitter as the crust cooled.

Beaming with relief and pleasure, Caleb Callahan went around and vigorously shook each man's hand.

"I want to thank you all for your support and your courage. Damn! I was the only one who had a stake in the matter. The rest of you risked suicide without any gain in prospect."

"Good works are of benefit to all men," said David Kalakaua. "All of us on these islands, we are all brothers. The English poet Donne said it best: 'No man is an island, entire of itself; every man is a piece of the continent, a part of the main. . . .' "

Luke scratched his stubbed chin and reminded them, "Only one problem now. How do we get back to the house, to Andria and the others? We can't cross that lava."

The new flow was widening and flowing vigorously.

"We'll just have to follow it down the mountain until it stops, then skirt around it and double back," said Kiano.

They started down, keeping a comfortable distance between them and the glowing river.

Chapter Eight

A fleet of small rowboats and catamarans ferried refugees from the districts imperiled by the fast-flowing lava from the beaches on the Kohala and Kona coastline to the larger rescue crafts standing offshore.

"Women and children first!" Andria, with the help of Lee, was directing the evacuation.

Many of the Hawaiians were reluctant to leave, arguing with some logic that no volcanic lava flow had reached the sea since the 1801 eruption of Hualalai. But when the tremendous earth shock hurled everyone on the beach to the sand as Mauna Loa's flank blew out, their doubts were resolved. Now everyone tried to get into the boats at once, creating confusion and havoc as several overloaded crafts capsized. Many of the men swam out to the big rescue vessels.

At last no more than a score of evacuees remained on the beach, including Andria and Lee. They were in the act of loading the last two boats, a paddle-wheel ferry and a large catamaran, when a man wearing only a loincloth raced down from the timberline shouting at the top of his lungs, "It's coming! The lava is coming! It's like a river from hell. We must all get away at once!"

Breathless, he piled into the ferry with Andria and Lee and ten other passengers.

"Engine on full power!" the skipper shouted, and

they pulled away from the beach with the side wheels whirling as fast as the engine could drive them, her steam boilers quaking from the strain.

They were halfway to their goal when a man, his face contorted in terror, pointed up at a high bluff down the beach.

"It's here! Oh, Lord, help us!" He crossed himself, as did other Christians aboard.

They watched transfixed as the great river of molten lava tumbled majestically over the rim of the bluff, and a waterfall of fire fell in slow motion into the sea below.

The ensuing minutes—how long exactly Andria could not determine, due to shock—seemed endless. A montage of cataclysmic proportion would be stamped indelibly on her subconscious mind for the remaining years of her life and haunt her dreams: Great geysers of steaming water shooting high into the sky all around them; the ocean floor writhing as if in the throes of fiendish pain; the eerie screeching of the high winds that were generated by the clash of fiery lava and cold water.

Quick thinking by the captain narrowly averted a disaster as an enormous maelstrom suddenly formed and seemed bound to suck the ferry into its bottomless vortex.

Then the sea began to boil like a gigantic caldron of water, bubbling and steaming furiously. All kinds of fish were hurled into the air, many of them falling back into the boat, as fully cooked as if they had been baked in an *imu!*

And then the real horror: as the winds rose and the cascade of lava continued without respite, a mighty tide was created that caused the sea to rush out from the beaches at breakneck speed.

Andria could only think of the Red Sea parting for Moses and his followers.

The ferry and the catamaran were carried out on the

crest of a huge wave. Three other craft, which had departed from the beach ahead of them, were destined for tragedy. When the oceanic upheaval began, the craft were so close to the rescue vessels that people already had their arms outstretched to clasp the rope boarding ladders. The boats were tossed about like wooden chips, and two of them were sent crashing into the sides of bigger vessels. A good many of their occupants were flung like rag dolls into the boiling water to die horrible deaths. Their screams of agony assaulted Andria's ears like the shrieks of lost souls ringing out from hell. With one arm she covered her eyes, and with her other hand, she held on to an iron ring in the ferry's deck for dear life.

Just as abruptly as it had begun, the direction of the tide was reversed, and they were hurtling back toward the beach on the crest of a tidal wave.

They were carried five hundred yards inland, almost to the timberline, then careened back on a long slide of water as the sea retreated to its natural condition.

Now the tiller took hold again, and with the captain at the helm, the side wheels drove her steadily out to the rescue ships. The ill-fated catamaran had been sucked into a maelstrom; all of her passengers were condemned to being boiled alive.

Those aboard the ferry were trembling with fear and were too weak to climb the boarding ladders. Ropes were lowered so that they could be hoisted aboard. They sat or lay sprawled on the deck with other survivors, eyes glazed, benumbed from the shock of their ordeal, as the ship set out to sea, heading for destinations further south down the Kailua coast, saved from the tenacious grasp of the goddess Pele.

There was a grand reunion supper at the Hulihee Palace, an intimate affair attended only by the Kamehameha clan and the Callahans, along with a few government dignitaries. Dress was informal.

King Kamehameha presided at the head of the banquet table. Understandably, the eruption of Mauna Loa dominated the conversation.

"The geologists at the institute say the flow may go on for weeks, even months, under the sea," the foreign minister advised them.

"What are the casualty figures so far?" Luke wanted to know.

"Officially none," Chief Justice Lee said with a straight face.

"That's ridiculous!" Andria said. "We *know!* We were there!"

"It is only when members of the *haole* are killed that casualty lists are issued," David said, a trace of malice in his voice that elicted a look of stern disapproval from Caleb Callahan.

"Not a *kanaka* or a *wahine* was killed from my plantation," Caleb declared.

"You actually keep records on each one of your workers, Mr. Callahan?" Kiano asked disarmingly.

Caleb flushed. "My lunas know each man and woman in their work gangs."

"And if a kanaka or two turns up missing, do you really believe that the luna of the work gang will report it to you? He will merely pocket the poor devil's wages and make do with what he has, work the remaining men twice as hard."

"Not on my land," Caleb maintained doggedly.

"And what of your plantation, young Mr. Callahan?" The king thought it prudent to change the subject. "I understand that you are fast becoming the pineapple king of Lanai, of all Hawaii, in fact."

"A slight exaggeration, Your Highness," Luke replied. "But I am doing very well, indeed. Far better than I would have dared hope when Scotty and I began our venture."

"How is Mr. MacIntire these days?" Kiano inquired.

"He has a touch of rheumatism, but after all, he's

well past sixty." He smiled. "How far past he won't say. No, for his age, Scotty is in fine fettle."

To the king's chagrin, the topic of annexation to the United States came up. His anti-American views were no secret, but he had no wish to taint the festive atmosphere of the evening by political haranguing.

Caleb Callahan was equally as inflexible in his pro-annexation views, and he was a powerful influence in the white establishment that was pressuring the government to draft a new constitution, more liberal than the one adopted under the reign of Kamehameha the Third. The current king, on the other hand, was calling for a constitution less democratic, one that would restore power to the monarchy and promote a revival of pure Hawaiian culture. If the king's efforts prevailed, the white men's ambition of making Hawaii into a republic would suffer a critical setback, and annexation to the United States—with the sure tariff benefits it would bestow on the sugar growers—would become a remote possibility indeed.

"Cannot some compromise be effected whereby in return for certain concessions on our part, the United States could be persuaded to remove the high import duties on Hawaiian sugar?" Prince David speculated.

"What sort of concessions?" the king wanted to know.

"I think I know what David means," said John Yee. "Never before in history has the presence of the United States been so strongly felt in the Far East as it has in the past decade. This extension of American influence in this part of the world requires an expansion of its Pacific fleet. Napoleon said that an army marches on its stomach. By the same token, we might say that a navy sails on drinking water and fuel. The Hawaiian Islands provide the indispensable link between mainland America and mainland China."

"No, never!" said the king, controlling his temper with effort. "Betray Hawaii's sovereignty by permitting the Americans to establish naval bases on our territory? I will not hear of it!"

"It is not my idea of an ideal compromise either, uncle," said the prince. "But in the coming of age of this once innocent and idyllic land, practicality must take precedence. Realism over idealism, if we ever hope to take our rightful place in the modern, industrial world."

"Well put, Prince David," said John Yee. "In pursuance of that course, I see no reason why we cannot conclude a reciprocity treaty with the United States."

"Bully!" Caleb said enthusiastically. "If that can be accomplished, the national income of these islands will double. No—it will *quadruple!* By George! Do you know what I think I'll do? I'm going to make a trip back to the mainland. Washington, I got a lot of friends there. Johnny Breckinridge, the vice-president, for one. I'll see what I can do to get the ball rolling in our direction."

"I do believe we are boring the ladies," the king said, with some agitation. "David, it was my impression that the Princess Kapiolani was to be present here this evening?"

"She was indisposed and sends her profound regrets, Your Highness," David replied without expression.

The truth was the princess's indisposition was due to Andria's presence at the dinner. From puberty, Princess Kapiolani had been assured by her parents that her betrothal to Prince David Kalakaua was a fait accompli. The royal family had given its blessing to the match. David himself felt a deep and sincere affection for the lovely Kapiolani and would have been perfectly content to marry her—but that was before Andria entered the picture.

After dinner the king and his statesmen, along with Caleb Callahan and a few select guests, retired to the king's library for coffee, brandy, and cigars.

Luke, Kiano, David, John, Andria, and Liliuokalani went for a stroll on the beach. The full moon seemed to fill up the sky, and sand and sea were laved in its silvery luminosity.

The quickening tattoo of native drums against the sensuous, high-pitched whine of nose flutes drifted to them from far down the beach. In the distance torches appeared like a swarm of fireflies.

"A *luau?*" Luke wondered.

"No, the *luau* has long been over. The *hula* has commenced. Shall we go down and watch for a while?" David asked.

"I'd love to," Andria said. "I never tire of watching the hula."

It was a good fifteen-minute hike, and the women removed their slippers and gathered their long skirts up about their thighs for comfort's sake.

Luke found himself casting covert glances at Andria. Her pointed, unfettered breasts strained against the fabric of her gown with every step. They were larger than when he had caressed them lovingly that never-to-be-forgotten day on the mountainside above the mission. His finger tips began to tingle as he thought of that magic interlude. He could close his eyes and feel the velvet texture of her skin. There was an ethereal quality about her beauty in the moonlight, but it did not overshadow the earthiness of the woman. Her long, slender, bare legs moved with the precision of scissor blades, calves arching proudly, her buttocks flexing with every undulation of her hips.

The revelers, seated in a circle within a ring of torches stuck in the sand, were clapping their hands to the rhythm of the drums. Prince David's party stopped just outside the fringe of firelight, so as not to break the concentration of the *hula* dancers, three lithe young girls with bare breasts that glistened in the torchlight.

"For more than forty years, the missionaries have been trying to ban nudity in the islands, but our ingrained sense of Polynesian innocence still prevails. The human body is an *objet d'art,* not an object of shame. I mean, would you take a beautiful vase or statue and swathe it in shapeless cloth to conceal its beauty?" Kiano sighed.

Luke had observed on occasions when members of the white establishment attended such affairs, the dancers' attire and movements were more conservative. This celebration was exclusively a Hawaiian party.

When the dance concluded, Prince David indicated that they should now join the gathering. "My friend Kono is the host. Come and meet him."

Kono, a squat and muscular man with features resembling those of an American Indian, welcomed them warmly. Like all of his other guests he wore the *kihei,* a togalike robe that was common to men and women.

"What will you have to drink? Kava, *okoleohao*— English scotch, if you prefer?"

"Has the entertainment ended for the evening?" David inquired after they were settled and had their beverages, served in halved coconut shells, before them.

Kono did not reply immediately, and an enigmatic smile played around his lips. He glanced at Andria and at Princess Liliuokalani, who were talking to each other. Then in a low voice he said to David, "No, the festivities have not ended as yet, my friend. But I am not certain that your sister and Andria would be comfortable with the pagan nature of the next dance."

David grinned. "You can't mean one of the ancient Polynesian or Tahitian mating rituals?"

"That is precisely what I do mean. You understand that participation is a prerequisite if one attends this function?"

"I will ask the ladies and let you know." David went over to Andria and his sister and explained the situation to them.

"Of course, the dance has become strictly ritualistic, playacting, if you will. In the old days couples actually paired up and went to the women's hut to consummate the union. Now the dance terminates before that phase." He smiled. "Although there are adventurers who prefer to adhere to the old customs and play the game to the natural conclusion. Shall we join in, or do you want to go back to the palace?"

Andria clapped her hands. I think it would be great fun to join in. What about you, Lili?"

"A mating dance! I wouldn't miss it for the world."

"You're going to have to change into more suitable attire," he advised them. "Much vigorous activity is involved."

Kono's financée took them up to a bungalow off the beach and outfitted them with loincloths, grass *pa'us* and *leis* made of *ohi'a* blossoms.

"I feel positively wanton," Andria said, inspecting herself in the parlor mirror.

The girl laughed. "That is how one is supposed to feel at a mating dance. Reckless and wanton."

Lili giggled. "If Uncle Alex could see me now, he would have apoplexy."

The three returned to the beach, and the dance began. The men and women lined up in two rows facing one another across a strip of sand ten feet wide and strewn ankle deep with a variety of exotic blossoms and flowers. At a sign from the *olohe*—the dancing master—the drummers began tapping their finger tips on the taut drum heads. They played ever so gently in the beginning, then gradually picked up tempo and began a crescendo. The flutes came in now, and all of the musicians sang out a chant:

> *"Oh, Laka, give grace to the feet of Poharku,*
> *and to her bracelets and anklets.*
> *Give comeliness to the figure and skirt of Luukia.*
> *To each one give gesture and voice.*
> *Oh, Laka, make beautiful the lei; inspire the*
> *dancers to stand before the assembly. . . ."*

There was a primitivism about this ritual such as Andria had never before seen in any of the multitudinous dances she had witnessed since arriving in Hawaii. A quality savage, sensual, and primeval. She shivered as a trickle of perspiration sent goose bumps along her bare spine. Her heart was beating furiously, and her breath no longer came so easily.

She was surprised when she realized that she was dancing along with all of the others; it was almost a reflex body language that her limbs, hips, shoulders, and hands were articulating without her volition. The frenzied monotone of the drums, punctuated by the whistle of the flutes, had a hypnotic effect on Andria.

Eyes glazed, she stared across the bower of flowers that separated male from female, scanning the line of men. Physical desire stirred in her loins at the sight of their hard, lithe, muscular bodies, rippling from head to toe from their rhythmic convolutions, patently sexual in expression. Her gaze held on Luke. His beautiful body was almost as bronzed as the kanakas'.

God! She recalled so vividly the sweet hunger that had possessed her when she had run her fingers over his flesh that one time they had been together. How ravenous her body had been for his caresses, his lips on her turgid nipples, his fingers stroking over her heaving belly and down between her quivering thighs. Andria closed her eyes and bit her lips to prevent herself from crying out her unrequited love, like a bitch in heat baying at the moon in mourning for a lost mate.

Everything was unreal now. Instincts, laying in hibernation beneath the thin veneer of civilized womanhood, were in full control. Undulating and gyrating, shaking and thrusting with their hips and buttocks, the women moved in a sinuous line from their side of the arena, around the bower of flowers, to the side of the men. Down the row they danced, appraising their male counterparts, never once losing the cadence of the dance. Then they circled around the men and moved back down the row behind them. Repeating the ritual, they danced in front of the men once again.

Only this time they danced slower and with purpose. A girl stopped in front of one man and stepped back into the bed of flowers as the others passed her by. Her smile was a wanton invitation as she stepped out of her grass skirt, removed her *lei,* and stood before him naked but for her loincloth. Andria caught a last glimpse of the two as the girl stepped forward again and slipped the lei around his neck. Without a word he took her hand, and the two of them trotted off together, melting into the darkness of the trees.

Again and again the ceremony was repeated, the ranks of males and females diminishing. Andria was only dimly aware that she was standing in the flowers before Luke, stepping out of her *pa'u.* His face shimmered wraithlike as it did in her frequent dreams of him. This, too, was a dream, of course. Consumed with lust, she stepped forward and placed the *lei* over his head.

Lost in lustful abandonment, he was powerless to resist her allure. Dazed, he took her hand, and they ambled away together while David Kalakaua looked after them, miserable and dejected.

They made love on a mattress of moss, soft as the bed of grass where he had taken her virginity.

Andria took his dear face in her hands and kissed him softly. "It is no use denying my eternal love for you, my darling."

"Nor my love for you, sweet. God knows! I've tried desperately to forget you!" He shook his head. "I feel like such a bastard, deceiving Leilani the way I've been doing for years."

"Your wife—yes—" He felt her stiffen beneath him. "What manner of woman is she?" She could not entirely hide the note of jealousy.

He looked into her eyes, reflecting twin images of the overhead moon, glittering like blue sapphires. "A wonderful woman. You two would like each other. That's the damnable thing about it!"

"You must have loved Leilani, or you would not have married her?"

He was wracked with anguish. "I do love her. I love her in so many ways." He hesitated. "But I have never loved her the way I love you, with my whole heart and soul and every cell of my flesh. You, Andria, you are a disease in my blood—no, hear me out. Neither you nor I can be held accountable for my treachery against Leilani, any more than if I had been taken away from her by plague or cholera. It all lies in the hands of the gods."

She shook her head, and tears dissipated the reflection of the moon in her eyes. "I understand. Oh, Luke, darling, make love to me again. Now!"

He entered her, and for a long while they held each other very close without moving.

"I never feel totally whole unless we are together like this," she whispered. "One body."

After the tender and profound emotion that she experienced at that moment, her orgasm was an anti-climax.

"What are we to do?" Andria asked Luke on the way back to Hulihee Palace. They were straggling behind the others. David Kalakaua had left the beach party soon after Luke and Andria had disappeared into the woods.

"The only honorable thing to do. I will return to my father's house with him in the morning. Stay until everything is back to normal at the plantation, and then I will return to Lanai and tell Leilani about us."

She squeezed his hand. "Poor Leilani. My heart suffers for her. To lose you whom she loves so dearly." A shudder ran through her body. "How she will hate me, and I cannot blame her."

"Did you hate Leilani when you discovered I was married?"

"At first. Until I learned the true circumstances of what happened. But this is different, Luke. You rightly belong to her. She is your wife."

He sighed. "I've never truly belonged to anyone else but you, darling."

"Just the same, I can't bear to even think about the pain I am causing the poor girl."

He stopped and pulled her around to face him. "It cannot be helped, Andria. There have been too many wasted years for you and me. From this point on, we will never be apart again for the rest of our lives."

They kissed chastely and continued on down the beach.

Next morning Luke and his father, along with Kiano, returned to the plantation. Except for a small parcel of land in the northwest corner, it was relatively unscathed, thanks to Caleb's idea to divert the main lava flow.

Luke and Kiano stayed on a few days to help restore order and get the laborers back into the fields. Andria had remained in Kailua-Kona at the request of the king and queen to attend a conference of the Hawaiian Board of Christian Missions, in preparation for the founding of Queen's Hospital.

On the night before Luke and Kiano were due to depart and return to Kiano's home on the northeast coast, father and son drank together on the veranda until after midnight.

"You fixing to go back to Lanai and stay put?" Caleb asked.

Luke shook his head. "No, I intend to return here and—" He hesitated.

"Stay with Andria," Caleb finished.

Luke sighed and slumped in his chair. "That's about it, father. I love her, and she loves me, and that's all there is to it."

"I told you that the day you came back here."

"I know you did, but I didn't want to believe it. Then when I saw her—when I touched her—when I—there aren't words eloquent enough to describe how we feel toward each other."

"So be it." Caleb raised his glass. "To you and Andria."

They drank solemnly.

"And to my grandchildren," Caleb said slyly. "You two won't keep me waiting too long, will you?"

Luke laughed and leaned over to grab his father's knee. "We'll do our level best. You know something, father, right now I feel closer to you than at any other time in my life."

Caleb slapped his son's hand with fierce affection and averted his head so that Luke would not detect the mistiness in his eyes. "Amen—my son."

A week later to the day, Luke stepped ashore on Lanai. Scotty was there to greet him at the quay. He pounded Luke's back and was grinning like a Cheshire cat.

"Welcome back, partner. We all missed you. How did things go on Hawaii? Did you option any coffee land?"

"No, I was too preoccupied with Mauna Loa. You heard about the eruption, of course?"

"Heard *about* it? We heard *it!* Sounded like the world was coming apart."

Luke told him all that had happened on Hawaii. Not quite all—Leilani deserved the courtesy of being the first to hear about Andria and him.

Luke put his luggage in the back of the horse-drawn wagon, and they started back to the house where Leilani was waiting for him.

"What in the hell are you grinning like a jackanapes for?" Luke asked curiously.

Scotty kept on grinning and winked. "You got a surprise waiting for you back at the house."

"What kind of a surprise?" For some reason Luke had the sensation that an icy hand had come down softly on his shoulder. He actually could feel the deathly cold fingers through the fabric of his shirt. The cold and merciless fingers of fate.

"You'll find out soon enough. Giddyap!" He shook the reins.

Leilani came running down the graveled path to meet him, her face aglow. She had never looked more radiant. Or more healthy. Almost too healthy, he thought.

She smothered him with hugs and kisses. In her own excess of love, she did not sense the reticence within Luke.

"Oh, my darling, I missed you so. If you had not returned today I would have died pining away for you."

He smiled stiffly. "You don't look as though you've been pining away. In fact you've gained weight."

Her delighted laughter, along with the hearty conspiratorial laughter of Scotty MacIntire, sounded exceedingly ominous to Luke.

"What's the big joke?" he asked tightly.

"Joke—oh, Scotty, listen to him! You silly, lovable man! You are so right, I have put on weight. And can't you guess why?" She stepped away from him and spanned her hands across her round belly.

Luke could only gape at her in speechless wonder.

"Darling, we're going to have a baby. You and I. Luke, Junior—I know it will be a boy. Oh, I love you so." She threw herself upon him and hugged him so tightly he thought his neck would snap.

Scotty was pounding his back again. "Congratulations, partner. You're gonna be a father. What about that! I took her over to Maui to see Doc Baldwin when she started to get the morning sickness. I figured what it meant, and Doc confirmed it."

"A baby," Luke said tonelessly.

"Yes, my one and only darling, a baby! Our baby!

Oh, I'm so relieved you're back home with me. You can't believe all the terrible calamities I invented. The boat would sink. The goddess Pele would destroy you." She giggled. "Or that you had run off with another woman! Go ahead! Tell me what a silly goose I am!"

"You are a silly goose," he said woodenly, forcing himself to smile.

Arms encircling each other's waists, they walked up the path and into the house.

Luke's heart was a ball of lead in his chest.

That night after Leilani had gone to bed, he sat down at his desk and picked up the quill pen.

My darling Andria,

How can I begin? What can I say? Where are the words? There are no words to express my eternal love for you. And at the same time there are no words to describe the sickness that eats away at my heart because of what I must now tell you. My darling Andria, I . . .

BOOK
THREE

Chapter One

Dear Luke,

I just learned that you have sold out all of your holdings to the Dole family and are returning to the United States with your family. I wish you good fortune and good health in the years to come. We shall miss you. As David says, you have become a true native son worthy of the appellation *nui* kanaka.

Your father continues to amaze everyone here on Hawaii with his inexhaustible stamina and energy. He is very disturbed, however, over the vigorous anti-polygamy campaign being waged back in the States and which is beginning to make itself felt here in the Islands. Charity has confided in me that she is seriously thinking of renouncing her place as his second wife and returning to California.

At long last David Kalakaua is on the verge of realizing his lifelong dream of becoming king. With the death of Kamehameha the Fifth, as you know, the last of that royal lineage became extinct, so a successor was chosen by popular election. Both David and the Dowager Queen Emma were soundly defeated by the liberal, likeable, pro-American Prince William Charles Lúnalilo. Still David's hopes were not dashed. He always said that Lunalilo was of frail constitution, and his ominous view proved to be accurate. The elected king scarcely reigned one year, and his death *has been attributed to the immense responsibility of the high office.*

The election race between David and his aunt, the dowager queen, has been a bitter and often unruly contest, with followers on both sides engaging in physical violence, intimidation, and bribery. Now the tide seems to be turning decisively in favor of David. If he is successful, I hope his victory will not go to his head. He has always had a fanatic lust for power and eminence, and an attitude of total ruthlessness with regard to the methods by which his goal can be achieved. I am not certain that he will be a benevolent monarch. No, that is not precisely so. I do think he may be a benevolent despot. Only time will tell.

Luke, please send my very best wishes to your wife Leilani and to your two lovely daughters. They must be quite the young ladies now. Even when I last saw them two years ago, they were very precocious.

Once again before closing, good luck, God be with you, and goodbye, dearest friend.

                                                   Andria

Andria just caught the tear before it fell onto her signature.

There was a gentle tapping on her bedroom door.

"Come in."

It was the Princess Liliuokalani, now married to John Dominis, governor of Oahu. Andria was spending a holiday with the couple in their stately white frame house on Beretania Street, across from Iolani Palace.

"What are you so excited about, Lili?" Andria inquired.

Lili was literally jumping up and down with joy. "It's official, John just came in. David has been declared the winner. He is our new king! Do come down and toast his victory with us, dearest."

"Of course. I'll be right along, as soon as I seal my letter."

Not long after that, David arrived, fairly bursting

with triumph. He swaggered, he strutted, he preened. His chest was inflated, his chin was tucked in tightly against his chest; somehow he reminded Andria of illustrations in history books depicting Napoleon Bonaparte.

He came into the library and embraced his sister and Andria. He Andria kissed him on the mouth. He shook hands with his brother-in-law.

"Congratulations, old man," said John.

"Isn't it marvelous?" David was not a man for modesty, nor was he a gracious winner. He rubbed his hands together, savoring the moment of victory. "God! I'd like to see the face of the old cow right now, dear Aunt Emma! If we feel any earth tremors, it won't be Mauna Loa. It will be the dowager queen blowing her top!" He slapped his knees and doubled over in laughter.

Andria and Lili managed stiff smiles and self-consciously avoided looking at each other. John Dominis cleared his throat and made a fuss of tamping down the tobacco in his meerschaum pipe.

To everyone's surprise and Andria's chagrin, David requested that Lili and John let him speak to Andria alone.

"Urgent state business," he said pompously.

"That wasn't very courteous of you, David," Andria said impatiently, after Lili and John had left the room. With unveiled sarcasm, she added, "Or would you prefer that I call you Your Majesty?"

David flushed. "That isn't funny, Andria. I was perfectly serious. This is private—state business."

"Just the same, you had no business dismissing Lili and John in their own house!"

"Oh, hell! If it will make you feel better, I'll apologize to John. Maybe I'll even give him a title worthy of the husband of a crown princess."

Andria rolled her eyes toward the ceiling in exasperation. "Oh, David, you are impossible!"

He gazed at her with admiration and embraced her again. "What a hellion you are, daring to talk to the king in such an insolent fashion. And I love you for it. Your pride, your courage, your imperial bearing. Oh, my darling, you are my equal. Not like my fawning consort, Kapiolani. It isn't too late, you know. You still could be my queen."

Shocked, Andria tried to push him away, but he was too strong for her. "David, stop it at once! You're a married man."

"She's merely a consort, not a true wife. I mean, the king can do as he pleases. If I decide to dissolve my relationship with Kapiolani, it shall be done as quickly as this!" He snapped his fingers.

"David! Let go of me!"

"Not until you let me kiss you once more."

She had no choice but to submit or create a scene that would bring Lili and John back into the library. Her lips were unresponsive as he pressed his lips ardently to hers. Angry, he pushed her away roughly.

"There was a time when you were eager for my kisses. To have my hands stroking your naked body. To have me enter you. Do you deny it?"

Andria could only hang her head and maintain silence. It was a sensitive nerve-ending that he could strike time and time again, knowing it would reduce her to humility.

He persisted. "Everything was ideal between us until *he* came back into your life. What a laugh! How it must devastate you to think that he gave up you, *the great love of his life,* for that little *wahine* slut!"

"Leilani is a sweet, wonderful woman and a fine wife and mother," Andria said quietly.

"Is that why you can't bear to look at their children? Always thinking that they could have been yours?"

"How can you be so cruel, David?" She brushed the back of her hand across her eyes. "David, don't you understand? How could Luke leave her when she was pregnant? He's too fine a person to do a dishonorable thing like that. I respect him for his decision. I—" She paused.

"You *love* him for it! You still love a man who is hopelessly lost to you."

"I do." Proudly she held her head high. "Don't you see? So long as Luke was dead to me, I could give myself to you. But when I discovered he was alive, everything changed. I couldn't go on with you, David, knowing that the greater part of me belongs to Luke. It wouldn't be fair to you!"

"Suppose you let me be the judge of that."

"It's no use, David. We've been over it a thousand times."

"And we will go over it a thousand more times. You'll see. In the end you will submit to my reasoning."

"Submit?" She smiled wanly. "What a typical word that is for you to use."

He held up his hands. "All right, let's declare a truce." He grinned. "Until the next time. Now about this business—I want you to come with me to America."

"To America? Are you mad?"

"I was never more serious. Let me tell you, I am not about to sit around on my *okole* like my predecessors, sipping *'awa* like some primitive Polynesian chieftain. I intend to make my presence known in the world. You'll see. In due time my name will be as familiar in Europe and America as the name of Queen Victoria.

He began to pace up and down with his distinctive foot-stomping style, hands clasped behind his back.

"My first goal as king will be to cement relations with the United States. Visit with President Grant personally, one world leader to another. Work out some compromise whereby the United States will remove this yoke, the sugar tariff, from about our necks. Naturally, I will take a delegation with me, and I am appointing you as a member of that delegation, Andria.

I cannot think of anyone who will make a better good-will ambassador. Will you accept?"

Andria was dumbfounded. "I don't know what to say, David. This is all so sudden."

He took her hands. "Don't do it for me. Do it for Hawaii. You have always been so dedicated to good works that make our nation a better place to live in. Even Queen Emma would agree with the soundness of my decision, and we scarcely agree about anything."

"Let me think about it for a time?"

He laughed confidently. "You do that. Now we must attend to the details of my coronation."

There was a knock on the door.

"What is it?" David asked irritably.

"It's very urgent, David," his sister called out. "John Yee is here to see you."

David strode to the door and opened it. He shook hands with John, who along with John Dominis, entered the room. "My friend, you look so grim," David said to John Yee.

"Things *are* grim, David."

"Don't talk foolish, John. John Dominis has assured me that the vote of the legislative assembly is a mere formality. My supporters outnumber Queen Emma's by better than six to one."

"Your support in the legislature, perhaps, but not among the people. Queen Emma holds a cherished spot in the minds and hearts of the islanders because of all the charitable works she instituted during the Kamehameha regime. There is a mob forming outside the courthouse right now."

John Dominis consulted his pocket watch. "It's just about time for the voting to begin. I must go to the courthouse at once."

"I'll go with you," David said.

"I would not advise it, David," said John Yee. "Your appearance there would incite a riot. Look, Henry Peirce, the American minister, is waiting for you at the

Palace. The *Tuscarora* is at anchor in Honolulu Bay, along with the British warship H.M.S. *Tenedos*. Peirce would like your permission to alert their commanders to the impending trouble and request, in case of a riot, that American and British marines be landed to restore order."

"Never! Permit foreign troops to perform a military action on Hawaiian soil that our own militia and police force are perfectly capable of handling without interference? Never!"

"David, don't be an ostrich," John Yee said with blunt irreverence. "Our police force has already deserted en masse. And as for the militia, the companies are so sharply divided politically that they might start warring among themselves. No, if there is an uprising, we must enlist the help of the Americans and British."

David Kalakaua slumped in dejection, his regal air of a few short minutes ago thoroughly deflated. "As you say, John." He turned to Dominis. "You had better be off, John."

"I'll go with you," John Yee offered.

"So will I." Andria went to the hall closet to get a shawl and bonnet.

"I forbid you to go, Andria," David called after her. "You heard what John said. There's a mob there in ugly humor."

Determinedly she pulled the shawl around her shoulders. Her blue eyes sparkled mischievously.

"You said I was your first choice for a good-will ambassador. Maybe I can promote a little good will among the mob. Come along, John."

The scene around the courthouse, where the legislative assembly was preparing to take an official ballot to determine who would be the next ruler of Hawaii, was foreboding. The supporters of the dowager queen were shouting and waving clubs in the air, as belligerent a mob as Dominis and John Yee had ever seen.

In the absence of the Hawaiian police, a small contingent of the white establishment, led by Sanford Dole and Charles Harris, were attempting to keep some sort of order. They were posted at the front and rear entrances to the courthouse. Although they remonstrated conscientiously with the dissidents to maintain law and order and abide by the outcome of the election, their efforts were met with increasing uproar and unruliness.

Dominis and Yee ran interference for Andria, and eventually they managed to battle their way into the building.

Dole frowned at Andria disapprovingly. "Ma'am, this isn't any place for a female. All hell is about to break loose here!"

Andria smiled at him pleasantly. "It won't be the first time in my life that I have been at that locale, Mr. Dole. By the way, my congratulations. I understand you have purchased all the holdings of Luke Callahan on Lanai?"

"Thank you, it was my good fortune. Callahan has one of the best spreads anywhere in the Islands."

They were interrupted by a clerk who came rushing into the lobby, waving a document in the air.

"It's official! David Kalakaua is the winner, thirty-nine votes to six for the dowager queen."

His voice carried over the crowd, and the word was passed along to those in the rear. The clamor swelled to alarming intensity, and the mob surged up to the steps of the courthouse.

"You'd better take cover, Miss Callahan!" Dole yelled.

Andria took refuge in the second-story courtroom where the balloting had taken place. The members of the assembly were in the process of breaking up their forum when she came bursting into the room.

Dominis, who had preceded her upstairs, rushed to a window and looked down at the street. "God! They're storming the building. Can we barricade the door?"

"We can try," someone answered him. And the legislators hurried to stack benches and chairs against the entryway.

The rioters had easily overcome the defenders at the courthouse doors and were rampaging through the building, vandalizing and ransacking offices, and calling, "Death to the traitors!"

Ultimately they concentrated around the courtroom where the assembly members were barricaded. "We've got them now," someone shouted. "I can taste their blood!"

A thunderous cheer went up. Forming a human battering ram, they pounded away at the heavy door. Inexorably the barrier gave way, inch by inch, and then at last it collapsed like a broken dam, and the rioters flooded the chamber.

The legislators battled desperately and courageously, but they were hopelessly outnumbered. One by one they were beaten into submission. Some were cast ruthlessly out of windows and fell twenty feet to the ground.

At the onset Andria clambered up on the judge's bench, armed with two gavels. The melee swirled all around her. Whenever an insurgent came within her range, she clubbed his head with the gavels. She floored a half dozen before an angry contingent dragged her off the bench.

"You traitorous wench!" a ringleader snarled. "What should we do with her, fellow *kanakas?*"

"Rape her to death!"

"Hurry!"

Lascivious hands tore at her clothing, and Andria fought back like a wildcat, scratching at her tormentors' eyes with her fingernails and kicking at their groins.

Her dress and petticoat were ripped off. Wearing only her lace-trimmed knickers and her camisole, she was exposed to their lustful stares. In another few seconds she would have been stripped naked, but then a provident cry went up from those rioters near the window.

"Troops! American and British marines. Flee!"

They broke off the fray and rushed out of the courtroom, falling over one another in their haste, and raced out of the building—as the newspapers later described the retreat, "like rats escaping from a burning barn."

On February 13, 1874, at Iolani Palace, David Kalakaua in the presence of the United States' minister Peirce and the British and French commissioners, was sworn in as the sovereign of the Hawaiian Kingdom.

That same afternoon the dowager queen Emma issued a statement supporting and recognizing David Kalakaua as Hawaii's rightful monarch and urged her followers to pledge their allegiance to him for the good of the nation.

It was the victory of a lifetime for David. "The reign of Kalakaua will be recorded in the history books as second to none, including the illustrious term of Kamehameha the Great," he promised.

At the victory celebration that evening, Andria was approached by Sanford Dole. "May I have this dance, Miss Callahan?"

"It will be my pleasure, Mr. Dole." She gathered up the long skirt of her ball gown in her left hand, and he led her twirling onto the floor.

"You look ravishing, my dear."

"Thank you, sir, and you look very handsome."

His eyes twinkled. "If I wasn't a married man, let me tell you—"

They both laughed, and impulsively Andria said, "Speaking of married men, do you know when Luke Callahan and his family are to leave for the mainland?"

"Last week in February. As I was telling you the other day, I got a good deal on his plantations. Oh, I paid a fair price, but I could have been persuaded to pay more. Callahan didn't bother dickering. He's anxious to get back to the States."

"Why is he so anxious?"

"Didn't you hear? His wife is very ill with tuberculosis. He wants to take her to a clinic somewhere in Europe that specializes in consumption, hopeless cases."

Her lips were wooden, without sensation so that it was difficult for her to articulate. "Hopeless? Oh, no—it—*can't* be so!"

"I'm afraid it is so, ma'am. Last time I was over there to finalize things, she looked like death."

"Death—"

Abruptly she stopped dancing.

"Miss Callahan, are you all right?" Dole inquired anxiously. "You're so pale of a sudden."

"I—I—it's just that the waltz always makes me dizzy. Would you mind if we sit down?"

"To be sure." He escorted her to a chair on the sidelines. "Would you like something to drink."

"Yes, please, a fruit punch."

She closed her eyes tightly. With every ounce of willpower at her command, she thrust the thought out of her mind: *Leilani dying. One day soon, Luke would be free of his marital obligations!*

"You are a detestable bitch, Andria!" she said softly. She thought that if she were holding a dagger in her hands at that instant, she would have plunged it into her heart to end the pain that was twisting her apart inside.

Chapter Two

On November 14, 1874, King David and his party—which included Henry Peirce, Governor Dominis, John Yee, Andria Callahan, and other Hawaiian dignitaries —left Honolulu aboard the U.S. *Benicia* for San Francisco. From San Francisco they would travel by train to Washington, D.C.

"He certainly didn't waste any time," John Yee said to Andria as they stood at the stern, watching Oahu diminish and finally vanish over the horizon.

"Do you believe he can accomplish his purpose, John?" she asked. "I mean, he has such extravagant dreams. World renown, confidante of presidents and kings." She smiled. "Sometimes he's almost childlike. Do you know what one of his principal ambitions is?"

John nodded. "To be the first world monarch to circumnavigate the globe. Can you imagine?"

"What I am afraid of is, that his idea of being a king is all play and no work."

John sighed. "Yes, and any lackey who bows and kisses his feet and tells him how wonderful he is, is eligible for a government post. You know, delegating authority to qualified subordinates is an essential quality of good leadership, but when authority is spread too thin among too many subordinates, a state of chaos is almost certain to ensue."

Andria agreed. "I remember that my mother's benefactor at the French legation in Canton used to say of China that there were too many warlords and too few warriors."

"Much the same as the American version, as frequently stated by Caleb Callahan, 'Too many Indian chiefs and not enough Indians.' Well, I must say that King David's odyssey to the New World is fraught with interesting possibilities. Time will tell. . . . Would you care to go below and have a cup of tea?"

"I'd like that." She took his arm, and they headed for a companionway that led down to the salon.

Over tea and biscuits served with jam, Andria suddenly asked, "John, how is it that you never have married? We keep hearing rumors about all of the predatory females in the Islands who are continually throwing themselves at you to no avail."

"That's not true. I see many lovely ladies and wine and dine them and—" He laughed self-consciously. "Are you trying to pry into my sex life?"

Andria blushed. "I'm sorry, of course not. It is just an enigma to me why such a handsome, successful, and charming man chooses to remain a bachelor."

He bit into a cake. "Variety is the spice of life."

"Not in my experience," she said softly, and her eyes went out of focus briefly.

"You are thinking of Luke," he said intuitively.

"That's absurd."

"I think you should get in touch with him and find out how Leilani's health is."

"I couldn't do that, John," she said, distressed.

"Why not? A truly compassionate inquiry won't alter the destinies of either Leilani or Luke."

After some thought she said, "Therein lies the point, John." Her eyes held steadily on his. "It would not be a truly compassionate inquiry. Need I explain?"

He shook his head and looked away. "I understand. Perfectly. It is why you would not marry David Kalakaua. Nor any of the other suitors who have sought your hand in marriage."

"We appear to have that in common, my friend."

"In common, what?" he asked warily.

"We are constantly avoiding the hooks they cast in our direction."

He laughed. "Hooks? You think of us as fish, then? Hah! That accounts for my adeptness in staying free and single. These ladies, they are employing the wrong instruments. Remember, Tongdlon is a turnip, not a fish. What they should be using is an earth spade. That is how one digs for potatoes."

Andria was delighted. "Tongdlon. It's been so long since I heard you called that. Big Turnip, indeed!"

John watched her in silence, in his head reciting a soliloquy:

What we really have in common, Andria, is that you have never married because you are in love with Luke Callahan; likewise, I have never allied myself with any one woman because I am hopelessly in love with you. I have been since the first instant I set eyes on you in the garden at the Mormon mission. Hopeless, because I saw from the start that you and Luke were made for each other, and neither one of you could ever have eyes for anyone else. And with my Oriental prescience, I am convinced that one day you will be together once again and enjoy true happiness until the end of time, here and in heaven.

The enthusiastic reception that King Kalakaua received in the United States seemed to justify his unwavering faith in his destiny to become an exalted ruler. Invitations from every major city in the nation poured into the royal suite wherever he stayed. New York offered to finance a full-week's visit for the king and his entourage. Washington, D.C., invited him for two weeks. His good-will tour was covered by every notable daily paper in the U.S.

"He's like the Pied Piper of Hamelin," John Yee mused to Andria as they stood on the sidelines watching him perform in the center of a gaggle of reporters, all swilling imported champagne.

The highlight of his triumphant visit was his stay in the nation's capital, where he was greeted by cabinet officers, senators, representatives, Supreme Court justices and by the vice president and President Ulysses S. Grant himself. The king's personal popularity notwithstanding, the majority of the members of Congress were opposed to endorsing any measure that would establish a reciprocity treaty with Hawaii that might eventually lead to outright annexation.

On December 18 the Congress hosted a lavish reception for the king and his party. The guest list read like a *Who's Who* of Washington, D.C. It had all the color of an inaugural ball. The men wore white ties and tails. The women were garbed in peacock raiment of every hue and fabric. On the dance floor the overall image was that of an array of pinwheels whirling in the wind atop a notions stand at a state fair.

Andria's gown had a myriad of stars on a background of midnight-blue silk; it was wasp-waisted, with petite balloon sleeves and a voluminous skirt. Her hair was done up in two rolls held in place by gold combs inlaid with mother-of-pearl, and she wore a simple headdress, *boutons d'or*.

As the evening wore on, the prospects of negotiating a reciprocity treaty seemed more remote. As John Yee saw it, the major hurdle was Hamilton Fish, secretary of state.

Andria took a different viewpoint. "There is only one man here tonight whose opinion counts, and that man is President Grant. If he can be persuaded, all other opposition becomes meaningless."

"And how do you propose we obtain the president's backing?" John demanded.

"I don't know," she admitted. "But there must be a way."

"Let's change the subject. Mister Fish is heading in our direction."

The secretary of state was a slim man with a military carriage and the proud profile of an eagle. He stopped before them, and honored Andria with a quick bow.

"Miss Callahan, Mr. Yee. Are you enoying yourselves?"

"It's been a delightful evening." Andria smiled. "I am disappointed in just two respects."

The secretary's eyebrows lifted. "I say, that will never do. You must not leave here with any disappointments, my dear. We will rectify that at once. What is your pleasure?"

"I have yet to have the honor of dancing with you or with President Grant," she said, tilting her head coquettishly.

Flustered, the secretary tugged at his cravat. "Oh, come now, a pretty thing like you can't possibly wish to dance with two old fuddy-duddies like myself and the president. All night you have been besieged by every young dandy in the room."

She fluttered her eyelids. "My taste runs to more mature and distinguished gentlemen. Ah, the 'Blue Danube,' my favorite Strauss waltz." She held out her arms to him.

"All right, by Jove, we'll have a go at it, you young vixen."

He clasped her right hand at shoulder height and put his right hand on the small of her neck, keeping a sedate distance between their bodies, and led her onto the dance floor.

"My wife says I have two left feet," he advised her, "so you undertake this venture at your own risk."

"You underestimate your ability, Mr. Fish. You are remarkably light on your feet."

After a minute of idle chatter, she asked him bluntly, "How do you feel about reciprocity, Mr. Fish?"

He stared at her, flabbergasted. "I don't imagine that a majority of the ladies present even know the meaning of the word."

"You might be surprised just how many ladies *do* know what it means, as well as being knowledgeable about other political topics."

"Then you must be familiar with the objections voiced by a good many Americans living in the Hawaiian Islands on the matter of reciprocity?"

"I am. They mistakenly believe that if we conclude a treaty it will postpone annexation to the United States."

"Exactly. Conversely, the sugar and rice planters here in the states claim that reciprocity will *lead* to annexation. And yet another faction is fearful that the terms of such a treaty would be dictated by California refiners such as Claus Spreckels, because high-grade sugars are not permitted free entry. In other words, 'damned if you do and damned if you don't.' It's a political hot potato, Miss Callahan. Undoubtedly it will be passed off quickly from hand to hand until it cools off and can be unobtrusively discarded."

He waltzed her to a side of the room where President Grant was conversing with King David and other members of the Hawaiian delegation.

"Mister President, this young lady has just voiced a most unusual request. She would like to dance with you."

Grant cast a mock scowl at his secretary of state. "What's so unusual about that, Ham? The young lady has good taste as well as exceptional beauty. I am honored, Miss Callahan."

Ulysses S. Grant was a man who gave the impression that he was larger than he actually was. He had a leonine head and impressive bearing that dwarfed the lesser men around him.

He removed the black cigar from his mouth and handed it, along with his water glass of whiskey, to an aide. Then he bowed to Andria and took her rather awkwardly in his arms.

Yet once on the floor, he proved to have a good sense of rhythm, and he was an assertive partner.

"You dance like a general," she joked.

"And how is that, miss?"

"You're masterful and decisive. You move boldly."

He laughed and winked. "Courage comes in a bottle. I told President Lincoln that once. And when members of his cabinet complained that I imbibed excessively, do you know what Mr. Lincoln told them? He said, 'Find out what brand he drinks and send a couple of barrels to all of my other generals.' "

Andria laughed appreciatively. "You must tell that story to King Kalakaua."

"I already have. He has quite a sense of humor, your king. Bit of a playboy, I think."

"He is that, only I would call it a keen sense of adventure rather than being a playboy. He really isn't frivolous. He is an extremely conscientious leader rather like yourself."

"Yes, I recognize that. I admire him for making this long journey himself when he could just as well have sent an emissary."

"The issue of reciprocity is much too important to King Kalakaua to trust anyone other than himself."

"Yes, I know that." His expression was grave. "I only wish I could hold out more hope to him than I can realistically. You see, this is a highly controversial subject."

"A hot potato, I know. Mr. Fish explained it to me."

"And what do you think, Miss Callahan?"

"Well, let us put aside the obvious benefits to the Hawaiian economy that a reciprocity treaty would produce. Let's consider what the benefits to the United States would be."

"I don't want to seem patronizing, Miss Callahan, but the United States is virtually independent, economically speaking."

"I wasn't thinking in economic terms, Mr. President. I was thinking of reinforcing the security of the United States, insuring U.S. dominance in the Pacific."

"Go on, this is highly interesting."

"I'm sure King Kalakaua has not spoken of it to you, because it would be a breach of ethics against the premier of New Zealand."

"What about the premier of Australia?"

"New Zealand—but he is acting as spokesman for Australia. For that matter, he is a go-between representing the British Empire. The premier of Australia has offered Hawaii a sizable loan to balance our budget and has guaranteed that Hawaiian sugar will be admitted duty free to Australia, New Zealand, Canada, and other British possessions. The French are prepared to equal that offer. Don't you realize what that means?"

"I think so. Hawaii will become an appendage of the British Empire. What you are saying is that the United States cannot risk *not* ratifying a reciprocity treaty with Hawaii."

"Not unless you do not care if we fall into the hands of the British and the French."

Grant was thoughtful. "This little conversation has been most enlightening, Miss Callahan. Will you join me in a drink?"

"I would be honored." Her eyes twinkled. "You never did say what brand of whiskey it is that you drink."

He laughed and winked. "State secret, my dear."

"I must remind King Kalakua to send you a case of our *okoleohao.*"

"That sounds very potent, indeed." He took her elbow and escorted her off the dance floor and over to a refreshment booth.

"What suits your fancy, Miss Callahan?"

"I like the pink champagne. It reminds me of an exotic Hawaiian wine."

"Champagne for the lady and whiskey for me, my good man," he told the bartender. He held up three fingers. "Neat, please."

When they were served, he proposed a toast. "To the peace and harmony between our two great nations."

"And to free trade between Hawaii and the United States," she added.

President Grant laughed. "Have you ever thought of entering politics, young lady?"

"Oh, but I have already," she replied with a straight face.

He cocked his head to one side and studied her intently. "Yes. In fact that was a clever piece of politicking you engaged in while we were dancing." He took one of her hands and kissed the palm. "The king is a fortunate man to have a friend and adviser such as you, one so beautiful, so wise, and so charming. Now, if you will excuse me, I see Mrs. Grant looking for me. And she has fire in her eyes."

As the president departed, John Yee sidled up behind Andria. "You seem to have made quite an impression on President Grant."

"And I think I impressed him with the urgency of getting Congress to pass a reciprocity bill."

"You are a remarkable woman, Andria Callahan."

A page boy approached them. "Are you Mr. Yee, sir?"

"Yes."

"Minister Peirce would like to speak with you, sir."

"Where is he?"

"Come with me, sir."

"I'm coming, too," Andria said, and they followed the lad out of the ballroom and down a corridor to a small study. Henry Peirce was standing before a blazing fire, warming his hands. He turned and smiled.

"Do come in, Mr. Yee. I'm pleased you came, too, Miss Callahan, inasmuch as what I have to say concerns you as well."

He led them over to a desk and picked up a lengthy telegraph dispatch. "This is in reply to the inquiries I have been making into the whereabouts of Mr. Luke Callahan."

Andria's hand flew to her throat, and her heart skipped a beat. *Oh, dear God!*

"You've found him, then?" John said excitedly.

"I believe so. I received this by special messenger from our ambassador in Bern, Switzerland. It has been ascertained that a Mr. Luke Callahan and his family are currently residing in Wunderbad, a small resort town in the Valais Alps. It has been a renowned health spa for centuries. The mineral springs reputedly have effected miraculous cures for hopeless cases that were given up by medical science."

"His wife, Leilani, has tuberculosis," Andria said tersely. "Is there any word—" She could not finish. She had no right to ask such a ghoulish question: *Is she still alive?*

The two men looked at her expectantly.

"You were about to say?" asked Peirce.

"Nothing, it's not important. Well, this is most welcome news, Mr. Peirce. We are both relieved to hear that Luke and his family are well."

"Family, to be sure—I meant his daughters. You said his wife *has* tuberculosis. I regret to say it must be in the past tense—*had*. Poor Mrs. Callahan passed away in November."

John Yee saw the blood drain out of Andria's face, and, as she began to sway, he went to her side and took her arm.

"Steady there. Are you all right?"

"Yes, thank you. I think I'll sit down if you don't mind."

John helped her as Peirce rushed to a server and fetched her a snifter of brandy. "Here you are, Miss Callahan. I'm sorry to have been the bearer of such distressing news. We will all mourn the death of Mrs. Callahan. She was a lovely woman, so I hear."

"A wonderful woman." Andria's hands were trembling as she accepted the glass, and she held it in two hands so as not to spill it. She sipped the brandy until it was gone, while John and the American minister chatted about the success of the reception for King Kalakaua.

"That reminds me, I must speak to President Grant and Mr. Fish before the affair breaks up." Peirce excused himself and left John and Andria alone.

"Well?" John asked finally.

"What do you think I should do, John?"

Without hesitation he answered, "There is no question of what you should do. You *must* go to him, Andria. Right now he needs you more than anything else on earth. He needs your love."

"And I need his love," she said in a low voice. "Dear God! How desperately I need his love!"

Chapter Three

A horse-drawn sleigh transported Andria from the railroad station to Wunderbad. There were three other passengers, two middle-aged women and a young, gaunt man with a hacking cough.

Which of the baths are you attending?" the stout blonde woman inquired in a German accent.

"I'm not here for the baths," Andria replied. She hesitated. "I'm visiting a friend."

"Ach, how I envy you. Would that I were here on a holiday instead of sitting in hot mineral water all day for my rheumatism."

"I wish I was sitting in a hot bath right now," the young man said. He tied his muffler tighter around his throat and shivered. "Does it do nothing other than snow in this Godforsaken country?" he complained to the driver.

"You don't like snow, you don't come to Switzerland," the old man replied indignantly, then muttered to himself in German.

Andria was delighted with the novelty of Switzerland, so unlike her beloved Hawaii except for the snow-capped summits of Mauna Loa and Mauna Kea. The grandeur and majesty of the landscape left her feeling breathless. A fairy-tale land, all sparkling white, set on the very top of the world, or so it seemed to her. Wherever one looked, north, south, east, west, snowy mountain peaks brushed the sky. The swirling white flakes fell on her face like wet kisses. She had never felt more exhilarated in her life. She flung up a hand to deflect a snowball hurled at the sled by a mischievous lad at the side of the road, and she laughed. The jingle-jangle of the bells on the horses' reins was sweet music to her ears.

The two women disembarked at a quaint inn in the heart of Wunderbad, and the sled proceeded to still another inn where the young man got off.

"Der Kurort is a spa famous for curing consumption," the driver said when the fellow was out of earshot. "But from the looks of that poor devil, it is going to take more than mineral water to fix those lungs."

Andria was reminded of Leilani and lapsed into silence, her good humor dampened.

"The Chalet am See is on the other side of town. Not too much further."

Despite the cold, the palms of Andria's hands were sweating, and the drumbeat of her heart made her uncomfortable. Now that she was here, the plan seemed weird and farfetched. One didn't travel across two oceans and one continent and then halfway across another, on the spur of the moment as she had done, and walk up to someone's door and knock and say, oh so casually, "Hello, Luke. I just happened to be in the neighborhood and thought I'd drop in and say hello."

She had half a mind to tell the driver to take her back to the depot.

"You're behaving like a lovesick schoolgirl, Andria!" she chided herself.

The road went up a slope for about a half mile, then the sleigh made a sharp turn around a hummock of white, and there it was, Chalet am See. A magnificent dwelling, strung out over the uneven landscape like a snake, built into the mountainside on three plateaus. The leaded-glass windows were aglow with light, and smoke curled up into the stormy night from three tall chimneys. The pungent scent of burning logs intoxicated Andria. She could almost hear the crackling of the flames.

As the sleigh drew up in front of the steps, a huge St. Bernard dog came trotting around from one side of the house and began barking. His gruff bark echoed back and forth from the surrounding mountains.

"Whatever is it?" Andria demanded nervously. She had never seen a dog even close to his size before. "A bear?"

The driver laughed. "Bear, is it? That is funny, madam. It's a dog, and a very friendly beast at that. He's named King. Come along."

He got down off the seat and went around to help Andria descend. "I'll bring your luggage presently." He walked to the back of the sleigh.

With mounting trepidation Andria approached the front door. King came trotting up to her, wagging his bushy tail. His enormous muzzle came to her chest level.

"Nice doggy," she said, reaching out a tentative hand to pat his head. "Good boy, King."

Before she could knock, the door swung inward and a pale trapezoid of light spilled out across the steps. A young girl was silhouetted in the doorway, her face hidden in shadows. She admonished the dog. "King, stop that silly barking."

Then she saw the sled and Andria. "I say, father, we have company." She called back into the room.

"Lucy?" Andria said as she climbed the steps.

The girl stopped. "Do we know you?"

Andria laughed. Swathed as she was in fur coat, boots, two mufflers, and a fur Cossack's hat, it was no wonder she was unrecognizable.

"Don't you remember me, dear? Andria Callahan, an old friend of the family's."

"Andria!" Lucy shrieked in astonishment. "Whatever are you doing here in Switzerland?"

"Andria!" She knew his voice even before he appeared in back of his daughter. Husky but gentle. A tremor raced down her spine. Then, there he was!

She hesitated on the threshold. "Luke."

They stood there motionless, gasping at each other. Speechless.

"I don't believe it," he said finally. He rubbed his eyes, not trusting what he saw before him.

"I'm real, honestly," she replied. "May I come in?"

"Of course! What's wrong with me? It's just the shock. I'm numb all over. Andria, dear." He took her hands and pulled her into the room.

Lucy threw her arms around her neck. "Andria, it's a true miracle. Do you know we were talking about you at supper last night? Oh, it's so wonderful to see you!"

Andria put an arm around the girl and kissed her cheek. "It's wonderful to see you. Wonderful." Her eyes cut to Luke, and her cheeks were warm with pleasure. Before he could look into them, she averted her eyes, afraid they would betray her. She was consumed with so much love for this man, yet dared not show it. Not so soon after his tragic bereavement.

"Here. Let's get those wet clothes off you, and then you must warm yourself before the fire."

He helped her remove coat, boots, hat, and mufflers. "Lucy, take these out into the kitchen and have Mrs. Muller hang them up behind the stove. And then call Lani." To Andria. "She's upstairs reading. Had a touch of cold and fever."

"Then she mustn't get out of bed. I'll go up to see her."

"In a minute, but first let's have a look at you." He stepped back and appraised her, head tilted to one side, pressing the knuckles of one hand against his square jaw. "Beautiful as ever," he said, and his eyes devoured her.

"I must look a mess after the long train ride. And—"

"You are gorgeous." He stepped closer and put his hands on her shoulders and stared into her face. "Your eyes, I do believe they are even bluer than I remembered."

"Just older." She smiled timidly, trying to muster up courage. "Luke—I—don't quite know how to say it."

"About Leilani." He nodded, understanding how difficult this was for her. "Leilani was a fine woman—and a fine mother. My two daughters, there is no greater gift any woman could have bestowed on a man."

"They're beautiful girls. Fine human beings. Like you and Leilani. How I grieve for the three of you, such a loss to suffer."

"A great loss. At least she did not suffer unduly. Not until just before the end. I had the best specialists in all of Europe. They could not arrest the disease. Wunderbad—coming here was a final, desperate attempt. She was happy here."

"It's so beautiful, Switzerland. And so much snow."

His expression hardened. "Too much snow. Two weeks without letup. There have been avalanches throughout Valais."

"But we are in no danger here?"

He shrugged. "Any time one lives on a Swiss mountainside with thousands of tons of snow and ice hanging over one, the danger always exists. But enough of avalanches." He took her hands and led her over to the hearth.

He moved a loveseat nearer to the blazing logs and bid her to sit down. He stood over her, his arms folded across his chest, contemplating her.

"We both know why you came all this distance."

"Please, Luke, it's too soon—"

"No, it's not too soon. All the years you and I have martyred ourselves so as not to hurt Leilani. God knows, I wouldn't have harmed a hair on her dear head. I loved her for what she has been to me, the children she gave me, but I can't lie to myself, and neither can you. What you and I feel for each other is an eternal flame. Neither time nor distance nor absence has ever been able to quench it. You came to me when you heard she was dead because you love me as passionately as I love you."

Andria buried her face in her hands and began to weep silently. Luke started to reach for her when Lucy came into the room.

"Your clothes are taken care of, Andria, and cook is brewing tea." She stared at Andria. "Andria, what is it? Why are you crying?"

Andria looked up and smiled through her tears. "It's nothing, dear. I'm just so happy to be here with all of you."

"And we're so happy that you are with us, aren't we, father." She went over to Andria and put her arms around her neck.

Luke, his eyes misty, too, embraced them both. It was a minute of silent communion, more expressive than any spoken words.

At last Andria said, "And now I must go upstairs and see little Lani."

"Little Lani?" Luke joked. "What about that, Lucy? Why, Lani is almost as big as this one."

"Not quite," the older girl sniffed. "Besides, I am much more mature and developed." She threw back her shoulders to show off her breasts, petite but assertive.

Andria and Luke laughed, and the three of them went marching up the broad staircase, arms linked together.

Because it was a special occasion, Lani, despite her fever, was permitted to bundle up and come downstairs for dinner. They ate at the long table in the large dining room with the beamed cathedral ceiling arching over them.

"This is such a magnificent chalet," Andria said.

"It was the work of Walter Schickhaus, the great Austrian architect."

"Chalet am See—what does it mean?"

"House by the lake. Didn't you notice the lake down the hill from the road? In summertime the view from the front yard is breathtaking."

Frieda Muller was a round, jolly woman who obviously enjoyed the hardy fare she prepared three times a day: fat sausages, golden eggs, home-baked bread, cakes and pies, knockwurst, bratwurst, liverwurst, pigs' feet, tongue, and on this night, sauerbraten with thick, rich gravy, highly spiced from days of pickling, served with fleecy potato dumplings.

"Not like Hawaiian cuisine, but formidable in its own right," Luke said, over an after-dinner cigar.

"It's absolutely marvelous. I think if I eat another mouthful, I will burst." Andria spanned her swollen stomach with both hands.

"Oh, but you must save room for Frieda's torte with whipped cream."

Suddenly the wind picked up with such ferocity that the chalet creaked and groaned from one end to the other. Luke bounded out of his seat.

"What is it, Luke?" Andria demanded.

"It could be the prelude to an avalanche."

"Avalanche!" Lani exclaimed. "Oh, daddy, I'm frightened!"

"No reason for fear. Not in this house. It was designed to withstand avalanches. The great stone bulwark out back, shaped like an arrow's head, will divert the snow around the house." He grinned in reminiscence. "Andria, do you remember my father's wall, how it saved the plantations when Mauna Loa erupted?"

"How could I forget." Despite his reassurances,

Andria became increasingly anxious as the house continued to creak and tremble. And now, above the banshee wail of the wind, there was another more ominous sound like thunder. It rose in volume and intensity, as did the quaking of the mountainside.

At its high point Andria had the sensation that a giant locomotive was bearing down on them at breakneck speed. The sound was terrifying but mercifully brief. Then it was rushing past them and down the mountainside, fading rapidly in the distance.

The wind ebbed as abruptly as it had commenced, and earth and house settled down peacefully once more.

"Is it over?" she asked him.

"Yes, I must go to the village at once. From the sound of it, the avalanche swept through the outskirts of Wunderbad on the other side. They will be mustering rescue teams."

Andria put an arm on his shoulder. "Do be careful, my—" She omitted the instinctive "darling" because of the presence of the children.

He smiled and said in a low voice, "I will be. You think I want to lose you again after so many years apart?"

She yearned to kiss him but resisted the urge. Luke, sensing the reason for her reticence, purposefully kissed Lucy, then Lani, and, lastly, Andria. He gave her a quick but sweet kiss on the mouth. Then he went into the foyer and fetched a heavy, fleece-lined jacket from the closet, along with high boots, a face mask, and a woolen cap. As an afterthought, he removed a pair of snowshoes from their hooks.

"I may well need these. I'll be back as soon as I can. You three sit by the fire and wait for me. Frau Muller will fix us a pot of hot chocolate when I return."

Lani clapped her hands in glee. "Oh, goody! Oh,

this is so much fun having you here! Andria, do you play cribbage?"

"As a matter of fact, I do. Your grandfather Callahan taught me back in Hawaii."

"How is grandfather?"

"Still healthy and robust, and he sends his love. Now, where is that cribbage board?"

Outside the snow was still falling, but the wind had subsided. Luke donned his snowshoes and slogged down the road toward the village. Fifteen minutes later he arrived at the village square, where a search party was forming.

Bewildered, frightened faces were pressed to the windowpanes in the buildings facing the square. The luxurious Valais Spa dominated the scene. Curious patrons were jammed on its open balconies, babbling excitedly and shouting questions to the townsmen in the square, who pointedly ignored them.

"What's happening, Klaus?" Luke inquired of a burly blonde giant.

"The slide missed the village, except for the farm house of the Schultz family on the outskirts. Carried the place all the way down to bottom of the valley."

"Well, what are we waiting for?"

Equipped with torches and sounding rods, the group of twenty started down the mountain, traversing it until they arrived at the path of the avalanche. The huge mass of snow and ice had gouged a wide swath out of the snowy terrain, wiping out everything—trees, shrubs, and wildlife. It was so clean and straight that it might have been machine made.

Following the trail downhill on snowshoes and skis, they soon reached the pileup on the valley floor, a sizable mountain of snow in its own right.

"All right, men," Klaus yelled. "Let's get to work." The fanned out around the base of the white mass, their torches held high and the long sounding poles clutched like harpoons in their other hands. Methodically they made their way up the steep, slippery incline, every few feet jabbing the poles down into the snow as deep as they could reach. It was an arduous and tedious operation, and it was almost an hour before the first cry went up:

"I've struck something!"

The searchers gathered around the discoverer and were joined by two shovel crews who had come up behind the forward contingent.

"Dig!" a chorus shouted, and everyone joined in. Those who were without shovels used their mittened hands.

Eight feet down they found the first sign—not of life, but of death. A frozen arm and hand stretched out of the snow as if clutching at salvation in the final moment before the soul departed the body.

They rapidly uncovered the man. It was Bernard Schultz, the eldest brother. Within another hour they had retrieved the entire family of five—father, mother, daughter, and two sons. The stiff bodies were shoved into burlap sacks and placed on sleds that the diggers had brought along. Then they began the long trek back up the mountainside toward the village.

They were halfway there when the wind began, shaking the crowns of the trees like rag mops, building to such force that it blew them off their feet. And the rising crescendo of thunder came in its wake, along with the trembling of the earth. All of it was far more violent than the initial avalanche.

"Oh, God, help us!" someone cried. "Look up there!"

Luke stared, transfixed at the spectacle far up the mountain directly behind the village. A wall of snow a half mile wide, it appeared, was moving down the slope, slowly at first and then gaining momentum.

The sight of it took him back to Hawaii, back to the glorious days when he and Kiano would compete in the ancient Polynesian water sport of surfing. Balanced precariously on the slim, sharklike boards made of koa wood, they would wait tensely as the gigantic wave hurtled toward shore. And the monster, roaring thunderously, would be towering over them, some of the foaming crests thirty feet high.

The descending avalanche reminded Luke of such a wave, a wave of snow ten times higher than any wave of water he had challenged. This time the element of challenge was nonexistent. No man could hope to come away alive from this encounter. Unless—

"Take to the trees!" Luke shouted. "It's our only chance. We can't outrun it or outflank it."

He kicked off his snowshoes, divested himself of torch and sounding rod, and ran to the nearest tree in a patch of forest to his left. Unpruned virgin trees, the branches were close to the ground, and Luke began to climb them as if they were rungs of a ladder.

Others were following suit. Breathless, his arms weary, Luke stopped when he reached a spot about ten feet from the top of the tree. Removing a rope from his mountaineer's belt, he sat down on a thick branch with his back to the bole and strapped himself firmly to it. He turned his attention back to the oncoming avalanche.

There was no escape for the people of the village and the patrons of the three luxurious spas. Many hid in their stone cellars, which would become their tombs. Others preferred the quick oblivion that the rampaging snow would inflict on them. Hardier souls remained in the taverns, drinking their beer and whiskey and proposing macabre toasts to God, to the devil, and to the better life hereafter.

Within two minutes after the wave rolled across Wunderbad, the city and all of its homes, public buildings, and the three baths were obliterated. There were miraculous exceptions. The four Skinner children were asleep in their common bedroom when the avalanche hit. Three died in their beds. The fourth was hurled out of a window and was borne along on the crest of the white wave until it stopped at the bottom of the valley. He was the sole survivor of the catastrophe. The father and mother were later found kneeling in prayer in the church, their arms around each other. A half dozen other villagers shared the good fortune of the Skinner boy and were carried along on top of the torrent of snow and ice until it spent itself; they received nothing worse than scratches and bruises.

Back at the chalet, Andria took the girls upstairs when they heard the first distant rumble and felt the tremors. Calmly she told them to lie down on a big double bed of sturdy brass and covered them with four thick featherbed mattresses. Then she got in with them and put her arms around them. "The important thing is not to panic. You heard what your father said. This house and the wall behind it are designed to ward off avalanches."

Lucy managed a brave smile. "I'm not afraid now that you are with us, Andria."

"Well, I'm frightened to death!" Lani said, and she began to cry.

The roaring grew louder and louder, and the house screeched in agony as if it were being ripped asunder, but the architect had done his work well. It remained intact even after the snowslide struck. Momentarily the retaining wall held fast, and great geysers of snow and ice shot off on either side of the house.

Then, as the pressure built up with ton upon ton of the snow pounding at it, it had to yield—but in one piece! The tremendous bulwark was pushed down to the back of the house, and then the house itself was uprooted from it's foundation and was carried downhill by the avalanche. Faster, faster, faster, like a runaway express train.

The children were shouting and screaming, but their voices were eclipsed by the thunder of the avalanche. Andria shut her eyes and began to pray, *"The Lord*

*is my shepherd, I shall not want. He maketh me to lie
down in green pastures. . . ."*

From his treetop perch, Luke watched in horror
as the ocean of white swallowed up the little village
of Wunderbad. From the breadth of the wave, awesome and luminous in the light of the full moon, he
knew full well that it must have demolished his chalet
and that Andria and his daughters had perished. His
one consolation was that within a few minutes he
would join them.

Impassively he watched the wall rush downhill toward the forest. He closed his eyes an instant before
it was upon him. The impact smashed him against the
bole of the tree, and he blacked out.

When he recovered, he was astounded to be alive.
And his astonishment grew tenfold as he realized that
he, along with the entire forest, was speeding down
the mountain almost as if they were being transported
on a gigantic sleigh. The snow mass reached the
bottom of the valley and continued on up the other
side of the valley until it lost all momentum. It came to
a great shuddering stop at last, and the shaggy crowns
of the trees swung from side to side and finally were
still.

"Is anyone else alive?" a voice called from an ad-
joining tree. A half dozen voices answered him.

"Do you believe this?" Luke shouted. The entire
forest has been transplanted from one side of the
valley to the other. Incredible!"

The survivors descended to the ground and con-
vened at the bottom of the valley.

"There's no hope for the villagers," Luke said, "but
we must try to find survivors. There may be a few
lucky ones like us. You go back to the village. I'll
join you later, after I find out what happened to my
chalet."

He waded through thigh-deep snow up to the main

road and headed away from Wunderbad, reflecting grimly that there no longer was a Wunderbad, with its picturesque Tyrolean dwellings, lively taverns, and lavish health spas. Just a flat expanse of blowing snow.

Along the way he picked up a pair of discarded skis that had undoubtedly belonged to one of the victims of the avalanche. He strapped them on his boots and took off again at a much faster pace.

Luke's heart sank when he reached the site where the chalet had once stood. Even the foundation was gone. He skied downhill, following the path of the mammoth slide all the way to the lake.

As he approached, he could scarcely believe his eyes. There, resting on top of a towering mountain of snow in the shallows near the shoreline, was the chalet. As far as he could tell, it was unscathed; in fact, it appeared so natural that it might have been built on this high rise of snow and ice.

Standing with his mouth agape in amazement at the miracle of it, he saw the front door open, and Andria appear with an oil lamp.

"Will someone help us?" she called to him.

"Andria! It's me, Luke."

"Luke?" her voice was overflowing with joy and gratitude. "Thank God. Oh, my darling, I never thought I'd see you again."

"Yes, that thought struck me, too, but the past has proven something, I think. You and I are destined to be one someday, one forever more. What about Lucy and Lani?"

"We're fine, father!" their voices called in unison from behind Andria.

"Come on up and get warm," Andria said. "I just got a fire going, and I'll brew some tea or hot chocolate. I'm afraid poor Frau Muller is indisposed. Her nerves. I told her to stay in bed until we're rescued."

It was a difficult climb up the precipitous, slippery

snowbank, but at last he staggered through the front door.

Andria and the girls embraced him, and even King came bounding out of the kitchen to greet him, barking and prancing around.

"Down, you big elephant," Luke ordered him. "The vibration of your heavy feet might send us sliding down into the lake."

"Is there any risk of that?" Andria asked, concerned.

"Not likely. I took careful note of the situation on the way up. This mass is as solid as the Rock of Gibraltar."

Sipping tea laced with brandy before the blazing fire, Andria and Luke sat on the loveseat holding hands. The girls sat cross-legged at their feet, drinking hot chocolate. They listened in glum and sorrowful silence while he narrated what had happened to the village.

"So Wunderbad is no more, and I think we will be leaving here as soon as rescue teams are dispatched by the military authorities in this district."

"Where will we go?" asked Lucy.

"Well, I have long-overdue business in Paris, The Hague, and London. That should keep us busy for a time. And when that is completed, we could go home to Hawaii. How many are in favor, raise you hands?"

Three hands shot into the air.

"Home," Andria mused. "What a marvelous sound it has."

"And you and Andria will be married there," Lucy said boldly.

Luke tried to sound severe. "Now, whatever gave you that idea, young lady?"

The girl drew up her legs and hugged them to her chest. "Because we're growing girls, and we should have the influence and direction of a mother. Will you be our new mother, Andria? Please say you will."

Luke and Andria doubled over laughing.

"That must be a historical first," Luke gasped. "Having one's sixteen-year-old daughter tender a marriage proposal in his behalf."

"And Andria accepts, don't you, Andria?" Lani piped up.

Andria threw up her hands. "And that is another historical first," she laughed. "Having one's twelve-year-old daughter accept for the lady in question."

"Then I suppose it's all settled." He leaned over and kissed her tenderly as the girls beamed at them.

Chapter Four

It was a dream not to be realized immediately, however, due to two separate, equally remarkable, events.

Soon after their arrival in Paris, Luke was dining with a business associate at the swank Courvoisier Men's Club. They were sitting in the main lounge, having demitasse with brandy, when Luke's companion, Louis Boussard, a broker, sprang out of his chair.

"*Sacrebleu!* Look who has just come in! Cecil Rhodes, do you know him?"

"Can't say as I do. Name sounds familiar, though."

"Bright young chap, you must meet him." He summoned a waiter. "Would you ask Mr. Rhodes if he would care to join us for a drink?"

"A brilliant statesman as well as a capitalist in your league."

Luke was surprised by the man's extreme youth. "You're joking! Why he can't be more than twenty-five!"

Rhodes came over smiling, his hand outstretched. "I say, Boussard, old chap, damn good to see you. How long has it been?"

"Two years ago when I was in London. Rhodes, I'd like you to meet Luke Callahan, formerly of Hawaii."

They shook hands, and Rhodes's forehead was furrowed. "Callahan—Callahan. You must be related to the Hawaiian sugar king, Caleb Callahan?"

"His son," said Boussard. "Luke's a bit of a financial king in his own right. Made a fortune on pineapple."

"Of course! Delighted to meet you, Callahan. Here in Paris on business or pleasure?"

"A little of both."

"He's looking for some good investments," said Boussard. What are you up to, Rhodes, these days?"

There was a pause, and the Englishman's smile was vaguely mysterious. "Have either of you ever heard of Kimberly?"

They shook their heads.

"Cape Province, South Africa. You can mine diamonds there the way they mined gold on the California Gold Coast back in the fifties. Practically pick them up off the ground like rocks."

Luke's ears pricked up. "Looking for capital, Mr. Rhodes?"

"Matter of fact, I am. No small potatoes, though. Our combine only accepts investors who want to put up a million or more."

Without batting an eye, Luke took out his checkbook. "How much am I in for? You name it?"

Rhodes looked startled, recovered, and laughed. "By Jove! I like the cut of your jib, Callahan. No nonsense chap. Man after my own heart."

Boussard chuckled. "The two of you are cut out of the same cloth. Big, rugged individualists. When you've set your sights on something, I would hate to be in your way, either of you."

It was true, there was a marked resemblance between Luke and Rhodes in stature and style. They both exuded courage and determination, tempered by a sense of gentleness.

"I'll put in two million for starters," Luke said. He was quizzical. "Tell me something, Rhodes. If you're as rich as Boussard claims, why do you require outside investments?"

Rhodes's eyes glowed with what Luke could only define as fanaticism. His voice radiated passion. "Diamonds and wealth are only a part of it—the tip of the iceberg. Africa, it's magnificent! A rich, virgin land virtually unsettled except for diamond hunters. It could become the largest and most productive of all of Britain's colonies. Yes, that is the foremost purpose of the British South Africa Company. Absolute control of all of South Africa. Those of us on the board of directors will become the most powerful men in the world. That is what you are investing in, Callahan: *power!*"

His verve was infectious. Luke felt an excitement growing within himself that he had not experienced since the early, adventurous days when he and John had followed Andria to Hawaii from China and when he and Scotty had started the first pineapple plantation on Lanai on a pittance and a prayer.

His reverie was marred by a flash of dissatisfaction. The other men observed it.

"What is it, Luke?" Boussard inquired. "Something displeases you?"

"No, no, nothing to do with what we've been discussing. I was just reminded of a mysterious benefactor who helped me get started years ago. Do you know, I've never met the man. Member of the Astor family, so I was led to believe, but a neurotic recluse. Refused to meet me when I was in the States on my way to Europe with my family. Bloody snob! I made him a ton of profit, far above his investment. No matter. Now to get back to Africa. How did you happen to travel there to begin with, Rhodes?"

"Was sent there for my health when I was seventeen." He smiled proudly as he said, "Within two years I had amassed a fortune from the Kimberly fields. One of my partners was a chap named Pierre LeFarge."

He removed his watch from his waistcoat. "Matter of fact, I'm supposed to meet him here tonight. He's late. Care to sit in at our weekly poker game, gentlemen?"

"No, thank you," Luke declined. "My family is expecting me back at the Hotel de Ville about now. Why don't you play, Boussard?"

"That game is somewhat too rich for my blood."

Rhodes rose. "Ah, here comes Pierre now."

LeFarge was a tall, erect man with a military bearing. In his late fifties, Luke deduced, a handsome, dashing man with the profile of an eagle and a full thatch of wavy, silver hair. A thorough dandy, he wore a velvet evening jacket over a shirt with a ruffled front and ruffled sleeves.

His English was perfect, with only a hint of an accent. Boussard and Luke were introduced, and they shook hands all around and ordered still another round of drinks.

They chatted about a variety of topics, and eventually Rhodes and LeFarge began to reminisce about their early days in the Kimberly fields.

"I took this young whippersnapper under my wing, or he would have perished like a baby bird that falls out of the nest," the Frenchman joked.

"Ha! Listen to this old frog," the young Englishman shot back. "Thirty years at sea—he knew nothing about living on land; what a greenhorn he was when it came to prospecting."

"Thirty years at sea?" Luke inquired.

"Yes. I was an officer in the French navy. Retired Commander Pierre LeFarge at your service, sir."

"Where did you serve?"

"As a junior lieutenant, I served in the Far East— China, Macao—during the Opium Wars."

"I've spent some time in China myself," Luke told him. "As a missionary in a Mormon mission up the Canton River from Macao. In the early fifties."

The matter was dropped there, except for one final

inquiry on Luke's part before he departed for the hotel. "Mr. Lefarge, have you ever visited Hawaii?"

"Yes, we made stops for food and water on our voyages back and forth across the Pacific. Why do you ask, Mr. Callahan?"

"You look so familiar. I thought we may have met on some casual basis, easily forgotten."

"I think not, sir. I was transferred back to France long before you settled in Hawaii." He grinned. "I have one of those commonplace faces."

Luke frowned. "That's just it. There is nothing commonplace about you at all."

Back at the Hotel de Ville, Andria sat in the parlor of their suite reading a letter from John Yee. The girls were attending the ballet.

Dear Andria,

As you must be aware by now, the reciprocity treaty was ratified last May, and David Kalakaua has emerged triumphant. To all outward appearances he is one of the most popular monarchs here since Kamehameha the Great. (You may recall David's boast on the day of his election.)

However, those of us who are closest to him and to government policy see some very dark clouds on the distant horizon. I honestly don't believe that he is temperamentally suited to rule this nation. David is a master of the bold stroke, such as his brilliant handling of the treaty negotiations. But he has little patience for the tedious minutiae, the humdrum, everyday business of government. To avoid these matters, he delegates every piece of authority to subordinates, who seem to be proving the validity of the old adage: "Too many cooks spoil the broth." Quite literally, they keep falling all over each other, and they engage in countless and constant intramural conflicts vying for still more personal power and for the king's favor. And you know how David's ego is gluttonous for flattery! If the trend persists for any length of time, I predict this regime will crumble under the weight of all the graft, corruption, and extravagance it supports.

David has too fine a mind not to recognize the suicidal course his government is following, so he is persistently blinding himself to what is happening: he is trying to escape from reality by traveling endlessly. His latest pronouncement is that he and Queen Kapiolani are shortly to circumnavigate the world. He has sent an advance order to London for two ornate crowns for himself and his consort.

Our immigration campaign has been a great success. In fact there are almost eighteen thousand Chinese in residence in all the islands, a nationality ranking second behind native Hawaiians, whose own ranks continue to diminish from leprosy, syphilis, and other debilitating diseases. The robust race of the ancient Kanaka is withering away physically and mentally.

Syphilis has affected the nobility, as well as the average man and woman. There are rumors that the royal bloodlines are plagued by impotency and sterility going back to Kamehameha the Fourth. Neither he nor his successor produced any issue. Nor have David and Kapiolani. There is no doubt in my mind that the monarchy is in its twilight years and that within the next decade or two, Hawaii will become a republic with a government run by the people and for the people.

But enough of this gloomy conjecture. Our country remains the most beautiful place to live in all the world. And all of us who love you are counting the days when you will be reunited with us here in paradise. . . .

Andria looked up as Luke came into the room. "Hello. How was your evening at the club?"

"Eventful, to say the least." He bent to kiss her.

"I was just reading the latest letter from John Yee." She put it aside.

"What does the Big Turnip have to say?"

"You'd better read it yourself. So, what were these events of the evening?"

He told her first about Cecil Rhodes.

She could not hide her distress. "Oh, dear, does that mean we won't be going home directly?"

"I'm afraid so." He sighed. "Perhaps we should enroll the girls in a good boarding school for a few semesters. I can't see them coming to South Africa with us."

"Why must we go to Africa? I'm sure Mr. Rhodes is an honest and capable man who will protect your interests."

"I have every confidence in Rhodes. It's just that—" His words trailed off, and a faraway look came into his eyes.

"You have the wanderlust, is that it, darling?"

He sat on the arm of her chair and put his arm around her shoulders. "I must confess that that part of the world has always had an exotic appeal to me. Darkest Africa—it sounds so exciting and mysterious."

"When do we pack?" she asked resignedly.

"Not for a few weeks. I still have business to wrap up in London. I'll head across the channel tomorrow. It won't take more than a few days."

He stood up, walked to a sideboard, and poured himself a brandy from a crystal decanter. He poured a smaller one for Andria.

"Thank you, I don't feel like it tonight, darling."

"I think you had better." He stood before her, an intent expression on his face.

"You sound and look so ominous." She accepted the glass.

"Ominous is not the word exactly. It could be quite to the contrary, depending on how you—" He hesitated.

"Depending on how I—I what? Goodness, Luke, don't keep me in suspense. What's wrong?"

He inhaled deeply. "Do you recall the name of your natural father? You said he was French and Spanish."

Andria pursed her lips and looked thoughtful. "It pained my mother so sorely that he deserted her, she could not bear to speak of him, and I was only an infant when he left. Let me see, though, there were occasions. . . . Yes, I think I have it now. His first name was Pierre—Pierre—oh, it's on the tip of my tongue."

"LeFarge," he said, his voice emotionless.

Her eyes were enormous with wonder. "Yes! Pierre LeFarge! But how did you know?"

"I met him tonight at the club. He's a partner of Cecil Rhodes. LeFarge is a retired French naval officer who struck it rich in the Kimberly diamond fields."

Andria shook her head. "No, no, no! You must be mistaken. After all, in France there must be numerous men with the name of LeFarge. Like Smith or Jones or Wagner or Callahan in England or America."

"No, there's no mistake. He was stationed in China about the time you were born. But the facts are immaterial. When I saw him, I was positive I had met him before. The fact is he looks like *you!* Rather you resemble your father. The likeness is uncanny. He's a strikingly handsome man, and his eyes are the color of blue sapphires!"

"It's impossible. I refuse to believe it."

"You'll believe it when you meet him."

"Meet him? That's out of the question. Even if it were true, I wouldn't meet him. I hate him for what he did to my mother. He's a cad!"

"So he was, but that was a long time ago. People do change. At least I think you owe yourself the indulgence of confronting him. Then you can behave toward him as you wish."

That logic intrigued her. "If it is true—yes! I owe my mother that, at least. To expose him before his friends. Does he have a family?"

"I don't know. The subject never came up. I'll find out from Boussard tomorrow. He's traveling with me to London."

"Give me another brandy, will you, darling?" she requested. "I'm so high-strung I'll never get a wink of sleep tonight."

"Then we must unstring you," he said, and there was a gleam in his eye. He took the glass from her and sat it on an end table. "But not with brandy."

He knelt down in front of her and undid the sash of her red velvet hostess gown. She was naked underneath. He parted the gown and leaned forward to kiss her breasts, teasing her nipples with his tongue.

"Oh, my darling!" she gasped, and a shudder ran through her body like an electric shock. She pressed her hands to the back of his head and drew him tightly to her bosom.

Luke's hands slipped inside the robe and around her waist. Gently he kneaded the silken flesh just above the swell of her buttocks. His mouth worked down her body. Her belly surged against his face as he kissed her navel.

"You're driving me quite insane," she murmured.

He felt the wild beating of her heart through a pulse in her groin. He parted her legs and lavished kisses along the insides of her thighs, moving slowly up.

She cried out and clamped his head in the vise of her thighs. Seconds later she writhed in the throes of orgasm. Words of endearment tumbled out of her mouth until she had spent her final spasm. She fell into a contented swoon, and he gathered her up in his arms and carried her into the bedroom.

"You must rest now."

"No," she protested in a weak voice. "I must make love to you."

"Not now, later."

"But you are frustrated."

"I'm at peace with the world. That is what true love

is all about. The pleasure of giving should equal the pleasure of receiving. I am quite content now. Almost as content as if I had shared your joy. When you have napped, I will come back to you, and we will make love together."

She took his hand and pressed the palm to her lips.

"My beloved. I love you so intensely that it drives a dagger into my heart."

"And I love you as much." He bent to kiss her lips. "I don't wish to wait until we return to Hawaii. I want to marry you here and now. As soon as I get back from London."

"Whatever you say, my darling. It matters little whether or not we have a preacher pronounce us man and wife. I am your wife now, and I have always been since the first time we made love on the hillside back of the mission."

"Nevertheless, it is my desire to 'make an honest woman of you,' as they used to say when I was a boy."

Andria fell asleep with a sweet smile on her face, and her dreams were all of Luke.

Chapter Five

The following Monday, after Luke's return from London, Andria reluctantly wrote an invitation to Monsieur LeFarge, inviting him to dinner the following Wednesday evening at eight o'clock. She grimaced as she lay aside the quill pen and put the note into an envelope.

"Monsieur LeFarge will be surprised to learn he is the sole guest at this dinner party—if one could call it that!"

Luke grinned. "No doubt he will also be surprised to learn that we are not Mr. and Mrs. Callahan, as you wrote in the invitation. But shortly we shall be."

He put the invitation in the inside pocket of his swallow-tailed coat, kissed Andria, and left the suite to deliver the missive.

The following morning Andria received a written reply to the invitation, along with a dozen long-stemmed roses, by special messenger. The note read, "I am honored and delighted to accept."

The intimate dinner party was to be catered by the hotel, and served in the suite's small dining room.

"I'm so nervous I can barely hold the comb," Andria told Luke as they dressed on that fateful night for dinner.

"You look divine," he assured her.

"Here, darling, help me with this snood." Her hair was done up in a chignon snood made of crocheted gold thread and dotted with pearls and semiprecious gems.

Her evening gown was made of pale peach organdy trimmed with dotted swiss.

LeFarge will deeply regret all of the years he's wasted, not knowing the pride of showing off a daughter so lovely and charming as you. To be without a daughter's love and attention."

"Please, Luke!" she said sharply. "Don't speak of me as *his* daughter! I loathe the man!"

"We shall see." He slipped into his black satin evening jacket and adjusted his black bow tie.

Andria bustled about the dining room, rearranging the silverware and the floral centerpiece. "These hotel waiters are so careless!" she said angrily.

Luke threw back his head and roared. "You certainly are overly concerned about making an impression on Monsieur LeFarge, considering that you 'loathe' him!"

"I'll ignore that!" She went off in a huff.

At five minutes before eight o'clock, they were sitting in the parlor before a crackling fire. Andria was gripping her sherry glass so tightly that her knuckles were white.

She started as the clock on the mantel began to toll the hour of eight. Precisely on the sixth chime, there was a knock on the suite's door.

"Oh, dear!" she breathed.

"He's punctual, we must say that for him." Luke rose, went to the door, and opened it.

"Good evening, LeFarge. Do come in, and let me have your hat and cape."

The two men shook hands.

"It was charming of your wife to invite me. I can't wait to meet her. Boussard says she is a rare beauty."

As yet he had not seen Andria, who was hidden from

his view behind Luke's vast bulk. Now Luke moved aside as the Frenchman entered.

"My wife, Andria. Darling, Monsieur Pierre Le-Farge."

"My dear lady." He stepped forward, took her hand, bowed low over it, and kissed her fingers. Then he straightened up and, still holding her hand, looked into her deep blue eyes.

"Boussard did not exaggerate. Rare beauty is a gross understatement. You are ravishing, madam."

Luke was watching him ever so closely. Andria wore a cool, waxen smile.

LeFarge continued. "I have been looking forward—" He broke off abruptly, and his face turned ashen. His hand, holding Andria's hand, was icy.

"Monsieur?" she said. "Is there anything wrong?"

He swayed and brushed a hand across his eyes. His voice was barely audible. "I—I—this is most remarkable."

"What is remarkable, LeFarge?" Luke asked.

"I—I—don't know quite how to say it. It is just that your lovely wife bears an uncanny resemblance to—to someone I knew many, many years ago."

Luke penetrated LeFarge's gaze. "Perhaps my wife resembles your mother, who was also named Andria," said Luke.

LeFarge let go of Andria's hand and looked at Luke in utter stupefaction. *"Mon Dieu!* How did you know my mother's name?"

"Because she was my grandmother, monsieur, after whom I was named," Andria said. And now her sapphire eyes glowed with the bitterness and resentment that had been festering inside of her all these years.

"Madam Callahan! What sort of distasteful prank is this?" He looked around wildly, like an animal at bay, seeking some route of escape.

"No prank, monsieur. My mother was Cho Lin Wong."

"Cho Lin! This is madness. I am out of my mind. This can't be happening!"

And he would have collapsed if Luke had not caught him underneath the arms. He helped LeFarge to the couch and set him down gently. "I will get you some brandy." He walked to the sideboard.

Andria hovered over the wilted Frenchman like a merciless avenging angel. He looked up at her and then quickly down at the carpet, thoroughly intimidated.

Luke held the snifter of brandy to his lips. "Here. Drink this and you will feel better."

LeFarge clutched the glass in trembling hands and sipped the fiery liquid. He was shaking so badly, the brandy spilled over onto his trousers.

"Our intent is not to torment you, LeFarge. Your astonishment and shock are understandable. It is the most incredible coincidence I have ever been witness to in my life. But what we have told you is the absolute truth. You married Cho Lin when you were stationed in Thailand and took her with you to Canton, where Andria was born."

Andria cut in sharply. "And where you deserted my mother and I!"

Slowly LeFarge brought up his head and looked into her eyes, which reflected only malice. It was an ordeal for him, but this time his glance did not waver.

"Then you are my daughter." He stretched out a hand toward her, a pleading gesture.

Andria recoiled as if from a snake. Luke could not help but be touched by the pain and guilt he saw in LeFarge's contorted face.

"I do not blame you for hating me. You have no way of knowing the true circumstances. There are always two sides to every story. I only beg of you to listen to my side."

Andria snorted derisively. "Listen to your lies? I think not!"

"Andria," Luke interceded, "do you recall a time

when you persuaded me to listen to my father? Soon after we were reunited? We live in a democratic society. Every man deserves to have his say in court. You are a reasonable and fair woman."

She shrugged and folded her arms underneath her breasts. "Proceed, Monsieur LeFarge."

He cradled his head in his hands and spoke haltingly, but there was a ring of truth in what he said that impressed Luke.

"You see, when my transfer came through—the fact is—I wanted to take you and your mother back to France with me. In spite of what you believe, I loved her very deeply—and I loved my daughter—"

Andria started to interrupt him, but a warning glare from Luke silenced her.

"Yes, I loved you both. In any case—Cho Lin—she was a strong-willed woman. She did not want to leave China. She did not want to make that long, harrowing voyage across half a world with an infant in arms. I could not change her mind, so I had no recourse but to leave the two of you in Canton."

"You promised my mother you would return for us," she said accusingly.

"And so I intended. But remember—I was in the naval service of France, the navy controlled my destiny. Those were chaotic times—we were fighting Algeria. I was badly wounded in action. There was a long convalescence—two years an invalid. Eventually I did return to China. There was no trace of Cho Lin or her child—our daughter."

He implored Andria, "You must believe me, God is my witness, I tried desperately to find out where you were, what had happened. But my time and my resources were limited. I was still a servant of the French navy." He threw up his hands. "I should have returned, tried harder, but by that time I had lost all hope. So many women and children had perished from cholera, the plague—I counted Cho Lin and you as two of the victims."

He took a deep breath and sat more erectly. "One thing—I never married again, out of my grief and love for Cho Lin and you. I served out a monastic existence until the navy retired me. Then I went to South Africa where I met Cecil Rhodes."

He stood up and faced her, his dignity restored by the catharsis of his confession. "My darling daughter, can you find it in your heart to forgive me? If not, I will understand. You will have achieved your revenge by deserting me." He opened his arms to her. "Andria?"

Luke watched her in fascination, not daring to breathe for fear of upsetting the delicate balance of all the conflicting emotions mirrored in her face, her eyes, the tautness of every muscle in her body.

He looked at LeFarge. Tears were streaming down his face. Then he looked back to Andria. The first hint, a softening around her mouth and eyes. Her shoulders were quivering. And then it burst through—a cry of relief, followed by a deluge of tears.

"Father!" she gasped and went to him.

He clasped her to his chest, raining kisses on her hair and her cheeks.

"My daughter, my wonderful, beautiful daughter."

Luke's own eyes felt damp, and he could not swallow the lump in his throat. Quietly he walked past them into the bedroom and closed the door.

It was definitely an occasion when three was a crowd.

After LeFarge had left and Luke and Andria were undressing for bed, she confided in him, "I still have reservations about him. He's a born charmer; all that he claims could be lies."

"I think we must give him the benefit of the doubt. I can swear to one thing. When he broke down, that was genuine emotion pouring forth unchecked. No one could fake a scene like that."

"Yes, I believe that was real. In any case, you're right, I will give him the benefit of the doubt." She smiled. "I must admit I am going to enjoy having a father."

"And a husband," Luke amended.

She laughed. "That was funny, too. When I told him that we are not man and wife, he pretended to be shocked. 'My daughter living in sin! Disgraceful!'

"Then he burst out laughing and said, 'It is of no consequence to me. Remember, I am a Frenchman.' "

Luke went to her dressing table where she was combing out her long hair. He slipped a hand down the front of her lace negligee and cupped her breast.

She slapped him playfully. "Now, stop distracting me until I do my fifty strokes." She winked at him in the mirror. "Remember I am part French myself."

And dutifully she let him lead her over to the bed.

Epilogue

Andria Callahan, convalescing from a bout of pneumonia, was thumbing idly through her scrapbook—her "book of memories" as she fondly called it.

The years following her marriage to Luke in Paris had been idyllic, marred only by the death of Caleb Callahan at his Hilo estate and the decease of her own father, Pierre LeFarge, in his Paris town house.

In his final letter to his daughter, written on the day of his death, there was an omen of his impending passing:

". . . and if I were to die today, it would be without a single regret, except my fervent desire that you and I had been reunited sooner. Whatever travails I had suffered before you came back into my life, my darling daughter, have been compensated for tenfold by the infinite dimensions of love and joy that you have brought into my existence. . . ."

Andria turned back the pages of the book to the sheet on which her wedding invitation was affixed:

Mr. Pierre LeFarge
requests the honour of your presence
at the marriage of his daughter
Andria
to
Mr. Luke Callahan
on Sunday, the ninth of June
at twelve o'clock
Saint Sulpice Church
Paris, France

The memories of that day flooded back as if it had been yesterday.

Most of the entries were newspaper clippings and letters from Luke's daughters by his previous marriage, both of whom were married and living in the United States.

She put her finger on an item from the *Hawaiian Gazette:*

> Mr. and Mrs. Luke Callahan and their daughters, Lucy and Lani, received an enthusiastic reception from the public, government dignitaries, and the press when they disembarked in Honolulu after an absence of six years. Luke Callahan, who amassed a fortune as a pineapple grower on Lanai, accrued further billions from his investments in South Africa's Kimberly diamond fields, and today is ranked as one of the world's foremost international financiers. All of the Hawaiian Islands welcome back this distinguished native son."

There were numerous news stories tracing the decline and fall of the Kalakaua dynasty. Ever riddled with corruption within government ranks, aided and abetted by the king's blatant disregard for the political chaos of his regime, it became, as one political journalist described it, "like a beautiful piece of fruit, shining with apparent health on the outside but eaten away inside by maggots."

David Kalakaua's one shining act of diplomacy, the obtaining of a reciprocity treaty with the United States, was overshadowed by his personal extravagance; his reactionary efforts to restore the ancient order; and his ideas of absolutism and divine right.

He did succeed in persuading the United States to renew the reciprocity treaty after his term had expired, but at the high price of deeding the exclusive rights to the United States to enter Pearl Harbor and maintain a coaling and repair station there.

Under pressure from the public, the press, and the powerful annexationist faction, Kalakaua found himself hemmed in on all sides. He resorted to his typical method of dealing with overwhelming problems. Escape!

Under cover of night, he boarded a steamer in Honolulu bound for San Francisco.

Andria thumbed through the album until she found the last newspaper reference to King David Kalakaua, from the *San Francisco Examiner*.

> Last evening the king of the Hawaiian Islands, David Kalakaua, was found dead by a valet in his royal suite in the Palace Hotel. Kalakaua was no stranger to San Francisco, nor to any of the other major cities in the United States and Europe. The "Merry Monarch"—formerly the "Playboy Prince"—was undoubtedly the foremost world traveler of his age. It is expected that he will be succeeded by his sister, Royal Princess Liliuokalani, wife of diplomat-politician John Dominis. The Princess Liliuokalani is a keen, intelligent, strong-willed woman who shares her late brother's royalist views. . . ."

Andria looked for more cheerful entries. A warm glow suffused her body, and she smiled as she looked at the two cards, one pink and one blue, announcing the births of her and Luke's two children, John Caleb Callahan and Martha Sun Ying Callahan.

She looked up as the bedroom door opened and Luke came into the room.

"Hello, darling. How are you feeling?"

"Much better, thank you."

He came over and kissed her forehead.

"Fever's down." He sat down on the edge of the bed

and put an arm about her shoulders. "Whatever are you doing?"

"Reminiscing over this old scrapbook. Do you know it's a rather thorough chronicle of our lives for the past twenty years?"

"I must peruse it myself, maybe after dinner. Martha won't be eating with us. She's invited over to the Yee's."

"How is John and his wife Uli?"

"They're fine. I saw John this afternoon at the Iolani Palace."

"How is Lili?"

His eyes dropped, and he put a hand over her hands. "I didn't want you to hear this until you were strong enough to bear the shock. Lili is no longer the queen. The monarchy was overthrown in a bloodless coup two weeks ago."

"Oh, no!" she said in distress. "I don't believe it!"

"It was inevitable, Andria, that the annexationists would have their way in the end. Don't worry about Lili. At present she is under house arrest at the palace."

"House arrest? Whatever for?"

"Her appearance in public just might incite her followers to stage a counterrevolution, and one that would not be without bloodshed. She plans to journey to the United States with John."

"Exile, is that it?"

He shrugged. "Who can tell about the future? One thing is certain. Before the end of the century, Hawaii will become a territory of the United States. Until then a provisional government will be established, with a president at the head."

"Who will it be, do you think?"

He smiled. "Sanford Dole and John Yee want to nominate me for the post."

"I think that's marvelous, darling."

"It's not for me, sweet," he said ruefully.

"Why not? You'd make a wonderful president!"

"With annexation only a few short years away, I can

be of more service to my country as an economic adviser and administrator. We're going to witness a mass wave of emigrés from the States in the next few years, if my hunch is correct. Hawaii will become the new American frontier. We have got to insure that the machinery of the economy can withstand the heavy load. That's where I can do the best job. Not bogged down in the bureaucracy of government. No, I told Sanford Dole that I intend to propose him for the job. I think he'll make a fine president. By the way, young John won't be home this evening, either. He's been invited to a *luau* at the Henderson's."

She smiled. "He has his eye on that cute little Betsy Henderson."

"Got a good eye for females, that lad," he grunted. "Takes after his father." He kissed Andria on the lips. Her arms went around his neck, and she murmured, "Inasmuch as we're going to be alone tonight, we should make the best of our privacy." Her sapphire eyes lit up, and she wet her lips with her tongue. "If you grasp my meaning?"

He held her more tightly. "Do you feel fit enough yet?"

"Fit as a fiddle and just as high-strung. I've been deprived for such a long time." Her hand moved up his leg and along his thigh. "Ah, I can feel your deprival as well." He kissed her, his ardor increasing, but he was interrupted by a knock on the bedroom door.

"Come in," Luke called out.

An exquisite girl of twelve burst into the room. She had her mother's eyes and her father's red hair.

"Martha!" Andria exclaimed. "What are you doing home? I thought you were going to dine with the Yees?"

"I changed my mind, mother. I got to thinking how selfish it would be, just when you're feeling better and no doubt yearning for a game of cribbage."

"A game of cribbage," Luke and Andria said in a doleful chorus.

"Yes. I intend to donate my entire evening to you, mother. Oh, what fun we'll have!"

"Yes, indeed," said Andria.

"Fun—" Luke mused.

Unexpectedly the two of them burst out laughing.

Martha stared at them in astonishment. "What on earth is so funny about a game of cribbage?"

"You wouldn't understand, love. Come over and give your old dad a kiss." He put an arm around her slender waist.

"Not quite yet, daughter," Andria said wryly. "But you soon will."

Luke Callahan took a deep breath of the spicy tropic air wafting through the open window, *maile, ohi'a* blossoms, oleander, and ginger.

He smiled at his two loves and said, "I could not dream of a world more wonderful or more complete than the world I share with you."